DAWNSTAR

The Starchaser Saga
Book II

R. DUGAN

DEDICATION

To Cassidy.
Happy birthday, Queen of All Angst.

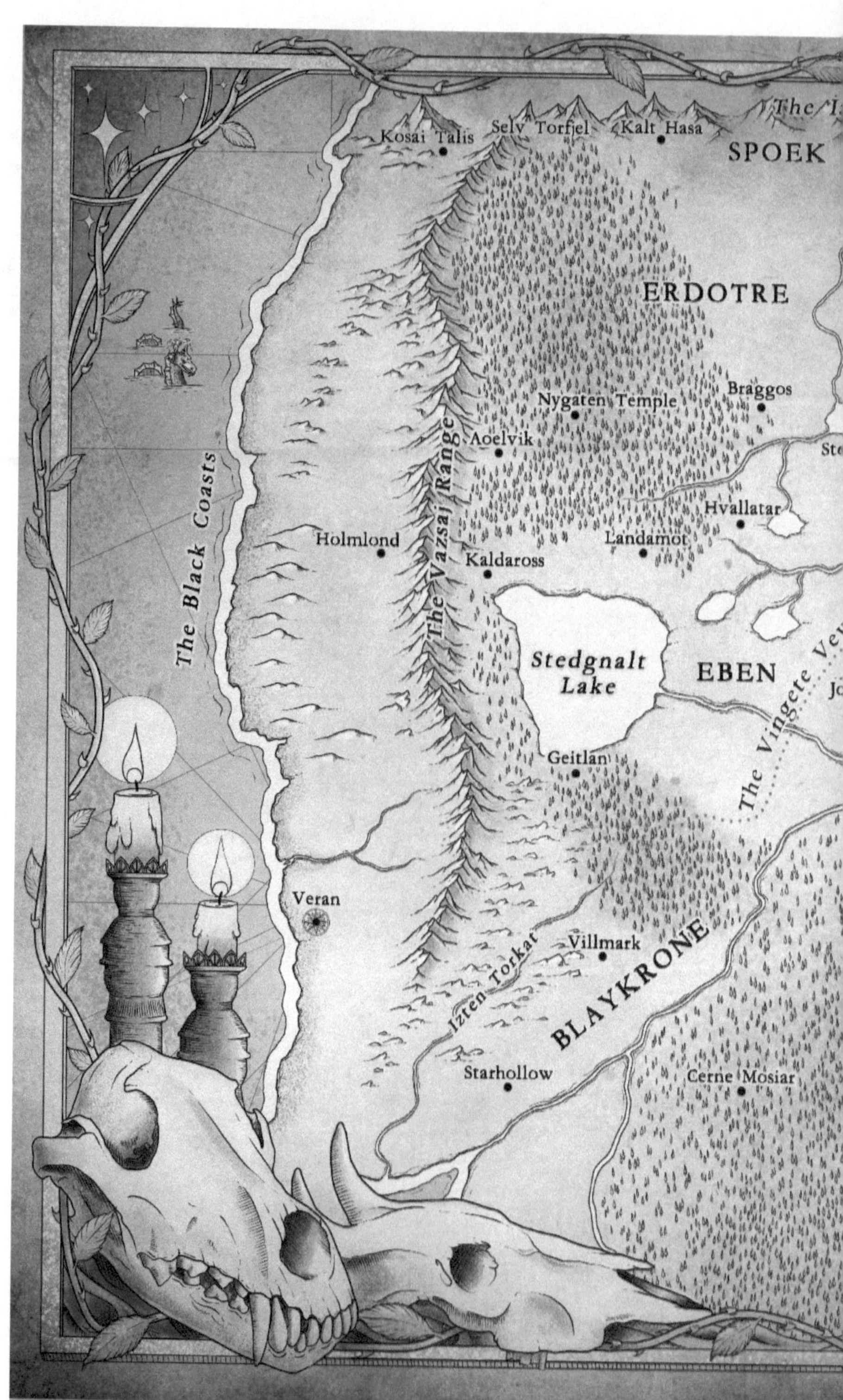

The Black Coasts
The Vazsaj Range
Kosai Talis
Selv Torfjel
Kalt Hasa
SPOEK
ERDOTRE
Nygaten Temple
Braggos
Aoelvik
Hvallatar
Landamot
Holmlond
Kaldaross
Stedgnalt Lake
EBEN
The Vingete Ve
Geitlan
Veran
Villmark
Izten Torkat
BLAYKRONE
Starhollow
Cerne Mosiar

nge
iralek
NORDBRAN
Azkai Temple
KROAKEN
Felstrond
n Hatcheries
Detlyse Halet
Keltei Temple
Niot River
idom
LATAUS
SVERD
The Wildwood
Soratt Temple
copr. 2020 Jessica Khoury

THE
LORD
OF
SAND AND
BLOOD

CHAPTER ONE

SOMEWHERE IN THE crossing between Kroaken territory's pale sands and the hard-baked dirt mounds of neighboring Lataus, Princess Cistine Novacek of Talheim lost the last threads of her fury. Where trees prodded the sky again and the surroundings became more familiar, relief eased the snarl of emotion that lived in her heart ever since she'd left her Warden and closest friend, Asheila Kovar, in the City of a Thousand Stars, and escaped into the wilds with a disgraced High Tribune and his cabal.

It was toward him that all her fury had been directed. But after days of walking, it finally simmered away; perhaps because there was only the two of them now. Thorne had sent the rest of the cabal ahead to Hellidom, the Sanctuary City below the Nior River's falls, days ago. Cistine could still see their faces as they'd gone: Tatiana and Quill wearing matching scowls; Ariadne, even quieter than usual; Maleck, his eyes sunken, with Ashe's sword Echelon strapped to his back. And Julian...

Cistine's suitor had fought her every step when she sent him away, and she'd been just as reluctant to see him go—fearing how much she'd miss the touches and warm glances that never failed to set her heart aflame.

Except they hadn't lately, eclipsed by fury. It was from that endless spool of rage unwinding through her body that Cistine had urged him, then ordered him, to leave with the cabal.

There was a conversation she had to have with Thorne, and Thorne alone.

In the dimness of midday under a sky masked with clouds, Cistine risked a glance at the High Tribune walking on her right side, where she could hear him. Her ruptured left eardrum kept the world out of balance, and the broken knuckles on one hand ached only a sliver more than the bruised ones on the other, which she'd smashed against Thorne's jaw several days before.

He'd taken that blow like he took most things: silently, and without flinching. Only his watering eyes afterward had made her regret lashing out with her fist. Hitting people had never been her retort of choice before she'd traveled north to Valgard in search of an alliance to protect her kingdom from the threat of war. But now that Thorne's cabal had trained her, she had more in her arsenal than witticisms from countless books mined in her father's library. And Thorne had made her so furious, stacking one betrayal on top of another, she hadn't known what else to do.

She caught him looking back at her now, his silver hair wind-tossed, blue eyes pale chips of ice in a faintly-stubbled face. He looked just enough like his father—the Chancellor of Kanslar Court, the man Cistine had hoped would help stymie a threat of war from Talheim's southern neighbors in Mahasar—that it sent a chill burrowing down the backs of her arms.

She'd found obsession, not aid, at the end of that desperate road. Chancellor Salvotor was no benevolent judge, he was a ruthless abuser with dragon scales under his skin and a lust for power in his heart. Cistine was only free of him because Thorne and his cabal had chased after her and her companions into Stornhaz and exposed themselves to the very man who'd driven them out a decade ago.

They'd risked everything for her, though she had run straight to the City of a Thousand Stars without so much as bothering to speak with Thorne when she learned his initial plan for her—a lure to draw Salvotor from within the impenetrable city walls.

But matters were different now. She understood that...understood *Thorne.*

As if he sensed the shift in her thoughts, he asked, "Does that look mean you're finished resenting me?"

Cistine let the slap of her feet—bound up in the rags of Julian's shirt, since she had no shoes—answer at first. Then she cleared her throat. "It means I'm ready to ask questions."

Thorne squinted ahead into the pale gray light. "I've been waiting for that."

Of course he had.

She opened her mouth to ask her first burning question, and Thorne held up a hand. "There's a reason I brought you this way alone."

They mounted a short incline in Lataus's hilly terrain and halted at the edge of a steep basin, its center a broad hole traveling deep into the flesh of the world. Cistine's stomach plummeted at the sight of it—and of the creatures crouched around it on broken haunches or fallen completely.

There was nothing like these great metal beasts in Talheim. Vegetation grew along their bellies and bird droppings painted their faces in war stripes. Spiraled siphons with sparkling glass bowls on the ends drooped from their rusted arms.

Cistine pressed a hand to her middle, nauseated by their strangeness.

"These are harvesters." Thorne sank to one knee, balancing his wrist on his leg. "And this is one of the smaller augment fields."

Cistine stared down at him, lips parting in shock. "That hole..."

Thorne nodded. "An augmentation well. Like the others, it was sealed after we lost the war, when Talheim offered the truce."

Cistine's father had fought in that war, had ascended from Prince to King during it, and as conqueror he'd forced Valgard to seal the Doors to the Gods and halt the mining of augments—the god-like energy blooming in the Northern Kingdom's core. But her father never told her the entire truth: the scars that war had left, or that there were still augments, already mined, in this kingdom—and its people used them.

People who were not so profoundly wicked as men like Julian's father always claimed.

Thorne gestured into the basin. "These harvesters are a kind of machine fed on augments. Lightning, mostly, that kept their moving parts in motion."

"Like a clock?"

"In one sense. But instead of winding them, we filled their depositories with an augment and sealed the door. They ran for hours, sometimes for days, tilling up more energy from Valgard's core."

Cistine sank to her knees beside him, grateful to give her feet some relief. "Why are they still here? Their parts must be valuable."

"The depositories were," Thorne said. "They were removed to house more augments in Stornhaz when the war ended. But moving these machines required augmentation, and with the Doors sealed, it was a waste to return them to the city."

Cistine stared at the peculiar machines, their angles too sharp, their design too rigid for this plain wilderness, and that burning question finally made it past her dry lips. "You said you've been searching for the Key to wells like this one. That you wanted to use it to open the Doors to the Gods and let augments flow back into the world. Why?"

"Not for the reasons you're thinking. Not for power or pride, not even to unseat my father," Thorne said. "For the people. The ones being treated by the medicos, the ones who relied on augmentation to help their crops in times of drought, after forest fires, during the harshest winters."

His answer cooled the fire in Cistine's belly. If she'd had such resources to preserve her own kingdom, would she reject them?

"I'm telling you the truth, Cistine," Thorne said when she didn't speak. "I wanted the Key for my people. I won't say it doesn't still interest me, but it isn't my focus now. The Key is only a legend. What we have if you and I stand together is more tangible. Knowing what you do now, are you still with me?"

Cistine couldn't muster an answer through the tightness in her throat. She ached to believe the promise he'd made—that he would find a way to expose Salvotor for planting his own men in the other Courts, replace him on the Judgement Seat, and put an army behind Cistine to push back the threat of King Jad of Mahasar and protect Talheim.

"I'm with you," she said. "To help you find a way to unseat your father, and to find Ashe. But I won't help you open the Doors, Thorne, and I won't help hand that Key to the Courts either."

She meant every word; but she hadn't gained reputation as Talheim's greatest court gossip by keeping her curiosity in check. During their days of walking, she'd been wondering about this Key; how it had been forged, *why* it existed, and who among Talheim's own people—even in the Citadel where Cistine was raised—knew of its existence and location.

"Understood." Thorne pushed himself up slowly, gripping the small of his back where he'd struck water shielding her from a fall. "And I'm grateful...for your help, and your understanding."

Cistine rose and dusted her hands on the tattered dress she'd worn since Stornhaz. "I know I burned my share of bridges when I left Starhollow, but I'm glad we mended this one."

"Some small comfort," Thorne chuckled.

"It means more than you know." Cistine rubbed her sunburned face and winced. "I just don't know how I'll manage with the others. Quill and Tatiana will hardly look at me."

"Remember what I told you when you and Julian argued at Villmark. Apologize for the harm, not for what you felt. Your hurt...that rests solely with me."

"Not solely. You shouldn't have kept the truth from me, but I didn't have to lead Julian and Ashe into danger just because I was angry. We carry that weight together, Thorne."

A familiar croak split the air, and Cistine turned south to face the sound—and the great raven who flapped across the basin's rim and alighted on her wrist. "Hello, Faer," she whispered, stroking the back of his head with one finger.

"Quill and the others must have reached Hellidom safely, then." Thorne stepped closer, running the palm of his hand down Faer's sleek plumage. "And now it's our turn, *Logandir*."

Wild Heart of Fire. The name, given to her by Thorne's allies after a disastrous battle in the Izten Torkat, poured new strength into her veins.

She smiled up at Thorne and found him already gazing at her, a small smirk crooking his mouth in turn.

And Cistine thought maybe he did understand how much it meant to her, knowing he'd determined long ago never to use her as bait. That even if fear had kept him from being honest, he'd abandoned cruelty and truly sought to help her.

Faer brushed out from under Thorne's hand, ascending to Cistine's shoulder, and only then did she realize how close she was to the High Tribune—sharing breathing space while they stroked Quill's trained raven.

Cistine turned her face into the wind, sharply cooler now and smelling of rain. Thunder murmured between the tattered clouds, the quiet voices of the True God and his lesser vassals discussing the fates of Cistine and her friends.

The gods seemed to be betting against them.

"I always thought it was more than coincidence," Thorne mused, "how the storms increase whenever the Court of the Conqueror sits in session."

"Do you think we're ready to face this one?" Cistine asked.

Thorne shifted his weight. "I don't know."

At least he was being honest, just as he'd promised. Even if such an unhappy answer, from someone as confident as Thorne, made the wind's bite seem much colder. "Let's go. The others are waiting."

With Faer on her shoulder, Cistine led the way toward Hellidom.

CHAPTER TWO

T HE RAIN FELL in earnest when Cistine and Thorne reached Hellidom's array of homes and shops, carved from the stone cliffs and pieced together out of wood at the base of the falls. It was a relief to return to the place where she'd trained, learned Old Valgardan language and history, bonded with the cabal and begun to see them as friends. Where Julian had asked to court her, where she and Ashe shopped for weapons together...

Eyes burning, Cistine followed Thorne past the garden he'd gifted her. The rain was doing it some good, but the plants needed harvesting. The Den's three large watermills churned and creaked, pressing the barrels of grain in the undercroft into flour that would help feed the city during winter.

Life carried on. Yet so much had changed.

Thorne opened the front door, and Faer flew inside first, alighting on one of the jutting dividers carved from the foyer's wooden walls and pecking the water from his wings. Cistine slipped in after him and stood shivering in the low light. For the first time in weeks, she wasn't certain what to do with herself in this house.

Ariadne appeared from the short hallway to the kitchen, strapped with glinting knives, her angled eyes gleaming just as bright as she leaned her shoulder to the wall. "You're dripping all over the floor."

"I'll clean it up later," Cistine replied through chattering teeth.

Ariadne raked her with a calm look, then disappeared back down the hall. Before Cistine could do more than cast Thorne a nervous look, Ariadne returned with a scratchy linen towel, tossed it over Cistine's head, gave her hair a quick, jarring rub, then yanked it down around her shoulders and met her eyes. "Your hand?"

"Aches?" Surprise lilted the word into a question. Though her gaze was calm as ever, there was something framing Ariadne's mouth and wrinkling the bridge of her nose Cistine had never seen before. At least not directed at her.

"No cleaning until the ache stops," she said. "I'll teach you exercises to help the knuckles heal properly."

Gratitude swelled in Cistine's throat so thickly she could only nod.

Ariadne snared her chin and held her gaze. "You did not deserve for him to hit you. I'm proud of you for hitting back."

Footsteps thudded in the hall, and Julian appeared behind Ariadne, dressed in his Talheimic vest and long shirt again rather than the black threads from Stornhaz that had unbearably matched Thorne's. When he breathed Cistine's name, Ariadne released her to his running footfalls and open arms, and she stepped forward to meet him. When she felt his heartbeat, the steady lift and fall of his chest, she relaxed. His touch eased her bone-deep shivers, and the smell of herbs and soap on his skin turned her knees weak.

These past two days were the longest they'd been out of each other's company since their argument in Villmark. She never wanted to fight with him that way again.

"Thank you," Julian said over her head to Thorne. "For bringing her back safe."

Cistine's eyes plucked open. Before she could speak, Thorne said, "She brought herself. I followed."

Cistine withdrew, looking up at Julian. His face was a mask of concern as he brushed the damp tendrils of hair from her brow. "There's food in the kitchen. Baba Kallah made cinnamon strawberry bread and venison stew."

"That sounds delicious." Cistine took his hand and tugged him toward the hall, casting Thorne a grateful smile over one shoulder. He nodded in silent farewell and turned down the bedchamber corridor where the cabal slept; Ariadne hurried after him.

Cistine and Julian entered the short, dim hall with its three doors—one to the weapons loft, two each to a bedroom—and all at once Cistine forgot about Ariadne and Thorne. She forgot about food. She even forgot she was holding Julian's hand.

Ashe's room was so *empty*.

Not that she had frequented it, especially after the shrapnel wound in her leg had healed, but Cistine felt the absence echoing the void chamber in her heart where her Warden had lived. Her things were still scattered around the bed: weapons she'd neglected to bring to Villmark, changes of clothes neatly folded on the side table as the King's Cadre had taught her. The mill wheel churned outside the window, striping watery gray shadows along the floor and walls where she no longer lived.

"Princess?" Julian gave Cistine's hand a gentle tug.

She let her fingers fall from his. "I'm not really hungry. I think I'm going to lie down."

She padded into Ashe's room, running her hand over the wooden bedpost and coarse quilt. She sat and nestled her fingers into the pillowcase, and a puff of soapy scent wafted into her nose—the mahogany-and-rose smell that had belonged to Ashe ever since they came to the Den.

Julian cleared his throat from the doorway. "Do you want company?"

A tear snaked down Cistine's cheek. "No."

While his footsteps retreated, she stared at the pillow, grooming out the creases. In her mind she saw everything happen again: the sewer's damp coldness below the courthouse, Ashe's face up above, framed by a watery sky. Her grimness, her strength—her determination. The flash of pain when she threw her precious sword down the shaft to Maleck. When she fitted the grate again.

When she ran.

Maleck's cries and Cistine's own sobs still echoed in her ears, blending with the wheel's groan outside the window.

Footsteps shuffled back across the floor. Cistine struggled to take in a deep breath, to steady her voice. "I said I didn't want company."

"Well, that's all good," an elderly voice croaked, "but you never said you didn't want *food*."

Cistine whipped around on the bed, wiping furiously beneath her eyes. "Baba Kallah! I'm so sorry, I didn't mean to snap, I thought you were Julian."

"I can't say I've ever shared that delusion." Thorne's grandmother entered with a food platter in one hand, fresh clothes draped over her arm, and her cane in the other fist, her ravaged left leg dragging. Cistine shuddered at the memory of the man—Baba Kallah's own son, Thorne's father—who had shattered that leg beyond repair.

"I'm sorry," she said when the old woman set the platter on the bedside table. "I thought the Chancellor was going to help Talheim."

"Yes, Quill and Tatiana told me." Baba Kallah offered her the clothes, and Cistine ducked into the corner to peel from her soaked, heavy dress and drag on the soft muslin pajamas. They carried the smell of soap and the garden—of the times before she'd run away to Starhollow, and then to Stornhaz.

She turned around, limbs heavy and heart even heavier, to find Baba Kallah perched on the bed. She looked strikingly like her son in some ways—just like Thorne when the light caught his features at certain angles—and yet all those edges were softer in the frame of Baba Kallah's folded skin and kind eyes. "You shouldn't read letters that aren't addressed to you, *Yani*."

Wretched, heartbroken laughter burst from Cistine, and she collapsed onto the bed as well. "It's not a mistake I'll ever make again."

Baba Kallah tucked Cistine's hair behind her ear, examining the bruised skin around it. "A mother never wants to believe her child is beyond redemption. But after what Salvotor's done to you, I'd kill him myself."

Cistine buried her face in her hands. "I don't know how we're going to fight him. How *Thorne* is going to fight him."

"I have some thoughts. But let's leave talk of that until you're feeling yourself again."

"I don't think I'm going to feel like myself until we find Ashe."

Baba Kallah looped a strong arm around Cistine's shoulders. "It's all right to cry when something is taken from you. Strength isn't defined by whether we show our grief, it's *how* we show it. Whether it rules us or we rule it."

The tears started again, slow and silent, dripping from her chin. "If we don't find her, or if the Chancellor does something terrible to her before we reach her..." Cistine sniffled so deeply, it turned to a gasp for breath. "Baba, I don't know what I'm going to do."

The old woman tugged her around until their heads rested together. "You must find your courage, *Yani*. You must tap the wells of power in your own spirit, and fight. When you do, I know you will hit back strong. You've been learning Old Valgardan...the runes of our ancestors. Now you'll learn to speak the cabal's language, to strike with all your might and make certain my son hears you roar." Her free hand gently stroked Cistine's wrapped knuckles. "If I had to judge by these, though, I would say hitting back will not be a concern for you."

Cistine laughed again through her tears. Baba Kallah kissed her temple and rose slowly, then thumped her cane on the floor, commanding Cistine's attention. Sternness lined her brows and mouth—the strength of the exiled mother who watched her son's wrath unfold from the shadows and prayed for someone to put an end to it. "Spend your tears in this room. When you leave it, you must be stronger than you were before. You must find a way to walk forward, do you understand me? So spend them here. Fall a princess. Rise a queen."

With a parting smile, Baba Kallah gave her privacy. Cistine sank into it, dragging Ashe's pillow to her chest, but hugging it was nothing like putting her arms around her friend's solid, reassuring warmth. It did not bring Ashe back to her.

Cistine curled forward, buried her face in the fabric that still smelled like her Warden, and sobbed.

Days of walking on wounded feet, of heartache and headpain, of grappling with the absence of Ashe, slammed into her like toppling into raging waters again. She huddled on her side, face hidden in the damp pillow, and wept until she couldn't draw a full breath without choking.

She barely noticed when she was no longer alone.

Weight depressed the bed; it could only be Julian who sat beside her, rubbing her back in slow circles. Knowing words would offer no comfort, he gave none, just his steady hand tracing patterns between her shoulderblades, down her spine, and back again. After minutes of that touch, gentle and undemanding, her muscles loosened and she no longer gasped for breath. She loosened her grip on the pillow and pressed it more firmly to her face, humiliation heating her cheeks.

"I didn't want you to see me like this," she rasped. "A princess should be strong for her people."

His only answer was to stroke her hair back and plant a featherlight kiss on her temple. And then he was gone, wafting a strange smell over Cistine.

Not herbs and soap, but blood and rainwater.

Cistine eased into sleep without realizing it and woke in darkness. To her relief, some of the weight, the tightness, had lifted from her shoulders.

Someone was speaking her name.

She sat up sharply and a blanket fell from her body—Julian again. But it wasn't his voice she'd heard.

Brushing the tangled, dirty hair from her face, she squinted up at Maleck, his bruise-stamped eyes and hollow cheeks painted in the city's glare through the window.

"Come with me," he urged.

Cistine swung her legs from the bed and hesitated when her abused feet brushed the floor. Her tears had dried now; it was time to gather that pain among the linens of Ashe's bed and leave it to grow colder as they did, to step across that threshold and be better than the wounded child who'd fled Starhollow and gotten her Warden into this mess.

She was not bait. She was not a victim. She would rise and step from this room prepared to do what was necessary to unseat a Chancellor, to save her kingdom.

Cistine picked up the sliced bread and cup of soup Baba Kallah had left and ate them while she followed Maleck through the entry parlor, down the cabal's bedchamber corridor, and into his room for the first time. Most of the narrow space was taken up by a four-post bed, a thick armoire hewn with opposing stags, and a bench that hugged the bay window. There was hardly room to sidle between the bed and armoire, where Maleck stopped and nodded to the wall.

He'd mounted Echelon, Ashe's prized sword and a gift from Lord Rion Bartos, on a pair of golden hooks above the headboard.

"I won't use it," Maleck said, soft and earnest. "I intend to keep it pristine for her return."

Not a question. Not a glimmer of doubt in his voice.

"Do you have any idea where the Chancellor sent her?" Cistine's voice was still hoarse from sobbing.

Maleck spread his hands on the footboard, bending forward and staring up at Echelon. "I have several. They'll take time to sort through, but I give you my word, I will not rest until Ashe is safe."

Cistine glanced at him shrewdly. His posture, the clench of his jaw, the feralness in his gaze...they were the same as in the sewer when he'd been prepared to climb back up and face the Vassoran guards beside Ashe, even if death took them both. Only the sound of his Name on Thorne's lips, a sacred word with the power to cut through a warrior's wildest will, had held him back.

Maleck Darkwind.

That day, Cistine had learned who he truly was. Not the death-god who patrolled highways in search of people to slaughter and caravans to raid, but her equal, her friend in the hunt to find Ashe.

He would help her bring her Warden home or die trying.

"I'm sorry I left Starhollow how I did," Cistine said. "I put Ashe in this position, and I *need* your help now, Maleck. I'll never find her on my own."

Maleck dipped his head. "Of course you have my assistance. And you have my apology, *Logandir*. Your anger was not without merit."

"Well, I forgive you, too." Cistine offered him a tentative smile. "And I'm grateful to share this hunt with you."

Maleck's cheek ticked. Then he turned again, and they stared up at the sword—a token of this vow.

Together, they would bring Ashe home.

CHAPTER
THREE

T HE PRISON CART gutted itself in yet another rut, snapping Ashe from a dream of her parents' bakery in Astoria. The warm smells of rising dough, fruity pie filling, and powdered sugar sank beneath the stink of waste and sweat in the wagon. Less-familiar scents of sun-soaked sand and hot rocks perfumed the arid atmosphere, as they had for the past several days of travel.

For the first time in her life, Ashe considered herself lucky to have seen war when she was twelve. Unfavorable conditions hadn't broken her spirit then and they would not break it now; not when she had a vendetta to repay against everyone who'd harmed her princess in this gods-forsaken kingdom.

She swiped her tongue along her cracked lips, peering around the cart. When they dragged her from the city of Stornhaz and threw her in the back of this cart, she'd become one of a half a dozen prisoners bound for gods-knew where—most with jutting clavicles and protuberant ribs, eyes sunken and cheeks caving inward, skin bonded to their skulls. The others never spoke, only moving when they licked sweat off their arms.

The silence had given Ashe plenty of time to grapple with the shock and fury after the battle in the courthouse where she learned augmentation still existed. What a *flagon* really was.

She'd taken the first few days in the cart to come to grips with the knowledge that somehow, Valgard clung to their augments after the war to seal the Doors. She supposed she should have expected that; these people were all conniving bastards, with perhaps one or two exceptions, so of course they'd found some clever way to cling to their power stashed in those innocuous little jars.

Now all she wanted to do was get her hands around their necks and pay them back for that deception. Instead, she was trapped in this cart, sweating mercilessly and healing from the beating they'd dealt her, her mind with her princess.

She prayed Cistine was all right. The last time she'd seen her—bleeding from one ear, hand, jaw, and temple swelling—Ashe had been ready to kill Chancellor Salvotor, the man responsible. Her only regret was that she hadn't gotten her hands around his throat before his retinue head, Devitrius, had drugged her and tossed her into this cart.

But here she was, days from Stornhaz now, and more than that from Cistine, from Julian.

From Maleck.

At least Echelon was safe with him. She hoped he'd use it to chop Salvotor's head off. If anyone in the cabal could reach the Chancellor and mete out the vengeance he deserved, it was a warrior who'd fought in the battle between the Middle and Northern Kingdoms. Someone capable of near-impossible killing feats; her equal in every way but heritage.

She pushed out the memory of how she'd felt when he burst into that courtyard with the rest of the cabal, searching for Cistine; of the way he'd looked at her from the sewer when she flung her sword down to him; of the echo of his cry, her name on his lips, while she led the Vassora away.

Maleck wasn't here. He couldn't help her. She had to help herself.

Ashe flexed her wrists against their leather bonds and brought her knees to her chest, one after the other, loosening her cramped muscles. The prisoners watched her with languished, unfocused eyes, and she ignored them. She'd given up trying to convince them to fight for themselves, to at least attempt to keep their minds and bodies ready for whatever lay ahead. It would be far worse than death, and she was determined to face it on her feet and with a blade in her hand if she could find one.

The cart struck another rut, tipping precariously to one side, and Ashe's head glanced off the wall. She caught a faceful of air between the wooden slats and sucked it down like a drowning sailor; with it came a distant, pungent reek and the nauseating grease of cooking oil.

Far away, above the creaking wagon wheels and plodding horses that dragged them to their inexorable fate, there was music.

Ashe's spirit would have known the sounds anywhere: drunk shanties belted out by croaky voices, and drums, sitars, and a flute or two, mostly played off-rhythm in a way that made even Cistine's pitiful childhood attempts at the violin seem passable.

The cart's progress slowed. Voices joined the music, singing and shouting gleefully. Ashe pressed her cheek to the wall, ignoring the splinters that dug against her skin, and inhaled deeply through the small seam as they trundled on. She smelled vomit now, mixed with barley grains and spice and rich perfumes that usually hovered around brothels in Astoria; cookfire notes, sizzling fruit, and something nutty.

A hand slammed against the wood, and Ashe jerked back, cursing. More hands joined in, hitting and flailing, rocking the wagon; the hoots turned to a slur of excitement, though Ashe couldn't make out what they were saying. Devitrius shouted from the wagon seat in a smug voice Ashe had already grown to despise, and the hands withdrew. The cart picked up speed, and when Ashe scooted back to the slat, she saw nothing but shadows.

The wagon rolled to a sudden halt, and she spun on her haunches to face the door. They'd stopped several times on the journey to water the horses, for Devitrius and his people to stretch their legs, but this was the first time they'd been near civilization.

The latch rattled, and she pushed herself up on one knee. Her other leg, wounded by shrapnel and still newly-healed, twitched with the beginnings of a cramp.

"No," Ashe hissed at it. If this was her one chance to run, she would drag that wounded leg behind her all the way to Talheim, where she'd ordered Julian to take Cistine. She would endure any pain to return to her princess.

The door eased open, and Ashe whipped forward, slamming it with her shoulder and breaking through.

A hand chopped her throat, stealing the breath from her body. She plummeted chest-first onto the ground, breasts throbbing, chin bleeding, lungs shriveling, no time to catch her wind before a boot flipped her onto her back. A blue-black sky met her gaze, stars blotting out when Devitrius loomed over her. "You're going to be very popular here, *korvat*."

Ashe lurched up and tried to sweep his feet with hers. He danced nimbly out of reach, chuckling.

"Get her on her feet," he ordered the Vassoran guard at the cart door.

Ashe didn't resist when the man took her elbow and drew her up. She was too busy taking stock of her surroundings, searching for any escape from this—

Desert.

Red sand dunes, a thin moon hanging low over the dark horizon, a small tent city with canvassed sides rolled up to the frame, and beyond them, white stone homes with wooden-shuttered windows and flat rooftops, all crowded around an oasis pond. Ashe didn't realize she'd shifted toward the distant sight of dark water until the guard snatched her backward against his chest, erupting pain along the places where his friends had beaten her bloody in Stornhaz.

Water forgotten, Ashe dreamed of killing again.

Devitrius lined up the other prisoners behind the cart, their eyes downcast, hands bound just like Ashe. "Listen here. You will go where the guard leads. If you stray to the right or the left, my whip will put you back in place. If you run, the Viperwolves will be unleashed to chase you down. That's an end no one wants to see. March."

The Vassoran guard towed Ashe around the wagon, and the other prisoners fell into step. When they passed between the bowing frond trees, Ashe caught her first glimpse of their destination.

Its height alone left her speechless. Symmetrical arches pocked the elliptical structure's outer wall, three levels high, its upper edge capped by half-roofs on struts. Pendants fluttered from the wall, moonlight tracing their imagery: four chalice-wielding women, a cowled figure, a man with a bow, a curl of shadow, a mace-wielding conqueror.

The symbols of the five Courts. Ashe longed to grind them into the sand.

Before the mammoth structure, two statues rose half the wall's height, halberds crossed and murderous faces opposing one another. The guards marched them underneath the crossed weapons, through a ground-level arch, down a short corridor, and through an iron gate Ashe's escort paused to unlock. The sandy arena beyond it, with its circumference of seats above a high, freshly-oiled stone wall, reminded Ashe of a hundred summer days spent in Astoria's great circus, yawning at her post while Cistine bounced and squealed over the dazzling equine performances and Julian bombarded his mother with questions about horse breeds.

She doubted this place was meant for the same balancing acts and prancing ponies.

In the very heart of the arena, they halted along a stone promenade peeking through the freshly-dragged sand. Ashe wrinkled her nose when the other prisoners clustered to her right, trapping her once again in the smell of waste and body odor; Devitrius and the guards boxed them in from both sides, discouraging escape.

And they waited.

There were three entrances in view: the gate they passed through and two more off to the left and right. One was directly beside an enormous box draped in garlands and twines of blue and silver lace. Everything else was stone seats and steps accessible from hidden staircases with a few niches between.

Another gate groaned open, interrupting her cursory assessment.

Make that *four* entrances. She hadn't noticed the last one at the arena's edge, buried below the sandline; but now a man mounted those steps and approached them. Muscle banded and sun-browned, his hair long and gold like a lion's mane, he halted before the prisoners, folded his arms, and surveyed the pitiful line they formed.

And Ashe remembered the war.

It was a vague glimpse of the first time Lord Rion had left her alone after he found her sneaking on their heels into the Northern Kingdom. She'd been posted on the front's quietest edge while he slipped away to relieve himself, alone for only a few moments when a boy with a strange face and dead eyes attacked from the dark gaps between the trees. Lightning augments had shattered the oaks to splinters on every side, and Ashe had dropped her sword in shock at the raw display of power; she'd fallen to her seat in the snow and scrambled back when he stalked toward her.

And then she saw how young he was, barely older than her. Swiping up her sword again, holding it two-handed, she'd *screamed* in his face, "I'm not afraid of you!"

He'd stopped. In that moment, she'd felt nothing but power. With her voice alone, without swinging her sword a single time, she'd brought the enemy to a halt.

That same power blooded Ashe's body now when she stared at this Valgardan who tried to intimidate them with his stormy gray stare. He was just like all the rest of them...nothing to be feared.

Ashe let her eyes fall to half-mast and stared right back.

"Nowhere near as impressive as the last bunch you brought me, Devitrius," the man said, his attention trained on Ashe. "If I didn't know better, I'd think you were trying to sabotage the games."

Devitrius chuckled. "Chancellor Salvotor had the same thought about you. That's why he sent me personally to observe the fighters."

The man tipped his head. "Then by all means. Observe."

With a mocking roll of the arm, Devitrius strutted away to the fourth gate. The guards snapped their heels together as the gray-eyed man prowled before the prisoners, observing them one by one.

"I assume you know why you're here, but on the chance you're ignorant, allow me to inform you." He faced them again, folding his hands at his back, and that movement stirred Ashe's unease.

It wasn't the posture of some scrappy pit rat; it was the way the King's

Cadre faced their Commander before dispatch each morning.

"This is Siralek," the man said, "the Blood Hive. In this place, pilgrims from the northern cities and elites from Stornhaz find entertainment like nothing else Valgard has to offer."

He scraped the sand with the side of his boot, and Ashe's empty stomach lurched with revulsion.

There were shards of *bone* hidden under this fresh sand.

"You are here as criminals deemed beyond rehabilitation. Your only chance to stay entrance into Nimmus a bit longer is to fight." He paused, letting his words settle in. "You will be fed and trained. When I deem you ready, you will fight man and beast on these sands until your last breath is ripped from you. If you're lucky, you'll have made penance with the gods enough that you'll see Cenowyn rather than the Sable Gates when your eyes close." He looked at Ashe again, his lip curling. "But I doubt that."

Ashe's tested her bonds, angling her body forward.

"I will determine your rank and status in the arena," the man went on, turning his attention from her. "I will personally see to it you're given enough training that they can make some sport of you before you're carried out on a pallet."

A prisoner whimpered softly, the first sound Ashe had heard from any of them.

"The testing will begin at dawn," the man said. "Until then—"

"Why wait?" Ashe interjected. "Why not test us now and see what we're capable of at our worst? Without water, with pitiful scraps for rations in our bellies, after days in a cart."

He swiveled back to face her, and she met his contempt with a glare. She'd been condescended to all her life for her choice to join the King's Cadre. Her parents lied to their upstanding friends about her occupation. Other Wardens discussed her behind her back and made training after the war an absolute nightmare. She'd quietly smashed apart every hurdle in her path and earned the right to defend Princess Cistine, to walk through the King's Citadel with her head high while lesser Wardens averted their gazes.

She would not bow before this lord of the sands.

The man addressed the nearest guard without averting his gaze: "Unbind her."

The leather cuffs disappeared, and for the first time in days Ashe had full mobility in her arms. She loosened the tight muscles between her shoulders with several swings and moved away from the other prisoners. She was certainly exhausted, dehydrated, and famished. But she'd been all those things and more during the war, and survived.

The man did nothing to limber up. As arrogant as he was good-looking, he faced her without any show of aggression except for that smug stare.

"Why don't we make this a bet?" Ashe challenged. "If you win, I'll submit to your pitiful training."

He raised a brow. "And if *you* win?"

"I get first pick of all the meals. And I have your name, so I can call you like a slave whenever I have use for you."

His jaw tightened sharply and true dislike narrowed his eyes. "A wager I'll gladly make, because there's no hope you'll defeat me."

"I take it you've never fought a woman before."

"Plenty of times. Don't flatter yourself—you're nothing special here."

How wrong he was.

Ashe snapped forward; with the advantage of surprise before he knew her style, she could get in one hit, perhaps ending the fight with it.

The man brought up his hand and slapped her clean across the face, setting her ear ringing and jerking tears from her eyes.

Ashe stumbled, the sand giving out under her feet. He caught her arm, swung her in a half-circle, and threw her to her chest. Stunned, spitting granules from her lips, Ashe pushed herself up and whirled to face him, fists raised to block the next slap.

His ankle swept both of hers and he caught her throat this time, flinging her backward onto her seat.

Again, she rose, more furious than focused. He wasn't trying. He wasn't even breaking a sweat.

She sprang toward him, tactics be damned. This time he boxed her ears, grabbed a fistful of her hair, looped an arm around her waist and dumped her over his shoulder, kicking her onto her stomach.

Choking on her own breath, ribs and back throbbing, Ashe couldn't move. She could barely draw air through her trembling lips.

He'd beaten her. She hadn't even landed a single blow on him, and he'd *beaten* her. Not since Rion had anyone *ever* devastated her so thoroughly in manual combat.

His boot ground into her spine, just like Devitrius in the courtyard while he and Salvotor decided her fate. "That was a valiant effort. No one has ever challenged the Lord of the Hive outright on their first day. Valiant...but foolish."

Ashe couldn't catch enough breath to spit that she was both of those things, always, and she didn't need to be told so from the likes of him.

The man crouched, pressing her deeper into the sand. "Welcome to Nimmus. My name is Aden. I'm here to lead you through the Sable Gates."

CHAPTER
FOUR

ASHE'S HEAD STILL rattled with shock after the guards laid hands on her again. With the other prisoners trailing like cattle to slaughter, they descended into the hole where Devitrius had gone.

She still couldn't believe it; he'd devastated her in just a few blows. This *Aden*—

She knew that name. Where did she know it from?

Sense slammed into her along with a deluge of cold water chasing the air from her lungs again. She was propped with her palms against a stone wall while someone cast water all over her rank body; rough hands tore her ratty clothes from her back and another bucket soaked her naked flanks, her skin seizing up on her bones. A pitted sponge scraped off a week of sweat, urine, and hard manure from her flesh; she tried to turn, to see who she owed this degradation to, but the sting of a crop across her shoulders jerked her back toward the wall.

When the cold water struck again, Ashe hung her head and prayed.

The guards bundled clothing into her arms, yanked her from the wall, and led her naked and confused through a pattern of stone corridors to a metal gate barring darkness beyond. They thrust her past it so forcefully her knees cracked on the floor; when she whirled onto her feet, ignoring a twinge in her injured leg, they slammed the gate in her face.

"Dress," one of them snapped. Then they left.

Ashe dropped the bundle of rags, pressed her hands to the walls, and followed them all the way around a circular cell, barely twelve feet deep, all solid stone. When she came back to the gate, she shivered so violently her fingers rattled the iron.

She slowly laid out her attire. The outfit was far more revealing than anything she was used to wearing, little more than a leather band for her breasts and gauzy skirts that fell to the mid-thigh. But at least they'd provided a wool cardigan to cover it.

Ashe dressed briskly, then sat against the wall with the cardigan's hood drawn up, rubbing her hands to warm them. As the shivers eased, she slowly found her calm.

She would survive this cruel fighting arena and escape. She would go home again at any cost.

Hours passed before Ashe had company; the door rattled, and when it swung open she was already up, grabbing a loose stone and stepping forward to meet this newcomer.

A hand caught her fist before she could smash the rock into the first inch of flesh she found. In the muted glare of torchlight shining from the corridor beyond, Ashe faced another woman: pale as soured milk, redheaded and freckled, scowling fiercely.

"We know all the tricks." Her voice belonged in this desert, dry and coarse like sand itself. "The way you tried to look at the guards when they scrubbed you, we knew *you*, too. How defiant you would be."

Ashe wrenched her arm free and took a step back. "You watched them bathe me?"

"We watch everything that happens here." The woman settled a bowl on the floor between them. "My name is Nimea. Let me be the first to formally welcome you to Siralek."

Ashe snatched up the bowl and forced herself to sip the thin broth rather than gulping it the way her parched throat begged her to. "Aden already gave me a warm welcome."

"You challenged him?" Nimea swept her with an appreciative look.

"Don't feel badly that he won, he's the strongest of us all. He's never walked away from a match without winning."

"I would think the same is true for everyone here."

"Winning isn't the only way to stay alive." With a jerk of her sleeve, Nimea exposed six notches on her forearm. "If you lose, but the crowd finds you amusing, they can cry for mercy. But that's not without consequences."

Ashe wiped her mouth on her wrist. "This is what the elite of Valgard find entertaining?"

"Not to hear them tell it at their fine suppers. But some still crave bloodshed, and the Hive gives it to them."

"I suppose it's one way to keep the prisons from becoming overpopulated. What was your crime?"

Nimea's smile was all teeth. "They call us *svakari*—because the common language of the Three Kingdoms has no word strong enough for traitors like us."

Ashe tossed the bowl into the corner. "Who did you betray?"

"In their eyes, the very heart of Valgard. And you?"

Ashe grimaced. "I loved someone so much, I ran into danger with them. It got me captured."

Nimea slapped Ashe on the back. "I think we've all been victims of that lapse in judgement a time or two." She marched to the gate. "Are you coming?"

Ashe prowled after her. "I thought this was my cell."

Nimea's laughter barked against the walls. "What makes you think you're so special?"

They circled a small bend just outside the chamber and entered a long hall full of empty doorways. Ghostlamps draped its spine, their eerie bioluminescence smudging the walls green-and-black as Nimea led her down a second corridor on the left, this one so narrow they couldn't walk side-by-side. Alcoves were hollowed from the clayish stone, each one as long as a body and as tall as Ashe's forearm.

Somehow, people were *sleeping* in them.

"Choose whichever one you like," Nimea said. "Though I should warn you, the rats have no qualms about nibbling on whoever takes the lower shelves."

"This is not a *bed*," Ashe seethed. "It's a tomb."

Nimea shrugged. "Welcome to the catacombs of Siralek."

At the rasp of a clearing throat behind them, Ashe and Nimea turned together. Aden leaned against the narrow corridor mouth, arms folded, head bent to the side, and assessed them with blatant suspicion. "I see you've wasted no time with this one, Nimea."

She shrugged. "Well, since your guards seemed content to let her rot of hunger in that cell..."

"They aren't my guards. I'm just another prisoner to them."

"To the Vassora, maybe. But the rest of the guards here?"

Aden's eyes flicked to Ashe, and she folded her arms and cocked a brow.

"At least leave some piece of her intact for tomorrow's exercises." Aden unfolded from the wall and strode toward the two women, forcing them to part for him. Beside Ashe, he lingered, cutting her a glance from the corner of one eye. "You may want to sleep on the lower beds. We choose warriors for the hardest matches from the top, and you aren't ready yet."

Like a specter, he vanished around a bend in the hall.

Ashe swiveled back to face Nimea, who blew a wayward strand of filthy hair from her brow. "Do whatever you like. The top is safest, but maybe Aden plans to change his tactics now that we have fresh blood."

Ashe rested her hand on an alcove sill and peered inside. Her skin crawled when something dark and many-legged scuttled along the back wall. "What's his story? This *Aden*?"

"Sedition. They brought him here to be made example of. Instead of crumbling like most do, Aden climbed," Nimea said. "Rumor has it he holds more than half the guards under his control now."

"Tales he could tell about them?"

"Or they're just terrified of him. Whatever his tactics are, he runs these catacombs like a Court of his own. Almost nothing happens without his knowledge."

"Almost?"

Nimea smirked. "You should sleep. Dawn will come quickly, and you'll have another taste of Nimmus with it."

Ashe swallowed her revulsion and climbed into an alcove one level up from the floor, lying nose-to-stone with the roof. Eyes clamped shut, she forced herself to breathe deeply.

She could do this. She would walk through fire and bloodshed to reach her princess, sleep wherever she had to, and kill anyone they put in her path. These lives meant nothing, these Valgardan prisoners already condemned to die. She would burn through them like fire through chaff.

No matter who she faced in that arena, man or beast, the only person standing in the way of her freedom was its lord—this *Aden*.

CHAPTER FIVE

CISTINE HAD NEVER seen so many downcast eyes and solemn mouths among the cabal. With a fair night's sleep behind her and one of Maleck's poultices oozing over her wrapped knuckles—and those held safe in Julian's hand—she took stock of their faces around the Den's kitchen table.

Thorne sat across from her at the opposite end, with Baba Kallah on his right and Maleck on his left. Beside Maleck, Quill gnawed on a cinnamon stick, frowning at the bowl of bran muffins before him. Julian sat beside Quill, his face a calm mask Cistine was grateful for.

Tatiana sat to Cistine's left, though she hadn't spoken a single word to her since they'd fled Stornhaz, the silence as deafening as her ruptured eardrum. Ariadne, next to Tatiana, pared her nails with a knife and stared down the table at Thorne. Faer flapped and croaked from his perch in the window beside the big-bellied stove, filling the quiet.

Finally, Thorne cleared his throat. "Cistine has heard me say this already, but it bears repeating. I apologize for my actions these past few weeks, for keeping the truth from you about the blood I share with Salvotor and my initial intentions with you. That was dishonorable, no better than what my father himself would have done. I ask for your forgiveness."

Cistine held his gaze, ruler to ruler. "You have it."

"You have our apology as well," Maleck said. "We kept Thorne's confidence out of respect for our leader, but that was no longer any excuse once you became our friend."

"I especially should have pushed him much harder to be honest," Baba Kallah admitted. "I am sorry, *Yani.*"

Cistine's eyes burned—not because they had lied, but because they were sorry for it. Every head around the table nodded with regret, even if it was grudging from Tatiana.

"I forgive you all." Cistine ignored Julian's quiet snort. "You had your kingdom to think of, I had mine. But from now on, I think we can all agree honesty would be best. Which is why I owe you an apology, too."

No one made a sound, though Maleck turned in his seat to pay her his full attention. Julian's fingers tightened slightly around hers.

"I'm sorry for leaving Starhollow how I did," Cistine said. "I behaved like a spoiled child, not a princess. I should've discussed my offenses instead of running from them."

"Apology accepted," Maleck said.

Ariadne's gaze drifted to Ashe's empty chair. "The lesson taught itself."

"Accepted," Thorne said.

"Accepted." Baba Kallah tapped the tip of her cane underneath the table. "I hope you'll think twice before reading other people's letters from now on, though."

"As long as I can expect honesty, I don't think I'll feel the need to." Cistine stared at Thorne, who had the decency to grimace.

"Tatiana?" Maleck rumbled. "Quill?"

They didn't look at each other, but their silent unison forged a cold wall across the table.

"Are we done here?" Tatiana asked. "I should be on patrol."

"Organizing your closet, more like," Quill said under his breath.

"Take a long dive off a short cliff."

"Following your lead."

"That's enough," Thorne cut in. "This meeting isn't just about the apology we owe Cistine. It's to discuss our movements going forward."

"Now that Kanslar has risen?" Ariadne asked. "Or now that you've faced your father for the first time in a decade and seen what he's capable of?"

Thorne drummed the tabletop. "Both. We know what Salvotor has been doing while Kanslar was out of session."

"Hiring expensive surgeons to graft reinforcements under his skin," Tatiana said sourly. "I sense a new trend in Valgardan fashion."

"It's no wonder he was so quick to act at the Conqueror's advent this time," Maleck mused. "He intends to stamp out our rebellion before the constellation sets."

"He's anticipating direct confrontation," Julian said, and Cistine swiveled toward him in surprise. He met her eyes and shrugged. "My father was the King's Cadre Commander. You think I don't know my way around a battle strategy?"

Ariadne cocked her head. "Julian is right. These aren't the blows we've swung against each other in the dark over the years. Salvotor was prepared this time."

"No surprise there." Quill flopped his augment-bleached hair over one side of his head, baring the long scar there—a wound that shocked the roots silver, just like Thorne's. "Considering his informants in the other Courts."

The cabal all looked around the table at each other, and Thorne to Cistine, who gripped Julian's hand until her fractured knuckles throbbed. Now that she understood the significance of the name she'd revealed to the cabal—Devitrius, one of Salvotor's closest confidants—the gravity of Quill's statement raked her skin with shivers.

"Thorne, this is too large for us," Tatiana said. "Too many parts in motion."

"I agree," Thorne said. "And the time of resisting from the shadows is over. Salvotor is ready to evolve the conflict. Are we?"

Ariadne grazed her flat hand down the bandolier of knives strapped across her front. "Yes."

Maleck nodded. "We have no other choice."

"That's why we're here, isn't it?" Quill said. "To find a way to put that *bandayo* in his place."

Tatiana folded her arms and tapped her polished nails on her elbows. "I'm in for it if the rest of you are."

Silence reigned. Thorne looked at Cistine again, startling her so much she sat straighter in her seat. "Me?"

"You have scars from him now, like the rest of us. Are you prepared to repay him for that?"

Julian scowled at him. "Ashe told me to get Cistine back to Talheim. That's what we're going to do."

Cistine pulled her hand from his. "I will never, *never* forget the sacrifice Ashe made in that courthouse, but it wasn't her choice to make whether I go. It's not yours either, Julian."

His eyes widened. "You want to *stay*?"

"Yes, to save Talheim. We still need Valgard's strength to discourage Mahasar, and we won't find any aid while Salvotor is controlling three of the five Courts." She grimaced. "Not to mention his interest in Talheim. If his plans succeed, we may find ourselves with enemies at both borders. You remember what our fathers said...we can't afford that."

Julian opened his mouth to protest, and Cistine cut him off: "I'm in this, Julian. For Ashe. For the Middle Kingdom. Are you with me?"

His jaw snapped shut, working furiously. After a heart-stopping moment of humiliating silence, he nodded.

Thorne dipped his head. "Baba Kallah?"

Her mouth puckered with aged stripes. "In offering a hand of spite to Talheim's princess, Salvotor does more than endanger this cabal. He risks open war with the Middle Kingdom...a war we couldn't win before, even with the Doors to the Gods open below our feet. He's always been dangerous to those closest to him, but now he imperils all Valgard. He must certainly be stopped, *Stornjor*. But carefully."

Thorne inclined himself, hands clasped and face toward Baba Kallah. "What do you suggest I do?"

She balanced her chin on her folded hands, tipping her cane slowly back and forth. "You have allies of your own within the Courts. Men and women of Traisende and Yager who were open to your talk of fairer rulings and just dealings before you were driven out. Now may be the time to meet with them, to treat openly and plainly."

"Would they really listen to him?" Julian asked. "No offense—he's been disgraced for a decade."

"True," Thorne agreed. "But I'm still Kanslar's High Tribune."

"How is that possible if you're in exile?"

"To unseat a High Tribune and have him stripped of his title requires a unanimous vote among the Chancellors and other Tribunes. According to our allies among the Courts, the motion over my title was stymied by one vote."

Cistine's skin prickled. "Who could've wanted you to keep your title?"

Thorne spanned his hands in a broad shrug. "No one who's bothered to find me in the past decade, but it gives us leverage with our allies. They'll need an incentive to stand with us, and my title, however buried, gives them that."

Cistine took Julian's hand again and squeezed it, excitement bursting through her. They could unseat Salvotor and place Thorne on the Judgement Seat, and at last, Talheim would have allies.

"You really think these contacts will agree to this?" Julian's question blunted the edge of her glee. "It's an awful lot to hang on a title and hope."

"It's entirely within reason," Baba Kallah said. "These are people with valiant hearts who stand for something good and true. If they know what Salvotor is plotting, they may be willing to offer us support. Perhaps even openly."

"What Salvotor is plotting,'" Cistine echoed. "You mean his intentions for me?"

Now it was Julian's hand that tightened, so sharply he pinched her knuckles. Cistine jumped and hissed, and Thorne's eyes shot to her.

"Most of these Chancellors are still nursing the wounds where your father and grandfather kicked them during the war," Baba Kallah explained. "They wouldn't be eager to enter into conflict with the Middle Kingdom again. And if Salvotor forced it on them, especially by uniting the five Courts..."

"They would be furious, and fight back," Ariadne finished.

"You have my permission to tell them," Cistine said, "if Baba Kallah believes it will sway the free Courts to our side."

"They might believe me," Thorne said. "But it would be better coming from your mouth."

Cistine swallowed, laying her free hand over her stomach as the thought of facing another Chancellor, another courtroom, washed through her. "I can't. I can't face them. They would never believe a foreigner, a *Talheimic...*"

"They would believe a princess," Thorne said, "if you stood before them as one."

Julian's hand was suddenly a cage around hers, just like the throne she was destined to inherit, and Cistine withdrew again and shot to her feet. "Excuse me."

She walked blindly down the short hall to her own room and out onto the balcony, where there was a door she could close. Trembling, she leaned against the wooden railing and stared out across the garden, wishing for a moment she was only a gardener, not a princess bound for a crown she didn't know how to wear.

The door opened behind her, and she recognized the heavy footfalls a moment before Thorne said, "You make a habit of disappearing when you feel overwhelmed, don't you?"

She buried her forehead on her folded arms, hiding from him. "It seems to be happening more often lately."

His heat wrapped around her from the side. Though he made no sound, she suspected he was leaning against the railing, too. "The first time my father ever forced me into a courtroom, I almost lost control of my bladder." Surprised laughter bubbled from Cistine, and Thorne chuckled with her. "I know, I know. Amusing now, but at the time I felt only humiliation. Never believe it's been easy to come from there to here."

"To leading the cabal?"

"That, and to making life-or-death decisions, or putting myself before Traisende and Yager where I can't control the outcome."

Cistine peered up at him, keeping her nose and mouth buried in the crook of her elbow. He was studying the garden as if the solutions to all their problems might be growing on the trellises there; and how she wished they were. "But you have almost a decade more experience than me with being a High Tribune people *do* listen to. I'm a princess, but I've only been a figurehead in Talheim. Purely seen, never heard."

"Was that the people's choice?" Thorne asked. "Or yours?"

She frowned. "A bit of both, maybe. Until my twentieth birthday, there was no reason for them to notice me except at parties or when I sat beside my mother during receiving hours. I started to prefer that...not being noticed in my title. It gave me the freedom to read and gossip and drink tea."

"That's what you have here. Freedom. If you choose not to face Traisende and Yager, I'll find some way to convince them on my own."

"Thank you, Thorne."

"But," he added, "you also have the freedom to stand next to me. We can begin to show them a possibility of Talheim and Valgard united. Even if we manage to unseat my father and I ascend to the Judgement Seat, I can still only put the might of our forces behind you for a few months at a time. If you want Valgard to stand with the Middle Kingdom against King Jad, we'll have to convince the other Chancellors as well. I'll do what I can to help, but this was always going to come down to you."

Cistine groaned. "I've been trying not to think of it like that."

"Politics are complicated, particularly when you're trying to win the favor of Chancellors. It's best to start small. And since Yager and Traisende are already sympathetic to our cause, you'll find no better ears to practice on."

"But I failed to even get in a word of my plans with Salvotor. He talked right over me. Ashe and Julian were right, I don't know how to be a princess who negotiates. Even you were manipulating me when we made a truce for my training."

Thorne shifted awkwardly, bending his head. "True. But what about when Quill was worried for Tatiana, and you still convinced him to train you the next day? Or when you commanded Julian's respect in Villmark? You weren't being manipulated then."

A touch of strength sizzled through Cistine's body—then dimmed. "But I wasn't trying to be a princess with them. Quill was my friend, and I wanted to help him. And Julian...Julian infuriated me. He made me want to fight for myself."

"You're thinking too much about what being a princess means. Stop imitating nobility, and do the noble thing. The rest will follow."

Cistine drew a deep breath through her nostrils, straightening up to grip the railing with both hands. "I think I can manage that."

"Then I have your permission to write to my contacts in Traisende and Yager that we'll meet with them?"

That heavy, long breath melted out of her. "Yes, on one condition. I want to meet somewhere private that puts us all on common footing."

Thorne's mouth tipped up. "I think I know just the place. I'll add political decorum to your training regimen until then, if you're ready to start again."

"Anything to keep my mind occupied. Who's going to teach me?"

"I am, if you'll have me."

"Of course I'll have you!" Cistine grinned. "Who better than a disgraced High Tribune to teach me the ways of Valgardan politics?"

"That may have been an insult, but I'll gladly take it," Thorne laughed. "It's good to see you smiling again."

He slipped indoors before Cistine could decide if she wanted to throw her shoe at him or stick out her tongue.

She settled for following him back to the kitchen instead.

Ariadne and Tatiana had already left. Baba Kallah pottered around at the counter on the far wall, mincing garlic for the night's meal, while Quill fed Faer a handful of stale bread. Julian looked up from the table when Cistine entered, his brows rising in silent question.

"I'm going to do it." The words filled her with a thrill of fear and anticipation. "I'm going to speak to the Chancellors with Thorne."

Julian's mouth settled into a scowl. "What did he say to you?"

"Only what I needed to hear to make my choice. Why?"

He folded his arms. "I just don't appreciate the way he manages to talk you into everything you don't want to do."

Cistine stared at him. "I'm doing what's best for Talheim."

"So, that's the line he fed you." Julian got to his feet. "At least I know who to go to when I want to convince you of something against your will."

"Excuse me?"

Julian flicked a hand. "Nevermind. Just try to remember we're not here to help *him*."

He left before Cistine could muster a comeback. Rubbing embarrassed goosebumps from her arms, she glanced at Baba Kallah, watching her sidelong from the counter; Quill, dropping his gaze quickly back to Faer; and Maleck, still sitting at the table, scribbling hastily on a thread of long parchment—the kind they used to send messages with the raven.

"He's just grouchy, that's all." She hated the words the moment they left her mouth—hated that she was apologizing once again for a spat with Julian.

When no one spoke, Cistine shuffled up behind Maleck's seat, laying her hands on the back of the chair next to his. "Thorne is going to help me prepare to face the Chancellors, but that means I won't be able to devote as much time to finding Ashe. Will you let me know if you find *anything* that might lead us to her?"

"Of course. Besides my cabal duties, finding Ashe is my priority."

He went back to writing, oblivious that Cistine was staring at him, or that her throat and eyes burned at the quiet dedication of this Valgardan warrior who placed so much value on the life of a Warden from a once-enemy kingdom.

Before she could question her own sanity, Cistine slid behind Maleck's chair and wrapped her arms around his neck, squeezing his powerful shoulders until his writing hand went slack.

"Thank you," she whispered. "For caring enough to even try."

He was motionless under her touch, and she started to pull away—embarrassed by her forwardness, afraid that some intangible line had been crossed with this death-god who was set apart from the rest of the world.

And then Maleck reached across himself and caught her elbow. He rested his chin in the crook of her arm and nodded, holding her gently but firmly in place.

Faer—fed and satisfied—took wing suddenly, gliding from Quill's shoulder into the hall. Without a word to any of them, Quill pushed away from the counter and followed, and Maleck spoke to Cistine without looking up: "Go after him. It's time we restored peace in the Den."

She wasn't looking forward to this conversation, or to the one with Tatiana; but it had to be done. So she gave Maleck one last squeeze and hurried into the hall. "Quill!"

He ignored her. Cistine broke into a jog, grabbed the hinge of his elbow, and yanked with all her might. "Quill, I need you to talk to me."

This time, he planted his feet and swung around to face her. His frigid demeanor, when he'd been so full of warm energy since the moment she met him, iced her muscles. "I have patrol."

"I thought that was Tatiana's excuse."

Quill shrugged away her hand, staring down at her, and the exhaustion in his face socked Cistine's belly. "What do you want?"

"To apologize for breaking your nose and leaving the way I did."

"You didn't break my nose. Just rearranged it a bit."

His curt retort ushered in something Cistine had never known in his presence: pure discomfort. "Storming off like I did wasn't noble or mature, I recognize that. But I did have my reasons."

"Because we lied to you."

"Yes, you did. But I do still consider you my friend, Quill. All of you. And I apologize for the hurt I caused."

"This isn't about me." He thumped his body against the wall, turning his face away from her. "Pippet panicked when you left."

Dry-mouthed, Cistine stared at him. Pippet, Quill's younger sister, had lived in Starhollow most of her life. After more than a decade in seclusion, she was beginning to dream of the world outside the meadow's confines— and that clashed with the cabal's fierce determination to keep her safe. "I didn't think she cared enough to notice I was gone. She hardly liked me, Quill."

"Pip feels more strongly than most people realize. She followed us, and we were too worried about you to notice. She almost made it into the wilds on her own."

Now it was Cistine's turn to lean against the wall, shoulder-to-shoulder with him, horror whipping the backs of her knees. Pippet was untrained, unfamiliar with the wilderness. And if she'd been found by the Vassora...

"Why do you think we were so far behind you?" Quill's voice was raw, teetering on a chasm of emotions. "We had to drag Pip back to Starhollow. The things she said to me when I locked her in her room to keep her from chasing after us again..." He grazed a hand over his mouth, drinking in deep breaths for several seconds. "I don't care that we were in danger. I care that my sister was."

Cistine dropped her gaze to the stitched-shut slash on his forearm, dealt in the fight to escape Stornhaz. She could still hear the concern in Tatiana's voice bordering on panic when she discovered that cut beneath Quill's armor. It hadn't been there before he used a fire flagon to carve them a path from the courthouse, but if it had, he would be dead, devoured by the augment he'd used helping her fight free.

Cistine took his wrist and brushed her thumb over the crude sutures. Maleck's work, possibly Baba Kallah's—a stitching job as wild and crooked as the entire cabal. "Well, I care about both. I'm so sorry for how everything happened. I'll swear on any stars you want me to...no more storming off. We'll sort out our problems face-to-face from now on."

Quill stared at her hand supporting his arm, and the wound he'd taken in the fight to rescue her. "And I promise not to keep any secrets from you, not even for Thorne. You're one of the best friends I've ever had, Cistine, but don't tell me I'm like a slaver again. I'd rather die the Second Death than be grouped with those *bandayos*."

Shame speared through Cistine. "Never again."

A slim shadow fell into the hall, and they both looked up at Tatiana's stony-faced arrival. "Patrol, Quill. Remember?"

He lurched away from the wall. "On my way, Saddlebags." Sliding his arm free, he glanced back at Cistine. "We'll train again once Maleck gives the word. In the meantime, keep up your stretches."

Cistine nodded and pushed herself up, smiling at Tatiana. "Before you go, can we talk?"

She met eyes cold as frost, a jaw square and sharp. "No."

Tatiana dragged Quill away before Cistine could muster another word.

CHAPTER SIX

No SOONER HAD Ashe's chin cracked the ground, fogging her senses and studding her eyes with starlight, than Aden growled, "*Again.*"

After two weeks, she knew exactly what that meant: gather your wits, get back on your feet, or suffer a staff to the back. Already her bare skin was freckled with bruises from the countless times she hadn't risen fast enough.

Digging her wrapped soles into the rock and lurching upright, Ashe picked up her own staff and swiveled, slamming weapons with Aden, forcing him back one step. Not quite a victory, but something to be proud of. She dreamed of pinning him with the staff across his larynx and pressing down until he *begged* to apologize for that first time he'd humiliated her. And all the ones since.

Every day, it was the same: ripped from her alcove, stripped of her cardigan and thrown into this stone chamber where she grappled with other prisoners for hours, then with Aden for hours after that. Occasionally someone shoved a sloppy bowl of beans and a cup of water into her hand. Then it was back to the floor, weapon in hand.

The only consolation in this monotonous routine was that Ashe had twenty years of Warden training in her arsenal and five years of sparring lessons in Talheim's seediest alleys before that. Most of these men, and the few women she faced, were scrappy street thieves or murderers for hire. One or two had decent clout behind their blows, enough to suggest they'd undergone training somewhere in their past, but none were a match for her.

Except Aden. This gods-forsaken *bastard*.

He was the only one she couldn't beat. Every time he knocked her to her knees with another ankle-sweep, another punch, another tackle she didn't see coming, it was that first slap to the face all over again. Not just hitting her...*humiliating* her, trying to convince her she was no better than an abused animal fit to be shoved around.

These thoughts hammered through her in time with their staves colliding, increasing the tempo. Aden smiled grimly, falling back two steps. Then he ducked beneath the swing of Ashe's staff, hooked her knees, and kicked her onto her back on the sandy floor.

"Again."

The catacomb gate clattered open, and the small pockets of sparring around them stumbled to a halt. Stern again as if he'd never smiled, Aden offered his hand to Ashe; she ignored it, staggering up to face the new arrival.

This man didn't belong here; his brilliant red jacket, dark pants, and groomed physique frightened away the dirt that clung to the prisoners' clothing. A pair of men flanked him, better-dressed than any catacomb guards.

"Aden." The man's voice lilted with false pleasantry. "I trust everything is coming along as expected with the new recruits?"

Aden inclined his head. "On schedule, Tribune Noaam."

Ashe plunged her staff into the sand and glared at this Tribune, hating every inch of him that reminded her of Thorne.

"Excellent," he said. "And what if I suggest we move the deadline closer by just one week?"

A harsh stillness settled over Aden. "Then I would say one day can mean the difference between a quick, dull battle or an entertaining one for men like these. We agreed, three weeks for new prisoners. That's the bare minimum where I can guarantee a fight worth betting on."

"Understandable," Noaam said. "Now understand *this*: I'll be entertaining my fellow Nordbran Tribunes this coming week, and I expect to show them nothing but the best entertainment. That means *everyone* must be up to form, even your newest fighters."

"Three weeks was the arrangement."

Noaam stepped forward, genial liveliness no longer hiding the subtle streak of killing potential in his bristling limbs and jaw. Suddenly he belonged among the shadows and sand in this dismal room.

Ashe tensed, knuckles whitening around her staff.

"The day after tomorrow," Noaam said. "Whatever that requires, Aden. Your best fighters. The bodies of these recruits. Your own blood in the sand. Remember that you're here to serve a sentence, and you can pay with your head if it comes to that."

Aden quaked with anger. In one breath, Noaam had put the Lord of the Hive beneath him.

Ashe tried not to smile, satisfaction fizzing through her.

"Consider it done," Aden finally said.

"Good." Noaam cast a doleful eye over the chamber, smiled blandly, and retreated with guards in tow.

In his absence, Aden cursed. "Ever since Devitrius..."

He tossed his staff to Ashe and walked toward the gate without waiting for her to catch it.

"Where are you going?" she snapped. "We aren't finished!"

"Find a different partner. It seems I have death orders to dole out."

Ashe saw her chance.

She dropped Aden's staff, gripped hers with both hands, and swung with all her might at his retreating back.

The wooden bar smashed into Aden's hips so hard, he tumbled straight to his knees. Several prisoners sucked in their breath. One whispered a prayer. But Aden simply crouched on the sandy floor and didn't rise.

Ashe smirked. "I said we aren't finished."

Aden was on his feet in one leap, in front of her before Ashe could raise the staff to defend herself. He caught her by the throat and slammed her against one of the stone support columns. The impact knocked the breath from Ashe's body, left her gasping as he lifted her. Bare toes scraping the ground, she stared down at him, and he stared back.

"It seems I have my first volunteer." Aden cast her to the side, and Ashe tumbled into a crouch. Fighting for breath, she wiped her mouth on her wrist and glared at him. This time, when he walked away, she didn't attack. She'd already done enough damage to her own plans.

The gate almost swung shut, but a slender hand wedged in the gap and fished it open again. Nimea towed her hood back as she slipped inside. "Impressive. I don't think I've ever seen Aden go down that hard, that fast. Well, outside my wildest fantasies."

"I would ask why you despise him so much," Ashe rubbed her bruised throat, "but I think it's clear enough."

"It's not only him, if you can believe it. He has the misfortune of sharing blood with a certain *bandayo* I have business with."

"And who might that be?"

Nimea's smile lurked with secrets too numerous to stay hidden in her shifty eyes. "No one who's going to be a concern of ours for very much longer. Now come have supper with me."

Possibly Ashe's least-favorite place in the catacombs was the mess hall, another low-roofed, dark hollow where everyone clustered in lines to retrieve their food. The few lucky enough to head up the line also claimed seats along the walls. The rest had to travel out into the musty corridors while they scraped their bowls.

Ashe was never lucky. She took her bowl of dates, dried fruit, and hard cheese and followed Nimea into the catacombs for solitude.

Today, there was no such thing to be found.

"Is it true you struck the Lord of the Hive in training today?" The question followed her from the mess hall. Scowling, she popped a date into her mouth and didn't look back.

"She did, I saw it with my own eyes," someone murmured.

"Straight across the back like a fretting mule—"

Ashe planted herself against the wall beside Nimea and ate faster. Faster to eat, faster to train for the fight Aden had promised for her outburst.

A prisoner she'd ridden to Siralek with appeared by her side. He looked no healthier with the layers of grime removed. "What was it like, striking that *bandayo*?"

Ashe pushed a handful of fruit into her mouth and stared at the wall across from her.

The next prisoner stepped directly into her line of sight. "He can be beaten, then?"

"Would you do it again?" someone added. "Would you show us how?"

God's bones. As if the Lord of the Hive wasn't human, just as breakable as anyone.

A crowd was gathering now, drawn in by the tale. If they hadn't seen her smash that rod across Aden's haunches, they'd heard about it by now. To Ashe's annoyance, several guards enclosed the ranks from behind; if they thought she was inciting rebellion, gods only knew how they'd punish her in ways that might make her unfit for the coming fight.

"Get away, all of you!" Nimea barked above the clamor. "Let the woman eat in peace!"

A good portion of them dispersed, grumbling, and the ones who didn't Nimea chased off with her fiery glare.

Ashe smirked. "So, *this* is what it feels like to have a personal guard."

Nimea polished off her own portion, hurled the bowl to the floor, then propped her hands on her waist. "I'm sure this wasn't the attention you hoped for when you struck him."

Ashe raised a brow. "Aden doesn't seem popular."

"He isn't, but now *you* are. How do you feel about that?"

"I feel like giving them the same treatment I gave him." Ashe polished off her ration and tossed her bowl onto the floor as well.

"You certainly gain attention just as quickly as him." Nimea started down the hall, and Ashe kept pace with her. "You continue to impress me. It's rare Devitrius ever brings prisoners to us personally, especially ones who don't behave like prisoners. You manage to keep your head high even when they do their best to humiliate you. And you *did* strike Aden."

Ashe smirked. "I know my way around weapons. And if that's what keeps me from looking as miserable as these other fighters, I'll hit Aden every day."

"I'd welcome that." Nimea threaded her fingers into her pockets. "I'll be watching your fight *very* closely. You have more spirit than all the prisoners they've brought to us in the last year combined. It would be interesting to see what Siralek makes of you if you survive."

"If?"

"Most prisoners who fight this early don't return to the catacombs. It may be that after you humiliated him, Aden wants to get rid of you."

Before Ashe could spit back that she would not be gotten rid of so easily, Aden himself rounded the corner ahead of them. He didn't slow his stride, but his eyes traveled between Ashe and Nimea, and a scowl jerked at his mouth.

So Ashe smiled, linked her arm through Nimea's, and walked faster— forcing the Lord of the Hive to move out of *her* way.

CHAPTER
SEVEN

CISTINE'S DECISION TO assist Thorne with his Court allies did not usher in good sleep. She tossed and turned night after night, trapped by the magnitude of what she'd agreed to do, and dreaming of Salvotor often when slumber did find her. Before her visit to Stornhaz, King Jad had played the villain's part in her dreams; but now, instead of his poisons in her body or his hand smothering her in the cradle, she dreamed that Salvotor chased her with augmented fire cloaking his body.

She woke long before dawn one morning, drenched in cold sweat yet again, with a soft call brushing her limbs.

Come, it whispered. *Come and see.*

That yearning had keened in her heart since long before she'd ever set sail for Valgard. It had once made her curious of what lay beyond this kingdom's mysterious, forbidden borders, but after so many revelations—the survival of augmentation, the nature of Kanslar's Chancellor, and the Key, whatever it was and whatever part Talheim played in it—she wasn't eager to go searching for another mystery.

She ignored the call while she dressed in darkness, snatched up baskets from the kitchen, and hurried out to the garden—only to find she was not the first one there.

Ariadne's figure was unmistakable even from a distance, propped against the fence, her sleek black hair falling arrow-straight over one shoulder. Cistine halted when she spotted her, frowning. "Ariadne?"

The warrior's shoulders jerked in a steep, silent breath. "You may have woken earlier than Quill for once."

"Bad dreams."

"Does the garden help?"

Cistine cautiously approached, setting the baskets at her feet and folding her arms on the fence. "It does. Soil makes sense. You reap what you plant and you can predict the outcome from how you tend it. I find that calming."

Ariadne slowly bobbed her head. "I used to as well. My family were florists."

Cistine blinked. The thought of Ariadne being raised by anyone but warriors was incomprehensible.

"They are quiet people without great ambition," she added. "They taught me that growing things is a disciplined practice and harvesting is an art. They showed me poisons and healing."

Cistine raked her lip between her bottom teeth. "If you know about healing, why did Maleck tell you to leave when Tatiana came home with that Tyve arrow in her shoulder?"

Ariadne was quiet for so long, Cistine made peace with never hearing an answer.

"I don't...bear it well when this cabal is in danger," Ariadne muttered at last. "None of us do, I suppose, it's a weakness Salvotor has always exploited. But Tatiana in particular is...difficult for me. Seeing her wounded is like seeing my own sister torn apart."

"Is it difficult for you when she's angry, too?"

"The way she's been since we returned to the Den, you mean?" Ariadne raised a brow. "What happened in Stornhaz upset her balance, which upsets us all. I'm no exception. So I came out here for peace...to see if that had changed."

Cistine looked from her inscrutable face to the lush plot of land. "Did *you* plant this garden?"

Ariadne nodded. "But it was too painful to maintain it. Too many memories. I left it to Baba Kallah and Cassaida and focused on weapons instead. I only help with the planting."

Yet here she was, the only other one awake among the cabal, lingering outside the garden as if she felt unwelcome inside it.

Cistine held up a basket. "I could use help, if you're willing."

Ariadne's eyes flashed to her, sizzling with something Cistine hardly dared guess was apprehension. But when she smiled, awkward and hopeful, Ariadne took the basket and followed her on careful feet into the garden.

They spent the last dregs of darkness among the plants, making up for lost time. Cassaida had done some harvesting in their absence, but Cistine hadn't seen her since their return to Hellidom, leaving plenty of work to be done. By ghostlight, they turned the soil and harvested potatoes, carrots, and onions. They walked among the fruit trees, filling one basket with apples and lemons and another with beans and pea pods. They didn't speak, and in that way it was like cleaning the Den; but there was a kindred spirit in the work which Cistine had never felt with Ariadne before.

This florist who wove armor around herself like a shield; this daughter of quiet people who'd grown up to take a sword in her hand. A cool strategist who saw hurt and tried with all her might to balance it.

Moment by moment, Cistine's feelings toward Ariadne thawed into something truly warm.

It was nearing dawn when Ariadne rose, taking up the baskets. "Coming for breakfast?"

"I'll be there soon. I just need a moment alone."

Ariadne took her leave without another word, and Cistine knelt, burying her hands in the rich loam until the chilly lower layers seeped between her fingers and cooled the ache in her splinted knuckles.

She shut her eyes, and for some time, simply breathed.

When the sky faded from core black to royal blue, Cistine finally returned to her room, where she discovered her training armor folded on the pillow like a note left to read.

It was time to return to the rock top.

She changed rapidly, excitement buzzing in her dirt-caked fingertips, and snatched an apple from the basket on her way from the Den. Racing the rising sun, she sprinted south, eating as she went. She was out of breath when she reached the rock top and hauled herself onto it, knowing without a doubt she hadn't beaten Quill.

And there he was: fists and knuckles wrapped, but today he was shirtless. A faint spray of wounds marked his muscled torso from the battle in the Izten Torkat where Cistine and Thorne had taken the plunge into the Muunvat River, and from the skirmish in Stornhaz. He was limbering up through a series of stretches when Cistine reached him.

"I'm sorry I'm late," she panted. "I was in the garden with Ari—"

Quill cocked his fist and smashed it straight into her ribs.

Pain exploded through Cistine's bones, bit into the muscles, and sank deep as she stumbled to the side. Clutching her ribs, she stared up at Quill.; he watched her with his head tilted, the breeze moving the white thatch of hair from his brow.

"Was that *punishment?*" Cistine yelped.

"You punched Chancellor Salvotor in the face and came back with a deaf ear and fractured knuckles. I wanted to see if you learned anything from that. It looks like we still have work to do." He sucked in his lip and whistled, and Cistine expected Faer to come floating from the niches in the cliff. Her stomach turned over when Thorne swung up across the rock top instead, garbed in training armor of his own.

"Please tell me I don't have to fight both of you at once," she begged.

Quill guffawed. "*Fight?* You can't even take a blow to the ribs! No, we're going to start small."

Thorne dipped his head in greeting, a faint smile on his lips. "I'm going to work with your muscles, if I have your permission."

Cistine nodded, holding her breath as he slipped behind her and gripped her shoulders. A shiver of dread winnowed from her skull to the base of her spine, leaving her tense and breathless.

"Your only task is to relax," Thorne added, as if that was simple when his powerful hands were inches away from her neck.

"It will hurt worse if you're tense," Quill warned. "And don't shut your eyes."

"You can only block a blow you see coming," Thorne agreed.

Cistine scowled up at him. "What about the ones I *can't* block?"

Quill stepped back, rubbing his jaw. Then he slapped his gauze-wrapped hands against his thighs. "Come here, *allet.*"

Thorne's hands slid from Cistine's shoulders. He circled around her side to face Quill. "Remember not to dodge."

"I'll do my best."

Thorne surged forward, and Quill dug in his heels, brought up his arms, and braced himself—a flutter of his abdominal wall tightening, his chest dropping when he breathed out—just as Thorne's fist knocked into his belly, shoving him backward on the stone. Cistine caught her breath at the blunt pound of fist on muscle, but Quill didn't even flinch. He straightened up, jogging the pain from his body. "Notice what I did?"

"You tensed?"

Thorne chuckled, and Quill rolled his eyes. "Bracing and tensing aren't the same. Nimmus' teeth, we have a ways to go."

The morning blurred by with Thorne's hands working Cistine's shoulders, helping her pinpoint different muscles she tensed each time Quill slid his fist close to her body. By the time the sun reached its zenith she'd become aware of just how different bracing was, how to sharpen her body rather than recoiling from the notion of pain.

"Being able to take a blow is just as important as being able to give one," Quill explained after they descended from the rock top and crossed Hellidom, the Den looming into view ahead. "Maybe more, even. I've been waiting a long time to teach you this."

"For some, defense will always be preferable to attack," Thorne added. "And there's no disgrace in that."

Quill clapped him on the back. "Others prefer knocking heads together."

"True. And just as many aren't given a choice between the two."

Before Cistine could offer a word of comfort for the heaviness in his voice, she spotted Julian on the Den's wraparound porch, arms folded on the railing. His gaze flicked to Thorne, then Quill, jaw tightening before he beckoned her.

"Love awaits," Quill drawled. "Go and get him, Stranger."

Cistine dug her elbow into his ribs at the same time Thorne cuffed him on the shoulder, his gaze on Cistine. "When you're done with Tatiana today, come find me. We'll begin your new lessons."

Cistine nodded, and with a quick, parting smile for him, she jogged to the Den and up the steps.

"You're a hard girl to keep track of these days." Julian turned to prop his elbows on the railing, keeping some distance between them.

Cistine folded her arms on her stomach, still heaving from training and the journey back. "It's only going to be busier from here."

"I know." He smoothed his hair back. "Which is why I need to apologize. I know Thorne isn't...controlling you. I just don't like seeing you walk down this path with him."

"I told you the bargain we struck after Stornhaz. If he can unseat his father, Talheim will have the help it needs. I *have* to walk down this road, Julian. And I *want* to."

"That." Julian pointed to her. "*That's* what bothers me. Since when do you want political schemes and meetings with other royals? You've been against those things since we were children. You used to beg me to help you sneak from the throne room during session!"

"But I'm *not* a child anymore, Julian. I'm of age now, and as long as I'm in Valgard, my duties as princess supersede my own desires. I wish you could *understand* that."

"I do, I just..." He groaned, stepping forward to rub from her shoulders to her elbows in long, soothing strokes. "I don't want to see them turn you into something you're *not*."

"They won't. But maybe this is a part of me. The books, the tea, the gossip...and also the treating and fighting. Do I have to always be one or the other? A princess of books or a student of warriors?"

Julian sighed, threading a loose tress from her temple around his fingers. "You're just not the same Cistine I knew. The one who used to flash her gloves and skirts at me every time I visited the Citadel with my parents."

Cistine groaned. "You *did* notice?"

"Every time."

"God save me, I was such a tease." Cistine buried her face in her hands, and Julian laughed.

"You're a more dangerous flirt now than you were then. Sometimes I don't think you even realize you're doing it."

She looked up sharply to find he'd moved into her breathing space, and for the first time in a fortnight his lips were so close…

"I have a job for you," she said quickly.

Julian froze, his mouth barely grazing hers. "I hope it takes us indoors."

The husky words tossed ice down her throat. Cistine took a careful step back. "Actually, it takes *you* to Thorne."

Julian's sensuous eyes hardened into onyx again. "I'm listening."

She told him everything about augments and the Key, and how Chancellor Salvotor believed it was connected to Talheim. Julian paced while he listened, drumming his thighs, flattening his hair, rubbing his stubbled jaw.

"You would think our fathers would've mentioned about augments and this Key," he growled when Cistine paused for breath. "You would think *Ashe* would've mentioned it."

"Do you think she knew? She didn't say anything when Baba Kallah told us about the flagons."

"If even *she* didn't, then our fathers are better liars than I thought." Julian slammed the heels of his palms against the railing and leaned his weight into his forearms, glaring across Hellidom. Wearing that furious mask, he looked more than ever like his father.

"I know they kept it secret for a reason." Cistine slid her hand up the hard ridge of Julian's spine as she stepped beside him. "But it's time we peeled back that veil. Talheim is in more danger than ever unless we do."

"And so are you." The anger cleared from Julian's tone like a parting stormcloud. He rested a hand on her head and brought her into the shelter of his side, his fleeting kiss to her hair sweeping warmth through her limbs. "Where should I start, Princess?"

"Talk to Thorne. He's been researching this Key since the Doors closed."

Julian dropped his arm to her shoulders. "*Why?*"

"It has nothing to do with Talheim. His concern was for his own kingdom, his own people's wellbeing. I don't blame him for that."

Brow still furrowed, Julian said, "All right. I'll see what I can find."

Cistine stretched up to kiss his cheek, and he turned his head abruptly, catching her lips with his instead. The contact was deep and hard, almost to the point of bruising—full of a need Cistine ducked hastily away from.

"I should go." She rubbed her sweating palms on her legs. "Training with Tatiana."

"Back to the old schedule?" Julian's disappointment was evident in his drooping eyelids and curt tone.

"I think we all need that normalcy."

He sighed, took her hand, and kissed her knuckles. "I'll see you tonight, Princess."

She said nothing to that. If he continued those kisses and beckons that obviously meant *something* more, she wouldn't be visiting him alone in his room again.

When Julian swaggered indoors, Cistine reclined into the railing, rubbing her middle. Her ribs still ached from Quill's punch and the muscles throughout her abdomen were almost feathery after so many flexes. She would have to add another exercise to her daily regimen to strengthen them.

"You and Julian haven't joined yet, have you?"

Cistine jerked, almost shouted in shock when Ariadne leaned around one of the porch's support posts. "How long have you been there?"

"I just returned from patrol. I didn't want to interrupt." Ariadne bent slightly into the column. "You didn't answer my question."

"Because that's not anyone's business but ours!"

"Why haven't you yet?"

Her voice was quiet, but her eyes glimmered earnestly, as if Cistine's reply was of some personal importance.

On any other day, she might not have answered. But now she was thinking of quiet things harvested in the dark, and the look on Ariadne's face now—the same as that morning at the garden fence.

Cistine folded her arms against her waist. "I made a vow to myself when I was a child, I would never *join* with anyone until I was absolutely certain they weren't pursuing me for my position. I won't marry for less than that, either."

"And you're not certain you have it with Julian?"

Cistine curled her unbroken hand into a tight fist. "It's still too soon."

She braced herself for Ariadne to call her straitlaced or naïve, to remind her of all the ways Talheim—with its courting rituals and stylish weddings—differed from the selection and claiming of *valenar* in Valgard.

Instead, she straightened from the post, resting her hand on the dagger belted at her hip. "Never give that away until you're certain. Hold tight to yourself, Cistine...tight, with both hands. Don't surrender your vow. It's more important than you'll know until you're on the other side of it."

She slipped into the Den, leaving Cistine flustered and confused, staring after her.

For the first time in as long as she could remember, Cistine wasn't hungry for lunch. She picked over a plate of venison and turnips for several minutes, then gave up and trudged to Tatiana's room, where she paused and wrestled a moment more with her frustration. How could simply knocking on a closed door be more unnerving than seeing Tatiana accept a bloodied knife from Quill the day they met?

Praying for strength, she rapped on the door.

"Enter at your own risk," Tatiana snapped.

Cistine poked her head into the room of dark crossbeams, crackling hearth, and plush sofas and bed. Tatiana stood by the wall, gazing up at the map strung above the fireplace with which she'd taught Cistine about the territory borders of Valgard that branched out from Stornhaz—Spoek in the north, Nordbran in the northwest, then Kroaken, Lataus, Unsverd, Blaykrone, Eben, and Erdotre, delineated like the spokes of a wheel from the capital. Tatiana's fingertips rested over Blaykrone—Thorne's territory.

Cistine cleared her throat. "I'm ready for my next lesson."

Tatiana's arm swung down to her side. "No more lessons. You clearly don't care if you're ready for anything, so why should I? You'll go charging off to Stornhaz when it suits you, and Nimmus forbid any of *us* thinks otherwise. Who are we to challenge a *princess?*"

Anger panging in her chest, Cistine perched her hands on her hips. "That's not fair, Tatiana. We all played a part in this."

"Fair?" Tatiana spun toward her. "What was fair about the way any of this happened? What was *fair* about Quill having to hear his sister tell him she hated him after he *locked her in her room* to keep her from chasing after us? What was fair about all of us running until our legs gave out all the way to Stornhaz, only to find you didn't heed a *single word we said?* No caution, no care with how you approached the Chancellor. You acted as if everything we taught you was a *lie!*"

Every word hit like another punch straight to her ribs. Cistine's hands slid from her waist, limp and heavy. "I didn't want to believe—"

"That we were right about Salvotor? You made that very clear. You took the word of a Guide from Veran and a few tales about this kingdom over us."

"Why should I have believed you? For all I knew, you were still using me to lure Salvotor from the city! I thought you weren't my friends!"

"That much, at least, you're right about." Tatiana stalked toward her, the anger boiling from her body a stark reminder that she was just as capable of killing Cistine as anyone else in the cabal. Cistine fell back from that fury, step by step. "We are not *friends.* Now get out. I have better things to waste my time on than you."

The door slammed in Cistine's slack-jawed face so hard it vibrated in her teeth. Somewhere down the hall, something fell off a wall, and a reprimand echoed from Baba Kallah's room.

Face burning with anger and humiliation, Cistine spun away from the closed door and stalked blindly back into the entry room, then halted, flexing her tingling hands. There were hours left to fill until weapons training with Maleck, if he could tear himself away from the hunt for Ashe for even a moment. And after Julian's advances, she didn't feel like seeking his undivided attention, either.

Thorne. She needed his lessons—something to distract her.

She went straight to his loft, outrunning the pit in her stomach in a fast jog up the stairs, and she burst inside to find him sitting on his bed, shirtless, tucking a bandage tightly around his middle. He froze when she entered, and they stared at one another.

Cistine recovered her voice first, though she had no idea where it had gone in the first place. "I'm starting to wonder if you're always shirtless when you come up here."

"And I'm beginning to think you're purposely seeking me out in compromising positions." Thorne reached for his shirt slung over the footboard. "Have I mentioned how I feel about your knocking habits?"

"I forgot. I just spoke to Tatiana, and now I'm..." she waved a hand, at a loss for words to express her dismay.

Thorne raised a brow. "I take it today's lesson was brief."

"There was no lesson. She's furious with me about what happened in Stornhaz, so she won't train me anymore."

Thorne frowned, getting to his feet. "I'll speak to her."

"No," Cistine sighed. "It's her decision to be in my company or not. I have to sort this out between us. The best way you can help is if you teach me what she won't."

Thorne regarded her quietly, his bare toes crinkling the pelt rug that stretched across the loft's wooden floor. "That is a queenly answer."

"Hopefully that means it's the right one," Cistine smiled heavily. "I'm too miserable to tell the difference right now."

"I know what will help with that." Thorne dragged his shirt over his head. "We'll start your first lesson early."

Speechless with relief, Cistine followed him down the steps into the kitchen, where he retrieved a pair of crisp apples from the bowl on the table and led the way out onto the balcony. He tossed one to her and crunched into the other himself, leaning on the railing. "Ask."

Cistine palmed the apple. "I want to know more about augments. Not how they were before, but how it is now. How you use them, how often, and whether they're as dangerous as Talheim says."

Thorne coughed quietly. "I have my suspicions you've already developed some opinions about that."

"Because of a few war stories, yes. But my father and Lord Rion never mentioned there were still augments in the world or anything about the Key, so I think it may be time for me to...reassess my opinions about augments. And the people who use them."

Thorne stared at the river. "The cabal would appreciate that."

"Then tell me."

"You eat, and I'll talk."

So she did, letting the water's music and the sweet fruit dull the edges of her sadness while Thorne's deep, accented voice wove the story of augmentation for her curious heart to explore.

CHAPTER EIGHT

THE THROB OF noise from the arena traveled through the catacomb walls, shaking stone dust and spiders loose from the ceiling above Ashe where she sat in the combat staging room, head in her hands.

Aden had made good on his word. The previous night, the guards had marched among the bed shelves, ruining any hope of sleep by calling out the fighters bound for the arena the next day.

Ashe was the first on the list.

She'd been out of her alcove the moment the last night watch patrolled past her bed, darted into the nearest training room, and spent the few bleak hours before midday putting herself through her paces, preparing for what awaited above.

At least they'd been decent enough to give her practical armor, a tough leather vest braided along the sides and front, long straps hanging from the waist to blunt any swing aimed at her knees or thighs. The high boots were well-worn and plated with greaves on the front, and Ashe couldn't help wondering how many other women had worn them. Whose sweat and blood was in her pores now?

As she sat there with that thought and the cacophony from beyond the gate pummeling her mind, she grappled with something she hadn't felt since she shut the sewer grate above Cistine, Julian, and the cabal.

Fear.

She'd accepted death for the choice she'd made. She'd been prepared to die since she was twelve years old, dashing off to the Northern Kingdom on the heels of an army; she'd been willing for twenty years to die for Cistine. But whatever awaited in the arena would be drawn out, bloody, and as agonizing as it could be for the sport of those whose cheers shook this room beneath the arena gate.

Lord Rion had fashioned Ashe from twelve years onward as his sharpest weapon, a woman who could solve any problem with a sword in her hand. But she'd always seen a finesse to battle, and she'd always chosen ones that served a purpose: the preservation of life. The salvation of her kingdom.

She wasn't ready to die for sport.

Aden's approach made no sound, but his voice cut into her thoughts. "It's blood they're baying for. No better than animals, really."

"They're your people," Ashe muttered.

"Does that make me responsible for their appetites?"

"If your purpose in life is to *sate* that appetite..." Ashe dropped her hands and looked up at him, clothed with a right armguard, a pair of greaves, and a broad belt that shielded his middle. He even carried a helmet with overturned horns under one arm.

"Your name may be first on the roster," he answered the question in her raised brows, "but the Lord of the Hive always takes the first clash. It's tradition."

"And then what?"

To her surprise, Aden crossed the stone room, sandals puffing spare sand from the cracks between the tiles, and lowered himself beside her. "Here is how this goes: I'll rile them with a few announcements and a match, likely with some pit animal. Once I've whipped them into a frenzy, they'll want to see someone less experienced against a fighter they choose."

"Someone else from the catacombs?"

Aden's lip curled. "Normally, yes. But Noaam's friends tend to be...selective about their shows. So it will be someone you've never fought or trained with, someone they may have bought from a slave market in

Kroaken's foothills on their journey here. They don't just want to see you fight, they want to see you flounder."

"They're particular about the kinds of shows they want, aren't they?"

Aden grimaced. "Siralek is entrusted to Noaam's family. They've been Tribunes under the good graces of Skyygan Court for generations, but the Tribunes over Nordbran from the four other Courts are desperate to have a hand in this place. So they bring fighters who they hope can loosen Noaam's grip by humiliating his warriors. And if they succeed without killing us, it's the lash for every survivor."

Ashe thought of the marks on Nimea's arm. "They'll take out their fury on us, but it's really Noaam they're trying to upset."

"You're keen on the uptake. In time, I think I could've made something of that fighting spirit."

Ashe glared at him. "As if I would let you. I won't be in this cesspit forever."

"No one leaves Siralek, not even on the traditional pyres of our forefathers. We're nothing more than carrion for the vultures in the end."

"I'll find a different way."

"There isn't one. The sooner you give up the ambition for it, the sooner you break their control over you."

Ashe smirked. Here, she had him. "They don't control me. I have a reason to fight."

"And that's where they hold you by the throat. As long as you're fighting for something, you'll give them a show. And as long as you do that, they own you completely."

Ashe scowled as Aden rose and fitted his helmet. "Then what's your excuse? Why do *you* go out there and show off?"

Aden glanced over his shoulder. "I have someone to fight for."

With that, he passed through the gate, greeting a dissonance of cheers so loud they shook more dust loose from the walls.

Ashe returned to praying, shutting out the echoes of Aden's speech, the roars of some beast unleashed up above, the crowd's hissing and groaning at the spectacle. Only when those groans turned to cheers did she finally look up again and realize four other fighters had joined her, each wearing leather armor similar to hers, their faces all sallow as turned milk.

The gate tumbled open, and Aden slowly descended the steps—bleeding, though not profusely, his right side painted in purple-ringed splotches. He slumped, shoulder to the wall, when he was out of the crowd's sight. "Your turn." His harsh tone dared Ashe to shy away or plead for her life.

She rose, swaggered past him, and snatched the helmet from under his arm. Fitting it on, she mounted the steps into the arena.

The glare of sun on sand blinded her the same moment the cheers deafened. She hesitated, shaking her head to clear her star-studded vision, cheeks aching from a harsh squint—and something slammed into her like a sack of rocks chucked against her body. She plummeted to her knees, and the cheering turned to riotous laughter.

Ashe staggered up and pivoted to face her attacker.

He might as well have been a beast, with those powerful shoulders growing straight into his bald, peeling head, and that furry dark beard. And his eyes...God's bones, those eyes. Full of mania, the violent need to kill, absolutely fixed on her.

He charged her, the cloth around his hips flapping wildly, and Ashe dodged. Her boots sank into the shifting sand when she flung her weight to the right, and she tumbled onto her side again, barely missing his attack. Derisive hoots clamored from the stands.

Cursing, Ashe lunged back to her feet. This time she spotted a glint of light back the way she'd come, buried in the sand.

Aden had left her a sword. How thoughtful.

Her gaze snapped back to her opponent, assessing his strengths and weaknesses. Bigger, buffer, but also slower. Like a drumbeat of ever-increasing tempo, her thoughts stacked on top of one another—plans, steps, notions of how to beat him.

She coiled her muscles—ignoring the faintest twinge in her scarred leg—and shot forward.

The man swiped at her, but Ashe skimmed beneath his attack, using the pliant sand to her advantage this time. She skidded on one knee, lifted the sword over her head, and blocked a downward thrust from his notched saber. The chime of blades together was like a gong ringing through her entire body, rattling the backs of her teeth. His driving blow nearly bent her in half over her own feet; she barely managed to thrust him off and roll out of reach.

She had no hope of beating him blade-to-blade. He'd break her guard in minutes.

Ashe swept the arena with a cursory glance, her gaze landing on the promenade at the center. Surer footing—and a broken railing.

Ashe feigned a slice at the fighter's ribs, and when he feinted, giving ground, she ran.

"Coward! Take her apart, Dorsta!" one spectator screamed, and with a thunderous roar, the man gave chase. Though the sand gobbled Ashe's boots with every step, her opponent almost skimmed over it, his shadow elongating behind hers, gaining on her heels with frightening speed.

She dropped and slid onto the promenade, skinning her knees, and white-hot pain met the sting at her core when Dorsta's blade slapped through the top of her arm—then pulled away. Not enough to deaden the limb, but it forced water into her eyes.

Dorsta laughed as Ashe somersaulted upright and backed away from him, clutching the blood into her arm with shaking fingers. "I *will* take you apart," he growled. "One piece at a time."

Judging by their cheers, the crowd would enjoy that.

Ashe refused to be fodder. She was a King's Cadre Warden, her strengths far surpassed an arena-reared criminal. She could *do* this.

Dorsta stepped forward, the sand on the stones puffing under his feet, and in a flash Ashe remembered Aden approaching her in the staging room, stirring dust with every stride.

She swept her leg, tossing an arc of sand straight into Dorsta's face, distracting him for a moment—all the time she needed to dash past him, step up on the promenade's railing, and plant a kick in the back of his neck.

Dorsta's knees cracked the stone like thunder, and half the arena gasped. The other half cheered when Ashe landed on his shoulders, wrapped her legs under his arms, and slammed the pommel of her sword into his head. The blow would've cracked most skulls, but Dorsta jerked backward at the last instant, catching the pommel just above his left ear. He followed through his own momentum, flattening Ashe to the stone beneath him and driving the breath from her body. Gasping, she jabbed the point of her blade into any part of him she could reach until he finally lurched off her.

Now they were both bleeding, and as they came to their feet, Dorsta watched her with new wariness; she was no easy feminine prey.

He rushed her this time, speechless and straight as an arrow, and she braced to meet his onslaught. At the last instant, she feinted to the side, circling him as the thrust of his strike carried him past her. She bent backwards below the sweep of his sword, parried it, and kicked his kneecap, buckling him to one side. Again he rose, just a hairsbreadth slower this time.

This was going to be a long game. She would have to stay one step ahead of his berserk charges and let his animal rage wear him into oblivion.

That's when she'd take his head.

Under the sun's pulsing heat, Ashe tempted Dorsta close time after time, let him think his blow would land, then employed new dodges. The promenade was her ally; she trusted the rock beneath her boots, and it rewarded her faith by enabling the swift, light dodges that had made her such a formidable opponent even against Rion himself. Every so often, she let Dorsta's blows land, just to keep him interested. She tested his weight and weakness and found the strength behind those strikes ebbing each time.

Strike, parry, escape; strike, dodge. The familiar chant belted in her head to the tune of the leather straps slapping her thighs, the armor creaking against her muscles, and Ashe smiled, slithering behind Dorsta yet again and slashing at his back. He bent away from the blow, but this time he overcorrected, stumbled, and caught himself against the railing.

There was her opening, with his flank exposed, his feet dragging as he struggled to pull himself back up. A crippling blow to the lower back, and his kidneys would escape.

Ashe braced the sword and charged in for the kill.

Dorsta dropped his sword and spun to his feet, snapped her blade aside with his elbow, and caught her by the throat. He smiled, huffing through his gritted yellow teeth, and Ashe knew.

He'd figured her out. He'd used her strategy to trap *her*.

Dorsta flung her, and Ashe's temple clipped the promenade's edge, jolting her brain against her skull like a wheel in a rut. The world went white as though the sun itself imploded, and her ears rang. She fought not to vomit as she rolled onto her belly and crawled away from Dorsta's looming shadow like stricken prey shot through belly.

The crowd was in a frenzy now, but even that quickly faded to a tumultuous murmur inside her pounding head. Ashe still crawled, but there was nowhere to go. She didn't even know where she was *trying* to go. Sooner or later, she would come to the walls of this sandy tomb, and Dorsta would jab his blade through her neck until it came out the other side.

She stopped crawling, heavy head bowing onto the sand.

Give up, her body begged. All she could do now was spoil their game and hope Dorsta gave her that quick death she'd hoped for. Just let him end it. Just...

Just two more steps.

She heard it. Like he was right there, crouched on the sand, murmuring above her head.

Just two more steps.

She lifted her head, eyes swimming with pain, head throbbing and brain trying to claw its way out from behind her eyes...

Holy God, she could almost *see* him. In the midday sun's shimmering mirage, in the shadows where the roofs over the arena seats stretched out, the dark blur became his arm, sleeved, gloved, his hand extended across the sand...reaching for her.

That will be two more steps than yesterday.

"Maleck," Ashe gasped, dragging herself forward.

His eyes became clearer—moody, dark pools flickering in the light. But there was another shadow moving beside her. Dorsta, closing in...the hunter sauntering after his kill.

Do not look at him. Look at me, Ashe. One more step.

She could nearly touch him. If she closed that distance, if she gripped his hand, this would all be over. She would go back to Hellidom, to that ridiculous riverside Den, to a real bed and to Cistine, and Julian, and to that guttering mirage threatening to disappear before her eyes.

"*Maleck!*" She shouted his name at the top of her voice this time, a ward against the darkness that wanted to climb across her vision, to end this. End *her.*

Get up, Ashe, Maleck whispered back to her. *Get. Up.*

Her hand was inches from his, but Dorsta's shadow blotted her out, erasing the light.

Talheim's Cadre. Not without its strength and nobility.

Ashe's fingers closed over Maleck's. His face broke into a smile.

Now. RISE.

The mirage, the hallucination, shattered. It wasn't Maleck's hand she gripped, it was another blade sunk into the sand.

Ashe flipped to the side, planted her boot in Dorsta's stomach, and knocked the breath from his body with one swift blow. When he doubled over, she shoved the sword straight into his heart.

Dorsta's blood spewed on the sand, on *her.* Ashe tasted it, felt it drip into her eyes, her nostrils, her mouth, and she surged up, screaming with rage. Ignoring the dizzying pound in her skull, she kicked him off her sword, flat on his back in the sand, where he lay without struggling, staring past her. Compelled by that bleak stare, Ashe swiveled to look.

She'd risen in the shadow of the Tribune's box where Noaam perched, smirking at her like a prized mare who'd just won him the most anticipated race in Valgardan history. Two men sat on his right and two on his left—three of them glaring at her. The fourth had a different sketch to his brow. Almost ruminative.

These were her true enemies, the ones who'd purchased Dorsta to kill her or be killed. And she *had* killed him—not on a battlefield, not to protect Talheim's royal family, but because they'd put a sword in her hand.

Ashe released the scalding hilt and stepped back, then fell to her seat in the sand. Pain thudded dully in her temples, and the world spun at a tipsy angle. A few spectators chuckled, but most were cheering.

She hadn't humiliated Noaam, and she wouldn't receive the lash. Not tonight.

The next thing Ashe knew, there were hands under her arms, guards lifting and guiding her back toward the gate. Four men dragged Dorsta through another doorway, leaving smears of blood in the arena behind him.

That could've been her. It almost was. The fight had been too close by far; if she was going to escape, she would have to do better than that.

All Ashe heard for many minutes was her own pulse and the scrape of her boots on rock while the guards half-dragged her through the catacombs; finally, they removed her arms from across their shoulders and dropped her onto a seat. She was too tired, too dizzy, too blinded by the hot turquoise imprint of the bright arena still in her eyes to take stock of where she was. She sat with her face in her hands for several minutes after the guards' voices retreated, waiting for her everything to correct itself.

When something clipped her shoulder and a curt voice ordered her to bandage her head, she squinted up at last.

This was a dim room lit by a single ghostlamp hanging from braided cords across the low ceiling, garlands of herbs and medicinal jars dancing lazily around it. To Ashe's left, a sturdy cot occupied a deep alcove in the wall, its blankets stained with old, brown blood. She perched on a low outcropping of bricks, another one across from her, bisecting the room. That was where Aden sat, wrapping his ribs.

"I said, bind your head," he repeated. "The medico is absent today. If you don't treat your own wounds, you'll die."

"So many things to kill us here." Ashe stooped over to retrieve the bandages he'd tossed to her, then thought better of it when her head gave a slow, wet throb. She kicked the spool up into her hand instead. "Why don't they just build a gallows and have it over with?"

"Because of that." Aden gestured to the roof, where the faintest echo of cheering could still be heard. "They're bored, crafty, and hungry, and they need something that can sate all three. Just as you did."

"You saw the fight?"

"I watch every new recruit in their first match."

Ashe unspooled the bandages and wrapped her bleeding brow. "And what do you think of me now, Hive Lord?"

"That you're a woman with something to prove. Who told you that you weren't a good enough fighter?"

Ashe scowled at him. "No one."

Aden slid off the wall and didn't bother to strap his armor back on. "Whose lectures are you hearing when you swing at me in training?"

"The only thing I hear when I fight you is the same thing I hear whenever you open your mouth: *Hit me, Ashe. As hard as you can.*"

"It isn't me you want to hit. Not really." He loomed above her, the spice of blood, sweat, and poultice wafting from his chest. "Who are you fighting against, Ashe?"

She bound the bandages around her brow and hurled the roll into his hand. "I was fighting Dorsta. And now I'm sore, probably concussed, and I'm going to bed. Assuming I have your leave to go, Lord of the Hive."

She didn't wait for him to give it. She had a battle to unravel in her mind, the consequences of which were currently rattling her hands like shriveled autumn leaves on a branch.

She was almost to the doorway when his voice stopped her: "*Maleck.*"

Ashe froze.

"I heard you call his name."

Ashe's pulse pounded with dread. "I was seeing things from this head wound. I don't know what I was saying. If it sounded like any name you know, *you're* imagining things."

Aden's voice was close behind her when he said, "Then you don't know Maleck, the most feared and despised of all the Azkai acolytes who survived the war between Talheim and Valgard?"

Ashe swung around to face him. "There must be plenty of men with that name in your gods-damned kingdom."

"Possibly. Yours wouldn't happen to have augment scars across his chest, would he?"

Ashe caught herself grimacing at the memory of those twisted, hideous marks, and Aden's mouth twitched.

"They mentioned the new batch of recruits might have ties to people we knew before." His gaze raked over her with newfound interest. "I thought it might be you. You have the exact sort of fire Maleck's always appreciated in women, even if he's too cautious to admit it."

"What do *you* know about him?" she snapped.

"We have history. I know he was Named by the one he protects: High Tribune Thorne. If you're familiar with Maleck, you've likely met Thorne as well."

Ashe jerked up her chin. "And if I have?"

"Then I have a job for you."

CHAPTER NINE

BEING HIVE LORD had its advantages; Aden didn't want for space like the other fighters. His sleeping quarters had a gate that locked from both sides, a dining table with a pitcher and cups, a central pillar lined with shelves, and a bed, mirror, and dressing table—all within four walls ringed floor to ceiling with human skulls.

Revolted, Ashe halted over the threshold, the gate clanging shut behind her. Aden nudged out both chairs at the table and sank into the one that faced her, folding his hands on his middle. "Sit."

"You expect me to sit in the middle of *this*?"

"Unless you want your skull to join theirs."

Either it was a weak attempt at humor, or Ashe was really betting her life against her revulsion. Scowling, she settled into the other chair and gripped the scabbed wound on her upper arm. The skin around it was hot with pain, but that was her anchor, keeping her focused despite her muddled, concussed head. "Who are they?"

Aden glanced up at the skulls. "Prisoners who came long before my time. The head of every fallen fighter was once boiled and lodged into these walls. Dissenters were brought here to be threatened."

"And now?"

"Now we destroy dissenters from within." He picked up the pitcher and filled the cups, pushing one toward Ashe. "Tell me what you know about Thorne."

Ashe tried to ignore the baiting slosh of water along cup's rim, keeping her gaze fixed on him. "Tell me why *you're* so interested."

"He didn't tell you? He's my cousin."

There was no masking the shock that unhinged her jaw.

That was where she knew Aden's name: the cabal dinner in Starhollow. One of them had mentioned Aden there, a man with a Tribune for a father. But this couldn't be the *same* one, in this pit, lording his title over her.

"Close your mouth," Aden broke her stupor. "Arkhomar scorpions like to roost in dark holes like that."

Ashe snapped her jaw shut and forced herself to assess him like she might a quiet room for a hint of trouble or a street for a wanted face.

She could see it, now that she searched; some resemblance to Thorne in that naturally-tan skin and those glittering eyes, though Aden's were gray and Thorne's were blue. And the way he watched her in turn was the same as Thorne when he put a blade to her throat the day they met.

Hate sparked down Ashe's spine at the similarities to a face that had caused so much grief. "Your cousin and I are not friends."

"That doesn't surprise me. But you do know him."

Ashe reclined in the seat, still gripping her arm. "My friends and I were his captives."

"Wrong," Aden said. "Thorne takes no prisoners."

Ashe gritted her teeth. "We were held with an understanding. He and his cabal trained my...the woman I serve." She jerked her chin at him. "What about you? If he cares so much for his people, why is his *cousin* rotting in a prison?"

"I'm here of my own volition." Aden sipped slowly from his cup, and Ashe had the feeling he was talking around something just like she was. "I've done things that make me worthy of this place and my title in it. What I do here is penance for my crimes, and I like to think I made something better of it. Until Devitrius arrived."

Ashe frowned. "What do you mean?"

Aden tipped his cup on its edge and spun it like a top. "You're still new to these catacombs, so no doubt it's escaped your notice, but not mine…the Hive has grown restless. Certain fighters have begun to slip from bed beneath the watchmen's eyes at night." He let the cup fall on its base and drummed his fingers against the rim. "I suspect Nimea is party to this."

"With the clout you carry, finding out what she's up to should be easy for you."

Aden bared a flash of his teeth. They were the truest tell of his powerful heritage—straight and clean. "Nimea has been vying for my position for some time now. We share a history that made her reluctant to cross me when I first came to Siralek, but she's cobbled together a following of her own among the seasoned fighters. I have the fear of the guards and the new prisoners like yourself. She has the veterans."

Ashe sneered. "Challenge is good. It keeps men honest and alert."

"Not this sort of challenge." Aden nodded to Ashe's water cup. "Thirsty?"

She refused to look down. "What kind of challenge is it, then?"

Aden folded his arms, muscles fluttering lazily under the skin. "Ever since Devitrius visited, Nimea and her acolytes have made themselves scarce during the night. My guards can't follow them wherever they're disappearing to. Now they come to me with requests to fight their own. These seasoned fighters, who've relied on their own circle for protection, rations, and training all these years, are arguing for the opportunity to kill each other."

Despite her dislike of him, intrigue sparked in Ashe's belly. "Strange."

"Indeed."

"Why don't you follow them yourself?"

Aden scoffed. "Because the moment they know I've grown aware of their actions, the patterns will change. Whatever they're plotting may accelerate. For the guards to follow a few loose fighters is expected. But for the Lord of the Hive himself to stalk them…"

"What a pity you're so important." Ashe swirled her cup.

"Do you know what else is important?" Aden asked. "Ever since Devitrius came, I seem to hear Thorne's name whispered in these catacombs more and more."

Ashe stiffened, raking one fingernail slowly along cup's curve. "And what are they whispering?"

"So far, little more than his name. But I feel it's no coincidence—the restless Tribunes, my best fighters begging to spar with one another, Nimea's movements in the shadows, the rumors that the new recruits had ties to people from our pasts...and now Thorne's name traveling like a specter through these halls."

Ashe licked her lips. "And what are you going to do about it?"

"I am going to hire a spy."

She locked eyes with him, and though his face remained still, cold, she knew. "Me?"

"Nimea has taken a liking to you. *Why* is beyond me, but it's a road. And as these desert nomads will tell you, a way in the sand is the finger of God."

Ashe glowered at him. "And what makes you think I'd be willing?"

"Because I have Noaam's ear," Aden said, "and in time, if you expose a plot Devitrius is hatching beneath our feet, I might be able to convince him to give you special favors. Possibly enough to get you away from this place and back to the woman you claim to serve."

Ashe's pulse thudded greedily. One fight in that arena had been more than enough; death had come too close today. The sooner she was away from this place, the better. "If I agree to this, I want something more in return."

"I expected as much," Aden sighed. "Name it."

"Freedom to train where I want, when I want."

Aden's brows flicked up. "I'll accompany you to every training session you take, wherever you take it."

Clever. He thought she might try to escape, as if she didn't know that running across the desert with no water, no food, and no horse would kill her in three days at most. Her escape would have to be more finessed than that. But if it was the only way he would agree... "Done. And can we see about finding me a better bed?"

"If you want to draw attention to yourself."

Ashe cursed silently. The alcove would have to do. "I'll see what I can find out about your fighters. And Nimea's involvement."

"Good. But know that if they learn you have ulterior motives and Nimea slits your throat for it, I won't interfere. This can't come back to rest on me."

Ashe rolled her eyes. "I'll defend your semblance of honor with my death. You can rest easy."

Aden lifted his drink. "Then we have an agreement."

Ashe lifted hers in turn. "To making oaths with the Undertaker."

They knocked cups together. And Ashe, finally, sated her thirst.

CHAPTER
TEN

WEEKS PASSED WITH training consuming Cistine's days and thoughts, leaving little time to panic about Ashe, Talheim, Tatiana, or the inevitable meeting with Thorne's allies. On the rock top, she continued to throw punches, and now when Quill threw them back she took each one, settling into bracing and blocking. Maleck walked her through the paces of knifeplay, simple strikes of his birch dagger Remany against her faithful Nail, and after every session she and Ariadne exercised her knuckles and worked the garden together, a quiet synergy between them that needed no words.

Cistine looked forward to her lessons with Thorne the most, where all her focus was on lessons in Valgardan decorum.

"Traisende varies little from Kanslar as it pertains to structure," Thorne explained one day. They retreated into the early-autumn warmth on Cistine's balcony, and Baba Kallah kept mostly-silent company, leaning against the railing at her grandson's side. "In any Court, the Chancellor is like a symphony conductor. He oversees the flow of conversation in a courtroom."

"Which we will not be in for this meeting," Cistine reminded him. "You promised."

"I did," Thorne smiled. "But you can't expect the Chancellor to conduct himself any differently whether he sits on the Judgement Seat or on a stool."

"Is that a hint? Will we be sitting on stools where we're going?" He had yet to tell her—or anyone, Cistine had learned from harassing Quill—about where this clandestine meeting would take place.

"As for proper conduct expected of us," Thorne went on, and Cistine jutted her tongue at him, which made him smile wider, "it's the Chancellor's game yet again. If he speaks, the room stops and listens. He's in command of the topic's flow. We show him the respect his title deserves."

Cistine tapped her pen against her chin. "No different from a throne room."

"I would imagine."

Baba Kallah rapped her cane against Thorne's shin. "And Yager?"

Thorne laughed under his breath. "Baba Kallah is...fond of Yager Court."

"Why?" Cistine asked.

"That isn't our story to tell...I know," Thorne said when she scowled, "you're tired of hearing that answer. But my silence was the price for their help over the years. If they agree to meet with us, it will mean they're ready to entrust that secret to Talheim. I won't make that choice for another Court."

Not like his father was doing with his spies and secret out-of-season purchases. "That's fair. I won't ask again."

Thorne settled his elbows on the railing. "What I can tell you is that Yager was the first ally of Sillakove, even before we left Stornhaz. Its people are cunning hunters and even better politicians. I've never met one who didn't have a clever secret up his or her sleeve."

Cistine frowned at that. She'd met three women sworn to Yager Court in Stornhaz and found them alarmingly like herself: naïve, vapid, and easily distracted by a good shopping venture.

And yet, one of them had warned her about Salvotor's reinforced skin.

"All right," she said slowly, "but what about conduct with them? Is it the same as Traisende?"

"In some ways, you need to worry about your conduct less than I do where Yager is concerned." Thorne gazed over his shoulder out into the garden. "But in others, they'll watch you more closely than anyone else."

Cistine's skin pebbled with gooseflesh. "Why?"

Baba Kallah laughed. "Women are *important* to Yager, wouldn't you say, Thorne?"

He tousled his hair, huffing with amusement, and Cistine smiled anxiously between them. If they could both laugh at that remark, then the Court's interest must not be something she needed to worry about.

Lessons in decorum continued over the days: how to carry herself, how and when to speak, and what subjects to avoid with the Chancellors. Woven among these necessities, particularly on days when Baba Kallah escaped the heat indoors and left them alone on the balcony, were the conversations about augments and flagons—how they functioned, where they'd been harvested, and how many the cabal had.

"Thirty." Thorne's admission rang over the thump of blows on a day Cistine couldn't sit idle, her head crashing like a tide with thoughts of conduct and meetings. She slung steady punches with her good hand into Thorne's palms, and he talked over the smack of her knuckles into his skin.

Dancing on the balls of her feet, Cistine met his eyes over her upraised fists. "How many did you begin with?"

He smiled. "Forty."

Brows flitting up, Cistine pummeled his palm again. "You really have used them sparingly."

"We've had no choice. Raiding Vassoran caravans and divesting them of steel—even *Svarkyst* steel—is one thing. If we broke into a flagon storehouse, we would be caught or hunted. And killed."

Cistine bobbed like Quill had showed her and struck again. "Will thirty be enough if this comes to a fight against Salvotor?"

"I hope," Thorne said. "That would require Salvotor to use the Courts' reserve...flagons that belong to all Valgard by rights and aren't his to use however he pleases. But he'll find a way around that important detail."

Breathless, Cistine halted her assault. "If Salvotor had the Key and used it to open the Doors, I don't imagine he would spread the augments evenly."

Thorne shook his head, straightening from his bracing stance. "He would find a way to control every harvester, every Door, every well of power himself. Maybe that's what his spies and influences in the other Courts are preparing for."

"Not only to control the flagon stores that already exist," Cistine murmured, "but to command the Doors when he opens them."

Thorne put up his hands again. "One more reason to outwit him."

Cistine took several steadying breaths, then attacked. "Tell me more about augments. How can they be used? What kinds are there?"

"Many. Some I've only heard of but never seen. The ones we stole from Stornhaz are mostly aggressive...fire, ice, wind, lightning, even darkness and light. Each flagon is tailored to contain the power of a specific augment."

Cistine punched his palm in two quick jabs. "What about the less-aggressive kinds?"

"Healing augments are the gentlest, to seal broken flesh, mend organs and limbs. There's no need for armor to protect against them. We have a few in reserve, just in case."

The notion of anyone in the cabal needing a healing augment for their wounds made Cistine's stomach drop. She hit harder this time, springing pain into her muscles. "It's a good thing you have armor to protect against all the other ones, or you'd have more wounds than anyone knew what to do with."

Thorne smirked. "That's only one reason the armor is useful."

Cistine met his eyes with the next blow. "What are the others?"

He caught her fist gently, halting her attacks. "Valgardans have learned to preserve the augments because they're a limited resource. For us even moreso. So if Tati, for example, breaks a fire flagon in battle, we share that fire among us until it burns out."

She stared at him, wide-eyed. "You can do that?"

Thorne moved his fingers to her wrist and bounded her fist open with a gentle squeeze. "Augments can be transferred. If two warriors wear reinforced armor, the conduits create a single, powerful current between them." He rested his hand against hers, palm to palm, fingers slightly spread together. "With our directive, the augment follows the course of the conduit to the other person's hand. Then they can use it, or guide it along their armor and transfer it again."

Staring at their joined hands, Cistine shivered. "I can't imagine what that feels like."

"The power?"

"The connection," she admitted, and Thorne's smile gentled. "How many times can you transfer it in a fight?"

"If we're wise about it, several. Quill, Tatiana, Ariadne and I once managed to share a single flagon between us in a battle."

Cistine dropped her hand, gooseflesh still sprinkling her arms. "I think I'd like to see that sometime."

Something like melancholy lurked in Thorne's eyes as his arm swung back to his side. "If you stay with us long enough to bring Salvotor to his knees, I have no doubt you'll get the chance."

It was lessons like these that kept Cistine focused and full of vision day after day; yet she struggled to sleep, when every night brought worries about Ashe and Tatiana and the others crawling back, setting her heart pounding.

She spent most evenings in the kitchen with Baba Kallah, drinking tea and discussing the old woman's life until they were both nodding off in their seats. Baba Kallah's stories of her girlhood home in the wilderness brimmed with mudslides and lumbering perils, and long summers chasing prey and playing warriors with her three closest friends; and of Stornhaz the tales were varied and fantastical, giving glimpses of city quarters and pockets of activity Cistine hadn't seen in her brief foray among its streets. Taverns and nightlife districts, haberdasheries and mess halls, hatmakers and dressmakers and vendors of every item known to man unfurled from Baba Kallah's long memory of a life escaping her *valenar* in all the wonders the City of a Thousand Stars had to offer.

If they ever returned there, Cistine had some exploring to do.

One night, after a particularly brutal day of training, anxiety and restlessness drove her from her bed much earlier than usual. She padded into the kitchen, rubbing her eyes, to find it was indeed occupied—but not by her usual companion.

"Julian, why aren't you asleep?" she whispered, sliding her hands over his shoulders.

"Working." He took her splinted hand and kissed her knuckles without looking up from the book spread out before him on the table. "There's tea. Hours old, and it's cold. Baba Kallah's out with Thorne, she asked me to wait up for you."

Heart glowing with gratitude, Cistine poured herself a cup, towed out the chair beside him, and propped her feet in his lap. "What are you doing?"

"Transcribing Thorne's notes on the Key. He didn't seem too reluctant to part with them, and I can see why. Half of this is runes and the other half is so sloppy, I doubt most people could read it."

She laughed, wrapping both hands around her mug. "But you aren't most people."

"My father's Warden reports looked worse than this. Maybe I missed my calling as a linguist."

Cistine stretched forward to look over his elbow. "He must've written in Old Valgardan to keep Salvotor from learning what he discovered."

"Clever. But now he's keeping *me* from learning, and I might punch him in the face for it."

She stifled another laugh. "How much do you have so far?"

"Not as much as I'd like to, given the amount of effort I've put into this." He gestured to his notes. "I spent half the night in the tavern talking to Tatiana. She's a chatty drunk, so she helped me decipher some of the runes."

Cistine parried a jab of jealousy that Tatiana would speak to Julian, but not to her. "What did you two find?"

"Well, judging by Thorne's research, closing the Doors involved some kind of ritual that forged a lock over their lids. That's what's kept the power from pushing through over the decades." He tapped his pen on the paper.

"They had to key the lock to an object of some kind to hold it in place. That's what Salvotor's looking for."

"Who performed the ritual?"

"Thorne refers to them as *visnprests*, or *prestas* for the women. Tatiana said they studied augments, you know, discovered their different functions and how to build a society around them. They still serve in all four temples."

"Like our priests and priestesses." Cistine vaguely remembered a similar conversation with Tatiana back in Starhollow.

Julian nodded. "But they did more than just intercede for the people or help them commune with the True God like our priests do. They spent so much time trying to understand the augments, I think they started to worship them. They even had to devote themselves to a life of celibacy so the *taint of life's pleasures*, I quote, *would not distract them from their calling*."

Cistine wrinkled her nose. "That's obsessive. Even priests and priestesses are allowed to have families."

"It's different here. I can see why our fathers and King Ivan were nervous about the North, if this is how their acolytes felt about augmentation. Devotion to an ideal like this can easily lead to notions of conquest."

"Strike before they strike you." Cistine sipped her tea. "But there was nothing wrong with using augments to power their cities, was there? It was when they started to abuse them, to worship them *instead* of the gods. That was where the danger sparked from."

"Some people would say that was just inevitable. That you couldn't have started down the first road without it leading to the second."

Cistine's palms sweated slightly. "What would we have done if we were in our fathers' positions when this became a concern? Do you think we would have waged war, or tried to find a peaceful solution?"

Julian shut his notes and stretched, rubbing Cistine's bare ankle. "I used to think I knew, but then you befriended augurs."

Cistine watched his face—drawn, and as tired as she felt. The only thing she could think to say was, "Yes, I did."

CHAPTER
ELEVEN

THIS WOULD NOT be Ashe's first time infiltrating a rebellious organization. Lord Rion had placed her on two such missions in Astoria— the first to unveil a small clutch of dissenters among the King's private council who questioned his wartime ascension, the second to foil an assassination plot by a few who'd believed Talheim was better off heirless than with its six-year-old princess, rather than a prince, set to inherit the throne. Ashe knew the steps to take, the ways forward to penetrate; so while she slipped into her new training regimen, she also crafted a strategy with tactics Lord Rion taught her back then. She constructed and finessed her five-pointed operation while she stretched out in her alcove each night and tried to ignore the scrape of its roof on her spine.

She had to admit, Aden was right to choose her. Nimea's blatant interest solved the first step: gaining an avenue with the leader. Still, she paced herself, focusing on her training rather than the infiltration while her head and arm healed. Each night when the other fighters surrendered to sleep, Ashe slipped out to meet Aden in the empty arena where the day's brutality lulled under the moonlight.

That's when Ashe ran.

She started small: three-meter dashes, back and forth. Then ten meters. Then fifteen. Each time she slid and altered direction, sprinting back the way she'd come, her muscles strained to adjust to the bow of the sand. Her legs cramped, then released, and she forced herself to run through the pain. She did this for hours, until sweat bloomed permanently in her pores and her shoulder-length hair itched with sand and salt. Aden watched from the promenade with those cool eyes assessing her every movement.

"You came away from your first fight with a concussion, a bloodied arm, and damaged ribs," he remarked one night when they descended into the catacombs, "yet your training regimen relies on dashing. Is that the only place you think you need to improve?"

"I'm sure you think I need improvement in *all* areas," Ashe scoffed. "But I was the one who fought Dorsta. I know what will kill me quickest in my next match."

She tried not to think of how near that loomed on the horizon—the day after tomorrow. She'd prefer to fight less and focus more on uncovering Nimea's plot, but as Aden had warned her two days ago when he announced the fight, that would arouse suspicion.

"If you're ever interested in a more rounded regimen, feel free to ask for one." He led the way from the staging room. "In the meantime, how far have you progressed with Nimea?"

Ashe tousled a hand through her tacky hair. "The second step is complete. I've marked her patterns."

Aden's brow flicked up. "My guards noted no patterns."

"Then maybe you need new guards. Everyone has patterns. They have patterned ways of *hiding* that they have patterns. It took me a few days, but I think I've cracked Nimea's."

The smallest of goading smiles graced his mouth. "And what patterns of *mine* have you made note of?"

Though she didn't appreciate that he knew she'd been watching him, waiting for a sign he'd renege on their agreement, Ashe decided to play his game. "I notice you always eat alone in that hideous room of yours."

"At least I have my own bed."

She rolled her eyes. "You take a special interest in the youngest of the recruits. And last week, you vanished completely for most of the day."

The spark of teasing in his eyes went dim. He lengthened his stride, abandoning her in the dim hall. "Get to your alcove. If you're discovered out of bed at this hour, it won't end well for either of us."

That was true. But had Ashe not been maneuvering already down the road to freedom, she might've let herself be caught anyway, if only to make life a bit more uncomfortable for the unpredictable Lord of the Hive.

If God had some mercy on Ashe, it was that she had one of the last fights of the day when the arena was already saturated with blood, toughening the sand while the sunlight weakened the crowd. Their lust for a good show had waned hours ago thanks to the two fighters killed and dragged off before Ashe ever set foot up above.

She kept to the promenade anyway, where footing was surest, and blocked the relentless attacks of her larger opponent. She let the crowd's lazy jeers incense the man until his blows lost their honed brutality and became quicker, more desperate. Then she knocked his legs out from under him, tossed him to the ground, and slid her blade clean through his throat.

She walked away before he stopped thrashing, stomach pitching at the ruthless waste of what she'd done.

Nimea waited for her in the staging room, the first time Ashe had seen her all day. Thoughtful eyes watched Ashe duck into the shadowy room. "You don't bask in their praise."

Ashe peeled off her close-fitting leather helm, freeing her hair. "I don't fight for glory."

"Then what *do* you fight for?"

"The chance to escape. And for vengeance."

Nimea cocked her head slightly. "That's a rare cause to find in this place. Most have given up the notion of all but surviving."

"Surviving's not enough if I can't repay the bastard who put me here."

"And this is how you plot your escape...by ignoring the crowd?"

"We all have our methods." Ashe shrugged. "Some of us play the crowd. Some of us creep from our beds and haunt the catacombs after dark."

She swiveled on heel and strode from the room to mask the gratification of seeing Nimea's eyes widen and her cinched arms unfold when she realized what Ashe knew.

With that, the third step was done. But even one more victory wasn't enough to erase what happened in the arena today.

Out of Nimea's sight, Ashe sagged against the wall and yanked off her gloves, then scrubbed her face with both hands. These were *Valgardan* prisoners she was killing; it shouldn't matter. None of it should.

But she could still feel the blood on her hands.

This was not what she'd trained for. It wasn't Talheim against Valgard or simple men against augurs—it was hatred forced at the tip of a sword, an imitation of bloodlust drummed up because a crowd demanded it.

She despised these desert nomads and the residents of Siralek. If there was any mercy in the world, someday Noaam would grow bored enough to pitch his fellow Tribunes into the arena. Let them get a taste of what it was like out there on the hot sands with steel thirsting for *their* blood.

"You can't let them see you like this."

Of course Aden had found her in this empty corridor. Torment on top of torment. "Leave me alone."

His voice approached from her right. "As long as you're here, you can't regret what you do. The ones you kill. The ones sent out to kill each other. Keep your head up and your eyes forward. You will not break."

As long as she was here. How long would *that* be? Would she even be the same person once she escaped?

"Are you hurt?" His voice was right beside her now.

Ashe growled at him.

"Answer me."

"*No,*" she snapped, dropping her hands.

"Then say you understand me."

"Why do you care if I do?"

"Because if you break, I lose my edge with Nimea." His eyes branded her, hot as the desert sun dying with the man she'd killed today. "*Say it.*"

Ashe set her teeth, but the words escaped: "I will not break."

His gaze, unbelievably, settled with something like respect—then hardened again, flicking past her.

Ashe expected to see Nimea creeping up on them, but it was a sallow-faced guard instead, bowing at the waist under their glares. "Summons from Tribune Sander."

Aden's brows leaped. "He hasn't set foot down from those stands in five years. What does he want with me now?"

"Not you." The guard's gaze flicked to Ashe. "He requested an audience with the fighter who killed Dorsta."

When the man scuttled away, Aden murmured, "Curious."

"Who is this Sander?" Ashe demanded.

"A member of Kanslar Court. And also, I suspect, the only man who didn't throw in his mynts to buy Dorsta from the slave market."

The hot, gritty breeze stroked every bruise and crevice of Ashe's wounds when she and Aden emerged back into the arena. The stadium was already empty, the patrons slinking into the coming night and the promise of a sandstorm in these high winds. Ashe had to squint to make out the silhouette of the Tribune near the promenade, flanked by two guards.

"That's far enough, Aden," the man called when they'd taken only a half-dozen steps from the gate.

Aden slowed, teeth grinding audibly.

"You two must be familiar," Ashe remarked.

"He served alongside Thorne in Kanslar. He's never been someone whose pyre I'd weep over."

"The feeling seems mutual."

Ashe's muscles quivered every step she took toward Tribune Sander. When she was a few meters from the promenade, he lifted his hand, and Ashe slowed to study his features. He was younger than she'd expected, perhaps a few years older than her, and when the sunlight struck his eyes, turning brown depths to liquid amber pools, she recognized him; he was the man who'd watched her so pensively when she killed Dorsta.

"Do you know who I am?" he asked.

"Tribune Sander of Kanslar Court," Ashe said. "I assume, Tribune over Nordbran territory."

"For a woman of such foreign accent, your knowledge is impressive. Where do you hail from?"

"Somewhere I doubt a Tribune of Kanslar Court has ever visited." Ashe resisted the urge to glance at Aden for some guidance as to where this meeting might be angled.

The Tribune's lips curled. "That may very well be true, but humor me."

"South."

"Unsverd, perhaps?"

Ashe's scalp prickled. It had to be coincidence that he'd guessed the territory where the cabal sheltered. "There's more to the south than just Unsverd."

"That much is true." Sander turned back the pale hood that wrapped both his head and shoulders. Cords of dark braids tumbled out, framing a tawny, full-lipped face, and he smirked at her like he thought she might be charmed.

He was an idiot, this one. Ashe folded her arms. "If that's all you wanted to know, I have training."

She started to turn, and Sander said, "Noaam tells me you were brought here from Stornhaz. Is that true?"

Scowling, Ashe swung back around to face him. "Does it matter? I'm *here* to entertain all of you. So unless my origins affect how much you enjoy the games..."

Sander burst forward, catching Ashe by the arm and yanking her close to him, engulfing her senses in the smell of cloves and smoky leaves. His grip was strong, but Ashe knew she could break it if she had to, flogging be damned. "There is a much larger game being played here than you can imagine. And if the rumors of your capture are true, then you are already playing it."

Ashe wrenched in his hold, and the Tribune released her.

"Dorsta was a test," he added. "Not of your strength, but of Noaam's. He passed, which is all the others care for. *I*, on the other hand, am far more intrigued by your victory."

Ashe stepped from his reach. "What test? The one where you're all vying for control over Siralek?"

Sander's eyes flickered. "As I said, well-informed. This prison is important. Its Lord is important. And you may also be important—more than any of them realize."

Ashe rubbed her stinging arm. "What do you want from me?"

"That you would prove yourself...and perhaps, in so doing, make yourself useful to the cause." He turned up his hood, masking his features in shadow again. "I will be watching your games very carefully. And for both our sakes, I hope you survive the next match."

He turned and strode from the promenade, toward the gates that led to freedom, gates Ashe longed to walk through—though she would never go on the heels of someone like him.

Still rubbing her arm, she strode back to Aden. He leaned against the arena wall beside the steps down to the catacombs, face fixed in its usual frown. "What did he want with you?"

"To discuss the weather." Ashe started down the staircase. "I'll see you back here tonight."

CHAPTER TWELVE

THE FOURTH STEP of Ashe's infiltration was a waiting game—one she tried to gather her patience for with other matches and long nights of training in the arena while Aden stood watch from the promenade. She learned to ignore his presence entirely, pretending he was one with the stone and she was alone, training like she had as a young girl on the outskirts of Astoria or in back alleys with thugs where none of her parents' respectable acquaintances would see; the bakers' daughter, spun together from sugar and flour and all manner of sweet things—but underneath, there had always been a bite of newly-minted steel.

Aden noticed it, too. One night, he sat up against the promenade railing after her twentieth sprint past him and said, "You're becoming quicker on your feet."

Ashe braced her weight with one leg flung out and bent the other, sliding to a halt. "After all these nights, I would hope so."

"Short, metered dashes are one thing. But how's your endurance?"

"How long have we been out here?"

Aden strode toward her. "If the goal is to outpace an arena beast with no purpose other than to devour you, sprints will only carry you so far."

Ashe readied a retort—then cursed when Aden slapped her backside in passing. She whirled to sling a well-deserved blow into his ribs, but he was already gone, sprinting barefoot across the sand.

Bellowing profanities after him, Ashe gave chase.

Aden ran as though they were on hard dirt rather than spongy sand, and though Ashe had indeed gained stability over short distances, her calves and thighs were soon screaming at the rigors of holding her balance on the longer sprint. When she started to flag, Aden checked his stride, falling back to keep pace with her. Ashe watched him from the corner of her eye, how his muscles bent, how he managed his balance and measured his breathing. She matched his rhythm and found the stitch in her side eased.

For a quarter-mile around the arena's edge, they kept in step with one another. When they slowed at last, then halted, Ashe's pains had faded into an all-over burn.

"You see?" Aden smirked. "You gain nothing if you don't variegate your regimen. From now on, you and I will run together every other night, then—"

Ashe straightened and slammed her knee into his groin. Aden howled in agony, staggering from the unexpected blow and dropping to one knee on the sand.

"If you ever touch me again without my permission," Ashe warned, "I'll break something the arena won't miss, but *you* certainly will."

"Noted," he groaned.

"As for the running, I agree. Tomorrow night?"

"If I'm still able after that blow."

"Lesson learned, I'd say." Ashe dusted off her hands and walked herself back to the gate, leaving him to stagger upright and limp after her.

It was two days later, over another sloppy meal of gruel, that Nimea finally approached Ashe at the mess hall's only table. Heart drumming at her unexpected company, Ashe focused on the meal when Nimea leaned on the splintered wooden edge and bent close to her shoulder to speak. "I've been thinking over what you said...about creeping around the catacombs.

Have you been following me?"

Ashe popped her spoon from between her teeth. "Maybe I have been. And maybe the whispers I've heard are intriguing to me."

"What whispers?"

"Rumors that you and I share a common enemy. The *bandayo* who put us here?"

Nimea's eyes narrowed. "And what is it you seek from me, Ashe?"

"To make sure the rumors surrounding *your* vendetta against him won't hinder mine."

"What's your quarrel?" Nimea's question was innocent enough, but the burning hunger in her gaze was another matter. If Ashe was Thorne, she would've feared this hungry desert creature lurking under the sand, plotting something against him.

"As if I would tell you," Ashe said. "From what I've heard, you and your allies would use anything to further your own agenda. If I have no part in that, why should I share information with you?"

"You think I should trust you enough to make us allies?"

Ashe raised a brow. "You want me to prove myself?"

"If you're as clever as you seem, and as well-learned of our intentions as you claim, you must know I wouldn't welcome you without a show of support."

Ashe finished her gruel and stood. "I'll keep that in mind."

She walked away swiftly, hiding her relief. The fourth step was finished—she had Nimea precisely where she wanted her.

On to the fifth: finding a means of proving herself to the suspicious leader of this anti-Thorne regime.

CHAPTER THIRTEEN

RIVER MIST TURNED the rocks along the Nior Falls slippery, and Cistine clung to the bulbous handholds, skin tingling, resting her weary muscles yet again. She was glad for the rope around her waist, which Quill had secured to a stone atop the falls long before their training began, and for the sunlight warming her back—the only thing that kept her from shivering in her damp armor.

"Keep climbing!" Quill called from several leaps above. "The ledge isn't going to come down to meet you!"

Cistine cursed under her breath. She'd been excited when Quill mentioned a change of pace in training that morning, something to break the monotony; she hadn't expected it would involve climbing a waterfall.

Grimacing, she hurled her weight up, grabbed the next stone, and continued to rise.

Midday was fast approaching when she crawled up the last slippery outcropping and found Quill basking in the sunlight at the Nior's riverside. When she nudged his sprawled-out leg, he squinted at her. "Finally! I was wondering how I was going to climb back down from here as an old man once you made it."

"Hilarious," Cistine panted.

Quill laughed and lurched upright, offering his hands to her. She rested her palms in his and he unwound the pale leather wrappings that protected her palms from the sharp stones and made it easier to grip handholds. "How did it feel?"

"Taxing." Cistine glanced over her shoulder at Hellidom, a shimmering streak of stone and wood far below. "But I did like you said. I didn't look down."

"That's good. Sore?"

"It's not really soreness. My arms feel heavy. And my fingertips..."

"Flex them." Cistine tried, but her shaking fingers would barely curve. "I figured. We'll rest here until you can move them. And let's add climbing to your endurance exercises from now on, partway up the rock face and down again. You never know when you'll have to climb from a tight spot, but you always want to be able to grip a sword afterward."

He hadn't brought either of his today, but Cistine felt safe when they collapsed on the brink, the Nior gushing to their right and the plains of Lataus's upper plateau spanning the horizon at their backs.

"How's your arm?" she asked after a few moments of silence.

"Hardly stings. I'm back to sparring with Tati. If I can survive her body-slamming, I can survive anything."

Cistine glanced at him from the corners of her eyes. "And how is she?"

Quill sat up on one elbow and turned his hair over the top of his head. "She's all right. Being back in Stornhaz shook her. She's acting like she did when we first came to Hellidom."

"I wish I could help. A shopping expedition, a good book, some tea...*anything*."

"She's not going to let you close enough to try." Quill removed a cinnamon stick from his pocket and wedged it between his teeth.

"I know, but I can't understand *why*. She wouldn't let me apologize, she wouldn't even hear me."

"That's what Tatiana does. I've seen her face down a band of charging Vassora and not give ground, cheat a pack of card players twice her size, wrestle a Sotefold wildcat like it was nothing...I've owed her my life more times than I can count. But something about seeing the cabal in danger, it's one beast she can't wrestle. She'll run away from it every time."

"I can't imagine her running from anything."

That got a chuckle out of Quill. "I never said she wasn't a conundrum. Her father is a tinker, so she spent most of her life surrounded by things she could fix. But when Salvotor came after Sillakove, she realized there are things you can't put back together the way they were before. None of us could be fixed after what he did to us, and she finds it easier to turn her back on those things. That's why she's shutting you out: because you were in danger in Stornhaz, she realized she could lose you, too."

Cistine wicked moisture from her calves with both hands. "You were in danger, too."

"You mean the flagon." Quill smirked. "I was a little reckless, maybe. But with Tati, I've learned not to *let* her hold me at bay. I plow right in and take whatever blows she swings. Even if she tells me she hates me, or she wants to kill me, I'll find a way to brace."

He nudged Cistine's ribs, right where he'd struck her the first time, and she laughed; but the humor sobered quickly. A small smile turned Quill's lips, but sadness framed his mouth and eyes.

"Does it always have to be you?" Cistine asked. "The one taking everyone else's pain?"

Quill slumped forward and stretched a kink from his back. "If not me, then who? Thorne has too much on his mind, so does Maleck. Ariadne carries enough...sometimes it's like she has the weight of our spirits on her hands, you know? And Tatiana can't manage it. So why not me?"

"Because you carry your own weight. When does it become too much?"

"It hasn't yet."

"Has it ever come close?"

He circled his arms loosely around his knees. "Once. Detlyse Halet."

The name pierced Cistine with dread so deep, her stomach turned. "You've been there?"

Quill flashed her a narrow look. "You've heard of it?"

"Salvotor threatened to throw me inside after I hit him."

He turned his hair across his head again, hiding the scar above his ear.

"Nimmus' teeth. I would've killed him. Whatever it cost me, I would've turned him to *ashes* if he'd done that to you."

Cistine stared at him, unsure if she should be flattered or shocked by the anger twisting his words.

"Detlyse Halet," Quill grated out. "You can't come any closer to Nimmus than that. I spent four days there when Salvotor learned I consorted with Thorne about Sillakove. I *still* have nightmares about it."

Morbid curiosity pushed Cistine closer to him. "It was that terrible?"

"There's a reason I chose the room with the most windows in the Den."

They lapsed into silence, and Cistine's mind filled the gaps in what he wasn't telling her: some place of lightless dark that caged both Quill's body and his wild spirit. Shivers, owing nothing to the dampness of her skin and hair, raced one another down her arms and legs.

Quill lurched suddenly to his feet and stretched. "But that's in the past, Stranger. About Tatiana, I don't suggest pushing her right now. You would have better luck boring through Stornhaz's wall with a hand drill. The only time she really opens up is after a few drinks, but that's not a place you want to send her, either. It's not good for her. Just give it time."

Cistine peered up at him in the banners of bright sunlight that shimmered from the water's flow. Talking about Tatiana, even briefly, had chased out the shadows of his memories from Detlyse Halet, leaving his face easygoing and open again. A small smile crept onto Cistine's lips in turn, and she couldn't brush it away before Quill glanced down at her. He smirked in return. "What in Nimmus is that look for?"

"Nothing," Cistine said innocently, climbing to her feet. "Were we about to leave?"

"Not until you tell me why you're grinning like that!"

She shrugged. "Suit yourself. I'll see you at the bottom of the falls."

Laughing, she swung herself over the edge and began her descent. Quill cursed and chuckled, following her down.

The Den was mostly deserted when they returned, parting ways just inside the door. Quill sauntered to his room to change into fighting armor for patrol, and Cistine headed toward her room.

Halfway down the hall, a gentle whisper pooled through her limbs. *Come and see.*

Gritting her teeth, she shook it away. She was in no mood for more of Valgard's strange, beckoning songs.

She quickened her steps to the kitchen, where she found Maleck asleep at the table. One arm curled under his head, the other outstretched, he'd dozed off with pen still in hand. A leather-bound journal sprawled open at his elbow, riddled with notes: conjectures and theories crossed out, several unfamiliar place names, some underlined, some with one question mark or more branching off from the end.

A tide of speculation in his hunt for Ashe.

Smiling so hard her cheeks ached, Cistine retrieved a blanket from her room and draped it over Maleck's shoulders, hugging one arm around his broad back and smoothing the blanket down. He stirred at her touch, burly frame curling, jaws parting in a yawn, and he turned his head to peer up at her with sulky, shadowy eyes full of dreams still winking out like stars in the pale dawn. "Cistine. Forgive me, I didn't mean to sleep."

"It's all right. One of us should be well-rested when we find Ashe."

Maleck sat up, gripping the blanket to his shoulders and holding Cistine's fingers against his arm while they both stared down at the journal.

A gentle tap on the window roused them, and Cistine spotted a flash of feathers in the glass behind the stove. She bolted to the window and lifted the latch, bringing Faer inside on her wrist. He nipped her fingers and scuttled along her arm, keeping the scroll on his leg from reach until Maleck joined them with a handful of fatty scraps from the night's roast. The raven eyed the offering broodily, then swooped to Maleck's elbow instead.

Cistine stuck out her tongue after him. "Traitor." Maleck smiled, teasing the note loose from Faer's leg and unrolling it one-handed. "What does it say? Is it from Thorne's allies?"

"No, this is from *my* contacts." Maleck scanned the note quickly, a spark of grim unease in his eyes that snuffed Cistine's eagerness and lit a fire of dread in its place when his gaze rose to her. "*Logandir,* would you do me the honor of accompanying me on a mission?"

CHAPTER FOURTEEN

CISTINE COULDN'T QUIET her clamoring nerves when she stole through the town of Jovadalsa two days later on Maleck's heels. A veil of poverty shrouded the decrepit buildings, where mismatched wooden slats masked holes in the faces of sloppy homes, and many roofs slumped with the weight of boards that kept out the temperamental rains. Jovadalsa had been constructed on the shores of a small inlet from the Ismalete River, then built gradually out over the water itself. Stone bridges linked to buildings on stilts, some of which sunk deep into the silt below. Gondolas whispered through the water like the stroke of dark fingers, their oars faintly illumined by ghostlamps swaying from their curved ends.

"What are they doing out so late?" Cistine whispered, shy of even her breath stirring the thick fog.

"These people will fish at any hour," Maleck replied. "The lake is their livelihood. They take nothing from Stornhaz—no rations, no building supplies—so the Chancellors pass them over for inspection. Most of Eben's Tribunes have never set foot in this city."

Cistine could understand why. Jovadalsa was the southernmost town in Eben territory and, according to the maps she and Maleck had consulted before departing from Hellidom, among the smallest. It warranted no attention from the Tribunes of the five Courts, but the lack of Vassoran presence was obvious in the dank, filthy avenues and the clefts between houses where men and women in rags peered out with eyes red-stained from drink and desire. Steel flashed in their hands, subtle enough that Cistine fingered Nail in reply. "Maleck..."

"I see them," he said, though he hadn't turned his eyes from the road ahead. "They rarely attack those who move in groups. Show no weakness. Hold your head high."

Despite her pounding heart, Cistine obeyed. She wondered if group safety was why Maleck had wanted her along; if so, he would've been better off with anyone else. Even in her training armor and with Nail, she hardly cut an intimidating figure. But she'd agreed to come along anyway, because this was a step on the path to finding Ashe that she *could* take; and in part, though she would admit it to no one but herself, she'd gone because Julian had told her not to.

"It's dangerous going off alone with him, Princess," he'd warned her. "I'm not sure Maleck is...all *there* enough to protect you if it comes to a fight. You asked him to find Ashe, let him do it himself."

He could've chosen no better argument to convince her to leave.

Cistine slapped away the memory of that short, heated exchange and focused instead on keeping stride with Maleck through the shadows. When he finally raised a hand, slowing their pace, Cistine tried to spot their destination, but every building around them had the same shabby, slanted look as the rest.

Maleck took her shoulder and gestured her through a small, curved doorway to the left, into a structure stretching over the lake. Reluctantly, Cistine stepped inside; through the sparsely-decorated entry room, she spotted a long, cornered counter and two tables. Beneath the counter, a set of steps led down to another level. Warm red light bathed the pale wooden walls and broke around a few patrons drinking at the tables.

"Is this a tavern?" Cistine asked.

Maleck nodded. "Private conversations draw less attention in public places than behind closed doors."

He shrugged from his bandolier and sword harness, keeping only

Remany. Cistine slunk after him, fidgeting and eyeing the other patrons while he hailed a grizzled barkeeper to the counter; before she could protest, a mug of mead was thrust into her hands and Maleck led her down the steps to the lower room, where the dark roof curved above them in gentle, spacious hollows bordered with untapped casks. Long wooden tables, framed by equally long wooden benches, took up one entire wall. Circular settings and another half-counter, littered with more casks and unopened bottles, populated the rest of the room. To Cistine's relief, the level was deserted apart from three men drinking at the counter.

Maleck led her to a long bench far from the other patrons and motioned her to sit with her shoulder against the wall, then slid in beside her. "Before we have company, there are several things you should know. Most importantly, your place here is to observe and listen. I ask that you not speak during this exchange."

Cistine frowned. "Why is that?"

"These men carry ancient fears in their hearts. They've agreed to meet with us because of old debts called to the reckoning, but the wrong question may send them into retreat."

"If they're so easily frightened, should I even be here?"

Maleck's cheek ticked with a small smile. "My endorsement is reason enough for them to trust you. The rest must be handled with a delicate hand. You're my ears and mind tonight, Cistine."

She tipped her head. "How do you mean?"

"When I speak with these men, it often clouds my judgement. I may be forgetful, or...I may become lost in myself for a time. If that happens, take my journal and make note of everything they've told us. When I've recovered, we can review what you've written."

Cistine's stomach churned with more than the musty tavern-smell and the mead's honeyed notes in her nostrils. She laid a hand on Maleck's scarred wrist. "Are you *sure* you want to do this?"

He stared across the room for a time before answering. "Yes. These men have ties to old paths where I can no longer go, places Salvotor may have sent Ashe. So only they can confirm if my speculation is correct."

Cistine wanted to kick the table's leg. She hated Salvotor for this—hated that by snatching Ashe, he'd demanded this pain of Maleck too.

"We should drink," Maleck said. "It will ease that frown on your face."

"I doubt that." Cistine eyed her stein uneasily. The last time she'd had a sip of alcohol, she'd practically burned her lungs.

"The trick to enjoying a good mead lies in knowing its fermentation. Dryer mead should be drunk at room temperature, as we're doing, but the dryness creates a burn. Sip, don't gulp. That will spare your throat."

"Like tea?"

Maleck smiled. "Just like that."

Cistine brought the stein to her lips and took a slow sip. The flavors of honey and anise tickled her sinuses, and the dry, warm burn traveled down her throat into her belly. This time, she didn't choke. "It's...good!"

"Indeed. I've always been fond of this tavern's brews."

"Do you come here often, since it's so close to Hellidom?"

Maleck sipped from his stein. "Not as often as I once did."

She peered around at the sparsely-decorated walls. They needed no embellishing; the warm lighting tones and the barrels created atmosphere enough. "Ashe loves taverns. She used to bring me along when she drank with the other Wardens."

"Then we have no choice but to bring her to this one when she returns."

The thump of boots on wood had Maleck sitting taller and gripping his stein tightly. Cistine wrapped her hands around hers as well, leaning against the partition wall as three men descended to their level and made straight for the table.

At first sight of them, Cistine's stomach plummeted. Their faces all bore that same collision of age as Maleck's, torn between a boy's youth and a man's graveness. They slowed at the sight of her, eyes dancing suspiciously between her and Maleck.

"I assure you," Maleck said, "she is no threat."

The men drew out seats across the table without further hesitation, facing them.

"Olaf. Gisli. Svan." Maleck pointed to the men in turn—one with a braid sprouting from the back of his shaved skull, one bald as an eggshell, and one with a mop of unruly curls...all with eyes that seemed sunken and void. But Cistine had learned not to judge that look the day she watched Maleck throw his own safety aside to follow Ashe into danger.

She bent her head to the men, and to her relief, they nodded back. They asked for no name, and she gave none. The moment their attention returned to Maleck, Cistine blended with the wooden panels at her back, an invisible observer.

"We were surprised you wrote to us, Maleck." Olaf had a voice of storm-churned seas, rough and pitchy. "It's been many cycles since we heard from you."

Maleck jerked his fingertips along his stein's intricate markings. "I've had other demands on my time."

"You're fortunate to have distractions." Svan's laughter was mirthless. "Something besides mead and harshbane to cool your sweats at night."

Maleck swirled his mead, then looked up at each man in turn. "Have you heard rumors of any flesh being traded in secret in this kingdom by someone other than slavers?"

Svan flinched. Olaf and Gisli traded long glances.

"Is that why you called us here?" Gisli asked.

"Yes. A foreigner in Valgard was taken captive by the Courts."

Again, that mighty wince, passed from man to man like a disease. Cistine suppressed a shiver, sipping her mead to warm the ice from her insides.

"I want to know," Maleck added with lethal quiet, "if you've heard where she is."

"Nothing," Svan muttered. "No stirrings at all from the old halls. Nothing from the trappers or the *visnprests*, either."

"And what of Detlyse Halet?"

Silence commanded the table, and Cistine's heart pounded. Maleck had not mentioned to her that Ashe might be there, in the lightless pit that had given Quill so many nightmares.

"No," Svan said. "We've heard no rumors at all of Detlyse Halet. But there are other whispers stirring...from Azkai Temple in particular."

Maleck's head slowly tilted, his lids falling to half-mast. "And what do these whispers say?"

Olaf fingered the reddish threads of his beard. "That the Bloodwights are stirring north of the Isetfells."

Maleck blanched. His hand shook, and he released the stein to grip the table's edge instead. "And *why* are they stirring?"

At his rough tone, iron-tanged fear mingled with the sweet mead on Cistine's tongue.

"The *visnprests* aren't certain," Gisli admitted. "But they spotted one or two on the ridges. Not attacking, merely watching. As if they waited for something."

Maleck surged to his feet, shoving the table away and pushing quickly around it, gripping the edge for balance. "Thank you for your report. We're leaving now."

He stumbled toward the steps, and Cistine offered a quick nod to the three men and bolted after him. He was already in the entry room when she caught up to him, sliding into his bandolier but fumbling to buckle the sword harness on. Then he crashed from the tavern, staggering blindly toward the nearest bridge. Cistine raced on his heels, heart in her throat, hands useless like the night Tatiana had been poisoned—not knowing what was wrong or how to help.

Maleck fell to his knees halfway along the bridge and dragged himself over to sit against its low stone railing, planting his hands on the cobbles. His eyes fluttered shut, and Cistine tumbled down beside him, gripping his bearded face in her hands. "Maleck, tell me what you need! What can I do?"

"Nothing." His voice dragged from his throat. "I need a moment to...to rest. Take the journal," he gestured to his pocket, "write what you heard. Hurry."

By the time Cistine freed the notebook from Maleck's pocket, his breaths eased into a trancelike slowness, retreating into some sanctuary within himself. Cistine's hands trembled to free the pen from the journal's spine, and she hastily jotted every word she hadn't understood, the name of that temple, *Azkai*, and then, *Bloodwight*. That last word she circled and underscored three times.

Just as she drew the pen across the page a third time, Maleck's head tumbled onto her shoulder, heavy with sleep.

Cistine stilled, wary of waking him with even the smallest movement, and reread the words on the journal page until her eyes blurred in Jovadalsa's dim glow.

She'd seen panic like that in her mother after her second miscarriage. Every little thing, every thought of the future, had reduced the Queen to hysterics. She'd slept for long stretches after these anxious episodes, while King Cyril locked the doors and sent away anyone who sought their company—even their daughter. Cistine had watched her parents curl around one another like a pair of protective wolves, guarding one another's hearts. Their *selvenar*.

Maleck had panicked just like that at the mention of these Bloodwights, at the mere notion of whatever was stirring north of the upper mountain passes.

That made Cistine afraid, too.

CHAPTER FIFTEEN

W HEN MALECK FINALLY stirred, it was slowly and with a quiet sigh. Cistine stretched out her legs, cramped from nearly an hour immobile, and he leaned away from her. With their backs still to the bridge wall, they stared at the sliver of like visible over the other side.

"Are you all right?" Cistine's voice was small in the vast darkness.

Maleck heaved a noiseless breath. "I will be."

She squinted up at him. "What happened in that tavern?"

Maleck drew one leg up slowly and wrapped his arm around it, thumbing a slow circle against his armor. "I traveled back to a place I've been running from for twenty years."

Cistine bit back her curiosity, waiting for him to gather his thoughts.

"I...did not come from kindly origins," Maleck explained. "My parents loved mead and strong herbs far more than they loved their children. My brothers were terrors in Stornhaz, always on the verge of being sent to Detlyse Halet. Eventually, to escape justice, they fled the city, and I made a home for myself in the symphony hall."

"I remember. You told Ashe and me about that in Villmark."

"Of course. Forgive me. At that time, I made my own way to the schools of Stornhaz to study law and music, where I first met Aden. But my education was short-lived."

Cistine's heart stumbled its beat. "Why?"

"My brothers returned," Maleck said. "To escape the Courts, they had sworn *visnprest* oaths, defended by temple rites. But during that short time, they also became...infatuated with the darker side of their studies."

Julian's notes, Thorne's notes, roared through Cistine's memory. "They were worshiping the augments."

Maleck's free hand tensed into a fist. "My brothers...recruited me, brought me to Azkai Temple where I met Olaf, Svan, and Gisli. There were others who...I don't know what became of them. I suspect they're gone now. We were all taught to use augmentation...and then, to abuse it."

"How?"

"No two augments affect the body the same. The touch of a fire or lightning augment to an unsheltered body will ravage it in seconds, but a wind augment can be withstood for even a full minute without armor. Healing augments can be given to those without armor at all. There are many more—dozens more—whose incremental use will not outright kill the augur. Those were the ones my brothers and their friends were most interested in. They believed that by imbibing gentler augments in small doses, drinking the power like mead or ale, we could become...other. Something greater than man. We were taken to test their beliefs."

Cistine pressed a hand over her mouth. "*Maleck.*"

"They allowed us to commune with our families at first, even to return to Stornhaz every few weeks to avoid suspicion. It was during that time I became familiar with Aden's family." Maleck thumped his head back against the bridge. "During my visits, Aden frequently cared for Thorne, Tatiana, and Quill. Though I came to consider them friends, I was ordered to tell them I was training to become a *visnprest*...nothing more.

"As time went on, ingesting the augment blends created...a chasm in me. I could no longer think clearly when I was away from Azkai. I began to tally time by the star cycles, as the *visnprests* do, rather than by the seasons and years. I was hurting the people I loved, so I withdrew. I stopped leaving of my own volition.

"And then...the war."

Here he paused, letting his leg slide down. He gazed blankly ahead for a moment before continuing, "My brothers and I fought against the Middle Kingdom. These people, we were told, came to end our ascension and take what was rightfully ours. The *visnprests* brought acolytes from all four temples, and we fought brutally in their name. I was fourteen at the time. I had no mind of my own, no purpose but to kill. And yet in those forests and plains, I battled warriors whose bravery was beyond measure. I faced a child like myself who screamed into my face that she was not afraid of me. It was as if I woke up from a two-year slumber, and I saw myself in her eyes...what I had become."

His hands, braced palms-up on his thighs, trembled. He closed them into fists again.

"I ran," he continued, "and I did not stop running even when Talheim and my own brothers chased me. I ran all the way from southern Unsverd to Stornhaz, back to Aden and his mother. They hid me until the Middle Kingdom won and the Doors were keyed shut."

"Your brothers did that, didn't they?"

Maleck nodded. "Afterward, they divested every temple of its augment stores and books and disappeared north of Spoek, into Oadmark—the wildlands north of our kingdom. The rest of us returned to our lives...or a semblance of them. Some made pilgrimages to the temples to become *visnprests* of a new and natural order: men of knowledge, not power. Others, like Olaf, Svan, and Gisli, can only cope with what we did and what was done to us with mind-altering herbs and drink. When they're numb, they occasionally communicate with the newer, kinder Order in the temples. But I can't reach out myself."

Tears streaked Cistine's cheeks, though she hadn't noticed when they started. She offered the journal to him. "That's why seeing them takes you away from yourself."

Maleck accepted the book. "It's also why I refuse to use flagons. I've drunk of those wells deeper than anyone in the cabal. I will *never* touch them again."

Cistine wiped her damp cheeks, stomach aching with grief for Maleck;

but though she couldn't bear to stoke his memories any further, she had to know. "Maleck, what are Bloodwights?"

The stillness overtook him again like a storm sidling down a mountainside. He shut his eyes. "Bloodwights are the culmination of the *visnprests'* dream. They are the men, my brothers among them, who fled after the Doors were shut. They are other, they are...remade of augmentation, disfigured, damaged, and not entirely human. Of all the beasts in Valgardan lore, all the creatures we have ever slain, Cistine, I fear them more. They are what I nearly became."

"How near?"

"Near enough that people still remember, and fear me for the road I was walking. It's all they can see me as to this day. Near enough that..." he rested a hand over his chest, his hidden scars. "At times, I wonder if I'm still a man myself."

Cistine grabbed the wall behind her and got to her feet, and though her hand shook, she offered it to Maleck. "People are wrong about you. You ran from the war because you wanted to be better than what they saw in you. And you *are* better, Maleck. Look what you're doing, why you're here. For *Ashe*."

Brows tweaking upward, he took her hand and pushed himself up, helping her bear his weight. "You wrote down what they gave us?"

"Everything. But there wasn't much. They haven't heard of anyone being abducted into the temples."

Maleck frowned. "Then I'll have to search Detlyse Halet."

Cistine's breaths snagged. "Do you really think Ashe might be there?"

"It's one possibility. The Lightless Pit houses prisoners who are deemed too dangerous to face the world."

Her knees wobbled. "Ashe is one of the most dangerous people I've ever met."

"We know that, but Salvotor does not, so perhaps she isn't there. Still, we must investigate. No stone left unturned."

Cistine could've cursed his nobility, his incessant need to prove something to himself and to everyone around him; to show the world he was capable of goodness, that he wasn't a creature of augmented evil. In the end, she could only say, "I wish you didn't have to go to any of these horrible places."

Maleck smiled softly and brushed her cheek with the back of his gloved hand. "I know that. But trust I will go carefully, Cistine. And that I will bring Ashe home."

She leaned into his touch, gaze tracking back the way they came. "Should we tell the others about that Bloodwight?"

Maleck stiffened, his hand dropping. "I'd rather not. After all this time, I don't know if they even remember what my brothers were like...and perhaps it's better that way."

Better for him, Cistine realized; it was easier if the others didn't think of those he shared blood with. Still, unease gripped her chest. "You don't think it's important they're lurking on the borders?"

"They have always lurked on the borders." Maleck offered her a smile that was meant to be reassuring, but strain lined his eyes. "Nothing in two decades has drawn them south of it. I doubt that's changed, *Logandir*. And I won't add to this cabal's burden with unfounded fears, when we have so many other near and present things to worry over."

CHAPTER SIXTEEN

ASHE'S PLAN HAD finally stalled. She couldn't think of any gesture grand enough to prove her intentions to Nimea—not without trading information about Thorne, which she might take for herself and leave Ashe no closer to knowing what these rumors were about. No closer to securing her freedom from Aden.

"Wouldn't it be easier just to assign her to a fight and let someone rip her apart?" Ashe demanded while she and Aden jogged the arena, cooling down from another run. "Her plans for Thorne would die with her."

"If only it were that simple," Aden grunted. "But this involves Devitrius as well, somehow, and Nimea's followers. Her death might send them into chaos, but it wouldn't be the end of things."

"You're probably right. But if I have to lose one more night's sleep wondering how I'm going to sidle up to that woman..."

"That makes two of us. I didn't expect it to take this long."

"I thought the Lord of the Hive could afford to be patient."

"Not when it pertains to Thorne. If there's something happening to him outside these stars-damned walls, I want to know about it."

"So do I, but brooding solves nothing."

"I don't brood."

Ashe halted, knocking her hair from her eyes, "Yes, you do. You're brooding right now."

Aden's frown deepened. "I'm ready to retire. So if you're through with training for the night..."

"Do I have a choice?" Ashe stretched, wrapping her hands around her calves and bending her legs. Even the scar on her thigh didn't so much as prickle anymore. She'd have to thank Maleck for his poultices if she ever saw him again.

Gods, she hoped she would. Perhaps more than she ought to.

"I learned something today that may be helpful to your plan," Aden said when they descended into the staging room, "Noaam wants women only for the next match."

Ashe swung back to face him as he slammed the gate shut. "For any particular reason?"

"He doesn't believe he needs one." Aden's harsh tone suggested he thought otherwise, but they both knew his influence over the fights only extended so far. "It's meant to be a surprise for fighters and audience alike, but we'll use it as an opportunity for you to sidle deeper into her favor."

"I thought I was doing this on *my* terms."

"Your terms, on my timepiece. More lives than yours hang in the balance."

Ashe couldn't argue with that. So the following night, rather than training, she sought Nimea out.

She was alone for once; Ashe had noted a cluster of people Nimea spent her time with, mostly men whose interest seemed reserved, almost reverential. They stormily eyed anyone who crept too close to Nimea, including Ashe herself. But tonight—perhaps anticipating the upcoming fight—Nimea fought alone in the room full of practice weapons. She moved with a dancer's grace, tossing and taking up staves and wooden swords and daggers, slashing through invisible foes.

Ashe leaned against doorframe to observe her, arms folded, and announced herself dryly after a moment, "It will be different when someone swings back."

Nimea's lithe feet twisted on the amber stone, bringing her in a pivot to face Ashe, sword resting on the hinge of her shoulder. "It depends on who swings." Her smile was as fierce as her eyes. "Nervous?"

Ashe brushed the weapon down. "Hardly. Just eager to have this over with so I can get back to fighting Aden for rations."

Nimea tossed the sword into a crate and stretched. "I've noticed you two disappearing at night. Where is it you go?"

"*I* train. He makes certain I don't escape."

"Don't let him intimidate you," Nimea laughed. "Underneath that sand and stone exterior, he has his weaknesses. They'll be the death of him."

Ashe studied Nimea, trying to measure out whether that was a threat or mere observation. "I look forward to that almost as much as I look forward to crossing swords with you tomorrow."

Nimea tipped her head. "Noaam must have something interesting in store for us. Or else the people he's entertaining have a keen interest in domination."

Ashe grimaced. "I wish there was something more we could do than be their entertainment."

Nimea's smile darkened. "There's plenty more to do these days, if you know which tunnels to look down." She clapped Ashe's cheek in passing. "I'll see you on the battlefield."

CHAPTER SEVENTEEN

BRUTAL DESERT SUNLIGHT scorched the sandy arena, turning it white as powdered bones. Ashe tried not to dwell on how true that might be when she followed her fellow fighters up from the staging room to the swelling roars from the Blood Hive's spectators—mostly men.

She slowed, trailing the nine other women selected from a shallow pool of eighteen, and checked her weapons by touch: both a sword and shield this time, though the latter was little more than a heavy iron plate strapped to her forearm. But today seemed less about surprise and more about a gruesome show.

Ashe's eyes sought out Noaam's special box, but it wasn't him she was looking for this time.

Sander's face was a cool mask as he watched the proceedings, giving no indication he cared how this fight went or that he was watching her with any particular interest. Yet when their eyes met, Ashe could've sworn he inclined his head slightly. That gesture was the closest to well-wishes she would receive from anyone today, and certainly from the Tribune who'd met with her in secret weeks ago. Someone who should've been betting against her, not for her.

Nimea fell back to Ashe's side. "Endearing, aren't they?"

"I'd like them to come down here and fight us themselves," Ashe growled. "Then we could cleave those grins off their faces."

They reached the promenade and gathered on it, taking a low, sculpted bow toward Noaam. He reclined in the observation box and waved them on, though toward what, Ashe didn't know. There was no one in the arena but them.

"Maybe we're meant to fight one another after all." Iza, a new fighter from the slave markets, trembled when she suggested it.

"Now where would be the fun in that?" Nimea purred.

A long, low rattle of moving metal sliced through the air—not from the catacombs, but from the largest of all the arena's entrances, straight across from the promenade. A dozen creatures sulked into the open, their short, arched bodies bent as if the ribs and spine vied for room, borne on bent knuckles with vicious claws hooking inward. Their long necks fluted into collars, their snouts and brows flat and smooth like a serpent's, ears cleaved low to their skulls.

"Viperwolves," Nimea cursed. "Lovely."

Ashe's mouth dried up like the sand under her feet.

The creature at the head screamed, a bird's cry and the piercing shriek of frightened child, and its collar broadened into a scaled parasol. Murky gray surfeit plopped from its fangs, sizzling where they struck the sand, and with a bunch and wriggle the Viperwolf sprang.

"Scatter!" Ashe knocked fighters away and dove off the promenade. They all twisted from the pack's reach except Iza; a hairsbreadth too slow to escape, the creature's jaws snapped shut around her ankle. Bone shattered and Iza tumbled to her knees, her scream silenced when a second Viperwolf tore out her throat.

Ashe hesitated for an instant, boots digging into the sand.

The girl had been no older than Cistine, barely a fighter, and she was already dead.

"Keep moving!" Nimea roared, snapping Ashe back to focus. She lunged away from the Viperwolves, putting enough distance between them that she could grip her shield, heft it, and turn before one caught up to her.

Despite its rawboned build, the Valgardan abomination slammed into

Ashe with the breakneck force of a landslide, burying her into the sand. Nothing stood between her vital organs and its fangs except her shield. She clashed her sword against the Viperwolf's ribs, but the scales deflected the steel, rendering her blows useless. Venom steamed on the shield when the creature hunkered down, pressing Ashe deeper and deeper into the hot grains.

But the sand proved to be her ally; the Viperwolf couldn't get enough leverage to truly pin her.

Ashe slipped her knee beneath the shield and heaved up with all her might, thrusting the Viperwolf off. She rolled away from the next lunge, let the beast plow face-first into the sand, then spun and hacked its neck—and there her blade encountered no resistance, spewing gray-blue blood onto the sand.

"Ashe!" Nimea shouted, and she spun on heel to find the other warriors rallying. Three of the nine had been ripped to tatters, but the others—stung with venom and rived by clawmarks—were back on the promenade, putting their backs in and facing the wolves.

Ashe darted to join them. The Viperwolves paced around their circle, spitting and snarling, venom burning small holes in the sand, their beady eyes regarding the fighters like prey.

"We need to spread out," Ashe hissed to Nimea. "They'll outlast us in this sun. They have patience, we have cleverness. Let's use that to our advantage."

"What did you have in mind?"

Ashe numbered the girls around the circle—Hadessa, Martina, Dilja, Briet, Nimea, and Ashe herself. One less Viperwolf than that, but the rest bounded in tight counter-circles, forming an organized pack.

The women would have to follow suit to survive.

Ashe raised her voice above the crowd's din. "Pair off and separate! One can distract while the other attacks. Go for the back of the neck where they're vulnerable."

Nimea shouted, "You heard her! *Go!*"

Hadessa flung her spear, forcing the Viperwolves to scatter, and drew a half-axe from the sheath on her back as she fled with Martina. Dilja and Briet formed another pair and shot off toward the closed tunnel where the creatures had emerged. Ashe grabbed Nimea and led her away from the promenade, and the Viperwolves gave chase.

But they didn't divide to attack the women the way Ashe had predicted. The whole pack shot after Hadessa and Martina.

Ashe skidded to a halt in a spray of sand. "Hadessa, behind!"

The girl didn't look back; her legs pumped faster, propelling her toward the wall. Without so much as a hitch in her step, she vaulted up the oiled stone and pushed off, somersaulting over the Viperwolves. As they churned and skittered, trying to turn, Hadessa grabbed Martina by the arm and hauled her away down the elliptical's curve. The audience jeered and pelted them with rotten food when they passed beneath the seats.

Ashe stared after them, her mind racing. Then she yanked off her shield, letting it fall to the sand.

"What are you doing?" Nimea snarled. "Have you lost your mind?"

"I don't need my shield for this. Just yours." She stripped off her sandals and let her bare feet grip the sand—hot and uncomfortable, but each step she took, she felt the ground, interacted with it more freely, like Aden did when they ran at night. "Divide the pack. We'll take them two by two. Just follow my lead."

"You are not in command here. I have tenure!"

"And I have experience in war! If you want to survive, follow me!" Ashe charged toward the Viperwolf pack. Nimea, cursing, gave chase.

With every stride, Ashe's muscles possessed the sand beneath her feet, grabbing and shoving, gobbling up the distance to the pack as they closed in on Hadessa and Martina. With several meters still between them, Ashe hefted her blade, stroked it lightly against the inside of her palm, and raised it to the wind.

The Viperwolves tossed their slender necks, flat heads swiveling up. The leader dug its claws into the ground and banked, turning sharply toward Ashe and Nimea.

"Turn your back on them," Ashe shouted at Nimea, "and get under your shield."

"Are you *mad?*"

"Just do what I say!"

Bellowing, Nimea swung her shield up, slid on her knees, and planted the iron dish toward Ashe. The Viperwolves closed in on her back; Ashe had one narrow opportunity before they decided Nimea was an easier kill than their bleeding prey.

Ashe huffed a prayer, then bolted forward.

Her bare feet slapped and rose from the sand. Twenty paces. Fifteen. Ten.

"Shield up!" she screamed. Nimea cocked it, and Ashe leaped, toes hitting the hot iron and blistering on contact. *"Thrust!"*

Nimea roared, pushing all her weight up, catapulting Ashe over the pack. She slashed her blade against every graceful neck in reach, severing spines and spurting blood with four well-aimed blows. Two Viperwolves fell dead to the sand and another pair darted away with ear-splitting wails.

The fifth plowed into Nimea, crushing her into the sand.

Ashe was on the beast before she could think, those venomous fangs an inch from Nimea's neck when Ashe wedged her sword under them, the filthy runoff freckling her blade. Nimea's dagger jammed across its neck from behind and passed through until it caught against Ashe's at the front.

The Viperwolf's severed head flopped into the sand.

Victorious shouts rose from the gate; the others had seen Ashe and Nimea's maneuver and replicated it. The last Viperwolves lay dead in the sand when Briet and Martina emerged from below their shields, Dilja and Hadessa wiping blue blood from their blades.

Ashe staggered backward, kicking the Viperwolf's body from Nimea's torso and offering a hand.

"Your foolhardy plan nearly killed me," Nimea panted.

"But my sword saved you. Remember that."

Nimea's eyes narrowed. "I will."

She let Ashe pull her to her feet, the arena around them thundering with the crowd's sated screams.

Viperwolf battles were a favorite of the Hive, judging by the stock of poultices for venom wounds. Ashe groaned when the salve soaked into her arm, cooling where the splatters from her sword had landed like hot oil. She doubted the other women were much better off, but they'd come and gone from the medico's room long before Ashe; when she should've been treating her wounds, she'd been cornered by the Tribunes instead.

Noaam had caught up to her in the staging room with a too-familiar clap to the shoulder. "I expected a much different outcome today, but this was far more entertaining. I haven't seen so many mynts and resources trade hands here since the first time Aden made mince of an Isetfell wildcat! Expect many, many opportunities to prove your worth in the Hive from now on."

And that was all Ashe needed on top of infiltrating Nimea's clan: Noaam singling her out for slaughter.

But it was Sander's presence that lingered in her mind. He'd stayed behind after the others ascended back into the arena, touched Ashe's elbow and murmured, "Well done. That cunning display of prowess caught Noaam's attention. That's precisely what we need."

"What *we* need?" Ashe had echoed scathingly.

"If you want to survive this place, yes."

Ashe did want to survive, but she wasn't sure she wanted a bloodthirsty Tribune's help doing it. Then again, she didn't want Aden's help, either.

A throat cleared in the doorway, and Ashe looked up sharply at the Hive Lord, summoned as if by her thought of him. "You're alive."

Ashe raised a brow, telling him silently what she thought of his observation.

His eyes narrowed. "Good." He left without another word.

"Goodbye to you, too." Ashe wrapped a bandage around her forearm and pulled it tight with her teeth, then sat back on her haunches with a groan.

"A sound like that can be taken for weakness in this place."

Ashe looked up swiftly again at the sound of Nimea's voice from the doorway, unusually quiet. She wore a necklace of bandages where the venom had dripped against her neck and hid them with her cardigan's upturned collar. But there was no hiding the darkness of her gaze.

"Is there anything that *isn't?*" Ashe scoffed.

Nimea's eyes narrowed even further. "Tell me why you did it. If you'd let me die, there would be one less person to squabble over rations and challenge in future fights."

"Maybe so." Ashe slid from the stone ledge. "But I told you, my ambitions here are for more than just surviving. I still believe you can help me accomplish those goals."

Nimea studied her for a full minute. Then she said, "Meet me in the mess hall after curfew tonight. I have something to show you."

CHAPTER EIGHTEEN

The GUARDS TOOK an inordinate time to rotate their shifts that night; Ashe trembled with energy by the time the sleeping hall emptied, freeing her to drop from her alcove and steal down the long, dark halls to the dining area unseen. Nimea waited for her there, a scrape of pale clothing and skin against the wall where she leaned, the dim glow from the ghostlamps in the corridor behind Ashe illuminating her body in the darkness.

"Your ambitions," Nimea said in greeting, "what are they?"

Ashe folded her arms. "What's *your* interest? You're the one who approached me first."

"There's a rumor that before you came here, you encountered Aden's cousin, Thorne. Is that true?"

Ashe scowled. The Hive Lord was doing the work for her behind her back, intimating her to this group who whispered his cousin's name in the dark. "We're familiar, but not friendly."

"And would your ambitions have anything to do with him?"

"Maybe. Maybe not. My business with Thorne is my own."

Nimea's thick brows slid up. "What if I told you I have the means to settle your score with him for you?"

Ashe's belly twisted. She forced herself to show no concern, no interest, no confusion. "I would ask for proof that you're not some ally of his, trying to trap me. I hear he has some influence in this kingdom."

"*Had*. And we aren't allies, I can assure you. Not anymore."

"But you were?"

Nimea turned her head sharply. The light silhouetted the curve of her cheek, her slanted, furious mouth. "Before I came here, I believed Thorne and I shared the same ideals. There were many of us in the City of a Thousand Stars who chose to follow his vision of justice. But when he left Stornhaz, he turned the entire might of Kanslar against us so he and his precious cabal of six could escape. Meanwhile, we were dragged from our beds and thrown into carts bound for Siralek."

Ashe stared at Nimea, heart thundering in her throat—with rage, not shock. None of this truly surprised her.

"There were almost fifty of us," Nimea went on, "but now only sixteen remain, and most won't speak to each other for fear of the pain in watching their friends die. We've struggled to survive in this Nimmus-pit the last ten years, praying for death or fighting against it depending on the day. So if you have no quarrel with Thorne, I have no use for you. But if your position here has anything to do with him—"

"It does. More than you can imagine."

Nimea turned back to her, that vicious frown shifting into a grin. "Then come with me."

She led Ashe carefully but confidently through patches of light and seams of darkness. Twice they stopped to shelter from passing guards behind the arches; Ashe wondered if their focus was usually so languished in these places, or if Aden was providing her yet another window of opportunity. She despised not knowing which movements in this game were hers and which were his.

Nimea finally turned down a smaller side hall and motioned Ashe to stand watch. Then she knelt and pried out a block of stone near the floor; judging by the powder surrounding it, it had been moved often, and recently.

"Shimmy through," Nimea ordered.

Ashe frowned. "That's an awfully tight fit."

"I've seen men twice your size make it. Are you going to stand there and make excuses?"

Ashe wedged her head and shoulders into the gap and wriggled through, holding her breath when the walls caught at her hair and arms. She emerged gasping on the other side, in absolute darkness, and rolled onto her back. She could only mark Nimea's arrival by the grate of stone dust falling around her body. When she emerged backwards, feet jamming into Ashe's side, Ashe swore. "You're out of your mind!"

"It's a necessity. We can't leave the block disturbed."

Ashe reached out both hands for something to anchor to in the blackness. "What is this place?"

"One of the sewage tunnels bricked over decades ago. Nothing comes down here but the waste from Siralek." Nimea struck a ghostlamp to life from the floor and raised it above their heads, the gentle pool of persimmon light paving cratered stairs down into a trough of filthy water. Ashe almost gagged at its rancid fumes, listing to the side, her hand plunging into a mess of tangled threads like hair sprouting from the wall. She jerked away, swearing, and Nimea caught her wrist. "Stop being so tense! They're just roots from the oasis seeking any moisture they can find."

She bounded down the steps and splashed straight into the wastewater, taking the light with her. Holding her breath, Ashe waded in on her heels.

For several meters, they trudged through the murky swill, and eventually Ashe had no choice but to breathe. She hiccupped and gagged at first, but by the time they slowed her eyes had stopped watering and bile no longer stripped her throat. They turned a corner in the sewer, and the light silhouetted four people perched on tumbles of devastated stone or ramshackle seats made of crates. Three men and one woman, none of whom Ashe recognized.

"Andras, Kalman, Tobor," Nimea introduced them by gestures, "and Rez." The woman, Rez, dipped her head, but her glittering eyes never strayed from Ashe's face.

"And who is this?" Andras, a beast of a man, shifted forward on his seat. Ashe half-expected him to spring down on her like a mountain cat.

"Someone else who despises Thorne," Nimea said.

"And why might that be?" Kalman, narrower and smoother than Andras in voice and features, tipped his head.

"Let's just say your former High Tribune hurt someone I love." The anger Ashe fed into those words was no imitation. "He used her as bait and she nearly died because of it. That's why I'm here."

"Pity you," Andras said. "That's why we're *all* here."

"That isn't reason enough for you to have joined us tonight." Rez turned her glare on Nimea.

"And where am I, exactly?"

"You're in the presence of those who lead the Tumult," Nimea explained. "We've spent ten years searching for a way to escape this place, return to the heart of Valgard, and kill Thorne and his cabal."

Andras curled his lip in disgust. "That *bandayo* left us to rot here while he chased power and that stars-damned Key to opening the Doors."

All the heat in Ashe's body pooled in her core, a small, pulsating kernel of shock and rage.

She hadn't heard mention of the Key to the Doors to the Gods in *years*. Cyril never told her what it was or what happened to it after the war, but she'd prayed it was forgotten, that no one in Valgard would believe it was anything more than a baseless rumor of a few zealots who hoped augments could be unleashed again.

But *Thorne* wanted it.

That seed in Ashe's gut bloomed into hate, pushing like fire all the way to her fingertips, and she slammed her flat hand against the wall, yanking the roots so hard they tore.

Tobor raised a brow. Rez snorted quietly, "*This* is what you bring to our ranks—a volatile, fresh desert flower who wears her emotions on her pretty face?"

Ashe jerked forward, ready to pummel Rez since she couldn't pummel Thorne, but Nimea threw out an arm to halt her. "She has something we lack. She's seen Thorne *recently.*"

In utter silence, they all stared at her, and Ashe met each pair of eyes in cold defiance. When no one else spoke, Nimea added, "We need details of Thorne's movements. Ways we can corner him."

"And how do you plan to accomplish that?" Ashe scoffed. "You're as trapped as I am."

Kalman sat forward on his perch, folding his hands in his lap. "Not for long, if you help us. Will you?"

It was a perilous slope she stood on now, pulled between her mission from Aden and the parts of her that wept and bled for Cistine's pain after what Thorne had done. She didn't know if she was lying when she said, "Yes."

Nimea's mouth turned in the beginnings of a smile. "The man who brought you and the other prisoners here. What do you know of him?"

"I know his name is Devitrius. He's the leader of Salvotor's private retinue."

"Not our first choice of someone to bargain with. He's as filthy a *bandayo* as any of them, as much as the man he serves. But this time he came to Siralek to do much more than escort a batch of prisoners."

"He's made us an offer," Rez grinned. "Freedom for anyone willing to take it...with a price."

Ashe's skin buzzed with exhilaration. "What do we have to do?"

"*You* won't do anything. That part doesn't concern you."

"Not yet," Nimea amended. "If you prove yourself through the information you give, then perhaps it will in time."

Ashe's enthusiasm blew out like a candle in strong wind. "What does Devitrius want *you* to do?"

"Two things." Andras folded his arms behind his head. "Stage our deaths and slip from the arena with just a bit of help from him."

"And once we're free," Nimea added, "we find Thorne and kill him, or kill his cabal and drive him mad so his own father can have him. We really don't care which, as long as they're all dead in the end."

"We've already begun matching off with one another to escape," Tobor said. "We've only freed two so far, but two may be enough."

Kalman nodded. "The difficulty lies in finding Thorne once we're outside. That's where we need you."

Sense pierced Ashe's burning vendetta like a stroke of light down this long, fetid tunnel. "Doesn't it bother any of you that Devitrius serves the man who put you here, and you're doing his bidding?"

"Listen to her, speaking like she knows our minds," Andras scoffed.

Nimea shot Ashe a pitying smile. "Salvotor upheld the law when he learned we forged a secret Court within Kanslar, but Thorne betrayed us outright to him, knowing what would come of it—the same way he betrayed your friend. Between the two, which would you want to kill?"

"I want them *both* dead."

"Then help us." Nimea stepped nearer to grip Ashe's shoulder. "First, Thorne. We'll win the Chancellor's favor through this test and move close enough to kill him, too. After that, we'll part ways with justice in our hands."

Sour temptation tickled the back of Ashe's tongue, but still she hesitated. She certainly knew where she could direct them, but dozens of other people lived there—Tariq the shopkeeper, Cassaida the grain mistress, and Baba Kallah, who was one of the gentlest souls Ashe had ever met despite her Valgardan blood. She couldn't trust these ruthless arena fighters not to use anyone as bait or, worse, hostages.

Putting them in the Tumult's path would be just as worthless as every life she'd wasted in these forced matches already. There had to be a better way.

Besides, she didn't even know if the cabal had gone back to Hellidom.

"I don't know where he is," she hedged. "But I can tell you how to draw him out."

The fighters exchanged glances. Kalman sighed. "That's something, I suppose."

"Threaten something that matters to him," Ashe said. "He came to Stornhaz when he realized he lost his bait."

"And what would you suggest we strike?"

"He was a Tribune, wasn't he? What about his old territory—Blaykrone, wasn't it?"

Andras rolled his eyes. "He's distanced itself from it."

"Not from what I've seen and heard. It's possible a threat to it would force him into the open."

Slowly, Rez sat back. Tobor scratched his lower lip. Kalman and Nimea were nodding already. "We'll need to dispatch another fighter," Nimea said. "Send him to tell Devitrius that Thorne is still territorial about Blaykrone. The rest is in Salvotor's hands."

"Is he going to kill anyone?" They were all Valgardans, and it shouldn't matter, but she didn't want to give Salvotor the satisfaction of the kill.

"Doubtful," Rez sniffed. "He's bound by law. He can't go hacking his way through Blaykrone."

"Oh, but he'll think of something," Nimea smirked. "That cunning *bandayo* always does."

Ashe peered down at her fingers in the ghostlit gloom and tried not to think that she was betraying not just Thorne, who deserved it, and not just his cabal, who were as complicit in his lies toward Cistine as anyone, but...

Maleck.

He would be caught in the middle of this, standing as close to Thorne as he always did, protecting him as fiercely as Ashe protected Cistine.

Pitting them against one another.

Guilt ripped through Ashe, yanking fetid air sharply down her lungs, and she suddenly wished she could take back what she'd told them, or find another way to frame it so Maleck could walk away. Thorne deserved this, but Valgardan blood or not, Maleck was the closest thing to a friend she had in this gods-forsaken kingdom. He'd taught her about its politics, about Nimmus and Cenowyn, about music and metal and the stars.

He didn't deserve this. He'd saved her leg. Saved her life.

Now it was too late. All she could do was pray he was every bit as lethal as she'd believed when she first saw his scarred chest. Nothing less would withstand the tide of the Tumult's hatred toward Thorne and his cabal.

Nothing less would survive what Ashe had put into motion tonight.

CHAPTER NINETEEN

CISTINE WAS GRATEFUL for training's familiar monotony when she and Maleck returned from Jovadalsa. She let her lessons consume fears of dark *visnprests* stalking the northern borders; she had little time to dwell on anything else when Quill put her through her paces so rigorously. He was tense about something, playing it off with sleek grins and jokes each day while Cistine took blows against the padding of her training armor and they climbed the stone cliffs together, but something was off in his eyes.

"Are you all right?" Cistine finally asked one afternoon when they descended from the rock top, the sun cooling in a warm disc toward the horizon behind them.

Quill sighed, raking his hair from his brow. "I'm worried about Tati. Ever since you and Maleck went off to Jovadalsa, she's been hitting the mead harder than usual."

Cistine frowned. "Is that...something she struggles with?"

"Not when she's on an even keel. But...Nimmus' teeth. She won't *talk* to me anymore. She's never shut me out this much before."

Cistine rubbed her sweaty brow with her wrist. "Should we tell Thorne?"

"It hasn't interfered with her patrols, so, no, not yet. I think I can still get through to her, I just need more time."

Cistine tucked a smile behind a cough and followed him into the Den, where the smell of roasted potatoes, vegetables, and sizzling meat greeted them. The rest of the cabal, Baba Kallah, and Julian were gathered in the kitchen for lunch, and Cistine's eyes went straight to Tatiana at the table, nursing a mead bottle and frowning at the separated halves of some Valgardan device: a half-dome with a small hole in the bottom and a smattering of empty pinpricks on top.

Quill swaggered up to the table and stole one half of the device. "When are you going to give up on this thing?"

"The moment I discover which holes to plug," Tatiana snapped. "Give it back."

Quill palmed the device from hand to hand. "Why don't you take it from me?"

Her foot crunched his knee, and he doubled up, howling in pain. She slid the device easily from his grasp with one hand, swigging from the bottle with the other. "Any more requests?"

Thorne looked sharply between them. "Enough, both of you."

Cistine collapsed into the last empty seat at the table with a moan of relief. Maleck glanced up from his notebook, smiling. "Another successful day of training, I take it."

"It's not over yet," Ariadne warned. "We have plans to go over for the garden aqueduct before the first freeze."

"And," Thorne added, "matters of decorum wait for no one."

"I'm looking forward to the torture," Cistine deadpanned.

Quill limped to the seat beside Thorne and sat, rubbing his knee. "If you're looking forward to it, we haven't tortured you enough."

"I beg to differ." Julian draped his arm around Cistine's chair, his fingertips brushing her opposite hip. "How were things today?"

"Brutal. But no worse than usual."

"That's our girl," Quill chuckled, and Julian's hand tightened around her side.

At the stove, Baba Kallah clicked her tongue, and Thorne was out of his seat at once, carrying platters to the table. "Book away," Baba Kallah said to Maleck. Reluctantly, he shut his journal and slid it into his pocket. "Whatever that is, Tatiana…*away.*" Grumbling, she snapped the halves of the device together and put it under her chair.

"What is that thing?" Cistine asked.

Tatiana took another swig of mead. "None of your business."

With everyone clustered around the table, Ariadne dipped her head in silent prayer. No one moved until she looked up again; then Quill said, "I'd like to say a prayer of my own."

Ariadne's brows rose, but she gestured him on.

Clearing his throat, Quill bowed his head. "Gods, we are thankful beyond words that Cistine did *not* have a hand in preparing this meal."

Cistine gasped in mock-offense, hurling the cup of water beside her place straight into his face. Chortling, Quill rocked his chair back in a swift dodge that sent half the water into Thorne's lap instead of his.

"Oh, no!" Cistine laughed, covering her mouth. "I'm sorry!"

"Hardly," Thorne growled playfully, starting up from his seat with a wicked smile. "*Yet.*"

Baba Kallah stuck her cane across the table, rooting both Thorne and Quill in place. "First, we eat. Then, we make war."

"Wise words," Ariadne said dryly. "Shall we?"

Cistine smiled as she tackled her portion, but her eyes returned incessantly to the empty seat where Ashe usually sat beside her—always the Warden on defense. No one else occupied that space, and from time to time she caught Maleck's attention wandering there too.

Thorne polished his plate too quickly to be healthy and leaned across the arm of his seat to kiss his grandmother's cheek. "Delicious as always."

"You spoil me, *Stornjor,*" she chuckled, leaning into his kiss.

"You could give Cistine lessons," Ariadne teased. "Quill was right, she needs them. *Desperately.*"

"I wouldn't mind," Cistine admitted. "Maybe they could replace my cleaning duties after dinner."

"Hm, fair try. But no."

Baba Kallah stretched her cane in front of Tatiana and Julian to prod

Cistine's shoulder. "If you like, I *will* teach you to cook these lovely things you harvest for us."

Ears hot with pleasure, Cistine nodded. "It would be an honor."

"Just don't ask us to try your first few concoctions," Julian laughed, and Cistine swatted his chest.

"Under Baba Kallah's tutelage, I'm sure even her first attempts will be noteworthy." Thorne winked at Cistine.

The Den's front door slammed open, the echo bolting through the whole house. "*Thorne!*"

The High Tribune shot to his feet, and the rest of the cabal lurched up after him, Tatiana a bit unsteadily. Cistine hurried around the table to help Baba Kallah from her seat as Cassaida stumbled into the kitchen.

Fear plunged through Cistine. She'd only ever known the grain mistress to be a pillar of calm when she worked with her below the Den; but today, fear blanketed the unfrozen half of her face and pulled down the corner of her branded eye and twisted mouth.

"Cassaida, what are you doing here?" Thorne demanded. "I thought you were visiting your family."

"I've just come from there," she panted. "But I joined a caravan of merches to make the return journey, and they told me..." Her face crumbled, mouth buried against the back of her knuckles. "My home—Geitlan, on the shore of Stedgnalt Lake. You know it?"

"Of course I do. It's the northernmost lumbering village in Blaykrone."

Cassaida's head bobbed, and a shiver crumbled her body. "It was buried in a landslide from the foothills of the Vaszaj Range."

Cistine caught her breath. Julian swore.

"Your family?" Ariadne demanded. "Oskar and the children?"

"I don't know."

"What relief has been sent?" Maleck asked.

Cassaida's wet eyes turned slowly from Thorne to Maleck. "None."

Thorne's hand slammed down on the table's edge and he pushed forward to take her shoulders. "*What?*"

"It's happening all across Blaykrone: there's no aid for the autumn hardships, the storms, the floods near the border with Eben. Stornhaz isn't sending help."

Baba Kallah leaned heavily on the crook of Cistine's arm. "God's bones."

Thorne's back lifted in a long, steadying breath—gathering himself. "Cistine, would you brew some tea for Cassaida? Then meet us in the room off the entry parlor. You know the one."

Cistine's heart wilted with shock.

The strategy room, where she'd listened in on the cabal's discussions about *Svarkyst* steel the first night she stayed here.

Hands rattling with haste, she brewed a pot of chamomile tea. Julian fetched a blanket from Cistine's room, draped it over Cassaida's shoulders, and helped her into Thorne's deserted chair. She rocked slightly and stared at the wall, one hand pressed to her mouth, the other covering her middle. She revived only when Cistine pressed the mug into her hands; her eyes focused, and she tried for a smile. "You're too kind."

"Please don't say that," Cistine begged. "If there's *anything* we can do to help..."

"Go to the High Tribune. He'll know what to do."

"Are you sure you want to be alone?"

"I'll stay with her," Julian offered. "I'm not much for Valgardan war councils myself."

Cistine met his gaze, stomach plummeting. He'd sensed it, too; with Cassaida's tearful report, something had changed for all of them.

Cistine sprinted to the entry parlor, around the wooden half-shelf, and into the room that encompassed the left-front corner of the Den. Windows took up half the walls, masked with drapes. A circular table spanned most of the room, wedged almost against the fireplace on one wall; a map of Valgard dominated the other. No one looked up from their seats when Cistine sidled into the last remaining place between Thorne and Ariadne.

"This has Salvotor's mark on it," Quill growled.

Thorne propped his elbows on the table and folded his hands against his mouth. "Yes, it does."

"Retribution," Baba Kallah said. "You struck him in his home, now he strikes back at yours."

Ariadne mirrored Thorne's posture. "He must have realized that between Stornhaz and the caravan on the Vey, Thorne's devotion isn't only to his own survival. It's to the people."

"And this is what he does with that knowledge." Thorne's eyes were fixed unseeing on the map.

"Is he going to start killing people?" Cistine asked.

Quill snorted. "You read too many books."

Thorne dropped his gaze to hold hers. "He's still an officer of the Courts, so it's unlikely he would. Instead he'll bury them under so many legal excuses for lack of aid, he might as well push the blade through them himself. Geitlan will only be the beginning."

"And where does it end?" Cistine demanded.

Thorne dropped his arms on the table, gaze hardening. For once, Cistine hated the honesty in his face. "It ends when I surrender to him."

She forced herself not to cringe at the thought of Thorne in chains, thrown into Detlyse Halet—or worse. "You can't go to him."

"I agree," Baba Kallah said. "This kingdom needs you and the aspirations you carry, *Stornjor*. Without them, nothing will ever change."

"I don't intend to give myself over to him," Thorne said, "but Blaykrone is my territory—my responsibility. Something must be done for them."

Tatiana crossed her arms and propped her feet on the table. "We can help them ourselves."

Thorne nodded. "Precisely. If Kanslar won't send aid, Sillakove will. Beginning with the strength of our own backs."

"To Geitlan?" Quill asked.

"At dawn," Thorne confirmed, "and we'll bring Cassaida along. She can help determine what can be saved and what can't." Pain flashed in his face, and Cistine's heart ached for him.

"And my journey to Detlyse Halet?" Maleck asked.

Thorne looked at him across the table. "I'm sorry, Maleck."

The warrior's shoulders peeled back, regret lashing in his eyes.

"Thorne, I beg you to spare me. This mission is important."

"I know. Finding Ashe is a concern this cabal will *not* forget. But we may be steps away from finding her, or leagues. Meanwhile, we know about Geitlan...we know what's out there. I can't spare one of my best during a crisis like this."

Maleck's gaze swept to Cistine, and she couldn't be certain—was he pleading with her? Or was that visceral emotion in his eyes because he already knew what she would say?

"Ashe would never put her own life before a village full of innocent people." Cistine hated herself for saying it, even if it was the truth. "I don't *want* to tell you this, but Thorne is right. Ashe will have to hold on just a bit longer."

Maleck looked at Thorne again. "Thorne, this—"

"Darkwind." A quiet command.

Maleck hung his head, braids sweeping forward to caress his hollow cheeks. The same resignation spilled through Cistine; Julian's research on the Key, her training, the hunt for Ashe...all of it would have to wait until Blaykrone's people were safe.

"I had best sleep." Baba Kallah hobbled to her feet. "These old bones don't like to rise as early as they once did."

"Baba..." Thorne began.

"Oh, yes, I am coming with you. Did you think this was all about you, *Stornjor*? Or have you forgotten I was raised on the shores of Stedgnalt before your grandfather took me to Stornhaz? I'll go to help those who remember that time, the families of the friends I once knew. They're often forgotten in a crisis."

Thorne gripped the arm of his seat, concern for the toll of the journey on his grandmother bright in his eyes.

"Thorne," Cistine interjected. "She should come. She's right, we're going to need everyone's help. *Everyone.*"

He groaned, settling back in his seat. "All right. I hear you."

And that, Cistine knew, was the only way they would survive the perilous days to come.

THE DAUGHTER

OF

STEEL AND THORNS

CHAPTER TWENTY

AFTER MORE THAN a week of silence from the Tumult—and no news of their success or failure in Blaykrone—and days of grappling with vicious spikes of guilt that left her squirming in her alcove, Ashe couldn't put it off any longer. She had to give Aden *something*, if not the truth; otherwise he might dispense with her entirely, destroying one of her potential avenues toward freedom.

Under the leering gazes of skull-ribbed walls, Ashe stepped inside the Hive Lord's dwelling and shut the gate. The latch's clatter brought Aden's head up where he sat at the table, poring over a list of names.

Ashe cocked her body back against the gate. "You were missed in training today. None of us felt the same without your lectures."

"Sorry to disappoint." He dropped his attention back to his papers. "Is there any particular reason you sought me out? Surely you don't miss me that much."

Ashe rolled her eyes. "I wanted to tell you I have an in with Nimea's people."

Aden pushed back from the table, grabbed the pitcher of water, and poured two cups. He slid one toward the opposite chair, inviting Ashe to sit. Slowly, she did. "Tell me everything."

Ashe brought the cup to her lips and hesitated, mulling over what to say. Aden had craftily withheld the truth of Nimea's imprisonment and her connection to Thorne, after all; secret-keeping and half-truths were a part of this partnership. "There isn't much to tell. They have a grudge against Thorne, and they think I do, too."

Aden snorted. "Offer your anger to a furious man, and he'll open his vault of treasures to you."

Ashe nearly bit back that Nimea was leaps ahead of him in whatever she was planning, and if not for Ashe, Aden would still be chasing whispers down the halls.

"Who else is allied to her?" Aden asked. "Who does she meet with?"

"They didn't give names," Ashe lied. "Three men and a woman. One was bearded."

Aden arched a brow. "The woman?"

Was he actually teasing her? She scowled at him just in case. "Yes, exactly. How did you know?"

"The catacombs have that strange effect." Aden bent back over his papers. "Inform me when you learn their names, and I'll keep them from future fights."

Frowning, Ashe leaned forward. "What are you working on?"

His pen halted. "The names for tomorrow's match." His voice was uncharacteristically soft. "Do you know how many of these matches I've rostered?"

"More than a dozen?"

He ignored her sarcasm. "It's never any easier. Less than half the fighters return every time. Those who do are often more bitter than before. So I have to decide not only whose death is permissible, but whose fury we can endure when the fight changes them."

Ashe studied him shrewdly—not as the man who'd beaten and ground her into the dust so many times, but the one who'd sat with her before her first match. The one who'd recruited her and offered her a chance at freedom. The one whose interest was the survival of his cousin, even if that cousin did not deserve it.

He was bent, she realized. Weary. He was here, and not in the training rooms lately, because the burden of choosing life or death for the people in this Hive was a weight too heavy for any man to bear. Even so, the image of Aden himself—as hard as the stone walls he governed, as unforgiving as the hot sun he sent these fighters to fight and die beneath—was indispensable.

Ashe couldn't fathom what the Hive had been like before he brought order to it, but the skulls on his bedroom walls begged to tell another story.

She rested her arms on the table. "The fights seem to be happening more frequently. Two or three times a week now. Is that unusual?"

Aden tapped his pen on the papers. "Yes. It used to be once every week, on the same day. The whole interim was spent preparing for it. Now…"

"Noaam is getting greedy."

Aden nodded. "In the presence of his fellow Tribunes, he can hardly afford not to. But without time to train all the recruits to the finest fighting standards, they're dying quicker than the prisons and slave markets across Valgard can repopulate them."

Ashe surveyed the paper, vengeance scraping at her chest. "You should send Noaam's favorite fighters into battle. All of them against one another."

Aden flicked up a brow. "And why is that?"

Ashe shrugged. "Why not? He doesn't care if this process is unpleasant for you, so make it unpleasant for him. Then, while the veterans and popular fighters are bound up with the arena, train the recruits hard and fast."

"That isn't how we do things."

"Maybe that ought to change. Noaam already shifted the game, Aden. It's time you caught up to him."

Aden stilled, his pen no longer flicking the tabletop.

"I'll consider it," he said. "In the meantime, I want nightly reports. Everything Nimea's faction offers you. If we can collect definitive evidence, some insight into a credible threat against Thorne or the cabal…"

"What will you do?" Ashe snorted. "We're prisoners here, and Valgard despises your cabal, in case you don't remember."

"Let me be concerned with that. Your only task is to pool the evidence itself."

Ashe fought the urge to roll her eyes. "As you wish. Am I excused?"

"Were you summoned?" Aden bent back over the table with a sigh.

As frustrating as this was for her, it must be twice as infuriating for him. And in ways she might not understand yet, it pained him to send these criminals to die a gory death rather than a quick one. "I'll see you in the arena tonight, Hive Lord. I'm not taking no for an answer."

Aden grunted, scribbling a few names on a clean scrap of paper. But when Ashe reached the gate, she thought she heard him murmur, "Thank you."

CHAPTER TWENTY-ONE

THE CABAL TRAVELLED west along the Nior River toward its eventual end in southern Blaykrone territory, where they would turn north toward Stedgnalt Lake. The way was mostly wilderness, dotted with trees thickening into forests, and Cistine was relieved the summer heat had passed. They rode in pleasant conditions, which gave her time to acclimate to a saddle again.

She hadn't ridden a horse in more years than she could count. Whenever she'd heard girls in Astoria daydreaming about riding barebacked across the fields into the Calalun Peaks, she'd yawned and gone back to her books. Having her pick of the royal stables—and being forced into posting lessons since she could walk—had left her with a sour taste toward horseback riding altogether. Now her sore haunches were unaccustomed to the saddle, and she was grateful to stop as often as Baba Kallah asked to, which spared her the embarrassment of admitting just how much her tailbone and legs truly ached.

"You could always ride with me instead of fighting that beast all the time," Julian offered one day, watching Cistine fumble to dismount. "I think I might be a better horseman."

That much was painfully obvious. He looked as sensuous and poised astride his white nag as he did whenever he swaggered toward her with that *look* in his eye like he would imminently kiss her.

But Cistine's soreness after days of alternately trotting and galloping along the riverbank made her cranky, so she snapped a bit more harshly than she meant to, "I'm *fine*, Julian. I have to learn to handle a mount myself."

He circled his horse around hers while she rubbed her aching hips. "Well, it's not as if you'll be doing much riding when we return to Talheim. Besides, this saddle is so cold and empty without you."

Cistine scowled at him, but his endearing smile eased her annoyance. When he hopped lithely from his saddle and kissed her, she was able to put the exchange from her mind.

But not far from it.

They made camp as they had every night before, and Cistine joined Baba Kallah at the fire to help prepare food: julienning vegetables she brought in her saddlebags, then watching her cook fish the cabal caught from the river.

"No more than three minutes to each side," Baba Kallah warned, "or the fish will blacken. Once it's well-seared, temper the fire and let it cook slowly through."

Cistine smiled sheepishly at Thorne as he passed by, sharing in one look the memory of the horrific meal she'd served the cabal in Starhollow. That recipe had called for a sear as well, but she'd assumed that meant thorough cooking on a high flame; she'd *seared* it for nearly fifteen minutes on each side.

Thorne's brows rose, and Cistine stuck her tongue out him. Chuckling, he shucked off his boots, rolled up his pant legs, bound his hair back with a cord, and waded into the river shallows to fish again.

He and Cassaida were the only ones still at camp besides Cistine and Baba Kallah. Quill and Tatiana had gone north, Maleck east, and Ariadne west, all on separate patrols. To Cistine's surprise, Thorne had offered Julian the southern track—and he'd accepted. It was good to see him taking cabal duties almost as seriously as he did his training for the King's Cadre.

One day, he would become a fully-recognized Warden, serving at her side like Ashe. And perhaps he would rule at her side as well. Julian Bartos,

King of Talheim.

Julian, taking casual rides along the courtyards with her sidesaddle behind him. Julian, lounging on the couches in Cistine's room—in *their* room—while Cistine read and sipped tea. Julian, on the ebony throne, resplendent with ideas for how Talheim should be overseen, how *Cistine* should oversee it...

Queen Cistine Novacek-Bartos.

"*Yani.*" Baba Kallah nudged her. "The fish."

Cistine blinked, her eyes dazzled by the light on the water, and her vision shattered. She was staring at Thorne, who'd forgone even a simple polearm for his task. He was catching fish with his bare hands instead, smirking as he slapped them from the water and onto the shore. The waning daylight turned his hair the same shimmering white-gold as the water soaking his pants despite his best efforts to protect the hems. Threads had escaped the tie at the back of his neck and grazed his temples while he studied the shimmers, watching for another catch.

He looked wild, unbound despite the very sense of duty that drew them toward Geitlan. His loyalty to Blaykrone was a natural as any other part of him; a ruler compelled by love for his people. A King who needed no throne.

Cistine stopped pressing the ugly bruise of melancholy on her heart and forced her focus back to the task at hand, mixing the filets with the raw peppers she'd cut and bringing them to Cassaida.

The grain mistress who'd commanded the Den's mills with so much vim and authority hunched on a cluster of stones away from the river now, wrapped in a heavy blanket, silently weeping. She scrubbed the blanket against her cheek when Cistine approached. "Forgive me."

"There's nothing to forgive." Cistine rested the broad leaf of food on Cassaida's lap. "If this is edible, thank Baba Kallah. If it's not, feel free to blame me."

"It smells delicious, but I'm afraid I have no appetite."

Cistine slid onto the rock beside Cassaida. "Your children—I think I remember their names. Hugo, Erik, Svetlana, and Greta?"

"Yes, that's them." Fierce pride and fear tore through Cassaida's voice.

"You told me they're all good hunters and even better fishers."

Heartbroken laughter rattled from her chest. "Oskar all but raised them in a boat on Stedgnalt."

"Then I think if anyone was to survive a landslide, and even thrive, it would be them," Cistine said. "They were most likely on the water when it happened, given the time of year, so I'd bet they rowed back to shore and found Oskar first. He must've been chopping wood, like you said he always does for the whole village in autumn. Then they pulled people from the rubble and now, just like their mother, they're keeping everyone busy and sane while they wait for aid." She rested her hand on Cassaida's arm. "Aid *we'll* give them."

Cassaida's strong fingers gripped hers. "Cistine, you are a good woman. Your kingdom will be fortunate to have you as its Queen."

Heat licked the back of Cistine's neck. "I didn't say...I didn't want to make you think that. I meant what I said."

"I know. That is why you'll be great."

Baba Kallah called to her, and Cistine was relieved to slide from the rock and out from under Cassaida's scrutiny, however kind it was. But fresh warmth splintered through her chest, entirely different from the flustered heat bathing her neck and ears, when Cassaida slowly picked apart the fish.

The pattern of riding and resting continued for many more days, and Cistine counted each one with mounting apprehension. Every hour brought new concerns—how many they would find alive in Geitlan, how much help would be needed, and what they would do once they'd saved those who could be saved.

Cistine almost wept with relief when Ariadne shook her awake one morning and announced they would arrive by midday.

They galloped most of the way, and no one complained of the pace— not even Cistine or Baba Kallah. Cassaida led the charge, riding low on her horse's neck as if they had become a single creature of four legs and hot hide and wind, flying arrow-straight straight to her family. In the dusty, pine-spotted foothills, they slowed but didn't stop—not until they crested a small embankment, and Cassaida dragged the reins so sharply, her mount skidded and screamed. Cistine and Thorne were the first to reach her side, and though Cistine had never seen Geitlan before its destruction, she still felt a stab of grief at the sight of it.

It was once a lovely village, of that she was certain: built on either side of a small inlet on Stedgnalt's shore, with bridges lacing its halves together. Now those bridges hung by threads, feeble as severed sutures in a wound reopened. Half the village lay buried in rock and mire, windmills snapped, homes devastated. The part that survived only stood because it was built on stone cliffs rising slightly higher than the landslide's reach on the other side of the inlet.

That slide...Cistine couldn't imagine what it had looked like, felt like, *sounded* like when it barreled down from the Vaszaj Range in whose shadows they now stood. The nearest mountain face had slid down into the valley, driving even into the lake in places, spearing small, dark fingers of rock and semisolid soil through the water.

"God's bones," Julian cursed, riding up alongside Cistine. "Look at this place."

Cassaida slipped from the saddle and ran, struggling over the rocky terrain toward the tall stone crop. Thorne dismounted and turned to the cabal. "Search the lower village, but tread carefully. Anything you knock loose may crush the buried structures."

The cabal nodded grimly and dismounted, picking their way toward the jutting apexes of whole wooden edifices shoved from their foundations, lying askance in the debris. Cistine offered a silent prayer for their safety, then slid from the saddle and turned to Thorne. "What can we do?"

"Go to the lake. Gather water and check the fishing traps. If the fishers have died, the baskets will be teeming. Empty them and bring them to the cliffbase, we'll haul them up to feed the people. Baba Kallah, are you prepared to cook for this many?"

"I'm always ready to feed hungry mouths." Distress carved lines beside her eyes. "Especially when they're in such need."

Cassaida called for Thorne, and he looked up at the steps lining the backside of the small cliff face where she descended, leading a taller, pale-haired woman who steps dragged with exhaustion and despair. When she reached them, she was winded and white-faced, tears tracking through the grime on her cheeks.

"This is Josefine," Cassaida said. "Geitlan's matriarch."

"When Stornhaz told us they could not send aid, we thought we were alone," Josefine rasped.

Thorne's jaw tightened. "Aid *has* come. Whatever you need, my Court is yours. Our arms and legs, our backs, are yours."

Josefine pressed a hand to her mouth. "*Thank you.* We thought we would bury our dead alone."

Thorne wrapped his arms around her, his mask of composure falling away to bare the true Thorne beneath—the man who hoped for a Valgard without these injustices, who built a secret Court on a dream of equality and fairness, a better future for people in places like Geitlan. Who sought the Key, not for power, but to spare his people, and dared to believe in Valgard and Talheim united.

Julian draped an arm around Cistine. "Let's go. Those traps won't empty themselves."

Cistine planted her feet, swiveling toward Cassaida. "Your family?"

"They haven't been found yet." She gathered a deep breath, anguish breaking in her gaze. "Our home is gone."

Julian tugged at Cistine. "Princess. Come on."

This time, she let him pull her away.

CHAPTER TWENTY-TWO

WHILE CISTINE AND Julian spent much of that day lugging baskets of fish to the winches that lifted them up the sheer cliff, the cabal worked in the lower village, climbing among the rubble of homes smashed to kindling, calling out to survivors. Cistine stole as many glances as she could spare across the inlet, reassuring herself they were all right.

Her stomach turned when she paused once to watch Thorne shed his shirt, plunge into a heap of debris, and emerge with a woman's bloated corpse flung over his shoulders. She couldn't tear her gaze from the appalling sight until Julian called her back to the shore.

When the sun began its descent and the traps were empty at last, Cistine busied herself beside Baba Kallah and Cassaida atop the cliff, cleaning and cooking fish, ignoring her protesting stomach while she removed the scales, tails, and heads. The shroud of death was inescapable, made all the worse by the lonely figure of Cassaida. Each time the cabal returned with more filthy, half-starved survivors in tow, she clung to Cistine's hand until Ariadne and Maleck helped the last unsteady man, exhausted woman, and weeping child up the steps to the houses.

Each time, Cassaida wilted when her family wasn't among them.

"I don't understand how Salvotor could *leave* them like this," Cistine hissed to Baba Kallah when Cassaida slumped off to retrieve more water for the cookpot, which hung over an enormous fire the villagers erected in the rock's center between the remaining homes. "Is his grudge against Thorne really so deep that he can leave innocent people to suffer for it?"

"Yes," Baba Kallah said. "And Salvotor's father was just as cruel. When I was with child, if I displeased him, he would leave me below the steps to the courthouse apartments. I was so heavy and swollen I couldn't climb them myself, so I would sleep on the ground waiting for him to return for me. He never did."

Cistine focused on deboning the filets while Baba Kallah cut them. It was the only thing that steadied her trembling hands. "I could never, in a thousand years, *ever* conceive of harming my people for a petty grudge."

Baba Kallah squeezed her shoulder. "That is why you will be an excellent queen."

For once, the notion didn't dismay her. In fact, it was thrilling, the thought of her entire reign being one long, loud scream of defiance in the faces of men like Salvotor and his father.

An angry bellow ripped through the air from the lower village, and all the weight crashed back into Cistine's chest at once. With a quick glance at Baba Kallah, she struggled to her feet and jogged to the cliff's edge, looking down at the ruins below.

Part of her knew who was shouting before she even looked. Still, it was a shock to see Quill and Tatiana wrestling at the mouth of a broken house half-buried in the hardened mire. The blows were not friendly; in fact, Cistine was certain she heard something crunch when Tatiana's elbow smashed into Quill's ribs. He resisted all the same, standing between her and the house and pushing her back by her shoulders.

"Would you give it a rest?" he yelled. "I'm trying to save your life!"

"By going in there *yourself*?" Tatiana snarled.

"I saw this place first, it's mine!"

"What if those beams collapse while you're inside?"

Quill gritted his teeth when Tatiana struck his ribs again. "As if it would be any better if they collapsed on *you*?"

"I'm not letting you make any more reckless mistakes!" Tatiana punctuated every word with another hit.

Quill abandoned her shoulders and grabbed her wrists instead. "Where's this coming from? You're usually the first one pushing me toward something dangerous! Why are you acting like this?"

"Because of that *stars-damned flagon* back in Stornhaz, Quill!"

Cistine blinked, her fingers curving tightly into fists.

Quill released Tatiana's wrists. "You think I have a death wish?"

"I think you *don't* think about yourself! No one in this cabal does! So I have to think for you, like I do for *everyone else!*"

"What in the stars are you two doing?"

Cistine sighed in relief when Thorne slid down a small slope in the debris to stand between his warriors. The gaze he traded from one to the other made her hot with shame on their behalf.

"Quill was trying to get himself killed," Tatiana seethed.

"And she was trying to take my place doing it!" Quill snapped.

Thorne grabbed their shoulders and forced them away from one another. "This is not the time or place for *either* of you to be taking risks. I need you both capable and alive. Now get back to work. And you," he revolved to face Quill. "You know why she's worried. Stay away from the dangerous heaps."

"This whole place is dangerous," Quill muttered, but he and Tatiana went their separate ways. The moment Thorne had his back to her, Tatiana ducked behind a ruin heap, uncorked a small flask from her pocket, and drank; then she dove back into the search.

Cistine rubbed her eyes with the heels of her hands, but she couldn't erase that unnatural image of Quill and Tatiana beating on each other.

It would be a long stay in Geitlan.

With the light fading into dusk, the cabal gave up unburying survivors for the day and one-by-one climbed the chiseled steps onto the rock. Quill arrived first, and one of the village women shyly handed him a rag to clean himself off. He offered her a cocky grin while he wiped his face and bare chest, and from her place by the fire, Cistine practically heard the girl swooning.

Tatiana took that moment to return, already sipping from her flask again. She scowled at Quill and the girl and went to sit by Cassaida at the fire, where most survivors huddled in whatever blankets their neighbors could spare. There were ten houses circled around the clifftop, already brimming with displaced villagers; they'd practically be sleeping on top of each other.

Maleck was the next to arrive, carrying a small child on his back, and Cistine hurried to meet them, snatching the last blanket from the pile as she went. She fluffed it out and wrapped it around the girl when Maleck took a knee and settled her on the rock.

"Was she alone?" Cistine whispered.

The grimness of Maleck's gaze said everything.

She swaddled the girl tightly. "I'm Cistine. What's your name?"

"Aleida," the girl whispered.

"I'll bet you're famished, Aleida. So am I. Let's see who can finish their bowl of fish broth first."

It was a contest Aleida was bound to win; Cistine managed no more than a few meager sips while she watched Ariadne climb up to join them. The warrior ignored the gathering altogether and went straight to the water barrel nearby, rinsed her face and arms, then retreated to the rock's edge and knelt, facing the lake. Head bowed, hands upturned on her thighs, she fell still as stone.

"She's praying," Baba Kallah explained as she limped by.

Cistine heaved out a heavy sigh. "I hope she says one for me. I don't think I can sleep if the gods don't send some sort of comfort tonight."

Baba Kallah smoothed a hand over Cistine's head and brought a second helping of soup to Aleida, who perched on Cassaida's knees. The nearness did them both good: the grain mistress chatted with her neighbors for the first time that day, and Aleida smiled, holding up her empty bowl to Cistine.

Cistine mustered a smile and stirred her own supper listlessly.

"You should eat." Julian knelt beside her, rubbing smooth circles on her back. "You'll need your strength tomorrow."

"I'm going to need it every day if I'm going to leave this place without my heart shattering."

"I know," Julian sighed. "This is the kind of cruelty you'd expected from King Jad. It's no wonder our fathers went to war against these people."

Cistine watched Maleck offer his portion to a group of hungry, wide-eyed children flocking around him. "Not all of them deserved that war."

"True. But they—"

"I don't want to have this argument tonight."

Julian kissed her temple. "All right. I'm going to bed. Care to join me?"

Ears flaming, Cistine glanced around to make sure no one had overheard, then hit his shoulder. "You already know the answer to that!"

He chuckled. "I know. Just trying to distract you."

Cistine wasn't certain that was true, but she really didn't want to argue with him tonight; so she let him walk away, drowning her biting retort with the next spoonful of cold soup.

Wood clattered, rocks tumbled, and Thorne joined them at last. Cistine's chest expanded in a long, loosening sigh of relief, and she smiled when the High Tribune's eyes scouted the circle—tallying survivors, numbering up the cabal, and finally resting on her. His mouth formed a half-hearted smirk in reply.

Baba Kallah limped to greet him, pushing a bowl of soup and a damp cloth into his hands. When Thorne stepped into the firelight, Cistine realized how badly he needed those things. He was bent with exhaustion, his face, neck, and bare torso painted with mud and blood. Some of it was his; a few shallow cuts bled along his pectorals and the tops of his shoulders, scraped raw from climbing in and out of the rubble.

He sat across the fire and slowly ate while the villagers dispersed. Cassaida rallied all the children and led them into one of the homes, while other survivors spread out blankets to sleep beneath the stars. Finally, the cabal left to tend their horses and form a perimeter around the clifftop. When Cistine finally finished her own portion, only she, Baba Kallah, and

Thorne remained at the fire.

She watched the High Tribune distractedly through the flames, her mind reliving the day's horrors and the people's plight until her fingertips sparked with restlessness, desperate to wipe away their anguish or find a way to hit back at it. And then she noticed Thorne hadn't moved in some time, and while he gripped the wet cloth in his hands, he did nothing to clean himself. In fact, with the way he stared vacantly at the fire, she wasn't certain he knew how hurt and dirty he really was.

She rinsed her bowl in the small bucket Baba Kallah had filled for cleaning, then crossed the fire. Crouching before Thorne, she slid the cloth from his hand and gently dabbed a cut above his brow. "Come back, Thorne."

He blinked, eyes flicking from the fire to meet hers. "Not your filthy sock this time?"

She pulled a face, and Thorne's cheek twitched—that smile trying to emerge again. "I'll have you know, it's Baba Kallah's dirty sock I'm using."

"At least her feet don't smell like a man's."

"Keep insulting me, and you can spend the night down in the lower village!"

"I feel like my mind is going to, whether my body does or not."

The humor evaporated as quickly as it came. "So is mine." Cistine shifted to clean the shallow gouge on his shoulder. "What took you so long to come back?"

Thorne looked down at the empty soup bowl between his feet. "I was tallying the dead while we searched today, but I wanted to wait until the cabal was gone before I moved most of them. They've seen enough of deaths they couldn't prevent...allies captured, friends sent to places like Detlyse Halet or worse."

"Landslides are acts of nature. They aren't anyone's fault."

"I know that," he sighed. "But when the cabal fled Stornhaz with me, Blaykrone became their responsibility, too. Every death may as well be a distant relative, someone who shared the cradle next to yours."

Cistine pondered that while she cleaned his wounds. "I think I know what you mean. Whenever I imagine King Jad attacking Talheim, even the southern forts full of people I've never met, it feels…personal. Like someone walked into my home and set my curtains on fire."

Thorne snorted with quiet laughter. "That's one way of seeing it."

"Lean back," Cistine said, and he did, baring a deep slash across his left pectoral. Cistine dabbed the edges of it. "How many other villages do you think Salvotor will leave like this?"

"As many as need assistance. He can be patient, it's months until Traisende's cycle. He'll withhold aid for every bit of that."

"Then we're going to have a busy few months, I suppose." Cistine spread the cloth over the cut, and Thorne's groan of quiet relief made her stomach clench. His strength held on like the stitched bridges below, waiting to collapse.

He rested his hand over hers, pressing the cloth tighter against his hot, hurting skin. "For the people's sake, I'm glad you were here today. I heard you making them laugh, and they need that now. Someone who gives them hope."

Cistine's heart pounded. "Then I'll keep giving it. As much as I have, for as long as it takes. That's what a princess does, after all."

Thorne's head drooped, but not fast enough to hide the smile that finally found a way through.

CHAPTER
TWENTY-THREE

DAYS MARCHED ON in Geitlan, full of skinned fingers and ravaging thirst, of rationing fileted fish and the few root vegetables not devastated by the landslide and passing them to the shocked, devastated villagers.

"It's inspiring, honestly," Julian said one day, filling another basket with leaf-wrapped rations. "Josefine says it's been a fortnight since the landslide, and they've already held out this long on sparse rations and cramped quarters. They refuse to leave their people behind."

"That seems to be a Valgardan trait," Cistine remarked. "And it's good they didn't. Look at how many the cabal has managed to unbury."

"Less today than yesterday." Julian slung the basket from Cistine's hands and onto his shoulder. "Less than the day before that, too. And there weren't as many fish in the traps this morning. I'm wondering if the landslide scared most of them into deeper waters."

"If it did, what does that mean for the village?"

"They'll need boats to fish. But I already spoke to a few men...the docks where they moored were destroyed. They're liable to starve if they stay here."

Gut plummeting, Cistine sat back on her heels and swept her gaze across the clifftop; most were tending the injured or elderly, some still asleep in their blankets though it was nearly midday. At the communal fire, Baba Kallah prepared a stock from the fishbones, wading through a sea of unruly, bored children desperate for a distraction.

"I'll take them," Cistine laughed when Baba Kallah swatted away yet another grimy hand reaching for the pot. "Julian?"

"Leave the rations to me." He kissed her quickly and moved to Baba Kallah's side.

Cistine clapped her hands. "Everyone with listening ears, time to listen!" The children spun toward her all at once, and she grinned. "Who wants to play a game?"

Under the sun's sullen heat, Cistine paraded ten children down from the cliff to the lakeshore. Cassaida had assured her they were all proficient swimmers—even the youngest at six years old—and raised with a healthy respect for the water. She easily divided her attention between the group splashing in the shallows, the one building mud huts, and the one skipping stones across the lake.

A boy named Ulric watched moodily from under his mop of sandy curls when Cistine skipped a flat stone seven times. "How did you get so good at this game?"

She ruffled his hair. "I used to practice from the docks at home."

"Is your home on a river?"

Cistine chose her next stone, and her answer, carefully. "For now, it is."

"Our home is gone." Voice small and quiet, Aleida bounced her rock into the water. "Cassaida says it's never coming back."

"That's true. But that means you have an adventure ahead of you now. You have to help your village find a *new* home."

"My father says there aren't enough of us to cut lumber or fish anymore." Ulric heaved another rock as far as it would go. "We're all going to freeze to death or starve."

Cistine frowned, crouching to rest her hand on his back. "Your father is wrong. Do you know who came to help your village? High Tribune Thorne and his cabal of warriors. If anyone can find you a new home, it's Thorne. He's done it before."

Ulric wiped his nose on his arm. "You really think?"

Cistine nodded and pressed a rock into his hand. "Let me show you how to skip a stone properly."

It was a gift to be surrounded with cackles and happy shrieks rather than the adults' coughs and quiet moans for the rest of the afternoon. They made imprints in the sand and dug tide pools, fished with long wooden rods using worms dug from the silt, and when the humidity licked their necks, they waded and splashed until there wasn't a dry head of hair among them.

Cistine stretched out on the shore at last, drying out while the children built fortresses of mud and stomped them flat again. At least they had this time to be children again, not just victims or survivors.

"Cistine!" A girl named Triss shouted from the shore where she'd waded out to wring her trousers dry. "Aleida's gone to the bridge!"

Sitting up sharply, Cistine followed the girl's wagging finger toward lower Geitlan—where Aleida had indeed wandered across one of the few remaining bridges. She was up from the shore in a lunge, at the bridge before Aleida's name formed in her mouth. The small girl clambered onto the house where Tatiana and Quill had fought their first night in Geitlan, and Cistine leaped up after her, snatching her in an iron grip.

"I told you to stay by the water!" she gasped, breathless with fright. "This part of the village isn't safe, Aleida! What were you doing?"

"I want to find my papa." Aleida stretched her arms out toward the whole devastated village. "*Papa...*"

That soft, miserable whimper raked Cistine's heart. She smoothed the girl's hair and kissed her head. "*Yani,* if your Papa was here right now, he'd tell you to be careful, wouldn't he? Because he always wants you to be safe. But this place is *not safe,* do you understand? You can't come down here."

Aleida twisted in Cistine's hold, filthy cheeks softened by tears, and twined her arms around Cistine's neck. "I'm sorry, I just want to see him."

Over Aleida's small shoulder, Cistine watched the lower village, bereft of all life and movement. The cabal must've returned to the cliff to rest and eat before they harvested more dead. It was a task better suited to fifty or a hundred Vassora, but all they had was their own strength.

"Let's go back to the others," Cistine said. "Maybe Maleck will let you climb his back like a tree again."

Aleida nodded, burying her face in Cistine's neck while she picked her way down the roof, back toward safe ground.

She felt the guttural, animal groan before she heard it, the home's frame shifting beneath her weight. The waterlogged wooden boards under her feet buckled and bowed steeply inward.

Cistine knew what was about to happen because it had happened before. But his time, there was no powerful body shielding hers from the fall. There was nothing between her and the void when the roof caved in under them.

Cistine wrapped herself around Aleida, both screaming as the wood gave way—plunging them into the buried house.

CHAPTER TWENTY-FOUR

FRIGID WATER SURGED beneath Cistine's body, a gentle, steady breathing. Dimly, she knew she was about to wake up on the Muunvat River's muddy banks. Thorne would be next to her, only she wouldn't have to pull him from the rushes this time, since he was already shaking her.

"Cistine!" A terrified cry. "*Cistine!*"

Oh, gods, her *back*...

Moaning, she opened her eyes to dim light, to dust and broken things—to the unseeing stare of a blue, bloated corpse, inches from her face.

Cistine screamed, sitting up so quickly she snapped her head against something solid. Clutching her brow with one hand, she dragged Aleida against her with the other and scooted away from a boy's body speared into the floor by a wooden beam through the left side of his chest. More beams wove above them, caved in like broken ribs, shutting them deep in the house's broken bowels. Judging by its tilted shape, the walls muted in darkness, the whole structure had swept off the mountain's lower slopes and into the village in the landslide.

Aleida whimpered, crawling into Cistine's lap, and even that made her back throb; she remembered the impact of something against her spine as she'd fallen. Measuring the gulf between the roof and the home's lowest level, she must've impacted against one of the beams and slid down it the rest of the way to the floor.

"Wh-where are we?" Aleida sobbed.

"Inside someone's home." Cistine curled an arm around the shivering girl. "And we need to be very, very still."

"Is...is someone there?"

Cistine swiveled on her seat, planting one hand on the mud-coated floor and squinting through a doorway on her right, toward that choked voice. There was a girl standing there, not much younger than the dead boy, her face and hair clotted with debris, eyes sunken, lips fissured with dehydration. She panted open-mouthed and stared at Cistine.

"How did you get in here?" her voice was as dry as her filthy face.

"We fell in. Is this your home?" The girl's head bobbed. "Did it fall from the mountain?"

"The slide carried us," the girl rasped. "And then...buried us. We couldn't reach the doors or windows. And Erik..."

Erik. A stab of recognition jolted through Cistine. "Are you...Svetlana? Or Greta?"

The girl clung the doorpost. "Greta. You know my name?"

"I know your mother. She came back for you. Are your sister and brother alive? Your father?"

"Papa is dying," Greta whispered. "Svetlana and Hugo are sick. I gave them all the food and water I could, but it wasn't enough. We're going to die here."

Aleida clutched Cistine so tightly, pain splintered through her back. "Is that true?"

"No," Cistine said. "None of us are dying. I *promise.*"

In mockery of her vow, the house's frame wrenched out another tuneless groan, daring them to guess which parts were failing around them.

A shadow eclipsed the pale wash of daylight above, the loose beams rattling with a shout: "*Cistine!*"

"Thorne?" Cistine squinted up at the hole, unsure if he was really there, if he could've found them already.

The High Tribune gripped the broken roof beams through which she'd fallen, fingers curling so tightly splinters must've dug into his palms. *"Are you hurt?"*

Cistine shifted her haunches. "Yes, but not badly."

Thorne twisted, yelling at someone behind him to do something, and then he swiveled toward her again. "Maleck is bringing a rope. Stay where you are."

"Not difficult," Cistine muttered. "Be careful, Thorne. The beams gave way under me, they won't hold you for long."

Thorne adjusted his weight like a man crossing thin ice. "We're going to get you out."

Greta sagged against the doorpost, snapping Cistine's attention back to her. A silent plea glinted in her tearstained gaze, and Cistine forced herself to think past fear, the selfish desire to escape, the revulsion at the corpse beside her and the hopelessness of the sheer *height* they'd have to conquer back to safety.

"Thorne," she said, "there are people down here with me. They're injured, they need to be taken out first."

Thorne said nothing, and Cistine didn't dare look at him. Whatever he was thinking so deeply about in that grim silence—however he was watching her—she didn't want to know.

"How many?" he finally asked.

"Five. Four children and a man."

"We'll start with the youngest."

Someone swore behind Thorne. *Julian.*

Cistine trusted Thorne to handle that argument. She said Greta's name and waited for the girl to focus on her. "Bring your siblings and your father to the doorway as quickly as you can."

Greta vanished back into the darkness. Cistine set Aleida at arm's length, brushing the tangled hair from her brow.

"You're going to leave first," she said. "Whatever happens, don't look down at me. Look at High Tribune Thorne with his pretty silver hair. I want you to think about just one thing: when you reach the hole, you have to tell him his hair should be *fuchsia* instead. Can you remember that?"

She made Aleida repeat it while scuffling happened above, until a thin, crude rope harness descended from the hole, snaking down over the beams and floorboards in a careful spool. When it reached them, Cistine tucked the loop over Aleida's chest and knotted it against her waist.

"Hold *tight*." She wrapped the girl's fingers around the hairy twine. "Remember. Keep your eyes on Thorne's hair."

Aleida nodded, burrowing her chin against her knuckles and staring up as the cabal heaved at the rope, drawing her slowly from the hole. Cistine turned her attention back to the doorway where Svetlana, Hugo, and Greta huddled beside their father's inert form. She couldn't see an easy way of pushing the man's body through the narrow gap beneath the crossbeams, but if they could loop the rope over his chest, and then, just for a few seconds, heft the wreckage higher...

"Hugo," she said, "show me your arms."

The boy rolled his sleeves, and to Cistine's relief, he had woodcutter's build, brawny and strong.

While they waited for the rope, she told Hugo her plan.

The moment the twine dangled within reach again, Cistine caught it and slid it along the floor, as close to the children as possible. Svetlana worked it over her father's head and below his arms while Greta propped him up and Hugo crawled over his legs, wedging under the beams.

Now was the time to learn if all the muscle she'd built in training was worth anything. Cistine slithered toward the gap and braced her shoulders to the beam. "Thorne! We're sending the father up to you next, he's the most badly hurt. As soon as I say, have the cabal pull with all their might, as quickly as they can!"

The rope rattled in response.

"Are you ready, Hugo?" He nodded, his face already beading with sweat. Cistine said a prayer and shut her eyes. "Thorne, *now!*"

The twine went taut. When Oskar's body slid from the doorway, Cistine and Hugo put their shoulders to the beams and heaved upward. Pain sliced through Cistine's damaged back and dug into her hips, pinpoints of pain popping and flaring like flagons shattering inside her body.

She retched with the weight and the agony as Oskar skidded past them and rose, drooping unconscious in the harness. Hugo bellowed at his sisters, and they crawled through the gap into the narrow opening near Erik's body.

"Hugo," Cistine sobbed. He dropped, scuttling past her right as she collapsed and rolled away to let the beams settle.

With a furious snap, several shafts gave way. A shower of wood slats, dust, and artifacts smashed into the floor, spraying glass and clay. Cistine flung herself over the children, the shrapnel bouncing from her training armor and smashing into Erik's corpse. A horrific stench fumed through the room where the shards pierced him, watering Cistine's eyes and filling her throat with bile. Greta vomited. They all wept.

"Cistine!" Thorne called. "Are you all right?"

"Not really," she gagged. "Hurry, Thorne."

The rope dropped down again, and again, and again—taking Svetlana, then Hugo, then Greta, who pressed a kiss to Cistine's temple before the cabal reeled her up past the unsteady, teetering beams.

Cistine was alone.

She pressed her back against the cool wall and shut her eyes. The humid reek of death choked the murky air, and the house creaked, a seven-beat song of decimation. Somewhere on the second level, a piece of furniture slid and cracked against the wall. A beam settled with a hollow cough.

Cistine squeezed her eyes tighter against the urge to look, hot tears streaking from her lashes.

She couldn't die here, crushed by fallen beams, another victim of this landslide—of Salvotor's treachery. She would not let his unjust punishment become her execution.

The rope's rasp brought her attention up to the gap again. It dangled ten feet above her head...eight feet...

The loop snagged the edge of a beam. And tightened.

"No." If they thought she had a hold of it... "Thorne, no!"

The beam jolted up as the cabal yanked—then dropped like a cut tree. Cistine hurled herself away as more planks fell, flattening Erik's corpse, sending up a storm of dust and rotten vapors...and the rope, her salvation, coiled up on the heap of fallen planks, threads caked in someone's blood.

Cistine slapped a hand over her mouth, choking on bile and fear.

People shouted her name above, some men, some women. And then, quietly, "Cistine, look at me."

She dragged her eyes from the rope to the hole above. It wasn't Thorne's face she saw now. It was Quill's.

"Listen, Stranger," he said around the cinnamon stick dangling from his teeth, "you have to climb out."

Cistine trembled. "*What?*"

"The beams won't last much longer," Quill's tone was calm, "and we don't have another rope. But if you can climb up *fast*, then you'll reach the hole before the beams give way. I can see a path through them. I'll guide you, just like the falls back home."

Cistine shook her head. "I've never climbed without a rope, Quill, I *can't.*"

"Cistine, you're going to be crushed if you stay there. If that happens, Julian will kill us all. So if you're not interested in saving your own hide...save mine?"

She stared up at him, and he flipped his hair casually across his head, but his hand was shaking. He was afraid for her. And if he was, then she could only imagine what the others were thinking, what Julian and Thorne—

But this was not about them. This was about her; because if she lacked the strength and courage to pull herself onto those beams, then she would rot in this house with Erik and no one would save Talheim. Just like no one could save her.

Cistine stumbled upright and braced her hands on the vee of the beams. "Which way?"

"Left," Quill said. "Grab and swing up to your left."

She took a deep breath, loosed a litany of prayers when she exhaled— and surged upward.

She didn't look back even when the wooden planks groaned under her skimming feet, following the bark of Quill's voice—left, right, straight up, right again. Splinters lodged into her fingertips, jerking tears from her eyes, but she grabbed harder and propelled herself faster when the first beam snapped near the floor.

And the rest began to crumble.

"No, no, *no!*" Cistine screamed, lunging for another handhold, and another, the hole yawning above her head.

The last plank buckled under her weight. Her fingers snagged the opening above, and for a moment she teetered dangerously over the empty drop into the house, a sepulcher of wood and mud and memory.

Then hands fastened into her armor, took her knife-belt and her elbows, and pried her through the hole. She crashed into Quill's chest and they rolled down the roof's slope, smashing into the dried crust of mud below. Someone else landed on Cistine's back just as the house gave way in a torrential crash of wood and stone, and with the slam of pain against her spine, she finally vomited—barely missing Quill's shoulder.

He rolled them both so she emptied herself onto the ground instead, laughing breathlessly in her ear. "See, what did I tell you? That was easy enough, wasn't it?"

Cistine gagged and choked on hysterical laughter, looking up to see who'd helped Quill hoist her from the hole.

Tatiana did not look back when she left Quill and Cistine on their knees beside the wreckage, walking away toward the cliff where an entire crowd huddled over Oskar and his children.

A curse carried over the shocked murmurs. Fists smashed skin, and Julian appeared, sliding to his knees and dragging Cistine from Quill's grip into the shelter of his chest. "God's bones, Princess! Holy *God...*"

Before Cistine caught her breath enough to reassure him she was all right, she spotted a sobbing Cassaida pushing through the crowd, falling on her knees beside her inert *valenar* and shaken children. They clung to each other, sheltering Oskar in their midst while Maleck knelt next to them with quiet reassurances and healing supplies.

Cassaida laid her head against Oskar's chest, folded her arms, and sobbed harder; and his hand lifted weakly and buried itself in her hair. As if some invisible tether bound them together, even in unconsciousness, even in sickness and agony, and he dragged himself from darkness for her—answering a call that drew him back to the one he loved.

Among the crowd, Cistine's eyes found Thorne.

Bloodied palms outturned at his sides. A bruise on his cheek from Julian's knuckles. Sweat drying in the threads of his hair. His eyes soft, watching her.

She wiped her mouth on her knuckles and dredged up a smile for him. He lowered his head, his gaze—a gesture full of more gratitude and respect than Cistine could fathom.

Then his eyes flicked up to her again, dancing with relief and mischief. *Fuchsia?* he mouthed.

Cistine heaved with shaky laughter again and shrugged. Then she let Julian lift her to her feet and guide her up the path to the clifftop.

Baba Kallah met them there, folding Cistine into an embrace that smelled like fish and herbs. She said nothing, tears glimmering in her eyes, and nudged Cistine to sit on one of the log seats. Julian crouched before her and set to task, pulling splinters from her fingers.

She'd never seen him so stone-faced, eyes chilled onyx, mouth a ridge of rock. She let him tend her wounds, shaking too badly to do it herself, and hoped his touch would ease some of the lingering terror. But that hope faded with each moment of cold, furious silence.

Baba Kallah brought bandages, looked between Cistine and Julian, then limped away. The moment she was gone, Julian started grumbling under his breath. "Of all the idiotic decisions..." he knotted a bandage around Cistine's bleeding left hand. "You should've let us pull you out *first*."

She wavered on her perch. "Julian, please, stop. I don't want to fight with you right now."

"And I don't want to see my princess crushed under a falling house." He jerked the second bandage tight enough to make her wince. "But that seems to be what's going to happen, whether I want it or not."

She was surprised she was still able to be furious, exhausted as she was. "Maybe it will, because I decide for myself what risks I take. I'll always consider your opinion, but the risks are still *mine* to take. No one else's."

"Well, we would all be grateful if you took a few less."

"Would Cassaida and Oskar?"

Julian scowled. "I just think Talheim needs its Princess more than you need to prove yourself to these people."

"I'm not proving myself to anyone," Cistine snapped. "I'm saving lives. And if I can't do that, if I can't put their wellbeing before my own, I'll *never* be the Princess Talheim truly needs."

Julian rested his hands on her knees, glaring up at her. "What about the Princess *I* need?"

She settled her wrapped fingers over his. "This isn't about us, Julian. It can't be."

His brow furrowed. "Then what in the gods' names are we even *doing*?"

He slid his hands out from under hers and walked away. Cistine gaped after him, hurt and fury crashing through her chest, certain at any moment he'd stalk back to her and apologize.

But he didn't. He disappeared down the trail, leaving her simmering in quiet rage.

How could he have possibly made it about them? A dead boy, a family reunited, a child saved...and somehow her decision was about *their* courtship? As if her concern in that Nimmus-pit should have been for *him*?

Indignation strangled her hurt, and in its wake anger rose unchecked. She snatched a blanket from the communal heap, stormed to the cliff's edge, and laid down with her back to the fire. She would sleep apart from everyone tonight, and she hoped Julian wouldn't come to find her.

Yet a part of her still ached when he didn't return, even after the other villagers did.

Despite her discomfort, the endless trembling while the adrenaline faded, she was nearly asleep when a shadow finally curled across her face. Someone tugged the blanket up around her shoulders, knuckles brushing her jaw, and the darkness was gone. A body settled not far away, filling her nostrils with the smell of blood and dust.

Old feet limped on the rock. A cane tapped the ground. "You should be asleep, *Stornjor*."

"I've tried. I can't." Thorne's quiet rasp. "I keep hearing that roof collapse. I keep hearing her scream."

Cistine shivered at the memory of boards giving way, the world-shattering snap of the home's very bones under her feet...

"No one died today," Baba Kallah said. "It was a good day."

"That's true. But if Cistine hadn't fallen into that hole, Cassaida's family *would* be dead. I wouldn't have reached them in time."

"You are not responsible to save every life, Thorne. That's what your cabal is for. Subverting your father has never been a matter of your wits against his. It's *their* might, behind yours, against his pride." A familiar shuffle as Baba Kallah walked somewhere and sat. "*All* their might."

Thorne shifted his weight. "She was magnificent today."

"It's amazing, isn't it? The things a clever woman can do that a cruel Chancellor cannot."

"Baba..."

She shushed him. "The stars are lovely tonight, aren't they?"

There was a smile in Thorne's voice when he answered, "They are."

Cistine cracked an eye and followed their gazes up to the vastness of the stars, like the night she and Thorne sat beside the falls in Hellidom and he taught her of the Courts. She could drown in the dark fingerlengths between one constellation and the next.

Thorne cleared his throat. "Aleida tells me you think my hair is pretty."

Cistine snapped her eyes shut again. "Leave me alone, you vain idiot."

He and Baba Kallah both laughed. "Go to sleep, *Logandir*," Thorne said.

And to the rumble of their voices as they discussed the future of Geitlan's people, Cistine did just that.

CHAPTER
TWENTY-FIVE

BY MORNING, CISTINE'S back and arms were so stiff she could barely totter around the camp and help with the meals. She doubted she could make the climb down to the shore with the children again even if nightmares of plunging through the ground itself, into the belly of Valgard, hadn't kept her thrashing all night; even if the strangeness of that dream, where she'd found a well of augments at the bottom and felt the call to bury her hands into it, hadn't roused her in a nervous fit before sunrise.

The cabal lingered in the camp today, lending their strength in laughter and conversation, and Cistine wondered if they stayed out of concern for her. Maleck asked her several times how she was feeling; Quill made it a point to keep her within sight at all times; and Ariadne stood post, arms folded, eyes narrowed, when Baba Kallah guided Cistine inside a house at midday to examine her wounds.

"Oh, stars," she cursed when Cistine's armor came off.

Cistine gripped her knees tight, shivering when the cold puckered her bare back. "How bad is it?"

"It appears you tried to tout a horse on your shoulders."

Cistine winced. "Or lift a crossbeam with all my might?"

Ariadne's eyes flicked up, meeting Baba Kallah's over her head.

"Thank your training this was not splintered bone," Baba Kallah said.

"You lifted it well, so these bruises will fade in time. Until then…"

"You might want to consider a dress with long sleeves when we meet with Thorne's allies," Ariadne said wryly. "Assuming they ever return our note."

"What about the pain? When can I go back to training?"

"Whenever your body says so. Trust me, you will know when it's telling you *yes* or *no*." Baba Kallah rolled Cistine's shirt down for her. "Don't fret, we have plenty to keep you occupied that doesn't require tossing grainsacks or moving houses with your bare hands."

Cistine laughed weakly as Baba Kallah kissed her head and limped from the hut. Ariadne twisted aside to let her pass, then returned to her post. "I need you to help me understand something, Cistine. Why were you on that roof in the first place?"

She shrugged, then wished she hadn't; not only for the pain, but this was no matter to make light of. "Aleida was in my charge. She climbed onto it first and I knew she was in danger."

Ariadne's eyes narrowed. "When we heard the beams crack, when you screamed, we thought you were dead…yet you still sent the others out first."

"I had to. You taught me that."

Ariadne cocked her head. "You'll have to refresh me on that lesson."

Cistine pried her aching body from the cot. "It's everything you *are*, Ariadne. The cleaning, the gardening, making sure I'm up at dawn, making sure I do my exercises. I thought it was just about *doing* those things, but it's not. It's discipline, isn't it? That's what you've been teaching me, like how you live *your* life."

Ariadne didn't speak. Her chest rose in short, shallow breaths, as if Cistine's words were blows to brace against.

"Discipline keeps the Den in order. It keeps the cabal strong. Without that…" Tatiana's face dashed across her vision, inebriated and furious, flask clasped in her hand. "We can't help anyone, even ourselves. Discipline in crisis lets you put others first." She halted before the strategist, mustering a smile. "You were there in that hole with me every second, Ari. I don't think I say this enough, but…I'm grateful for you."

Ariadne took Cistine's face in her gloved hands and held her stare with a gaze bright as fire. "I hope you know that none of us would've left you down there. *I* would have come in after you, even if it only meant you wouldn't die alone."

She pressed her lips to Cistine's brow, then turned away and led her out into the sunlight.

It wasn't until sunset that Cistine saw Thorne—or Julian. They arrived at the fire together, with twin scowls and heads bent in deep discussion, just as the last villagers left the circle for the night. Julian's eyes shot to Cistine—wrapped in a blanket, sitting beside Quill—at the same moment her gaze settled on him.

With a sigh, Julian lowered himself onto the log with her and slid a gentle arm around her shoulders. "Forget everything I said to you last night. I was still panicking, that's all."

Cistine nodded tiredly, nibbling on the last of her filet. Thorne picked up a shard of kindling and prodded the fire, bringing the flames lower so he could see the cabal gathered around the circle.

"We're approaching a crossroads," he said. "Julian and I checked the fish traps at dawn and dusk today. They were empty both times."

"And the wildlife has yet to return after the landslide," Maleck noted.

"Baba Kallah says we have two days' worth of food left at most if we ration," Thorne said. "But winter isn't far away. Even if we found a food source tomorrow, there isn't enough shelter for these people. They're short on woodcutting tools now, so keeping their hearths lit would be difficult."

"And there's nowhere they can easily build a garden," Cistine added. "The ground was compromised in the landslide."

Thorne nodded. "I think we all know what that means."

"They can't stay here," Tatiana sighed.

"Where do you suggest they go?" Ariadne asked. "Most villages in the foothills are full to the quiver with their own people already, and it's too late in the season to ration for so many new hungry mouths."

"There is one place they can go," Thorne answered, "where they'll have food, and we can find them shelter. Above all else, they'll have peace."

Quill's head jerked up, fixing Thorne with a stare so fierce the flames themselves shrunk before him. "No."

Thorne stared back, undeterred. "Starhollow is secure, it's broad enough to house this many people. If we empty the archer camp, send Magnus and his men further south, there will already be tents for the survivors."

"You want to bring strangers into my sister's home?"

"Baba Kallah and Cassaida both vouch for their integrity."

"Who would they tell, Quill?" Ariadne scoffed. "Salvotor left them to rot. If anything, I suspect they'll all leap at the chance to keep a secret from him."

"Ariadne makes a fair point," Maleck agreed. "And Starhollow is not ours to give or withhold. It belongs to Valgard. We simply keep Pippet and Helga's presence there a secret."

"For good reason," Quill growled.

Tatiana sat up and braced her hands on the log, glaring at him. "Pip isn't the only one who deserves peace and safety. These people are suffering *right now*. Don't you think if Thorne's scheme with his allies goes to plan, Helga and Pip could use the hands in Starhollow while we're busy? We won't have to worry we're neglecting them, we know they'll be taken care of."

Quill bent forward, clasping his hands. "You trust these strangers with Pippet's secret?"

"They're Blaykrone refugees, Featherbrain. They're just like us now. Besides, have you counted the number of children here? Pippet will go into spasms. She's never had playmates her own age."

Quill's jaw ticked. He twisted his head away, and Thorne glanced at Tatiana. From that look alone, Cistine knew the argument was over.

"Fine," Quill grunted. "But when we bring them to the river's mouth, I'll go on ahead and speak to Pip and Helga myself. If they have an issue with this, then so do I."

"We'll address that if it arises." Thorne glanced at Baba Kallah. "Agreed?"

"Agreed, *Stornjor.*"

"Moving them will be the issue," Maleck said. "We only have our mounts, and plenty of weary bodies to journey with."

"We'll go at their pace," Thorne said. "Let the injured and the children ride the horses with one of us as a scout. The rest will move among the people and help however we're needed."

Cistine was already nodding when Julian said, "Cistine should ride."

"I injured my shoulders, not my legs," she said. "I can walk for a few hours at the very least."

Julian threw up his hands. "I'm trying to look out for your wellbeing. When did this become such a point of contention for you?"

"Would you two take your lover's spats somewhere private?" Tatiana grumbled. "This has been a bore since Villmark."

Cistine's bristling temper snapped its tether. "Like privacy mattered so much to you and Quill in front of Cassaida's house?"

Tatiana's brows jolted upward. "What is that supposed to mean?"

Quill sidled away from Cistine. "I didn't ask to be part of this."

"Don't think I haven't noticed," Cistine spat. "You treat him like you treat me...the same way you treat everyone you're scared to lose!"

"Cistine." Thorne's voice was quiet. "You are dangerously close to crossing a line."

She flashed her focus to him; he watched her without contempt, but his eyes blazed in warning.

She sat back and cinched her arms against her middle. "I'll decide when I need to ride a horse. *If* I need to."

"That settles it, then," Baba Kallah said. "I suggest we leave at dawn."

"Agreed." Thorne's face was a mess of shadows when he stared toward lower Geitlan. "I think we've found all the survivors we ever will."

CHAPTER TWENTY-SIX

A MOTLEY ARRAY set out from Geitlan, horses carrying the wounded, young, and elderly. Ariadne rode before the assembly and the rest of the cabal walked among them, distracting with conversation and helping them over the rough terrain. Cistine fell in with Cassaida's family the first day; Oskar, still muddled with infection from a gash on his chest, slept in the saddle, but Greta, Hugo, and Svetlana, walking beside their mother, were full of chatter. And Cassaida practically glowed.

"I don't know how you manage it," Cistine admitted after conversation about Svetlana's sword practices lulled in the midday warmth. "With Erik gone…"

Cassaida wrapped an arm around her shoulders. "Oskar and I will grieve when the children sleep. While they're awake and with us, we'll show them they're safe to mourn for their brother, that we'll lift them up while they hurt. And that they are enough for us, even without Erik."

Unexpected, overwhelming tears stabbed Cistine's eyes, and her stomach churned. Mumbling an excuse, she slipped away from Cassaida's family and walked blindly to the edge of the assembly, where she could weave through the trees with only her thoughts for company.

For some time after, they were strange, unpleasant ones.

She wasn't surprised Thorne found her; he'd been prowling the fringes ever since they left Geitlan. He fell quietly into step with her, his thumb threaded through a pack slung over his shoulder. "Feeling overwhelmed again?"

Cistine shrugged—and winced when her bruised shoulders twinged. "I was thinking about my parents, actually. Something Cassaida said...it made me think of them."

Thorne tipped his head and didn't answer.

"My mother had two failed pregnancies after me," Cistine explained. "Mostly I know what Ashe told me about how difficult it was for them. But I do have one memory of my own: I was standing outside their bedroom, asking to come in, and my mother was crying so hard it terrified me. And...I remember the Wardens closing the door in my face and my nanny leading me back to my playroom."

"And that stayed with you."

"I was *sad*." It surprised her how clearly she remembered the feeling now when she pressed into it. "They didn't come to see me for almost a full day both times she lost the babies. And I think...I felt like they wanted that child more than me. That one princess wasn't enough. Maybe they wanted a son, or...someone more interested in the throne."

Thorne was quiet for a moment, looking ahead into the thick pines. "Or perhaps you resisted the throne because you felt that, in their eyes, you were already unworthy of it."

Cistine's feet snared to a halt on the dirt. A terrible weight crashed into her chest, the churning in her gut finally given a name by his suggestion. She covered her mouth with her hand, her breaths petering out.

Had her parents' actions made her feel she was unfit for the throne?

Thorne was in front of her at once, resting his hands lightly on her shoulders. "Cistine."

"I think...I think you're right," she rasped. "After the second miscarriage...that was when I gave up swordplay. I started to read more, to spend time by myself in the library. Reading about other people, other *lives*..."

Tears burned her throat and eyes. She'd never even considered how the deaths of the siblings she'd never known, and the way her parents withdrew afterward, had made her feel lesser…as if they'd hoped for something *better* than her.

A better ruler. A better child. A better legacy.

"Cistine." Thorne squeezed her shoulders. "Look at me."

She dragged her focus to his eyes; no longer chips of ice, but sun-kissed pools of clearest blue, fixed earnestly on her face.

"You are enough," he said. "For your people. For your throne. You are *enough.*"

Tears slipped over her lashes and cooled her trembling lips. "They shut me from their grief. They made me a stranger."

"They didn't know any better," Thorne said. "Grief is fickle, everyone faces it differently. But whatever they wanted from their other children, they have *you.* And you are the queen Talheim needs."

Cistine buried her face in her hands, hating that she'd realized this now, on foreign soil, before the High Tribune of Kanslar Court no less, and that she couldn't stop crying in front of him.

Thorne gripped her wrists and brought her hands down from her face, ignoring her moan of humiliated protest. He took her damp cheeks in his hands and made her look at him again. "Cistine, listen to me. You are *more* than enough."

He kissed her brow and backed away from her, returning to his patrol—leaving her to grieve privately.

Cistine unearthed another hazy memory as their journey south continued: playing dolls with Ashe while they waited for her parents to come for her. She remembered the soothing balm of her Warden's presence, the peace breaking when her mother came into the room. Teary-eyed, her cheeks red from sobbing, Queen Solene had opened her arms to her daughter, begging for her love.

She'd run to Ashe instead. And she wanted to run to Ashe now.

She told Julian that, though she didn't tell him why, when they stopped to make camp. He hugged her to his side, rubbing his thumb gently against her arm. "I know, Princess. I miss her, too."

His kisses soothed her that night. But her dreams were chaos again, and she woke more tired than when she fell asleep.

She told no one else about her parents except Baba Kallah. While they cooked the first game the cabal managed to bring down in the morning, Cistine explained what Thorne had helped her see. She was crying again by the end, and Baba Kallah brushed the tears from her cheeks, then helped her gather up the venison meat and bring it to the fire Ariadne and Tatiana built.

"It amazes me, the capacity to feel hurt, and to give it, even without meaning to," Baba Kallah mused. "I think that's why my *valenar* and Salvotor became the men they did. Their ability to love and to feel empathy were calcified to protect their hearts."

"Maybe that was what happened to me." Cistine tipped the meat into the cast-iron cookpan. "Maybe I hardened my heart to the throne because I already believed I wasn't worthy of it. I thought my parents were lying to me when they made me heiress and inheritor, that they wanted someone else for the title."

Baba Kallah tapped a gnarled finger over Cistine's chest. "And now you know a woman who defends herself, who cleans up her *own* messes and places other lives before her own—she is a worthy Queen. So you chip away the hard parts over your heart, and you forgive them. Then you'll heal that wound."

"That may be harder than it sounds."

"Yes, it always is." Baba Kallah frowned. "That is why I worry for Tatiana, with the drinking and the snarling. That's how the calcification starts...by pushing everyone out beyond reach, running to something else rather than facing your problems."

Cistine used a skinned, chiseled stick to push the venison slabs around. "How do I stop it from happening to Tati?"

"You cannot face it for her. But think of what allowed you to face your own hardened heart, and there you are."

Cistine glanced over her shoulder at the huddled mass of Geitlan's citizens, and Thorne moving among them. She wished he'd look up, catch her gaze, but his focus was on his people where it belonged.

For the next several days, Cistine pondered Tatiana's hurt in place of her own, which soothed the ache and allowed her to revive from her stunned grief. She distracted the weary children, who complained often of the cold, foggy weather settling over the foothills. Soon they were all soaked with chilly rain.

"This is miserable," Cistine muttered one day as she and Maleck walked among the people, handing out rations for the long day's travel. "Some of us are going to be sick long before we reach Starhollow."

"It's only a few more days on foot," Maleck soothed. "Even at this pace we've set."

Cistine wrapped her arms around herself, shivering. "I'd like to be there *now*, before we catch our death of cold."

Quill was suddenly on her other side, swinging his arm over her shoulders and rubbing her bicep briskly. "Noted! Add *swimming in the ice-cold Nior* to your training regimen."

Cistine groaned. "I should learn not to speak around you at all."

"Finally! I thought this day would never come!"

"I despise you."

Quill bent his head over hers, resting his cheek on her hair—sheltering her from the rain. "If Faer was here, I'd offer to have him roost on your head."

"After what happened when he last roosted on Tatiana's?" Maleck said. "I thought you'd learned your lesson."

Quill coughed. "She threatened to run me through with my own weapons."

"What happened?" Cistine asked.

"Bird droppings. Hair."

Cistine wiped her face on her damp sleeve, which did nothing to clear her vision as she peered ahead through the misting rain, picking out the cabal from among the crowd. Ariadne took the left flank, Tatiana wove her way toward the right, and Thorne rode point today, his hair streaked to his armor by the rain. It would need a trim soon, unless he wanted to tie it back. Or braid it like Maleck did. She wondered if he would submit to let Baba Kallah cut it when they—

CRACK.

The sound came from the cliff face to their right, an echo so familiar Cistine's heart knew it before her eyes registered what was happening.

A scream broke from her throat as a black-shafted arrow plunged into Thorne's side, throwing him from his horse.

CHAPTER TWENTY-SEVEN

BABA, GET THE people out of here!" Taking charge in the bedlam following that archer's strike, Quill shoved Cistine to the side, drawing one of his swords. "Mal—*cliffs!*"

Maleck unsheathed Starfall and Stormfury and shot toward the dark hills—toward whoever had fired the arrow that wobbled in Thorne's side as he tried to drag himself up.

Cistine darted around Quill and splashed through the mud, her throat aching, and when Thorne twisted to look at her she realized she was screaming his name. She dropped beside him, grabbing the arrow's shaft, and he gripped her wrist in turn, breaths seething between his gritted teeth. "*Gently.*"

Cistine pried the arrow out, and with a gasp of relief she found it was only faintly spotted in blood partway along its tip. Thorne's battle armor had stopped the arrow. If he hadn't been wearing it...

Thorne cursed suddenly, scooped an arm around Cistine's side and rolled them away from the wailing descent of a sickle-sword that bit through the damp soil where Thorne was a moment ago. He kicked the weapon from the wielder's hand and pulled Cistine up beside him all in one fluid movement. The assassin—garbed head to foot in deep lavender clothing, long flaps of cloth looped around each other with an iron mask affixed over his features, and trembling with the strength of a brawler—wheeled bare-handed and flung himself at Thorne, who shoved Cistine aside just before he fell to the ground again.

"Get the others to safety!" Thorne cracked the man across the face, flipping their positions so he wrestled on top.

Cistine skidded back to the people, herding them with her arms flung out and turning them east, away from the cliffs. In the chaos, she spotted Quill and Tatiana intercepting two more assassins; a fourth was already locked in combat with Maleck, hacking brutally at his head and chest.

Ariadne dashed past Cistine, tossing a bow and quiver to her. "Guard these people with your life!" She charged on toward Thorne, fishing something from her pocket as she ran.

Cistine shrieked with rage when a hand wrenched her shoulder. She spun, and Julian caught her elbow before she could hit him across the face with the bow.

"Run, Princess!" There was madness, almost fury in his gaze, and Cistine knew exactly what he was thinking of: the last time she'd held a bow in her hand, with the Vassoran carts, with the flagons...

No sooner had Cistine thought it than she heard glass shatter and Ariadne scream Thorne's name. She slid through the mud toward him, and Thorne, still wrestling the assassin, stretched out his hand to meet her.

It was no more than a kernel, what Ariadne held—a seed of power. Yet Cistine *felt* it, like she had in the courthouse when they faced Salvotor. Her hair stood on end, answering its furious call.

"Cabal!" Thorne shouted. "*Eyes!*"

They whirled away from their enemies, arms over their faces, falling to their knees in the mire. Thorne opened his fingers, taking the power from Ariadne's hand into his own.

Arresting, unbearable light erupted from Thorne's palm. Julian pulled Cistine's face against his chest as the flash of a breaking sunrise unfurled through the trees, and the assassins screamed when it blinded them. The icy power licked the nape of Cistine's neck and turned her body stiff in Julian's arms. He grunted, and she smelled hot skin and singed hair, but she didn't *feel* it…

Against her eyelids, the light winked out; yet the impression still sizzled in her veins, not just in her eyes. Her whole body trembled with its roaring dynamism, the augment's energy settling inside her bones, coiled in her muscles and ligaments. There was a strange, ethereal hum as it went dormant inside her chest, quiet as dusk.

Tatiana shouted a warning.

Cistine pushed herself away from Julian, dropping the quiver, reaching for an arrow as the only assassin wise enough to cover his face during the augmented attack reached the High Tribune—and broke his defenses.

A blade, black as the dredges of night, pierced through Thorne's armor and into his side, spraying blood.

Cistine tried to haul the bowstring back, but her shoulders popped viciously, and she sobbed with fury and pain, falling to her knees. Julian dropped beside her as Quill whirled to his feet, lunged onto the assassin's back, and ran him through. His sword slid from the sheath of Thorne's skin and clattered into the mud. Along with the High Tribune.

Cistine cried out his name again when his knees impacted the ground. He tipped dizzily forward, one hand holding his ribs, the other plunging into the muck to hold him upright. Ariadne reached him and grabbed his head, pulling it up as the rest of the cabal knelt around him. Thorne cursed and argued something with Quill, who snapped back to his feet and stormed over to Cistine and Julian. He crouched in front of them, resting a hand on Cistine's head. "Where are you hurt?"

"It's my shoulders, it's nothing. Thorne?"

"He'll live. He's more winded than hurt. That augment takes a lot to control, especially since you can't see where you're aiming."

"But that sword…"

"I said he'll be fine, Cistine."

"It was *Svarkyst* steel!"

The rain hollowed Cistine's shout, but she knew by Quill's flinch that she was right. Steel mined from the Black Coasts could cut through their thickest armor without much resistance; the proof was bleeding in the circle of the cabal now, hidden from Geitlan's people, who were huddled some ways off in the trees.

Quill turned his hair across his head, his breath ghosting on the chilly, damp air. "They were all carrying it. Maleck took a beating, too."

"How did they get them?"

"I don't know." Quill's eyes were as bleak as his voice. "I don't know, Cistine."

She shivered. "Salvotor did this."

Julian tightened his hold around her. "We don't know that."

"Who else would arm assassins with *Svarkyst* steel?"

Quill frowned. "That would be new."

"She's right." Thorne raised his dull voice over the rainfall. "Their purpose was to reach me. Nothing else explains those focused strikes." His eyes found Cistine's when Quill swiveled aside to face him. "Which is why you have to travel to Starhollow without me."

"Don't," Tatiana said flatly. "Don't even start that talk with us."

"However they found me now, they can find me again. If I traveled anywhere but straight to Stornhaz to surrender to him..."

"Thorne," Quill said. "This is *not* happening."

"Would you rather they followed me to Starhollow?"

Quill's jaw shifted furiously, but he didn't argue. Panic sliced through Cistine's chest.

"Let one of us accompany you," Maleck urged. "Two blades are better than one."

"No. I need all of you to keep the people safe."

"You're a fool," Ariadne snapped.

"I'm your High Tribune." Thorne's tone was cool wind and razor-edged metal. "And you will obey this command. Get the people to Starhollow. I'll come by a different route once I'm certain I'm not being followed."

Cistine opened her mouth to protest—

"*Stornjor.*"

None of them saw Baba Kallah come back or even heard her mount approach through the rain. But her face...Cistine saw not only her resemblance to Thorne now, but to Salvotor; the mouth set like a sword, the eyes brilliant steel keening in the light.

"I forbid you to go," she said.

Thorne's throat bobbed. "Baba..."

"*No.* If you would walk away now, then what would be there to stop you from walking to your father if you thought it would keep everyone safe? What have I told you? One wild seed sprouts an untamable harvest."

"And if they follow us?" Thorne muttered belligerently.

"Then you fight them. You show them why, after ten years in hiding, you are still *free.*"

She wheeled her horse and nudged it into a gallop back to the people. And there was no more argument after that.

CHAPTER TWENTY-EIGHT

I T'S BEEN WEEKS. Do you and Nimea ever do anything but *discuss* matters?"

Aden's disbelieving snort struck Ashe like a whip when they dashed side-by-side down the Hive's sandy length, the moon's lidless eye keeping watch from above. "What did you expect? That she would welcome me with open arms?" she panted. "I've tried to pry out information about Devitrius. All they'll tell me is that he spoke with them during his visit."

"That's *all?*"

"Yes!" Despite the cool night, Ashe was sweaty and sore, pushing herself more than usual with her next fight the following dawn—and that shortened her temper to a smoldering wick. "They don't trust me, Aden. It's going to take some time."

She couldn't bring herself to tell him that she'd met with the Tumult several times since they'd dispatched fighters to lure the cabal from hiding. Nimea still hadn't given any report of whether that mission was successful, but she'd told Ashe enough stories about things the Tumult had suffered in Siralek that she hoped it had been.

So she remained silent, even if it added to the frustration that already painted Aden's scowling features. "I'm aware that these kinds of infiltrations don't happen in a matter of days. But I'm..."

He slowed, wiping his arm along his brow. Ashe checked her stride to match his. "Worried about Thorne? I'm worried, too."

"For the lady you serve."

"She isn't with him anymore. I was actually thinking of Maleck." That was perhaps the first truth she'd offered him in days—the birthplace of the guilt that gnawed her whenever she spoke to the Tumult, or thought of Blaykrone in danger or the cabal attacked.

Aden's eyes cut to her. "And does he share that concern?"

Her ears filled with a roar of memory, the way Maleck shouted for her from below that grate when she charged the Vassora. No one—not even Cyril or Rion during the war—had ever said her name that way, as if they'd crack apart the foundations of the world itself to come after her. "It's...difficult to say."

"Maleck is an enigma." Aden led the way back toward the gate. "He's always been."

"I take it you've known each other a long time?"

"He was the first friend I ever had aside from Thorne, and cousins hardly count for friends."

Especially if that cousin was Thorne. "What was Maleck like back then? Just as brooding and quiet?"

Aden smirked. "Livelier, if you can imagine it. When I first knew him, his passion was to become a pianist, with a sprinkling of law on the side. It wasn't until his brothers came back for him that he—"

Aden broke off with a sudden bellow of pain and crashed to his knees, a thick arrow jammed into the back of his shoulder. A second projectile tore through the meat of Ashe's side, thudding into the sand before her. Gasping at the sheer burn of it, she tumbled down beside Aden, gripping her bleeding ribs and searching the stands frantically for some hint of their assailant.

There. Close to Noaam's observation box, she caught the flirt of dark cloth with even darker shadows. A glint of moonlight on an arrow shaft as the archer drew again.

"Move!" Aden snarled, grabbing Ashe's elbow and towing her toward the gate. She ran blindly, ignoring the pain that cracked through her side and into her hip with every step closer to the stairs, to safety. Aden fumbled with the keys single-handed, and Ashe watched behind them in the vain hope that this attacker, whoever he was, would muster the courage to jump into the arena and face them head-on so she could snap his neck.

Instead she spotted the lethal arc of another arrow hammering toward Aden's neck.

Ashe shouted and barreled into him, knocking him against the stairwell's uneven wall. The shaft in his shoulder broke and the next one sailed past them, through the gate, into the staging room.

Aden's arm looped around Ashe's back, flattening her to the wall beside him as they waited for another attack. The hot stench of blood and sweat was all over them, and adrenaline spun Ashe's head.

This was not happening. She was not going to die here without so much as a fight. After everything she'd survived already, she would not be shot down by some cowardly assassin.

"Give me those!" She ripped the keys from Aden's hand, unlocked the door after several swift attempts, and let Aden push her through. He dove in behind her, kicked the gate shut, and picked up the arrow. Then he kept running, with Ashe on his heels, until they ducked for cover behind the first arch in the long hall.

Aden dropped into a crouch, clutching his shoulder, fingers winding around the arrow shaft but not pulling it out. Ashe fell to her seat beside him, heart thundering like a team of horses. "What in *God's name* was that?"

"If I was a betting man," Aden groaned, every word wet with agony, "I would wager a Tribune just tried to weaken Noaam's hold over Siralek."

Ashe doubled forward, gripping the stone that shimmered before her eyes. "By killing the Lord of the Hive?"

"And the most intriguing fighter to have crossed that Hive's threshold in a decade." Aden's breaths petered out from gasps to dry-heaves.

Ashe groaned. "As if we didn't have enough to worry about."

Aden didn't answer. He'd passed out.

CHAPTER TWENTY-NINE

EXHAUSTED AND SORE did not begin to describe how Ashe felt after spending most of the night having her ribs bandaged and waiting for a guard to extract the arrow from Aden's shoulder. Despite the commotion from the arena, the darkness of sleep dragged her eyes while she lay on the staging room bench.

She was doomed.

A boot nudged her ankle, and Ashe bolted upright, sucking in a harsh breath. Pain pulsed like hot embers around the rough stitches in her side.

"That was a Nimmus-cursed night." Aden eased down on the bench beside her. "Did you sleep at all?"

"Barely. You?"

He snorted. "With this dressing on my shoulder?"

They both glanced at the mess of cloth bulging like a pauldron from his arm.

"What did you glean from the arrow you picked up?" Ashe asked, fitting her shield over her back with heavy arms.

"Nordbran in make. The serrated head is meant to make the quarry bleed longer. The nomads would track their prey, both human and beast, for miles by the bloodstains left on the sand."

Ashe grimaced. "No wonder you passed out."

Aden cut her a cold glance. "If you tell anyone here about this—"

"And what would I stand to gain from that?"

Aden made a fist with his right hand and slowly knocked it into his open left palm. "You dragged me to the medico's room. And you pushed me away from that second arrow."

Ashe shrugged. "Warden's training."

"That isn't how the arena functions. We don't save our own."

"Nimea seems to think otherwise. So do her people."

"Nimea is an idealistic fool. She always has been."

"Better an idealistic fool with a soul than a clever man without one," Ashe retorted. "You told me Noaam owns my life as long as I have something to fight for. I'm not just fighting to escape...I'm fighting to still be *me* once I do. I refuse to become like Dorsta, like..."

She caught herself just short of saying it, but Aden understood.

"Like me," he finished. "Someone who signs away the lives of others to kill and be slaughtered."

"I didn't mean it that way."

"But it's how you see me. The clever, soulless man." Aden got to his feet. "Give me your helmet."

Ashe squinted at him. "What?"

"Your helmet. Give it to me." Aden grabbed the helm's left horn. "I'm going to fight in your stead."

Ashe coughed with incredulous laughter, towing back on the right. "No, you are *not*!"

"Which of us is Lord of the Hive? I'm taking this fight in your stead."

"Why?" Ashe snarled. "You humiliate me every day when we train. Don't tell me you care if I make a fool of myself in front of them!"

"This isn't about you. It's about proving to the Tribunes that *I* am still standing. They need to see that their stunt in the arena yesterday did not break me. The moment they smell weakness, they'll come down hard and fast against Siralek, and I can't afford that."

"Your left arm is useless," Ashe argued. "You could die."

"Then I die. But first I give them something to remember me by."

He ripped the helmet from her grasp and walked out through the gate, leaving it ajar in his haste. Cursing, Ashe struggled to her feet and hurried after him. She emerged into a fume of arid wind and cheers—exultant cries that shook the Blood Hive's walls, stirring the sand on the steps—and didn't quite know what she was going to do now. Tackle Aden, maybe. Snatch her helmet back. Scream in his face that he was *not* her protector, he was not her Lord of blood and sand no matter how loftily he thought of himself...

Then she saw him in the arena, and all thought came to a dead halt.

If she didn't know better, Ashe would never suspect he was injured; strutting across the sand like that, like he needed nothing but the crowd's praise to survive. And they offered it to him flagrantly, pumping their arms and screaming themselves hoarse, spurring him on toward the figure who waited at the promenade.

Not a catacomb fighter. This criminal was built from mountains of muscle; scars disfigured his arms, his chest and neck, his face under a razor-curved helm. No doubt he'd pinned countless opponents and withstood their close-quarters attacks while he crushed the life from them.

Shadowed inside the stairwell, Ashe watched the two fighters meet on the stone promenade. The grizzled man said something to Aden, his chapped lips peeling apart in a taunt; Aden dragged the tip of his sword against the stone, rocked his head loosely against his shoulder, and swiveled toward the observation box where the Tribunes sat. Ashe followed the gesture.

Sander caught her interest first. He lounged in his violet-and-white robes, cleaning under his fingernails with his thumb and paying the arena no mind. But the Tribune beside him...

He made Ashe crave a sword in her hand. The way he almost came up from his seat, clinging to it by the arms and watching Aden like a specter, mouth agape...

It was his assassin who'd shot them.

Aden fitted his helmet and took several long strides back. The mountainous fighter tipped down the mask attached to his helm, shutting it just shy of his throat; then he reached behind his back and unleashed a weapon Ashe had only seen in ancient Talheimic museums: a short pole affixed with a triplicate of chains capped in sturdy iron barbs, black as volcanic glass, winking slyly in the sun.

The Mountain roared and surged forward. Aden feinted back, curved nimbly aside, and charged the man's flank.

Apart from training, Ashe had never really seen Aden in combat. The Mountain he faced was pure, raging mass, berserk with bloodlust. He plowed forward like a horse-drawn reaper, that flail casting its three slender arms out before him. With each heaving swing, Ashe imagined those barbs sinking into Aden's flesh, stripping out ravenous portions of muscle—and her heart slammed into her throat again and again.

But the bloodshed never came. Aden moved like a cut of lightning, his form flawless. He exerted no excess energy, made no attempts at grand gestures of might or prowess. He stalked the edge of the Mountain's reach, taunting him with brutal shouts like some starved, arena-bred beast, keeping the man spinning and that flail always casting just short of its intended target. Each time its hooks dug into the sand, the crowd roared louder and Aden's smirk grew.

And up in the box, that bearded Tribune scowled deeper.

The match continued for several minutes that way: Aden smoothly dodging, forcing the Mountain to wear himself down; the Mountain, incensed, pirouetting and striking again and again to no avail.

At the height of the battle, Ashe finally noticed the hitch in Aden's movements.

It was so subtle, she almost dismissed it as her eyes playing tricks on her; but after another harrowing swing, the flail grazing past Aden's side and him twisting out of reach, she knew it wasn't her paranoia.

Aden winced every time he rolled that left shoulder back.

The Mountain stumbled—no. He *hesitated*, and Ashe's guts knotted.

He'd seen it, too.

Aden lunged in, his steel raking the air in a sun-stroked arc, clanging against the flail's metal links as the Mountain pivoted his arm backward. In a complicated swivel, he trapped the sword inside the chain.

Aden had the good sense to let go before the Mountain whirled and swiped at him. But now he was disarmed, and the Mountain had the long-range flail and the short-ranged blade. He sheathed the latter in his belt and charged Aden, the flail's barbed spheres threshing the air. Aden slithered from reach, but there was no mistaking this time that he flinched when he arced his body.

His bandage blushed with new blood.

Ashe flattened her hand to the wall beside her head. "Stay ahead of him, you bastard. If that flail reaches you…"

The Hive Lord darted past the Mountain, stepped up on the promenade railing, and pushed off, aiming a knee for the man's unguarded back. The Mountain slammed the flail's shaft backward into Aden's toned stomach and flipped him onto the sand. He rolled, snarling profanely as his shoulder raked the ground. A trail of blood followed him.

Quiet stole over the stands.

"No, no, no…" Ashe chanted. "Aden, get on your feet. Get up!"

He was slow to rise, clutching his shoulder and blinking sand from his eyes as the Mountain approached, flail picking up momentum, sailing higher and harder and faster. Aden rested on his knees, eyes flicking rapidly as he planned, but from her position in the stairwell Ashe saw the pain arresting his focus every other second.

He was outmuscled, unarmed, with nothing to fight or shield himself with.

Shield.

Hers was still pinned to her back.

She thought of nothing but the cold metal under her fingers when she loosed it and charged up the steps. The crowd roared with shock and the fever of anticipation as Ashe burst into view, planted her feet, and heaved the shield up with both hands. Sander shot forward in his seat, showing the first spark of interest in the fight.

Ashe ignored him, the crowd, and the Mountain. She roared Aden's name and let the shield fly.

Her bellow snagged the Mountain's attention for an instant, but no longer. He reared his arm back and brought the flail sailing down—

Straight into the shield, cracking metal on metal with a boom like thunder when Aden caught the heavy disc and rolled to his back, bracing it with all four limbs.

Then he was up, sweat-streaked, bloodied, but grim as a scythe, slamming the shield three times into the Mountain's chest before the man could recover from the flail's last swing. The third strike landed high, and Aden pushed up—sending that wicked helmet soaring to the ground.

Another hit, shattering the man's nose. Another dislocating his shoulder. Aden swept out his knees and pounded the shield's edge into his throat. The Mountain went to his back, and Aden gripped the shield with both hands and slammed it downward.

Serrated metal sliced through scarred flesh, muscle, and bone. Ashe stood rooted on the sand, palms torn where she'd grabbed the same jagged edge that just decapitated Aden's opponent.

The silence was deafening.

Then it disappeared in a storm of cheers so loud, Ashe winced. Aden cast the shield aside, retrieved his sword, and walked away from the body. He snatched Ashe's arm and marched her down into the staging room, slamming the gate behind them.

"What were you thinking?" he demanded.

Ashe perched her bloodied hands on her hips. Now that her concern had faded, she was ready to be furious, and as usual he gave her every reason to be. "I was thinking that if you died, I'd have no way to escape this place."

"The use of any weapon not left for you or brought on your person into the fight is considered a dishonor. That means *Noaam's* dishonor...it means the lash for me."

Ashe's breath caught. "God's bones."

"It means the lash," Aden repeated, dragging his hand down his face. "It also means I'm alive to face it."

Ashe blinked.

The Lord of the Hive—battered, sand-caked, and unsteady from the match—dropped his arm and stared at her. "What did I tell you about saving lives in this place?"

"What makes you think I listen to a word you say?"

Aden grunted, mouth twitching. "Fair enough."

He brushed past her, moving slowly, painfully, toward the corridor's mouth, and Ashe turned to face him. The sequence of battle repeated in her mind: the smoothness of his movements, the cleverness of his strategy. If he hadn't been hampered by that wound in his shoulder, she never would've needed to intervene.

"If that had been my fight," she said to his retreating back, "I wouldn't have known what to do. I've never faced a flail in battle."

"They're favorites here. Gruesome when they strike, but not quick enough to end a match before it sates the crowd."

Ashe grimaced. "You should teach me how to fight against them, otherwise I'll be killed the next time I have a match. Assuming you don't intend to steal that one from me, too."

"I'll teach you." And then he was gone.

Ashe made the long walk to the mess hall alone, her stomach churning with adrenaline, with despair and fury that saving someone's life would earn him the lash. Nothing about this place was sensible or fair. She couldn't wait to leave it behind.

It was in the gruel line, as usual, that Nimea cornered her. Ashe was almost fatigued enough to tell the other woman to leave her alone—until their eyes locked.

Nimea's fiery glare was hot enough to melt the strongest steel.

"What happened?" Ashe demanded.

"We just received word through one of the Vassora," Nimea growled. "We did as you suggested: gave word to the Chancellor to withdraw his support from Blaykrone. Sure enough, Thorne made himself available."

Ashe's heart raced. "And?"

"Of the four men we sent, only one survived to bring word: Thorne is still alive. Now he's in the wind."

CHAPTER THIRTY

Perched on her usual crate above the fetid waste-current, Ashe watched Andras pace. Like the rest of the Tumult, he trembled in rage at the report they'd received along with the newest batch of criminal recruits.

"Where did they catch up to Thorne?" Ashe asked.

"Just south of the Blaykrone village of Geitlan," Nimea grunted. "You were right, Ashe. It was the perfect strategy to draw him out. They nearly had him, too. The people slowed him down."

Ashe frowned. "What people?"

"Refugees, according to the report," Rez said. "From Geitlan."

Ashe bent forward, fingers digging into the crate. "Thorne was *leading* the refugees?"

"Yes, and it should have been the perfect window of opportunity, except those *bandayos* forfeited it!" Andras kicked a chunk of stone from the pile at Ashe's feet, sending it skipping into the dark. "One of us should've gone."

Ashe bit the inside of her cheek. "Were there any casualties?"

"Does it matter?" Kalman rubbed his temples.

"Yes, because there were more people than just Thorne there! And not all of them deserve to suffer as much as he does." She'd expected Thorne to be exposed, out in the open, not leading refugees somewhere. Where would he even take them?

There was only one place in southern Blaykrone Ashe knew the cabal thought was secure—somewhere they'd dragged her as a furious, screaming knot of panic and rage, with Maleck's arms locked around her waist to keep her from leaping off a cliff after her princess. She could still hear his voice, a desperate rumble in her ear.

No, Ashe, no—Thorne is with her, he'll bring her home, steady, listen to me, breathe—if you leap in there, I'll have to go after you—

Starhollow.

"We'll just have to try again," Nimea mused. "Rez, you'll lead the next party."

"With pleasure," she preened.

"Where to, Ashe?" Kalman asked.

Everyone—even Andras—stared at her now. Sweat gathered under Ashe's collar, as humid as the root-choked tunnel.

If she put the assassins on the cabal's trail to Starhollow, it would put Pippet and Helga in harm's way. That sweet, sassy girl who reminded Ashe so much of a younger Cistine; and her caretaker, who'd been kind enough to help Ashe fix poultices for her wounded leg and sat up drinking tea with her when fear for Cistine kept her awake.

"I don't know where he's gone this time, but I think I know *how* you'll find him." She closed her eyes, picturing the map Cistine had shown her on the wall in Tatiana's room. "The Vaszaj Range. If you fan out along the Izten Torkat as far west as Veran, you might find something."

At least, she hoped they would. East was a better gamble to intercept the cabal, but it also placed them closer to Starhollow. Ashe wasn't fond of those odds.

"The Vaszaj Range," Nimea repeated. "He did have some interest in those old war camps. Villmark, for one."

"Then I should lead," Kalman offered. "Rez is better suited for combat than scouting."

Nimea nodded. "Ashe, can you convince our beneficent Hive Lord to assign Kalman a fight? You seem to have gained his trust."

If there was any accusation in those words, Nimea hid it well, but Ashe couldn't shake a small, quiet pang of dread.

And if she dreaded this—gods, what was she doing?

"I'll see what I can manage," she grunted.

"Good. In the meantime, we'll send out more fighters. How many do you prefer, Kalman?"

"With the one still out there in Blaykrone?" Kalman stroked his chin. "Only one more. Otherwise, it may arouse suspicion."

"He's right," Andras said. "I'll send them out in my next match."

A sprinkle of stone dust floated down over their heads. For a moment, the Tumult was quiet, watching the roof.

"It's time to leave," Nimea decided. "Andras, you lead."

He stalked down the waste-filled corridor, bidding none of them goodbye. It was the same way they always left the tunnel: quietly, one after the other, and always with many moments between them. That way, if anyone was caught, they couldn't be tied to the others.

Rez was the second to leave, then Tobor, then Nimea with a tip of her head, leaving Ashe and Kalman alone. The scholarly fighter stepped up to her side, arms folded, looking ahead. "I hear you were meant to fight today, but Aden took your place."

Ashe's skin prickled. "He stole the glory for himself."

"So the rumors say. I find it all very curious how things have progressed with you. You bring us word of Thorne, and it proves out, but then our fighters die in the attempt to trap him. Success and misfortune have smiled on us equally since Nimea brought you into the Tumult. A scale perfectly weighed...that's very rare."

Ashe turned her glare on him. "If you want to suggest something—"

"I want *you* to send me from the arena."

The request was hardly what Ashe had expected. "Why me?"

"Because either you'll do it, or you'll hesitate and I'll kill you myself. Either way, all my questions will be answered."

CHAPTER THIRTY-ONE

Wary from the fight against the would-be assassins, the assembly of refugees moved hastily, crossing a narrow bridge at the Izten Torkat's mouth and entering the lower cliffs. Their surroundings were familiar for a few hours, a memory of the day Cistine, Maleck, and Ashe went on patrol from Villmark and ate berries on the hill's edge, looking into the river; then it all become the same drab monotony of rocks, trees, and dirt again. Cistine kept a watchful eye on their surroundings, but never saw another attacker.

Either the cabal had killed them all, or the survivors were keeping a healthy distance.

She desperately wanted to reach Starhollow, wash the stink of travel from her skin, and help the people settle into their new home. And she wanted to stop worrying about being attacked whenever they slept.

The end finally came in sight one evening when Quill joined her by the riverbank where she washed her hands of the day's weariness, and crouched beside her. "I'm off to meet Pip and Helga, so I need you to take my place on patrol tonight. And watch out for Thorne. He's trying to prove he's still the strongest of us, but he's been tossing and turning every night since the attack. His side hurts."

"I'll chase him off if he tries to follow me."

Quill shifted. "During the fight against those assassins, when you saw

Ari and Thorne use the augment. What did you think?"

Cistine met his eyes. "Are you asking if I was afraid of them, seeing them fight as augurs?"

Quill shrugged.

"Thorne had to put those assassins down before they put down all of you. I'll never resent him for that." She chose her words carefully, to say what had taken months to learn—in her talks with Ashe, in her time with Maleck and Thorne, and in her own thoughts chasing around the things her father knew, the lies he taught her, and what she saw with her own eyes. "Augments are a weapon, like your swords. If you use them to keep this cabal and these people alive, then I support you. If you use them to oppress or kill the innocent, then you deserve to be stripped of them."

Laughing, Quill ruffled Cistine's hair. "One of these days, Talheim is going to have a sensible queen on its throne. I look forward to seeing that."

Cistine pulled a face and leaned her head on his shoulder. "Be careful."

Quill touched her spine lightly. "For your sake, Stranger, always."

She didn't see him again after that. Her patrol with Julian passed as quietly as every day and night since the attack in the foothills.

The following morning dawned dreary again, the clouds fed to bursting on a blustery autumn wind. Half an hour of walking went by before Cistine realized the river's flow on their left had slowed somewhat.

Julian took her hand. "We're here."

They climbed a short incline of stone and trees and emerged in Starhollow, and Cistine's heart shrank and expanded all at once at her first glimpse of the spacious horizon. Good memories and terrible ones collided here: swimming in the pond behind the cottage, walking with Tatiana through the blooms, weaving flower crowns with Pippet and Helga while the cabal patrolled the borders; fleeing in the rain, smashing Quill's nose, thinking the cabal was only interested in using her as a lure.

A long, lonely caw split the air, and Cistine answered with a whistle that brought a dark body spearing straight from the sky to alight on her wrist.

"Faer," she laughed. "*There* you are."

"He must have traveled to Hellidom," Baba Kallah mused from behind her. "And when he didn't find Quill, he sought him here."

"Clever bird."

Faer flapped up to rest on her shoulder, and though the weight and the prick of his talons were uncomfortable, Cistine didn't dislodge him as she led the crowd of weary villagers down from the hill.

At the archer camp, Baba Kallah and Cassaida rallied the people together but still held a distance of some twenty yards; Cistine and the cabal went on ahead to find Quill. Cistine's heart lodged in her throat as they approached the cottage, light burning in its multicolored windows and smoke curling from its chimney. She squeezed Julian's hand with all her might when Faer took flight again, soaring toward the three figures who hurried out to meet them.

Pippet—slight and dark-haired, a sharp contrast to her brother's musculature, but with a face like his in every way—leaned against his side. Her gray-haired nanny, Helga, trailed behind. As Faer alighted on Pippet's shoulder, she came to a halt, and the cabal closed the distance to meet them. Pippet looked at Cistine first, her eyes shrewd.

Cistine swallowed a lump of guilt and grief in her throat. "I'm sorry I left without saying goodbye, Pippet. Do you forgive me?"

"Maybe. Do you still have my picture?"

Cistine nodded. "Quill gave it back to me. I keep it with my books."

Pippet quirked her mouth to one side. "Then you can stay. And so can the people you brought with you."

Cistine grinned, and Pippet's answering smile was a part of every good memory she had of this place: rich amber sunlight, flower crowns, dinner around the table with the cabal—

Ashe.

Pippet glanced past them—and frowned. She walked straight to Maleck, who held her gaze without speaking; after a long moment, she tilted her head. "Mal, why are you sad?"

His back rising and falling with a labored breath, Maleck knelt before her. "Because I have lost something very precious to me and I don't know how to find it again."

Heat washed Cistine's eyes as Pippet rested her hand on Maleck's unshaven cheek, looking deep into his eyes. She offered her straw doll to him. "Tazra is a brave warrior. She can find anything. She'll help you find what you've lost, and she'll keep you safe while you search."

Maleck weighed the doll in his hands as if it was the most priceless thing he'd ever held. "I'll carry her with me into every battle."

Pippet's thin arms circled Maleck's neck and he hugged her against him, draping his chin over her shoulder.

"Well," Helga said when Maleck straightened, Pippet still clinging against him, "let's see to these refugees of yours."

She all but ran in the lead, head high and skirts gathered in her fists, toward the archer camp; they'd barely broken into sight of the milling refugees when Helga shouted, "*Kallah!*"

The cabal's elderly matron wobbled out from among the ranks—stiffer than usual after so much time astride a horse—and made straight for Helga. Despite the hitch in her stride, Baba Kallah moved with twice her usual vigor. "Helga, by every star in the sky! I never thought I would see this place!"

"Or *you!*" Helga swooped her arms around Baba Kallah, both speaking over one another like delighted children.

"Look at you," Baba Kallah crowed, "as gray as silver birch!"

"It had to happen sometime, didn't it? We can't always be the envy of Stornhaz for our glorious youth."

"With your pouting lips and your enormous eyes! You always over-imagined their envy, *malatanda.*"

"Sister of my spirit," Thorne translated for Cistine. His eyes danced with delight as he watched his grandmother and her friend embrace again, still laughing—almost weeping with joy.

"I didn't pout!" Helga scoffed. "That was always Sigrid, the absolute tease. Have you seen her?"

"Not once. Or Iri, not since we left Stornhaz. She stayed with the Order."

A flicker of movement drew Cistine's eye: Ariadne, shifting her weight subtly, a shadow passing through her eyes. The same shadow stole across Helga's face, then cleared. "Well, I'm glad to see *you*, Kallah. That leg...Quill was telling the truth, everything Salvotor did. We should have fled with Sigrid when she left Stornhaz."

Baba Kallah shushed her, gaze flitting to the cabal with a strange, peaceful sort of knowing—lingering the longest where Thorne and Cistine stood, side-by-side, grinning at her.

"No, Helga. We are all precisely where we need to be."

CHAPTER
THIRTY-TWO

I T TOOK CISTINE two vigorous dips in the pond to scrub her skin and training armor clean. When she finally returned to the cottage— barefoot, damp-haired, and exhausted—the cabal waited for her: Thorne, Ariadne, Baba Kallah, and Maleck at the table, Tatiana perched on the trunk below the window, Julian leaning with arms folded against the wall, and Quill in the reading nook, thumbing idly through a small book. Pippet and Helga, Cistine assumed, were readying for bed.

"Scones on the table," Quill announced.

Cistine hesitated when she reached past Maleck for a pastry. A scroll lay next to the plate, bound with a thick, gold-leaf cord—expensive. In Talheim, it would've indicated royalty. "What is that?"

"A note for Thorne," Ariadne said. "Helga says Faer brought it almost a week ago."

Guarding his side with one hand, Thorne waited until Cistine chose a scone and settled into the seat between Maleck and Ariadne before he picked up the scroll. The cabal held its collective breath, sending the room into a dark spiral of silence while he studied the contents with a furrowed brow and tight jaw, eyes jumping back and forth across the script several times.

Finally, he set the note before himself and looked across the table at Maleck. "Veran. In a fortnight."

Maleck's breath crashed from him. Tatiana swore quietly and took a pull from her flask. Ariadne sat back, folding her arms. "Are they both coming? Traisende and Yager?"

Thorne nodded. "They're leaving separately to avoid arousing suspicion. It's safe to assume Salvotor is watching them closely, searching for a way to infiltrate their Courts. But if the Wayfinders and Hunters are as clever as they claim to be, they'll find a way."

"Two weeks," Maleck mused. "That leaves us little time to cross the mountains."

"And less time to help the rest of Blaykrone," Cistine murmured.

Thorne's eyes flashed to her, leaden with pain. The tear in him between his duty and his territory boomed around the silent room.

"You cannot go everywhere, *Stornjor*," Baba Kallah said gently. "The kingdom needs you."

"What good am I to my kingdom if I can't protect my own territory?" Thorne muttered. "What faith can the people of Valgard place in me if Blaykrone crumbles while I fight for my right to the Judgement Seat?"

Cistine wracked her exhausted mind, trying to think of a solution, a way to solve both problems at once, to be versatile enough to keep their word to Blaykrone's people and to each other.

"Magnus." His name burst from her, a spectral thought taking wing with a lilt of surprise.

Quill cocked his head. "What about him?"

"You could send Magnus and the other archers." Cistine's chest warmed as the thoughts angled through her, kicking up speed while they flew. "The refugees have already taken over their camp. Leave one or two on guard here and send the rest to help Blaykrone. Tell them to spread the word that they're under your orders, Thorne."

He held her gaze across the table, the air fizzing with something Cistine hadn't truly felt between them in weeks: excitement. Hope, even—that they could accomplish two tasks at once, by their own might and the hand of archers opposed to the Courts.

"Baba?" Thorne said.

Baba Kallah pressed her lips tightly, deep grooves framing her mouth. "I see the wisdom in it. Helga says the archers have grown restless waiting for orders here. Let them spend their energy out in Blaykrone under the cause—rallying support for Sillakove's name."

"They could bring more refugees here," Quill offered—an unexpected but welcome concession. "The ones who can't rebuild, anyway."

Ariadne nodded. "Send them out and have them come back by winter, and when the snows close the passes, everyone here will be safe. With God's help, by the time the spring thaw comes, Salvotor will have lost the Judgement Seat. Then we can help Blaykrone rebuild."

Thorne nodded slowly. "I'll speak to Magnus in the morning."

"Well plotted, Cistine." Ariadne's quiet praise raised a proud flush to Cistine's cheeks.

"That's thinking like a queen," Quill agreed.

Julian flashed her a smile, but something akin to sadness flickered in his eyes.

Maleck folded his arms on the table. "Perhaps we could spare one archer from the ranks to scout Detlyse Halet?"

Thorne's brows slowly lifted. "You really believe that's where Salvotor has Ashe?"

"No one has proved otherwise. And every day we ignore the possibility is another day she may rot in lightlessness."

Tatiana scoffed under her breath, rough words echoing into her flask.

Maleck faced her in his seat, perching his arm on the back rest. "What did you say?"

She held his gaze with icy-eyed defiance. "I said you should give up the search. Spare yourself the heartache. Let go of her."

"Of Ashe?" Cistine snapped. "*Never.*"

"You'll all be better off if you do. Stop chasing what you can't find. You're just asking to get knocked on your knees."

Quill growled under his breath, and Maleck said, "We *will* find her."

"Let's say you do." Tatiana took another swig, and this time the reek of strong spirits wafted from her pores. "What then? Either she's damaged beyond recognition or you find her corpse hanging from a door. Maybe Salvotor had his way with her, sullied her into his personal plaything so Talheim will never take her back."

Retaliation did not come from Cistine, though she pushed back her chair and shot to her feet. It didn't come from Maleck, though a furious snarl ripped from his chest.

It was Ariadne who lunged and slung a punch straight into Tatiana's cheek, smashing her head to the side. Tatiana's blood—from biting her tongue, maybe—plopped on the floor.

Cistine froze, still holding onto her chair.

Tatiana spat and slowly turned her head back toward the cabal, her glittering, intoxicated stare daring any one of them to land the next punch.

Thorne rose. Foreboding as a quiet wind before a world-ending storm, he walked around the table's edge to stand between his warriors. "Ariadne, walk."

She shook out her knuckles and left the cottage. Thorne looked down at Tatiana, and she stared back, defiance in the shimmer of her bared teeth.

This was not the friend Cistine made when she first came to Valgard. This hateful creature, making comments like that about Ashe, who she knew Cistine was desperate to find, who Maleck cared for so much that he'd go down the darkest roads of his past to search for—

There was no love in Tatiana's actions. No mercy.

And there was no mercy in Thorne when he ripped the flask from her hand and hurled it to the floor, fracturing it in pieces. "I have waited for you to solve this problem on your own—whatever it is you aren't telling us. But the time for excuses is over. If I see you drinking again, I will remove you from this cabal and from my confidences. Do you understand me?"

Tatiana stared at the shattered flask, mutinously silent.

"*Dawnstar.*"

Her head snapped up, lips cutting back in a snarl at the sound of her Name. But her barbed viciousness slammed against the adamant wall of Thorne's glacial eyes, his folded arms, his heaving chest. High Tribune and warrior clashed silently, neither one backing away from the other's fury.

Cistine shivered at the tension souring the room.

Finally, Tatiana muttered, "Understood."

Quill loosed an audible breath, staring at her with grief-stricken eyes—seeing precisely why she'd said what she'd said, and already forgiving her for it.

But Cistine didn't. She pushed aside her chair and stormed from the house to find Ariadne.

The cabal's strategist paced just over the threshold in short, sharp circles. She halted when Cistine emerged, the light from the windows illuminating her still-bleeding knuckles.

"I'm glad you didn't just let her say those things," Cistine admitted.

"I shouldn't have done that. I love Tatiana like my own flesh and blood, but when she's in these drunken fits, I don't know what else to do except hit her." Ariadne spread her hands in a helpless shrug. "You speak to me of discipline, but she has a way of finding the seams in my armor like no one else can."

"I don't think anyone is disciplined *all* the time. I wanted to hit her, too."

"I'm glad you didn't. I'm not certain your friendship would survive that, much less your knuckles."

Cistine twisted her mouth at the teasing reminder. "But yours will?"

"My knuckles, yes. Our friendship..." Ariadne flexed her hand. "It goes deeper than any of this. Tatiana is fortunate it does, or that remark tonight..."

She trailed off, then jerked her head and walked away from the cottage. Curiosity raging, Cistine followed her across the dusk-swallowed meadow into the belly of Starhollow, where insects chirred sleepily in the tall grass and frogs croaked behind them along the pond's edge. Shadows soon suffused the cottage, no more than a whisper of shelter and home at their backs. Still they walked.

"I was going to be a *visnpresta*."

Cistine flicked a glance at Ariadne and saw something different tonight in her stern mouth, her eyes damp in the faraway moonlight. "Do you want to tell me what happened?"

"What always does? Salvotor." Ariadne thumbed blood from her knuckles. "My whole life, I wanted to serve the True God however I could, and joining the Order seemed the best way. My sister, Saychelle, shared my ambition. We began training the day we were both old enough and never once looked back. Iri was our mentor...you heard Helga and Kallah mention her today."

"She's a *visnpresta* too?"

Ariadne nodded. "The moment the four women traveled from Stedgnalt's shores to the City of a Thousand Stars, Iri heard the calling on her life. She went straight to the temples. Later, she guided us to them."

"I don't know much about *visnprests*," Cistine admitted. "Only what Maleck and Julian have told me."

"They speak to the gods, minister to the people, keep records about augments and such. Now with the Doors shut, they spend a good deal of time acting as mediators between the True God and the common man."

"That must be a heavy weight."

"It is, so every *visnprest* and *presta* takes a vow of chastity. One's focus must be entirely on serving the gods in whatever temple they're assigned to after training."

"No wonder you're so good at discipline. You must've completed your training years ahead of schedule."

"Months," Ariadne corrected with a small smile. "But I waited behind for my sister. She became...bored with the life of a *visnpresta*, particularly when she began to listen to Thorne's ideas about changing things. There were several laws and rules about the Order my sister wasn't fond of. That law of chastity especially."

Cistine kept her gaze ahead, letting herself see nothing but the distant, dim outlines of the mountains. "Were she and Thorne...lovers?"

Ariadne shrugged. "You would have to ask Thorne. I certainly advised them against it. To break those vows was to spit in the face of God. I couldn't bear to see her do that, even if I was afraid she'd scorn me for it." She gazed across the meadow, a deep furrow slitting between her brows. "I followed Saychelle everywhere those days, half to keep her from trouble and half because I'd never taken the time to pursue other friendships. I've never been good at them. I was always better at speaking to God than people…but I had Iri, and Saychelle. And Iri had not forsaken her friendship with Helga and Kallah, which placed my sister and me directly in Thorne's path.

"Whatever Thorne's purpose with my sister, it wasn't academic. And he didn't want to place Iri in an uncomfortable position, being at the head of the acolyte school in Stornhaz. But he knew I was her prodigy, so he came to me with his questions about ancient lore…and some less-ancient things. The war between Valgard and Talheim, the stories of a Key that could unlock the Doors. He wanted to make certain his father never learned what knowledge the *visnprests* had to offer about such things."

Cistine grimaced. "Salvotor found out, didn't he?"

"Not about the Key, not from me. But when Aden betrayed us, he gave Salvotor my name, and he must've strung together why Thorne and I were friends. I assume that's why…"

She halted and rested a hand on her hip, staring toward the mountains, but Cistine knew she wasn't really seeing them anymore.

"The moment Kanslar Court rose that season, Salvotor called me to his personal apartment to meet. I thought it was for my dispatch, that he had chosen a temple for me." Her face hardened, fingers clenching against her side. "That was not what the visit was about."

She was quiet for so long this time, Cistine's horrified mind filled in what had happened to Ariadne that night. And, to some extent, *why.*

"Afterward, he nailed my body to the door of Aden's home by my wrists and shoulders." Ariadne turned up her sleeves, baring the circular, gnarled scars Cistine had noticed the day they met. "Aden found me, he kept me from bleeding to death. But during that time I was hanging on his door, Salvotor captured Quill and Maleck, whipped Thorne, and broke Baba Kallah's leg."

Cistine pressed a hand to her mouth, sickened at the surgical precision with which the Chancellor had struck Sillakove Court to their deepest parts. "Why did he do it?"

"Because a *visnpresta* who has any carnal relations is no longer fit for temple life. Even if we had stayed in Stornhaz, I would have been excommunicated. He destroyed my dream and left me strung up as a warning to the others that he was coming to destroy theirs, too."

"Ari, *gods...*"

"I was broken for a long while after that. I forgot how to pray, how to live...how to breathe. I didn't know what to do with all the years I'd spent learning things. Gardening reminded me of my family. Healing reminded me of my training. I was aimless for a long time, until I stumbled across Maleck training with his blades one day. I'd known he was a warrior, but until I watched him drilling, I didn't understand what that meant. It was another form of discipline, one I had not been cast out from. So I begged him, and he helped me find a new practice to devote myself to."

Cistine couldn't even begin to fathom the courage it took to survive such violent abuse and come back from it strong enough to keep fighting.

Ariadne's hand slid from her hip to rub her brow instead. "Tatiana *knows* all of this. She barely left my side when we first came to the Den. She was the one who helped me survive those first few Nimmus-cursed months when I felt like I'd died on that door. For her to say something like that in my presence...she was asking to be hit."

Cistine wondered if that was one more step toward what Baba Kallah feared: Tatiana calcifying her heart. "Thorne broke her flask."

"Good. Tatiana is a cruel drunk. I can't discuss her anymore tonight."

Cistine changed the subject: "What do the *visnprestas* know about the Key?"

Ariadne pinned her with a frown. "That it was a very strange ritual that closed the Doors. It demanded a sacrifice to seal a path the gods themselves first opened. To open the Doors again would require just as much of a sacrifice. More, even."

"And Thorne is all right with that?"

Ariadne folded her arms, tapping her elbows. "It's been more than a decade since he first came to me about this. I told him everything I knew about the Key back then, and he's still hunting, even though he's had every chance to creep into Talheim and search for it there since we were cast out of Stornhaz."

She glanced over her shoulder toward the cottage's outline swimming in the eye-watering dark.

"If you want the truth," she said, "in the deepest part of his heart, I don't think he *wants* to find it. I don't think Thorne is truly ready to pay the price to unleash augmentation into these lands again."

CHAPTER THIRTY-THREE

To ASHE'S SURPRISE, Aden was awake and in his usual place at his table when she came to request a fight with Kalman. No trace of discomfort remained from his lashing.

"You're looking remarkably well," she remarked in greeting.

He didn't look up from jotting the latest list of combatants. "Because the punishment hasn't happened yet. Noaam delayed it until a fortnight's worth of rosters are filled out."

Ashe raised a brow. "You're stalling."

"Perceptive."

"Well, as long as you're working on them today, I have a match to request." She reclined against the gate. "I want to fight one of Nimea's people. Kalman."

Aden's gaze shot to her. "The scholar. Why him?"

"I think he suspects what we're up to." It wasn't quite a lie. "He's too close to Nimea's ear. I need him removed without raising suspicion among the others."

Aden sat back in his seat, pen tapping the table. "I'll arrange it."

In the following days, Ashe drilled with Nimea instead of Aden—letting the Lord of the Hive believe she was winnowing deeper into the Tumult's graces while Nimea taught her how to feign Kalman's death using a small weapon smuggled in by a guard Nimea paid off.

She bared the black-bladed knife during their first training session. "This is a *Svarkyst* blade inlaid with a Tyve paralytic. It slows the pulse and rigors the body to imitate death. But if the antidote isn't administered rapidly, death *will* set in."

"I've heard of these blades." Ashe took the knife from Nimea. "They can cut through any armor, can't they?"

"That they can. The trick is to slide it in subtly during the fight. *Svarkyst* is forbidden in a Blood Hive battle, but if you pierce the armor between the ribs, it's barely noticeable. The medicos will carry Kalman from the arena and then, if all goes to plan, administer the antidote within ten minutes."

"I can manage that."

"Good." Nimea took back the knife. "You'll have to imitate a true killing blow. These crowds are particularly fond of a snapped neck or a crushed sternum, but it's ultimately your choice."

Her choice how much she wanted to play the Blood Hive's game and embrace its ways.

Not until the day came did she decide how she'd do it, when she faced Kalman across the promenade. With the crowd already simmering in anticipation above them, they bowed to each other, his breath wafting on her face. "Let's see who lives and who dies, shall we?"

Right then, she knew.

The fight began with a familiar cadence: sandals circling the ground, swords and shields upraised, ready to thrash forward at any moment. When they did collide, ferocity drove Kalman's blows; a hidden wellspring of energy lay behind that sinewy body where even a trained Warden couldn't see it.

Thorne was deeply in trouble with these people.

Circle and clash, clash and circle. The crowd roared, not sensing for an instant that Ashe and Kalman feinted rather than truly fought. Yet even that felt like deception; Ashe pulled her blows twice as much as Kalman. He goaded her with alternating strikes, testing where her measures lay and whether he could cross them.

Gritting her teeth, Ashe plowed in, her sword a glistening ribbon that mimicked a falling star. Kalman grunted and fell back, feet skidding slightly on the sand, and Ashe pirouetted and kicked his legs out from under him. He slammed to his knees on the ground.

Ashe stepped back, giving him time to gain his feet while she stirred the audience, spreading and pumping her arms, coaxing the cheers like a concerto. Let them believe she was prolonging the match for their sakes. Let them believe she was just another fighter here for the glory, the bloodshed of survival...

"Don't turn your back on him!"

Kalman's shield slammed into Ashe's spine, shooting sparks across her eyes. She tumbled to her knees, narrowly shifting clear of the kick aimed at her ribs, and hopped to her feet again—but now her back throbbed in time with her heart. Black and blue would paint her skin by this time tomorrow.

She had no time to see who'd shouted that warning. Kalman rushed her, jaw set, eyes flashing like he might make good on his threat in the catacombs and kill her. She kept her sword up, catching every clash of his, but her muscles would only withstand a honed barrage for so long.

Between strokes, Ashe switched arms—blocking with her shield and thrusting all her weight behind it. Kalman staggered backward, but when Ashe dropped to sweep out his feet again, he leaped and brought his sword hammering onto her shield with a mallet's might. Ashe's arm rotated from its socket, shooting pain down to her hip. Screaming the pain away, she swiveled out from under his next blow and staggered away.

"Keep him in front of you!"

Aden. He stood at the top of the steps, the same place where she'd watched his fight, and cut his arm subtly toward Kalman's right. When the enraged fighter charged her, Ashe stripped off her shield—useless with her shoulder dislocated—and danced backward, keeping his side in her sights.

They circled and struck twice, weapons wheeling, Ashe blinking pained sweat from her eyes. Her arm was a throbbing mess, but she winnowed her focus past it. Kalman had given himself over to the fight entirely; this only ended when she managed to slip the *Svarkyst* blade between his ribs...or when he beheaded her.

She dodged his spate of stabs and slashes, her back drenched in sweat; twice, her knees hit the sand when Kalman's weight overpowered her, and both times Aden shouted at her to get up, to keep moving.

"Watch his right side!" The roaring crowd almost masked his voice now. "His *right!*"

And there it was: a subtle hitch in Kalman's stride, likely from an old injury that hadn't healed properly. Of course Aden knew about it; he likely kept a detailed list of every injury incurred by every survivor in a match.

Ashe gritted her teeth and rushed Kalman's left side. When he twisted to avoid her blind attack, she mirrored him. Pivoting on heel, she smashed her opposite foot into his right hip, sending him tumbling backward onto the promenade. She landed on top of him, yanked his sword from his hand, and sent it skidding across the stone. Pressing her body down the length of his, she freed the *Svarkyst* dagger from her vest and slid its tip between his ribs.

Kalman's breaths caught; his eyes widened and he stopped struggling.

"You see?" she breathed. "I *am* on your side."

She picked up his head and slammed it against the stones, cushioning it with her own knuckles to break the jarring impact to his skull. Kalman went limp, his breathing slow.

Ashe staggered to her feet, the audience cheering her name like some hero or living god. The Hive welcomed her as one of its own.

Sickened, Ashe staggered straight into the catacombs and to the healing chamber. It was empty when she arrived, the medicos seeing to Kalman, but the moment her haunches touched the solitary cot Aden's familiar swagger sounded off the walls. He made straight for her, sat, and put out his hand.

Swallowing a sigh, Ashe surrendered her dislocated arm to him.

"I didn't expect to see you out there watching the fight," she said as he rotated her arm against the socket. "I thought that was forbidden."

"Intervention is, if they catch you."

"Were you trying to make us even?"

"Yes. A life for a life. It's not the Hive's way, but it's how I was raised."

"Well, I appreciate how you risked humiliating Noaam again. I could've gotten the lash for that."

"Better that than Kalman taking your head."

Her arm snapped suddenly back into place, and she howled with surprise and pain, buckling forward. Aden caught her gently by the collarbone, pushing her upright.

"This is nothing compared to the lash," he told her. "You've gotten away easy."

She studied his face, solemn and blank, but his jaw like steel. "It's happening tonight, isn't it?"

He nodded. "All the rosters are finished."

"Does it frighten you, knowing it's coming?"

"It once did. Now I refuse to count the lashes. I try to think of something pleasant enough to outweigh the pain."

Pain that, this time, *she* had brought on him—unwittingly, by saving his life. It was as much her burden to carry as his.

Ashe nudged him, smirking when he glanced at her. "You could always think of me. I'm sure that will cure any pain you feel."

Aden scoffed. "You're my greatest source of pain."

"I won't argue with that. But I've been told I'm also a great source of pleasure."

This time, the Lord of the Hive burst into laughter, coarse and cocky, and Ashe was glad he could laugh despite what was coming for him. The sound gave her hope that he might survive the Hive's punishment relatively unscathed, after all.

Maybe they both would.

❧

Ashe dreamed of fighting Kalman again that night, this time with the intent to kill. When she finally managed to blow through his guard, his face dissolved into Maleck's, a plea flying from his lips just as her polearm slammed through his belly. Pained eyes locked on hers and he crumbled to his knees, bleeding to death on the sand. Ashe grabbed his hand and hauled against his faltering weight, screaming at him to get back up, to get on his feet; and he squeezed back, but it felt less like a reassurance and more like a parting.

Someone *was* grabbing her hand. Shaking her.

The guard let go of Ashe's wrist the moment she woke. His dark eyes glimmered in the wash of ghostlight that painted his thick, stubbled jowls from the lamp in his other hand. "Get up. You've been summoned."

Ashe dragged herself from the alcove, binding her cardigan tightly around her waist. "Aden?" He must be truly hurt after all, if he was asking to see her.

The guard shook his head. "He's still recovering."

"Then who?"

The man's bright stare fixed on her scowling face. "One of the Tribunes."

CHAPTER
THIRTY-FOUR

TWO GUARDS ESCORTED Ashe from the Blood Hive, one holding the lead to the shackles on her wrists, the other to the manacles on her ankles. If she attacked either one, the other could turn on her before she put her face toward him. A third rope affixed to an iron collar around her neck, threaded into the belt of the man who led their march from the arena.

This wasn't the first time they'd done this.

With the cool night wind raising gooseflesh on her arms, Ashe entertained several notions of what was coming, each more unpleasant than the last. The best she hoped for was that Noaam wanted to congratulate her for her fight today, but more likely the Tribune who'd sent the assassins after them realized his error now and sought to kill her and Aden by separating them.

The guards ushered Ashe between the nomadic tents bathed in blue, gold, and creamy-red ghostlight. The air smelled heavily of herbs and yeast, and she tried not to breathe too deeply. Whispers wandered after them, wondering drunkenly if this was truly the fighter who'd beaten Dorsta and half a dozen others like him; the one who'd led the women in such a lethal display against the Viperwolves.

The one who'd run from the catacombs to save the Hive Lord.

The whispers changed to jeers as they went. More than half the men among the tents demanded her buying price, and Ashe wanted to gut them all. If bartering the fighters for coital spates between battles wasn't a practice already, these bastards with their wagging tongues were going to put thoughts in Noaam's head.

She breathed out in silent relief when they reached the stretch of pale stone buildings. Most windows were dark, but the guards marched her toward one of the few whose upper rooms still glowed. The wood-latticed windows, set above a narrow walkway, were latched.

How much force would it take to break one?

The guard holding the tether to her ankles only had to knock once, and a stern-browed woman ushered them into the warm trappings—fine architecture, fires glowing in low pits, and plenty of beaded, dyed pillows to perch on. A handful of women were doing just that, glancing away from their books and crafting with lazy interest when the guards led Ashe up a staircase into the house's brighter, airier upper room.

Tables and sofas comprised the seating area, gauzy vermillion drapes decorating the stone walls; and Tribune Sander perched on the largest couch, sipping from a fluted glass smelling strongly of fermented grapes. He'd traded the robes that protected his skin from the sunlight for a turquoise vest hugging his pectorals and hips, binding his dark curls back with a scarlet sash that deepened his tawny eyes.

"At last. You certainly know how to keep a man waiting." He gestured to the guards with a lazy finger around the glass stem. "You may go."

The guards dropped their heads along with the chains and excused themselves, leaving Ashe bristling before the Tribune.

"I'm glad it's you," she said. "Better than Noaam after what he did to Aden tonight."

"Punishing a man for having his life spared," Sander said. "That sort of behavior proves Siralek would be better off in different hands."

"Like yours?"

Smile as enigmatic as his eyes, Sander set the glass aside and approached her. Ashe tensed for his fingers around her throat or another punch to her still-healing face, but instead he produced a key from his pocket and undid the shackles on her wrists. "This precaution was Noaam's orders. He'd simply be heartbroken, you know, if something happened to me."

"I can imagine," Ashe deadpanned, her thoughts swirling. Every action he took pointed toward one dark conclusion.

"Noaam's family roots are deep in Nordbran's sand." Sander lowered himself to the shackles at her feet. "They were among the last Tribune households to still own slaves. Not employ them...*own* them."

Feet free at last, Ashe shifted them a shoulder's width apart. Sander rested one hand on her cheek and undid the collar with the other.

"Sometimes," he went on quietly, "I think they took hold of this place as an excuse to continue slave work under a legal guise."

The collar thudded to the floor.

Ashe ripped back, knocked his arm away, and cast around the room for a weapon. Though the walls were bare beneath those veils, a pitcher of wine sat on the nearest table. She snatched it up and whirled to face Sander again. "I know what this is."

"I'm sure you don't." Voice lilting with tipsy amusement, Sander held up both hands. "Or else you wouldn't be threatening me with more wine."

"You're not going to touch me."

"Well, you're right about that. I have twenty-seven lovers, I'm not looking for a twenty-eighth here in Siralek of all places."

Ashe didn't dare lower the jug even when he sauntered back to the couch and lounged again, sipping his wine. "If this isn't about your appetites, then why in the gods' names am I *here*?"

Sander frowned. "I take it the Lord of the Hive hasn't introduced you to the concept of sponsorship." When Ashe didn't reply, he gestured to the couch opposite his. Slowly, she sank down onto it, haunches practically melting into the first soft surface she'd sat on in weeks. "Sponsorship is when someone with plenty of mynts in their coffers endorses a long-lasting fighter and enters them into higher-stakes matches inaccessible to the unsponsored."

"And I assume there's some benefit for the fighter risking her life in those matches?"

"The sponsor supplies them better rations, for one. He also has some say in which battles the Lord of the Hive assigns them to. In rare cases, he can purchase them some time away from the arena."

Ashe gripped the wine pot's handle tight enough to separate the dry seams.

She wouldn't have to wait for Nimea to entrust an assignment to her. She might not even have to wait for Aden's help to escape.

And of course he'd never mentioned this possibility to her; because if she knew there was another way to escape Siralek, even temporarily and on Sander's leash, she wouldn't have agreed to search for the truth behind the threat against Thorne. So Aden had painted himself as her only salvation.

Ashe gritted her teeth. "Has Aden ever been sponsored?"

"It seems so, though by who is Noaam's secret. He knows we would ply that person for intimate knowledge of how to defeat Aden."

"No honor among traitors."

"Betrayal is a nebulous concept. It may be that Aden's sponsorship is of such a nature he thinks other fighters are better off without it."

Ashe set the pitcher on the table. "Would he be right?"

Sander shrugged. "That all depends on the sponsor."

"And what kind of sponsor would *you* be?"

His mouth curved with appreciation. "I'm prepared to offer you a stipend of five mynts a month, with an additional two for every arena match you take beyond what the Lord of the Hive assigns."

"In other words, more dangerous fights that *you* choose for me."

"Precisely. In addition, I'll purchase for you one day's escape from the Blood Hive into Siralek's market to shop, or to the oasis to bathe, every fortnight."

There was a trick in this. There had to be. "Why me? I've only been in this arena a few weeks."

"True, but I've seen you fight. Clearly you're no inexperienced street rabble, and in this struggle I'd like to have a survivor in my corner. Someone who fearlessly humiliates Noaam."

Ashe rolled her eyes. "You want to use me."

"Everyone is using everyone else for something. What matters is whether you can achieve your ends together or whether the manipulation happens in secret."

Resting her spine against the couch's swooping back, Ashe spread her arms along its silky wooden frame. "You have my interest."

Sander refilled his wine glass. "Yager and Traisende's Tribunes have been called back to Stornhaz, which means somewhere in this kingdom, something more important is happening than this endless struggle for the Blood Hive. With the competition whittled down from five to three, things are going to become *far* more interesting."

Ashe gripped the couch frame with both hands. "How so?"

"There are already rumors that the Tribunes of Tyve and Traisende have employed their own methods to undermine Skyygan's hold over this place. Rumors of Tyve poison in the food and water, weakening the fighters bit by bit."

Though her stomach rebelled at the thought, Ashe believed it. The gruel certainly tasted like poison. "And Traisende?"

"I've yet to discover. I'm not popular with the other Tribunes at the moment. They're looking for ways to undermine Kanslar at every turn, so I find myself surrounded by not just rivals, but personal enemies. I thought it best to seek a powerful ally before someone else snatched you up."

Flattery. They were moving up in the world. "And what makes me so powerful?"

"To them? That well-conditioned body of yours. To me...I'm rather fond of the rumors that you once colluded with High Tribune Thorne."

Ashe shot him a daggered glare. "He's popular around this kingdom, that High Tribune."

"To me more than most. Our steps could collide if all goes to plan."

"What plan?"

"Let me sponsor you, and someday you may find out."

Ashe slid from the couch and went to the window, peering through the latticework and out over Siralek's nest of revelry; beyond it, nothing but desert for miles. The blade at her back pressed deeper every day, and if she didn't find a way to balance all these matters, it would run her through before she ever saw her princess again.

But she'd already put a morsel of faith in Aden, and one in Nimea, despite her vow that she'd never trust a Valgardan again. Now she was meant to trust Sander—another *Kanslar* Tribune, no less.

Still, he knew things she didn't.

"I want the whole truth," Ashe said. "Sooner or later, I'm going to find out why you sponsored me. It might as well be now."

"Even if that knowledge would drive you to deny my offer?"

"If you don't tell me, I'll absolutely deny it."

Sander snorted. More wine splashed into his cup. "Noaam is ready to up the stakes in these fights, so here is what I intend to do: I'm going to enter you into the most dangerous matches, place you in lockstep with the greatest legends in the Blood Hive's history. Our names will be bound up together so my greatness rises with yours. Perhaps high enough that I will replace Noaam as the Tribune who oversees the Blood Hive."

"What is so important about this gods-forsaken sand-riddled tomb?"

"It's full of the most dangerous people in Valgard, including dissenters who harbor knowledge of other Courts, matters of law, even augmentation. Control Siralek, and you may very well control the flow of secrets in this kingdom. And believe me, the other Courts despise Kanslar enough to search for any hidden truth that will destroy it."

"Then you're protecting your Court."

"I'm protecting myself, my twenty-seven lovers, and my tamed wolf."

"What does that have to do with *Thorne*?"

"Once our joined notoriety soars high enough that the people would prefer to see you a living god rather than a trampled fighter, this years-long bid for the Blood Hive will end. I will *finally* be free to go where I wish without the Chancellor's constant, aggravating attention *always* crawling up my spine. I'll buy you from this Nimmus-pit, and you will take me to Thorne so I may give him what he deserves."

That was hard to argue with. And if Thorne died at the Tumult's hands before Sander reached him, that wasn't Ashe's concern; she would still make

Sander believe she was leading him to the High Tribune.

She returned to her seat on the couch. "Let's say I agreed to sponsorship. What next?"

"You begin training for the chariot race at the month's end. In the meantime, I make it clear to Noaam that there are certain lines he may not cross with you."

Ashe rubbed her palms on her knees, wincing at the drag against her scabs. Accepting this offer opened another avenue—a third escape if Aden died before he got her out, or if the Tumult never allowed her to fake her death and pursue the cabal herself.

Lord Rion had taught her a clever card player would stack the deck in such a way her opponents never suspected it was all in her favor.

"Draw up a contract," she said. "I want everything on it that you said...the allowance, the rations, and the escape to the oasis. And I'm prepared to sweeten the offering...all I ask in return for this information is that you do something about it."

Sander tensed. "Very well, I'll do my best."

"That Tribune with the pale hair and beard, always braided..."

"Dusan of Traisende," Sander supplied.

"He sent an assassin to kill Aden and me. That's why Aden was flagging in the match last week."

Sander thumbed his lower lip. "So that's Traisende's angle. While Tyve poisons the fighters, Traisende kills them between matches."

"Can you stop them?"

"I can't prove there's anything *to* stop, but I'll have my men patrol near the arena at night. As for Tyve..."

Even in silence, Ashe knew they shared the same thought. There was no way of knowing what slow-acting poison was in the water, the food, the very air of the catacombs. "Maybe you should include fresh water along with those rations in the contract."

Sander's smile was humorless. "Yes. I think that might be best."

CHAPTER THIRTY-FIVE

THE DAY CISTINE decided to resume her training—whether Quill thought she was healed enough or not—broke with a storm brewing above the mountain peaks in low, furious drapes. Despite the dampness seeping into the cottage cracks and the knots of pain clumping in her shoulders, Cistine yanked on her training armor and took the stairs two at a time down to the dining room. To her surprise, Thorne was in Pippet's usual chair, studying a map and flipping an unbitten apple in one hand; the girl who usually took that seat, sketching between slurps of porridge, was nowhere to be seen.

"If you're not going to eat that..." Cistine plucked the apple from Thorne's hand in a pirouette past the table.

He folded his arms behind his neck and stretched so deeply his body arched from the chair, amusement erasing the lines of tension around his eyes. "And where is the Princess off to in such a hurry that she can't find her *own* breakfast?"

Cistine took two bites of the apple while she backed toward the door, covering her mouth with her smallest finger. "To intercept Quill on patrol. Which way did he go?"

"Southwest." Thorne bared his palm and Cistine pitched the other half of the apple back to him. "Good luck with training."

"And you with your map!" Grinning, Cistine blew him a parting wave and darted from the cottage.

The breeze was almost wintery, and she was glad of her close-fitting armor while she tracked Quill's footprints toward the gentle inclines beyond the cottage. She spotted Ariadne and Maleck after half a mile, distant shadows giving Quill a wide berth on one of the hilltops—and, to Cistine's surprise, Pippet as well.

The siblings' furious shouts carried on the blustery wind.

"Stop, Pip," Quill was saying when Cistine slipped between Ariadne and Maleck. "We're not having this conversation."

"I know we aren't, because you never want to talk to me—you only want to tell me what to do!" Pippet snapped.

Cistine nudged Ariadne. "What's happening?"

"One of the archers told her where we're going next. Now she wants to help."

"She was particularly quiet during our walk this morning," Maleck added under his breath. "She asked what happened to the villagers. When we refused to tell her, she went straight to Quill."

"You're not coming with us," Quill's tone smoothed over like adamant.

"*Yes, I am!*" Pippet stepped up into her brother's face. "I'm *going* to leave this place and there's nothing you can do to stop me! You can't keep me prisoner anymore, I want to *help!*"

Quill gripped her shoulders. "Pip, listen to me. You don't understand how dangerous the rest of Valgard is, what those villagers have been through. I can't let the people who hurt them hurt you."

"Then I won't go to any villages, I *promise.*"

"No, it doesn't matter where you go. It's what they'll do if they find you, because you're my sister."

Pippet wrenched free. "Then I wish you weren't my brother! I hate you!"

Quill stiffened, eyes widening with the same pain as when Cistine had struck him and fled from Starhollow. Then he pulled his composure around himself again, that shell of unflappable calm the cabal could throw their blows against and never shatter. "You can hate me if you like. I can't make you feel differently, but I *can* keep you from leaving Starhollow. Your safety is my responsibility, and I'll protect you as long as there's breath in my body."

"Then I wish you would die so I can finally *leave!*" Pippet broke his hold and bolted for the cottage, her furious sobs floating back to them on the wind.

Quill stared after her, hair tugged in the wind, his devastated expression nearly dragging tears from Cistine's eyes. "Maleck, you take patrol. I'm done."

"Quill..." Cistine began.

"I'm just done."

They watched him trudge away, bent-backed, head hung.

"I'll look in on him later," Maleck said after a moment. "Make certain he's all right."

He hurried away to take Quill's patrol, leaving Ariadne and Cistine on the hill with the damp-smelling wind wrapped around their bodies.

Ariadne broke the silence. "Well, what do you want to do with your morning?"

Cistine stared after Quill, her body feeling far too heavy now for training. "I want to weave flower crowns for the children."

"Good. I want to help you."

Storms rolled across the meadow by midday, the skies a dark eddy that matched the mood in the cottage. Pippet stayed in her room, with Quill outside the door; it was almost sunset when he gave up waiting for her to emerge and plodded back down the stairs. Dull-eyed, he swept the hair away from his scar and stared at the table, where Cistine and Ariadne wove flower crowns. Halfway through the day, Tatiana had trudged downstairs herself, sallow and coated with sweat from head to foot, and sat in the reading nook to stare out the window.

For the first time in hours, she looked away from the glass, fixing on

Quill with chilling focus. Then she swung from the reading nook and stood before him, hands loose at her sides. "What do you need?"

"To fix this," he said.

"You can't. You're never going to be able to make this right, because you're not safe for her. None of us are."

"Tatiana," Cistine snapped. Ariadne motioned for quiet.

"We can't protect everyone, and we brought this life on her," Tatiana bore on, "because we were too busy with ourselves back then. With our dreams, our ideals, with *Detlyse Halet—*"

Quill exploded forward, slinging a punch toward Tatiana's ribs. She blocked it effortlessly with her elbow, stepping backward toward the door as Quill swung again. And again. And again. They hit the ground in a tangle of arms and legs just through the doorway and Cistine winced when someone finally landed a resonate hit.

But as painful as it sounded, she understood it. She'd walked back into Villmark with that same helpless rage after her first real argument with Julian, and Quill had put up his hands and told her to hit him. He'd taken her grief and humiliation and anger and stored it up in himself, just as he'd done for Tatiana countless times. Now it was Tatiana's turn.

Cistine returned to her task, but her fingers shook and her eyes itched. Even after the rain stopped and the low cloudbank lifted, bringing a golden glow to the room, her mood stayed dull; she plucked listlessly at a plate of fresh salad from Helga's garden for supper, sitting across from Julian while he flipped through a book. She wanted to ask him what it was about, but she was too tired to care.

At last, she gave up on her appetite, kissed Julian on the cheek, and retreated upstairs with the flower crowns in her arms to the room all the girls shared. Pippet drowsed on her and Tatian's bed, her back to the door, curled around three different dolls. Cistine winced when her steps creaked on the wooden floorboards, and Pippet stirred, swirling around in the sheets to face her.

Silent, they stared at one another. Cistine's dry mouth couldn't call up a single word.

At last, Pippet said, "Are those for me?"

Cistine nodded and let the crowns tumble onto the bed, and Pippet chose a weave of roses and forget-me-nots for herself. After careful deliberation, she offered a crown of lavender and birch to Cistine. "You can sit with me if you want."

Cistine took the crown and sat cross-legged beside her. "You know, I haven't always been allowed to go the places I wanted to, either. My father wanted to keep me close. In fact, he'd have an absolute fit if he knew I was here." Something she tried desperately not to think about.

"Then your father is mean, and he doesn't love you," Pippet said. "Like Quill doesn't care about me."

"No, he isn't mean. Neither is Quill. They *do* love us, Pip, that's why they do these things. They want us to be safe."

"But I don't want to stay in Starhollow anymore! It's for *little* children. It's too small for me."

Cistine drew her lip carefully between her teeth. "You know what I always do when the world seems too small? I read books. They'll take you anywhere you want for a little while. You can go to other kingdoms, you can live a different life. And best of all, you can go back to those places whenever you miss them—as many times as you read that book."

Pippet's eyes widened slightly. "Helga gives me books to read about arithmetic and augments and things. They're not like that."

"Well, maybe I'll have to bring you some other books. Ones that can take you away from Starhollow."

Pippet sat up taller. "Can you tell me a story from those books?"

"Well, I've never really tried storytelling..."

"Would you, though? For me?"

Cistine bit her lips together and settled the crown on her head, much lighter than any ceremonial tiara she'd worn in Talheim. "I'll do my best. What do you want to hear a story about?"

"Tazra." Pippet wrapped her blanket around her shoulders. "Take Tazra and me away from Starhollow for a little while."

Cistine stretched out on her back beside Pippet, folding her hands over her belly. "Hm. Tazra. Well, once, long ago, legend has it Tazra was crowned warrior princess of the Wild Islands..."

Cistine didn't intend to fall asleep. One moment, she was weaving inelegant, stammering stories for Pippet about the daring Tazra; the next, she was waking up with her cheek resting on Pippet's head while Helga knelt beside them. Cistine sucked in a breath, and the nanny lifted a hand for peace. "She'll be happier when she wakes. She always is."

"I gave her a flower crown and told her a story," Cistine whispered. "I hope that was all right."

"It was the best thing for her today, to talk with someone who isn't cabal. Pippet is changing as she grows. You learn to swim in her moods and avoid the undertow, but on days like today we can only ride out the storms together."

"She's lucky to have you as her nanny." Cistine extricated herself gently from the blankets. "Someone who can weather all kinds of storms."

"Not as easily as I once did." Helga smoothed a hand over Pippet's hair. "Fear ages the body. And I do fear for her. The thought of leaving..."

Cistine swallowed. "Do you think you ever will leave Starhollow?"

"I hope so, but Quill is right. There's no going until Salvotor is dealt with and the kingdom made safe again. But Pippet doesn't understand the danger. She's been kept safe all her life."

"I know what that's like. But sooner or later she has to learn, Helga. Otherwise she'll be like me...running off into a world she doesn't understand because no one taught her any better."

"I pray you're not right about that. Hopefully we can keep her content here until that world is safe enough for her." Helga sighed, unease clouding her eyes. "But knowing our Pippet, it's only a matter of time."

CHAPTER
THIRTY-SIX

I T DIDN'T TAKE long for Aden to learn of Ashe's sponsorship. Before she'd even received her first stipend from Sander, the Hive Lord cornered her outside the training rooms with a lethal scowl and a heavy hand on her shoulder, turning her to face him.

"There you are," Ashe said. "How—?"

"I just received orders from Noaam to enter your name in the chariot races at the end of the month. Why?"

Grimacing, Ashe shrugged his hand away. "Because while you were flat on your stomach recovering from that lashing, Tribune Sander sent me a personal invitation to his quarters in the city."

Aden was so close that even through his light linen shirt, Ashe saw his breathing stop. "Is he sponsoring you?"

"Yes."

Swearing, he punched the stone next to Ashe's head. "You should have rejected his offer!"

"Why? So you could keep me ignorant, like you did by keeping the truth about sponsors from me in the *first* place?"

Aden looked swiftly up and down the corridor, then motioned her to follow him with a jerk of his head. Ashe stalked on his heels, blood boiling; this was the first time she'd seen him since he took the lash, and she'd been about to ask him how he was—had even been glad to see him upright after just a few days absent from training. And he wanted this to be a *fight*?

Fine. She would gladly give him one.

Aden didn't speak until they reached his chamber. He walked past the table this time and sat on the foot of his bed while Ashe leaned against the broad stone divider, arms cinched, glaring at him.

"I didn't tell you because most fighters don't know they can be sponsored," Aden explained. "You're no exception."

"Why? The opportunity for better rations and time away from this place..."

"It isn't worth it for the fights they place you in...chariot races, man against beast, and fighters deadlier even than Dorsta. Ask Nimea if you don't believe me, her allies snatched up every sponsorship that came their way when they first arrived. Fifteen died inside a week. Sponsored fights are a death sentence to all but the most accomplished warriors."

Ashe's guts quivered. "Like you?"

"You're asking if I'm sponsored?" Aden grimaced. "Yes, I am, but my sponsor has uses for me that keep me alive. My importance to the Hive is an added layer of armor for me. You have no armor and no hope."

"How do you know I'm not useful to *my* sponsor that way?"

"Because you can still walk without pain."

Ashe sucked in a breath. She knew *exactly* what he meant. "So the slaves do get purchased sometimes...for joining."

Aden rubbed the back of his neck, then raised his eyes. "They used to. Now it's forbidden."

"Noaam?" Ashe snorted. "I didn't realize he cared."

"*I* forbade it." Aden's guttural tone stopped Ashe's gallows humor in midswing. "Sometimes that *bandayo* likes to make a public reminder that he bought *me*, not the other way around. But as much as it's in me, I *do not* allow rape in this place. I can't protect these women from the fights, but I will protect them with every ounce of my power from that pain, that humiliation and abuse. They deserved better."

Deserved.

It had happened before. To some of them. And maybe...

He said he was useful to his sponsor, but that Ashe couldn't be, not in the same way—because of how she walked today.

Limbs heavy, chest tight, she slowly approached the bed and sank down on the edge beside him. The question was on her lips, but how could she even say it?

Aden stared down at his hands. "Ask."

She swallowed. "You?"

For a moment, silence.

Then Aden nodded.

"Female patronesses are rare. But I did discover one...or rather, she found me. After she'd purchased me several times against my will, I decided if I must endure it, I'd reap some benefit. So I wrote up a bargain of sponsorship. Now she impresses on Noaam not to sell the women fighters to high bidders. And in return..."

"You go to her whenever she asks."

Aden bobbed his head. "And to her friends. Whoever asks for me, really. It was another reason Noaam delayed the lashing. I was...summoned, and they couldn't afford damage before the deed." His lips twitched in a humorless smirk. "I'm told I'm the perfect specimen."

Ashe couldn't believe he could joke about it, paint himself and his value in such a flippant, deprecating light. He'd sold himself, his own body, to shield others. "Well, if it's any consolation, I'm more useful alive than dead as well, albeit not in the same way."

"Tell me."

"I can't. It's written into the contract. Everything I discussed with my sponsor remains between us."

Aden gritted his teeth. "At least tell me you'll be training in the chariot."

"Every day I'm not fighting."

"Then I'll reorder your matches to give you more time to practice. Keep your focus where it matters."

Surprise washed away the stain of her pain, echoing his. "Really?"

"I owe you my life more than twice over. I won't repay that by leaving you unprepared for a sponsored match."

Ashe dipped her head. "Thank you."

"Go." Aden nodded toward the gate. "And never breathe a word of this to anyone. I'm contracted to silence as well."

"Then why did you just tell me?"

"Because I'm tired of keeping this secret." Aden's mouth ticked in a smile. "Besides, I didn't tell you. You guessed."

Ashe thumped him on the shoulder. "Clever bastard."

He pushed her off the bed by the back of her head. "Get out."

Still smirking, Ashe went to the gate, then slowed and looked back.

Aden had bent forward, resting his head in his hands. In that posture, awash in the never-dying candlelight, she saw him differently. Here was a man who tried with all his might to come across as stern and unaffected, careless of every soul who walked into the Hive and every one carried out again on a pallet. And yet he'd sold himself for them. Given up his autonomy again and again to keep them from accruing shame and hidden injuries beyond the arena's threats. He'd taken Ashe's match from her, allowed her to train. And he'd come to her as soon as he learned about the chariot race.

Maybe he wasn't as callused as he'd led them all to believe.

"Aden." Ashe waited for him to look at her before she added, "I'm receiving special rations from my sponsor. You should share them with me. Don't eat or drink what the Hive offers anymore."

Suspicion narrowed his eyes as he read in her tone what her contract forbade her to say.

But he didn't challenge her. He simply nodded.

CHAPTER THIRTY-SEVEN

A PASTEL AUTUMN sunrise roused Cistine four days after the storms blew through Starhollow. From the moment she woke, her muscles burning in that coveted, invigorating way from training with Quill the previous day, strange peace bloomed within her; an almost reckless certainty that things were going to go well from now on.

They would leave Starhollow and treat with Thorne's allies in Veran for aid in unseating Salvotor. They would find Ashe. They would break Salvotor's hold over the other Courts and bring aid to Talheim.

"What are you so happy about?" Julian asked when Cistine skimmed past him at the table, planting a kiss on his cheek.

"Can't a princess be cheerful on a glorious, sunny day?" she grinned.

"Not when she's been sulking the past two weeks." Julian hooked Cistine around the waist, bringing her to his lap. "Don't think I missed how you were crying on and off most of the way from Geitlan."

"Oh." Cistine tamed a wayward thread of hair behind her ear. "That."

"That." Julian nuzzled her neck. "Care to tell me what's had you so concerned, Princess?"

"Besides the Key, and augments still existing, and the Chancellor, and Ashe?" Julian nipped her earlobe, and she laughed breathlessly around a delighted shiver. "Well, in the forest, on our way here, that was about my parents."

Julian stilled. "What? Why?"

Sliding her fingers through the cap of his dark hair, Cistine told him of her conversation with Cassaida and memories about her parents after the miscarriages. The only detail she kept to herself was how Thorne had comforted her that day; she doubted Julian would appreciate it.

Afterward, he remained quiet, his knuckles stroking her side from ribs to hip, his brows knitted pensively. Cistine brushed the hair from his forehead. "What are you thinking?"

He shrugged. "I don't know. Nothing."

Cistine sat back in his embrace, resting her hands on his shoulders. "Julian."

Another shrug. "I just think you might be trying too hard, Princess. You're blaming other people for how you are, when maybe you just never wanted the throne at all. I mean, how could you really know what you wanted back then? You were so small."

Cistine could muster no retort, tongue shriveling with shock. His indifference stung after the gravity of this revelation and what it meant to her—how it had unbalanced her entire sense of herself, of her past, and made her understand angles of her thinking and choices that had been so unclear before.

How could he not see it?

"It's not a bad thing that you don't want to be a queen," Julian added hastily. "You don't need to make excuses for being who you are. But I don't think it's fair to blame your parents, either. They're not the kind of people who would neglect their daughter, even in grief. Besides, that was a long time ago. You're probably remembering it wrong. My mother says time changes memory..."

She wasn't misremembering. The finer points, perhaps, but not the door shutting in her face. Not the way she'd run to Ashe instead of her mother. And the tears scalding her eyes were not sadness, or relief, or whatever Julian assumed.

She was *furious*. Furious that she'd opened up this portion of herself to him, and now he twisted her raw emotion to suit his image of her family: the benevolent rulers and the Princess who did not want to be Queen...just the way he liked it. The comfortable image *he'd* created.

The steps rattled as Pippet charged down them, her daisy-plaited dress flapping against her ankles. She leaped down the last two stairs, laughing. "I win again!" Faer alighted on the banister with a rogue squawk, ruffling his feathers indignantly.

"Good morning, Pippet." Cistine slid from Julian's lap, grateful for once to be out from under his hands.

"They're here!" Pippet announced. "The children are here!"

Her enthusiasm coaxed a smile from Cistine—relief that Pippet and Quill had made grudging amends two days ago, and now she had the other children to distract her.

All at once, they tore through the front door like a stampede of colts, flinging themselves onto the reading nook, climbing up at the table, and making faces at themselves in the mirror. Ulric and Aleida crashed into Cistine's legs, wrapping their arms around her, and their eager hands dismantled her anger. She was laughing before she even knelt to hug them.

"What are we going to do today?" Aleida asked.

"I thought we might play *Follow the Princess*." Cistine picked up the braided flower crown hanging from the banister and scolded Faer when he nipped her fingers.

"That's my cue to go be useful somewhere else." Julian finished his breakfast, kissed Cistine's cheek, and waded out through a sea of children all trying to grab his legs.

"What's a princess?" Aleida asked, wide-eyed.

"A princess...is a ruler from a different kingdom," Cistine explained carefully. "She's like a Chancellor."

Ulric snorted. "That's ridiculous. Women can't be *Chancellors*."

Cistine flicked his nose. "A woman can be whatever she wants." She handed the flower crown to Pippet. "Why don't you choose a princess to lead us today, Pip?"

Pippet grinned, turning the flower crown in her hands while she surveyed the cluster of girls dancing on the balls of their feet at the notion of being crowned leader for the day, their eagerness blazing like midday sunlight. To them, the crown was no burden or shackle; it was an opportunity to make the rules and lead, to see where paths of power would take their small, enthusiastic feet.

No matter what Julian believed, no matter what he said, Cistine had been like them once. She could see it as clearly as if her younger self flocked among these children, a girl with braided hickory hair and bright green eyes bobbing in the crowd, flailing her arms, begging to be given the crown she'd been born to wear.

That girl had gotten lost, swallowed in grief, stripped of the sense of her own potential and worth. And Cistine desperately wanted to find her again.

"Hmmm," Pippet hummed. "I choose...I choose..." She smirked, the expression alarmingly like her brother's, and perched the circlet on her own head. "*Me!*"

She bolted for the door, a knot of shrieking and moaning children jumping on her back, trying to pull the crown from her head. Laughing aloud, Cistine scooped up Aleida and raced after them into the bright, sun-splashed meadows of Starhollow.

Cistine hated the moment when everything changed. After hours of rock-skipping and sunbathing and dancing at Pippet's commands; after a picnic Helga brought them on the pond shore, potato cakes and meat pies and a pitcher of black tea. It was when she thought of her conversation with Julian again that her spirits spiraled downward, a darkness not quite eclipsing the enjoyable day, but profound enough that her belly tensed and the hair prickled on her arms.

She lay on the pond shore, a cluster of children dozing around her, thoughts in turmoil while she listened to the others splashing in the shallows. Memory made her just restless and distracted enough to be startled when Pippet dropped cross-legged beside her under the willow tree and placed the crown on her head. "I'm done for today."

Cistine removed the circlet and twirled it between her fingers. "It's heavier than it looks, isn't it?"

"Yes. But I liked it! I want to be a princess when I grow up."

"Well, what if you became a Chancelloress instead?"

Pippet wrinkled her nose. "Ulric was right, we don't have those."

"You can be the first, then." Cistine plopped the crown back on Pippet's head. "Chancelloress Pippet, warrior of Starhollow."

Pippet giggled, stretching out on the sand, and Cistine laid down next to her with eyes closed. She let the sun warm the tension from her muscles, let her cares soak into the sand and slide away into the water to drown.

A shadow fell across her face. "Sleeping on patrol. This could be a problem."

Cistine snapped back to full consciousness so swiftly her heart pounded, and she glared up at Thorne as he loomed over her, smiling. "My ears work as well as the rest of me, you know!" She pushed herself up, rubbing sand from her hair. "Well...one of them does. I was still keeping watch."

Thorne's brow creased. "Your hearing is still compromised?"

"A bit."

Pippet pounced to her feet, wrapping her arms around Thorne's waist, and he mussed her hair. "Go tell your brother Cistine and I are taking patrol."

She pouted. "But I'm *tired*."

Cistine nudged her. "Princesses have to do what's right, even if they don't want to."

Pippet heaved a sigh and whistled to the other children and Faer. Crown firmly in place again, she led them yipping into the distance, Faer leading the way toward wherever Quill was making his rounds.

"Why us for patrol?" Cistine asked. "Is something wrong?"

"Not imminently, but I wanted to discuss the meeting with our allies in Veran. Among other things."

As Cistine got to her feet, another blustery wind funneled down from the peaks around Starhollow, texturing the sky with small, dark clouds. In the distance, rain threatened yet again over the mountains. "You were right about the storms during Kanslar's season."

Thorne smiled. "There's a brilliance about storms, though: they don't last forever."

Cistine smiled, too, and followed him away from the pond toward the distant hills.

CHAPTER THIRTY-EIGHT

TALKING WITH THORNE came easily now. Where awkward pauses and cautious glances had filled their forced conversations when they first met, there was comfort enough to discuss the difficult subjects these days.

"Things seem better with the cabal," Cistine remarked as they walked, deep grass hugging their ankles. "After you broke Tatiana's flask."

"I'd hoped it wouldn't come to that," Thorne admitted.

"Did you know she had a problem?"

"Not as soon as I should have. I've been...distracted. Between Blaykrone, the meeting with the Chancellors, and then Geitlan. It should've come to my attention weeks ago that she was spiraling."

"No one can blame you for being distracted."

"I hold myself accountable for this cabal's wellbeing first, before everything. But I didn't notice how badly Tatiana was hurting or how fiercely she was fighting against that, not until she wounded the rest of you with her words. I'm sorry I let it go that far."

"I think I'm partially to blame for the way she's behaving," Cistine looked ahead toward the hills. "Quill says when I went to Stornhaz, it...affected her. Badly."

"Her feelings toward you are no excuse for how she treats the rest of us. And that drinking...she's been clever about it. Staying wet to quiet her anxieties, but never enough to set things off. But the secrecy is what concerns me. She knows she has a problem."

"Has this happened before?"

"Not since we left Stornhaz...not that I'm aware of," Thorne sighed. "But Tati did have a bit of a drinking issue when she and Quill frequented the taverns in Stornhaz. We helped her keep it in check for the most part. Now I wonder if she's drowning more than she's ever let any of us see."

Cistine grimaced. "Have you spoken to her about it?"

"I've tried these past few days. Something tells me it's not my insight, or *my* friendship, she's missing."

The statement hung uncontested when they reached the shallow foothills and started to climb.

Thorne broke the silence again while they navigated the dark stone croppings. "I'm also concerned about traveling to Veran. If those assassins survived the skirmish in the woods, they may find us again once we're traveling."

"You don't think that was an isolated attempt?"

"Whenever Salvotor changes his patterns, I've learned to assume the worst. He'll be satisfied with nothing less than my head."

Cistine's stomach pitched as if she'd plunged through a roof again. "Nothing?"

Thorne tapped his ribs. "Unless they came just to warn me that they could break through my defenses. But I doubt that. The message seems to be that either I die out here, or I go to him and die on my knees. I've run short on time for a counteraction."

"Well, he doesn't know what we have," Cistine said. "Traisende and Yager. We're not out of time yet, Thorne, not all the way. Salvotor may be clever, but we're the ones concocting strategies underneath his ridiculously shiny, reinforced nose."

Thorne chuckled quietly. "You know, your devotion to your books does you credit with insulting your enemies."

Cistine jutted her tongue, trumping the blush that crept into her cheeks. "Don't tease me. I love my books."

"I was being serious." Thorne nodded ahead to the gradually-steepening cliffs. "Are your hands ready for climbing again?"

Though they weren't entirely, still bruised from the climb out of Cassaida's home, she forced herself to follow him along the rocky shelves anyway. Thorne struggled just as much with the wound in his side; it became a test, a gauntlet of hurts they conquered together, the conversation filled up with punctuated, groaning breaths while they hauled themselves by handholds up the cliff.

"Where do you think the assassins came from?" Cistine panted when she paused to rest, clinging to the rock face.

Thorne waited on his knees on a ledge above her, trembling with exertion. "I have several theories, none of which bode particularly well for us. Where my father found these men was unconventional most likely, judging by the way they fought. Ariadne would say it shows he's desperate, and that means we worry him, but I don't see it that way."

"Ari *would?*" Cistine echoed. "You haven't asked her?"

Thorne shook his head when she scrambled up to join him. "I haven't discussed this with any of them."

She sat back on her heels, spreading and curving her cramped fingers against her thighs. "Why not?"

He looked at her, and for a flicker, like the first crack of lightning in an otherwise quiet sky, she saw his pain and fear. "Because it terrifies me, thinking that after all this time, he may have the upper hand. Worse, that he plans to attain it by killing me, and he came as close as he did..." He pressed the heel of his hand against his side. "I can't tell them. They need me to have a plan, a purpose...*something* that makes all this running and hiding, and Hellidom, and places like Geitlan, *worth* it."

Cistine's chest ached at the gleam of his gaze which told her, more than words ever could, just how close he was to losing control; to letting his cabal see this vulnerability he'd so far only felt safe to share with her.

At the depth of that trust, the heat traveled from her chest to her throat and branded her eyes. "We should keep climbing."

And they did—hand over hand, up toward a tongue of stone

protruding from the cliff face. The higher they traveled, the damper and cooler the air became, until Cistine's fingers seized against the handholds. But when they reached the cliff's zenith and Thorne offered a hand to help her up, she forgot the chill for a moment, her senses captivated by the sight of Starhollow spread out below—a sea of grass encompassing the cattle and tamed deer paddocks, the gardens and cornfields, the distant speck of the cottage.

A place that almost felt like home.

Lightning sizzled in the clouds; a low, ominous toll of thunder rattled the mountains. When the first raindrops pattered gently on the stone around them, Thorne stepped up beside Cistine. "Every time Kanslar's constellation rises, I always wonder what will happen when the lightning falls. Whether this will be the season that breaks us."

"Ten years, Thorne," Cistine reminded him. "No one has broken you yet."

"True." But he didn't sound convinced when he leaned his head back and shut his eyes.

Cistine gazed across this small slice of Cenowyn most thought they would never obtain. Somewhere down there, Quill was on patrol with his sister and a flock of children; Tatiana was trying to find her way back to stable ground. Maleck was searching temples for Ashe in his mind, and Ariadne was fighting enemies the rest of the cabal would never understand. Julian, Baba Kallah, and Helga were helping Geitlan's people heal. And Thorne...

He was beside her, head tipped back, eyes still closed as the rain slicked his hair to his scalp, tightening his clothes against the muscled relief of his chest. Cistine wondered what he'd felt when the assassins pushed through the cabal, trying to reach him. She wondered what *they* had felt when they met his strength...if his power had been everything they anticipated. Did he surprise them by how hard he fought, the same way his perseverance on the brink of hopelessness surprised her?

And why was her hand closing into a fist? Why was she angling her body, why was she *smiling* when she hefted her arm, when she took aim for his chest—

For a flash as Cistine's foot slid against the stone, in the jagged cut of lightning above, Thorne smiled, too.

His palm opened, catching her punch on the meat of his hand. When she wedged her leg between both of his, he trapped her with a twist of his knees and circled her arm behind her back, spinning her to face the valley again.

Gasping with laughter, she ducked, swiveled, and slithered from Thorne's hands, turning on him with a succession of blows he smoothly deflected. When he retaliated, she braced, feeling the shift in her muscles with feet planted and core tight—though Thorne softened his blow just before it glanced against her side.

It tested without doing harm, as he so often tested her.

They grappled in the rain beneath the might of the mountain storm, dancing through battle-patterns so beautifully familiar after all those long mornings of training, and though Cistine had never fought with Thorne before it felt right, somehow. It all made sense.

It wasn't about hurting or hitting. Like Quill and Tatiana, they took the pain from one another, shared the burdens. Made each other better.

The thought distracted her, made her grin, and Thorne plowed in, catching her next punch in his fist again and towing her in an arc. Her feet skidded on the stone before he slung her down on her back, planting his foot lightly on her belly. His eyes sparked, daring her to retaliate.

Cistine slammed her fist into the back of his knee, and he buckled over her with a cackle of shock, catching himself in a straddle with his hand beside her head. His girth blocked out the next fork of lightning further over the valley. His hair dripped rainwater down her cheek, and his quick, heavy breaths painted her face. Grazed her lips, even, as he bent over her.

His other hand was on her hip. She hadn't noticed he'd put it there to stop her from wedging her leg between them and pushing him off again.

She was flat on her back, chest heaving, throat cold with exertion, and Thorne braced himself over her, shielding her from the rain. His throat, too, pumped with labored breaths, and his eyes were wild from the fight.

But the fear, the devastation, had dissipated.

"You're ready," he said, and she could taste the words as close as his face was to hers.

"Am I?" she whispered.

Thorne's eyes dilated, scanning her from brows to lips. He sank his head in one slow nod. "For your battle armor."

He sat back on his heels, and Cistine scooted away, propping herself up with both hands.

"When we reach Veran, take your pick from the vendors in the House of Steel," Thorne said. "Let the cabal advise you on reinforcements, but choose whichever one appeals the most to what you need. Have your armor tailored while we're there."

Cistine pushed the rain-soaked hair from her brow and stood. Her muscles tingled in patches that would ache the next day, but for now she was exhilarated, carried on a wave of adrenaline so fierce it left a metallic taste in her mouth. "Is this how you wanted me to be before I went to Stornhaz?"

Thorne slowly climbed to his feet. "In a way. But ever since you told me to help you or stay out of your path, I realized that in fire, if not in muscle, you were already a match for my father...and I didn't want you to go at all. I didn't want to see what would happen if your fire and his ice collided."

"And now?"

"Now I know it doesn't matter what I want. I'm not here to tell you if you'll meet him in battle. My purpose is to make sure you're equipped, whatever choice you make. And judging by how you fought today..." he studied her for a moment, then smiled. "You're going to need that battle armor."

CHAPTER THIRTY-NINE

Cistine AND THORNE descended back into Starhollow well after dark, cold and soaked, entering the cottage to a sight that warmed better than the heat from the steaming pot-bellied stove.

Tatiana and Quill shared the reading nook, feet stacked, books in their laps; Baba Kallah, Helga, and Julian played cards at the table; Ariadne stirred a pot of rosemary and beans on the stove, with Faer on her shoulder intimately inspecting the contents. And Maleck...

Cistine suppressed laughter.

Maleck sat beside Baba Kallah, features chiseled from stone, holding absolutely still while Pippet braided the hair back from his brow in long twists and animatedly retold the story about Tazra—as if it was the most natural thing in the world to tell tales while braiding a death-god's hair.

Thorne cleared his throat and propped his soggy shoulder against the doorpost, grinning. "Almost finished, Maleck?"

"If you must know," he deadpanned, "we were about to pleat the daisies in."

Thorne rolled his hand in a generous bow. "Oh, then by all means. Beauty before all else, *allet.*"

"You would know," Tatiana jibed without glancing up from her book. "I remember when you used to take hours in front of the mirror."

"It's true," Baba Kallah cackled. "You were hopelessly infatuated with your own hair."

"Still hopeless," Ariadne and Quill chorused.

"But no longer infatuated, thanks to my father." Thorne went to the table and planted a kiss on Baba Kallah's cheek, then on Pippet's head. She wiggled away from him to pin the tiny daisies into Maleck's hair.

"Where were you two?" Julian asked without looking up from his cards.

"Training. I mean, patrol." Cistine glanced swiftly at Thorne, who didn't seem to share her pressing urge to qualify their time in the foothills. He joined Ariadne at the stove, helped himself to a ladle full of stew, and earned an elbow to the ribs for it.

"Quill's not patrolling tomorrow," Pippet announced without looking up from her task. "We're going to swim and then he's going to help me write Tazra's story for the children."

Helga glanced up, smiling at the offering of peace between the siblings. But Thorne said quietly, "Tomorrow, we leave."

A hush blanketed the room. Thorne's back heaved in a silent, heavy sigh, and now Cistine understood why he'd needed to escape Starhollow. What had finally brought all his fears simmering to the surface.

Pippet's hand fell to Maleck's shoulder, and he reached back and squeezed it.

"Right." Quill's voice, like his face, was stony. "Duty calls."

Thorne turned to face him, propping his haunches against the edge of the stove. "You know I wouldn't pull you away if it didn't."

"Already?" Pippet whispered. "Again?"

"Oh, Pip." Tatiana got up from the nook and wrapped an arm around the girl's shoulders. "We'll be back before you have time to miss us."

"But I always miss you!" Pippet's voice shattered with tears. "All of you."

"How about if I bring you something from Veran?" Quill offered. "Something to make up for it."

"A storybook?"

Cistine fought back a smile.

"Better," Quill said. "I'll bring you two."

Pippet sighed. "I suppose so…"

Maleck tapped the back of her hand. "I'll keep Tazra with me so she can see all the splendors Veran has to offer. Then you can decide if it's better than Cistine's Wild Islands."

The girl threaded her arms around Maleck's neck from behind and leaned her weight against him. "I'd rather Tazra stayed and *I* went. But I want to hear all about her adventures when you come back."

"We won't be gone long," Thorne assured them while Ariadne ladled the stew. "And if we return with what we need, we might be able to start looking toward a future where no one has to be left behind anymore."

Pippet and Quill straightened, swapping wide-eyed glances.

"Do you really mean that?" Pippet breathed.

Thorne nodded. "But that hinges on our success in Veran. It means we *have to* go."

Pippet nodded vigorously this time. "All right. Then you should leave as soon as you can."

Quill flashed Thorne a grateful smile.

"Thank you." Cistine took the bowl of soup Thorne handed to her and perched on Julian's knees to eat. The first bite chased out the chill from her body, and one by one the rest of the cabal rose to retrieve their portions.

"It's time I left as well," Baba Kallah said, and Helga made a strangled sound of distress. "Oh, I know, *malatanda*. It's been too terribly short of a time, but Hellidom needs its matron."

"Not as much as *I* need you," Thorne teased, setting the next bowl before her. "I don't suppose you'd travel to Veran with us."

"These bones only have so many journeys by horseback left in them, *Stornjor*. Best not to risk being stranded in Veran when this leg decides to quit."

"When will I see you again?" Helga asked.

Baba Kallah laid down her cards and reached out to take her friend's hand. "When the four wayfinding stars rise to light the way for the traveler bold enough to seek. You know you'll always find me then."

Helga's eyes filled with tears, her only reply a kiss to Baba Kallah's gnarled knuckles.

Dinner passed in silence after that; no one had the heart to remark on Maleck's hair, or the silent tears on Helga's cheeks, or the fact that both Thorne and Cistine were bruised and moving stiffly when they gathered the dishes and brought them to the kitchen. Helga simply pressed a bottle of tincture into Cistine's hand after they washed and stacked everything.

"For the pain tomorrow," she said with a knowing smile, and Cistine thought that kind gesture was the end of the day's surprises.

But it wasn't.

In her dreams, she returned to that craggy mountain shelf. In the valley below, the courthouse of Stornhaz broke up the soil at the heart of Starhollow, crushing the paddocks, the trees, even the cottage. Up above the great spires and domes, Cistine and Thorne wrestled for sanity and strength again, until he flipped her and pinned her to the stone.

Everything was the same—the storm, the hand on her hip, his face blotting out the light as he bent over her and lowered his head.

Except that this time...

This time, he kissed her.

THE
VESSEL

OF

CUNNING AND DESPAIR

CHAPTER FORTY

THE BITTER WIND of churning horse hooves kicked hot grit into Ashe's eyes. She squinted over the dark fabric shielding her nose and mouth toward the turn coming up again, that gods-forsaken corner where she *always* lost control...

"Bank, Ashe!" Sander shouted. "Tuck the reins and give the whip to the outside horse!"

Gritting her teeth, she did as ordered. The horses strained in their harness and swung wide into the turn, carving a rut in the sand that would've catapulted her into other fighters close by in a true race. Ashe cursed as they rounded the bend.

"Slow them," Sander bellowed. "Now! Slow them down!"

She curbed the slack on the reins and the foaming horses eased from a dead gallop to a hasty trot. Sander's servants rushed forward to subdue them by their bridles, bringing the chariot to a halt.

"How was that?" Ashe demanded as Sander hurried to join them, sunlight licking his robes the same green-and-blue as the oasis behind him.

"Better. One might even say impressive, given it's only your second time without Aftan in the chariot with you."

Ashe threw an appreciative smirk toward the elderly charioteer who calmed the horses with sugar cubes. He'd once been a fighter in Siralek himself, sponsored by Sander's father and trained to legendary heights of chariot racing that eventually won him his freedom and a position in the family household. For weeks now, he'd taught those same lessons to Ashe on Siralek's outskirts, and though it was a skill she'd never use again once Valgard was at her back, at least she was finally acclimating to it.

"I want to try that turn again," she told Aftan when he went to unclip the horses.

"Don't you think you've had enough?" That casual voice, not Sander's or Aftan's, but laced with icy contempt...

Groaning, Ashe swung around to face Aden. "They let creatures like you out of the Blood Hive?"

"Not unaccompanied." He leaned against a tree at the oasis edge, crunching casually into one of its fruits. "The guards are somewhere behind me. I was just on my way to meet with my sponsor."

Ashe glanced at Sander, but he did his best to pretend Aden was a mirage, keeping his back to the Lord of the Hive while he chatted with Aftan. Whatever was between these two men, she wanted no part of it. "If you're looking for your sponsor, you came to the wrong place. Keep looking."

"She has yet to arrive," Aden drawled. "I thought I'd see what activities have kept the Hive's latest novelty so occupied these last few weeks."

He knew precisely why she'd shirked their running sessions and slept so often straight through combat training. There was no real reason he should be looking in on her. "Well, now you've seen. So if you'll excuse me, it's time for another lap."

Aden shoved off the tree and joined them, smoothing his hand down one horse's powerful haunch. "How is your control, I wonder?"

She gestured at the chariot bed. "There's room for you to find out."

"Ashe..." Sander warned.

Aden seized the lip of the brass-colored wood and swung up beside her, shoulder knocking into hers. "Let's see what sort of a charioteer you are."

Ashe snapped the reins and set the horses trotting, and Sander towed Aftan away.

They took the first turn slowly, as Aftan had instructed, letting the horses ease into the pace. But in the first long stretch around the oasis, Ashe snapped the reins, setting their hooves pounding on the familiar track. Stones flew from beneath the wheels, jouncing Ashe and Aden upward, their boots leaving the cart for seconds at a time. Aden laughed, a powerful, ruthless sound kicked from him by the adrenaline of the steady gallop and the occasional jolt of tension, and spread his arms—one hand on the chariot's front curve, the other behind Ashe, bracing her body.

The next leap sent her slamming backward into his hold, hands tight around the reins as she fought the momentum. They neared the second turn, and she readied the whip.

"Don't," Aden said. "Let the horses navigate the curve themselves."

"Aftan told me—"

"I know what the old man said." Aden's head sank, his chin nearly grazing her shoulder as he peered ahead. "Do as *I* say. Give them their heads."

Ashe wasn't certain she trusted him about this, but with the curve closing in it was too late to turn them her way. So she gave the reins slack and let the whip fall.

The horses stretched their necks into the bits and charged at the turn. Aden arched forward, his shoulder pressing into Ashe's back, fastening her in place as the chariot swooped to the left, wheels lifting and skidding, tipping the entire cart precariously to one side. Ashe chanted a prayer against the moist cloth around her mouth as the chariot teetered, wobbled...

And slammed back down. They skirted the oasis's outside edge, tossing sand into Ashe's face until she choked on it, and flew through the second open stretch where Sander and Aftan ran alongside them, ordering them to slow the horses.

For a moment, fingers dancing on the reins, Ashe wondered.

What if they didn't stop? What if they ran the horses deep into the desert, abandoned the chariot, and rode barebacked all the way to freedom?

She looked up at Aden. He leaned back on his heels, watching her.

The horses slowed at Aftan's whistle, the moment lost. Ashe's arms slackened, Aden hopped from the cart before it stopped, and Sander strode up to join them, his face a sandstorm of fury. "I think that's enough for the day. I'll have the guards escort you back."

"*My* guards can see to her." Aden motioned Ashe to follow him, and because she preferred his company over the annoyance in Sander's eyes, she went.

"How did you learn to race?" she asked when they were out of earshot.

"Not with chariots, but Maleck and I used to race the roads of Stornhaz. You learn to allow your beast, whatever its nature, to navigate the turns smoothly. If you fight the curve, you only create trouble for yourself."

Once they passed through the oasis, the guards from the Hive fell into step behind them, quiet as shadows. Ashe tried to ignore them as she pulled a small hanging fruit from a fronded tree and bit into it. The sweet nectar made her mouth hurt, but at least it wasn't poisoned by Tyve's Tribune.

Neither spoke until they were among the pale structures of Siralek's wealthy guests. Then Aden slowed and Ashe matched her stride to his. "For both our sakes, I hope you're getting closer to unraveling the Tumult's plans. The whispers about Thorne have nearly halted altogether, and that concerns me."

Ashe grimaced. That was her doing: she'd finally convinced Nimea to keep mention of Thorne between them, and only in the tunnels. She couldn't afford to have Aden overhear things and grow more suspicious. Not when she was doing...whatever she was doing with the Tumult.

She really couldn't define it anymore—all the clandestine meetings, all the talk of who would go next if Kalman failed, all the conjectures, even the bets about which of the cabal would die first defending their precious High Tribune. Whenever those conversations arose, Ashe tried not to think of Pippet and Helga mourning Quill or Baba Kallah's face when she took word of Thorne's death.

They were all Valgardans. It shouldn't matter.

"I think I may be close to dragging the truth from her," she lied quickly, changing the subject. "Do you plan to have supper with me again tonight?"

"I'm afraid I won't return in time for that." Aden stopped in the middle of the road, and she turned to face him. His gaze was fixed on the house to his left, a glint of regret in his face. "But you're welcome to dine in my chamber alone if you prefer. Certainly better than the mess hall."

That was true, even if Ashe would be better off eating with Nimea to keep up appearances. She didn't really know who she was trying to fool anymore; she lied to everyone these days. Even herself.

"The chariot match is in three days," she said. "At least try to be available for *that*."

Aden smirked, turning his eyes back to her. "After today's display? I wouldn't miss it for all of Valgard."

CHAPTER
FORTY-ONE

THE JOURNEY TO Veran proved manageable despite the frequent autumn storms, the mood full of hope for everyone except Cistine, who couldn't chase off her dream from the night before they left no matter how hard she tried. She avoided Thorne's gaze and recoiled with guilt at Julian's touches, feeling like a traitor in the depths of her heart to him, to his affections, and to herself.

In the thick darkness of the passes each night, while one of the cabal stood watch and Cistine tried to sleep, she reminded herself she was a princess, true to her vows, not fickle of heart; she was loyal to Julian, and not about to be swayed by a dream.

No matter how many times it recurred.

It wasn't until they reached the paths above Veran that she finally shed the embarrassment, guilt, and detestable intrigue of that dream and focused on what she was here to do. What lay in the balance had nothing to do with courtships and suitors; and that duty was *all* she could think of, with skin prickling and bowels in a riot, while they navigated the horses down a long path toward the great expanse of the Agerios Sea, the three Houses—Aliment, Steel, and Wonder—and the winding streets of the city that was its own territory under The Loom.

Maleck checked his mount's stride to match hers. He had a light, easy touch on the reins, not hacking the bit the way Cistine wanted to when facing the steep slope before them. "Something's been troubling you since we left Starhollow."

Cistine thinned her lips. "I'm worried about the meeting."

"You'll do fine!" Quill, breezy and arrogant, enclosed her from the rear. "It's not you who has to prove yourself, it's Thorne, really. This is his scheme, after all."

"But I have to show them Talheim is worth standing beside. This won't *end* with Salvotor being unseated, that's only where it begins for me."

Quill scratched his jaw, frowning. "True."

"What's more," Maleck added, "they know Thorne well enough to have stood at his back thus far. But Cistine...what do they know of her?"

Ariadne rode up on Cistine's other side, peering down into the city. "If they knew as much as we do, who would need a meeting?"

Warmed by his trust, Cistine looked down the slope into the steep avenues, winding falls, and gondola channels of Veran. When she focused on those narrow whips of water where the gondoliers ferried merches and townspeople from one House to the other, heat sprang to her eyes.

How had it been *months* since she and Julian and Ashe had been here? Her Warden, so eager to explore the House of Steel, shopping for clothing and jewelry for hours at Cistine's behest; opening Cistine's eyes to her own naivety, which had given way to recklessness, leading her to meet Quill...

Her hands fisted the reins and her thighs gripped her horse's barreled sides tightly. The creature balked, sliding to a halt with hooves planted where the ground evened out, and Julian's mount stopped abreast of hers. He took her chilly hand in his warm one. "Princess, what's wrong?"

For the first time since they left Starhollow, she clung to his fingers. He squeezed back, confusion stark in his night-dark eyes, compassion framing his mouth. "Ashe would have loved to come back here. I didn't go with her to the House of Steel, but I would have this time, for as long as she wanted."

Julian's hand slid from hers so sharply, Cistine blinked away her tears and looked at him. He wasn't gazing at her, but at the city. And he said nothing about her sadness—or about the secret thoughts she could see, plain as anything, lurking in his eyes.

❧

"Patrol." Thorne's voice drew Cistine from her memories of Ashe and her nervousness about Julian's sudden distance the moment they entered Veran's cluttered avenues. "Ariadne, your eyes are on the streets. Maleck, above. Quill and Tatiana, you'll trade with them at sundown."

"I have something I need to look into," Julian said. "Spare me for tonight?"

If he was being petulant, Thorne didn't take the bait; he nodded him away, and Julian kissed Cistine's brow before slipping into the foot traffic filling the street. Maleck and Ariadne hurried after him, Quill and Tatiana taking the lead together, which left Cistine little choice but to walk beside Thorne.

Mercifully, he didn't mention how she'd avoided him through the mountains. His eyes roved the street for any hint of trouble, and she tried to imitate him, though curiosity slowly burned away her awkwardness. Finally, she blurted out, "Where are we going?"

"To an inn my contacts mentioned in the letter, though I've never heard of the place before."

"Does that make you nervous?"

Thorne glanced down at her. "To not be in control of the where and when? Yes. But concessions must be made, that's why it's called a negotiation. Our allies may be testing us to see how far our trust extends."

"Clever of them."

"Clever is what we need."

They rounded a steep grade in the street, and Thorne halted. Though his mouth didn't gape as Cistine's did, shock peaked his brows and widened his eyes.

A sprawling inn lay before them, walkways on the first two levels cordoned in by lace-thin railings and posts almost too slim to support the weight of the sloped blue roof; not to mention the third story, with its half-moon balconies accessible through draped openings overlooking the street on the building's front and the city and sea on its back. The open corner turret hummed with the chatter of occupants at white-iron tables. Flags bearing the symbol of Kanslar flapped from the spired rooftops.

"Well, stars," Tatiana cursed under her breath.

Quill whistled. "I don't think I've stayed anywhere this impressive since Stornhaz."

"Something to be said for clever, *wealthy* allies," Thorne said wryly, leading them into the parlor full of small, intimate two-person seating arrangements clustered by low-burning hearths. Thorne made his way directly to a recess where the innkeeper abided, and Cistine fidgeted by the door, feeling horrifically underdressed in her filthy training armor. She muttered a plea for civility to Quill, who helped himself to a handful of peanuts from a bowl and then swiped the entire dish from the table when Thorne returned.

"Our allies purchased us an upper suite," Thorne announced.

"How do you know it's for us?" Cistine asked.

"Because it's under Faer's name."

Three levels of stairs ended in a long, cozy hallway lined with doors on the uppermost floor. Thorne unlatched the last lock on the left and led them into a broad parlor framed with small sleeping alcoves behind whitewood arches and ivory-and-scarlet curtains. In the room's dead center, a table with a bowl of fruit and a pitcher of drink awaited them. Steps led down from behind it to a span of couches and chairs all cramped together, hearths burning on opposite walls. Three open arches, strung with lavender veils, separated the parlor from the balcony.

Cistine dashed past the table, took the steps in one lunge, and ducked outside to see the city from above.

The pocket of the Agerios lay as dark as the encroaching sunset along the horizon. The stars blinked open like feline eyes above it, their lazy glow joining the crescent moon's light; yet Veran still respired in light and music, and Cistine's heart rubbed against her ribs at these familiar sights and sounds. This balcony, and the room behind her, were more like Astoria than anywhere she'd set foot since Talheim.

"A city that never sleeps." Thorne's quiet voice brought her around on heel. He leaned against the middle arch, arms folded, watching her. When their eyes met, he smiled and joined her at the railing. "What do you think of this place?"

Cistine cleared the thickness from her throat. "Well, your allies are certainly generous."

"I believe that's a good sign. They wouldn't waste the mynts if they didn't think we were worth it."

"Or else they think your favor can be bought."

Thorne laughed. "Now you're truly thinking like a queen."

Cistine shivered at the praise. She needed to be that, as well as a diplomat and an ally to Valgard, if she was going to sway the favor of Yager and Traisende Courts. Thorne had prepared her as much as he could, but it all rested with her now; Talheim's future cradled in her shaky hands.

"The meeting isn't for another two days," Thorne continued. "If you want to find your battle armor, now would be the time. I recommend bringing Maleck or Ariadne with you. They're the most familiar with the different reinforcements and how they interact with augments."

Cistine shot him a shrewd glance. "Are you assuming I'll learn to use augments?"

"I'm assuming that when we cross paths with Salvotor again, you'll want armor well-made enough to divert *his*."

"You can do that? Channel an enemy's augment?"

"If you're sharp enough to catch it at the right angle when it's flung at you. It can take years to master, though some have more talent for it than others."

Before Cistine could ask whether he thought *she* possessed some scrap of that talent, a fight broke out in the parlor—Quill and Tatiana mock-battling over the best alcove. With a long-suffering sigh, Thorne stalked inside to put their argument to rest, and Cistine leaned against the railing again, fretting quietly about what two days from now would bring.

Some hours passed before she went indoors, ignoring her friends at the table in favor of a private alcove. Its rounded recess, with a simple bedside shelf and luxurious mattress, turned cozy once she fanned the concealing drape into place. She changed into the pair of freshly-washed bedclothes left on the pillow, which swallowed her completely in their large folds, and climbed under the covers.

She swiftly drifted to the verge of dreams, a shadowy place where Maleck and Ariadne arrived in a flurry of whispers, traded places with Quill and Tatiana, and vanished into their own alcoves. She floated off to a cliff face, to a rock outcropping—

To a hand on her shoulder, and a voice, urgent in the dark. "*Princess.*"

Cistine bolted awake, scrambling upright so quickly she forced Julian away. He loomed beside the bed, profile silhouetted by the light of a single ghostlamp on the parlor table. He smelled sweet and sticky, like sweat and fruit. But it hadn't been warm in the city, nor could she fathom why he smelled that way; or why he was trembling when he sat on her bed.

"Where have you been?" she whispered. "What time is it?"

"The middle of the night...almost morning, I don't know. I don't care. Princess, I need to ask you something."

Cistine tried not to growl at him as she wiped the blurriness from her eyes. Her forehead throbbed and her face itched with exhaustion.

"I don't know how...gods, I didn't think it would happen this way," Julian mumbled almost to himself. "This *soon.*" He ran a trembling hand through his hair. "I was going to wait. Give it a few more months, a proper courtship in Talheim like we talked about, but...after I saw how you felt about being back in this city, I thought, why not now? Why not bring some light into one of the darkest times of our lives?"

Cistine took his wrists. "Julian, tell me what's wrong."

He swiveled to face her—slid off the bed and onto one knee, turning his hands so they now gripped hers. But then he released one and pulled a small, circular object from his pocket, its metal glittering in the dimness.

"Princess." Julian cleared his throat. "Cistine. Would you...do you think you'd consider becoming my wife?"

CHAPTER
FORTY-TWO

CISTINE STARED UNSPEAKING at Julian's earnest face, his bright pink ears, his trembling mouth—and the tiny circlet he held out to her, its gold band tipped with a pink stone carved into an open rose, as lovely as the first rays of sunrise over Starhollow. And as unexpected as jamming her foot into her boot and discovering a snake inside.

"Princess?" Julian prompted. "You should breathe."

Cistine sucked in air so fast she squeaked and pressed a hand to her mouth. "I didn't think you...I didn't expect...*Julian!*"

He chuckled nervously. "I know! Neither did I. I went for a walk just to clear my head at first, but then I saw this ring and I realized how perfect it was. Delicate and beautiful and just...perfect, like you. That's when I knew I had to do this. I had to ask you to marry me."

And now he had. Why was she hesitating? Why did her mind scramble for an answer when it should've been so simple? It was *Julian*. She had daydreamed of this moment since she was thirteen years old.

But could she really trust her dreams anymore?

Cistine slammed the thought away. She'd committed herself to being with him; she was only hesitating because she was exhausted, distracted. That was the *only* reason she'd kept him on his knee this long.

She didn't need a Talheimic courtship ritual to prove where her loyalties lay. She'd made her decision.

Cistine swept her hair from her face and bent forward. "Julian, of course I'll be your bride. Nothing would make me happier."

When he smiled, his face radiant like the sun, Cistine believed it was true. He slid the ring onto her finger and scooped her off the bed in an embrace, and she laughed, gripping his hair with one hand, stretching out the other to admire the betrothal ring behind his back.

She had made a vow to Julian. Queens did not renege on their word.

For the next two days, no assassins, no Vassoran presence, no contention or grief of any kind distracted Cistine from the upcoming meeting. Or from the ring on her finger.

When she wasn't shopping in the House of Wonders for an ensemble that would, she hoped, make her presentable before the Courts, Julian stayed with her, stroking his thumb over that ring, admiring it with an endless smirk. None of the cabal asked about it; to them, it was simply a piece of jewelry.

Cistine didn't know why she hadn't told them otherwise.

Their second day in Veran dawned bleak, a coastal storm rolling thick into the harbor. While Cistine finished picking listlessly at her breakfast of cherries and fresh bread, Quill burst in from watch, startling her upright at the table. His clothes were damp, eyes shrouded with intensity.

"They're here," he announced, "and they want you to meet them somewhere else."

Thorne swung up from his bed, face stormy. "Where?"

"A tavern, the *Black Mirror*, back room."

Thorne towed a hand through his hair. "They're keeping us unsteady, not letting us become familiar with our surroundings before we meet."

"Testing us again?" Cistine asked.

"Most likely. Do you have what you need?"

She patted the closed satchel at her feet. "I'm ready."

Julian came up the steps from the seating area, hands in his pockets. "We're leaving?"

"*You* aren't," Quill said. "Thorne and his accomplice, that's all they'll meet with."

Julian's teeth clicked together. "No."

Tiredly, Cistine said, "It isn't your choice, Julian. They agreed to meet with us. If it's only on their terms, so be it."

"It could be a trap, Princess. A way to separate you from us and take you back to Salvotor in chains."

Cistine searched Thorne's face for any truth to that rumor. He shrugged slightly—allowing for the possibility, but doing nothing to dissuade her.

It was jarring how simply the words came from her lips, "I'm still going. We'll be all right."

Julian shot a murderous glance toward the wall. When Cistine stretched up to kiss his cheek and whisper a farewell in his ear, he didn't even look at her. It stung, particularly after two days of bliss, but she did her best to brush that aside when she followed Thorne from the inn, out into the chilly, foggy morning.

The narrow streets folded between the buildings, where Veran's smells hugged their clothes: oil and brine and fish at war with perfumes and fragrant mists. Cistine lengthened her stride to match Thorne's and swallowed against the pounding of her heart once they left the House of Aliment and neared the House of Wonders. The light that paved the cobblestones in broad, jagged dapples changed color, the smells richened with cooking fat and mead, and in that glow and scent there came a subtle shift in Thorne. His head rose and his shoulders rolled back, his stride turning to a casual swagger one beat away from hands sliding into pockets. He looked more the High Tribune now than the man who'd been on the run for ten years.

They halted outside one tavern among the many, and Thorne pointed to a covered wagon at the curbside. "This may be your only chance to change."

Cistine climbed inside without hesitation, stumbling on the furs in the footwell. If she paused to think about what she was doing and the role she would fulfill today, she would grow faint. She couldn't afford that today.

It was for Talheim that she stripped off her training armor, banded herself with boning, and struggled into the dress. For her people that she swept up her hair from her neck and tamed it with an ornate butterfly clip. For her family that she slid on the flat shoes rather than her boots and rolled all her armor up into her satchel.

Her hands stopped shaking when she emerged onto the wagon's raised step. Puddles of last night's rain gathered in the dip between cobblestones, and in their reflection, she adjusted her bodice. The material cut jaggedly in the shape of crisp autumn leaves to match the sleeves joining the fabric at the back, hiding the lingering bruises on her shoulders. The wine-red folds clung somewhat to the curves of her developing muscles but flowed elegantly from waist to mid-calf.

Practical, to some extent, if they needed to run. Commanding enough, in color and cut, for her to be taken seriously.

Cistine swung down from the wagon's step, holding her skirts clear of the puddles. "I'm ready."

Thorne, who reclined on watch against the cart, swiveled his head and blinked, scouting her with a long look that made her feel shy all over again. She smoothed out the waist and tried not to draw too much attention to the bodice.

"Perfect." He offered his arm, and together they entered the tavern.

The interior assaulted Cistine's senses with sound, sight and scent, all a sharp reminder her last time in Veran. She tried not to think of how much skin she exposed as they reached the counter. Several barmaids perked up when Thorne leaned his powerful forearms on the rutted wood. "I have an appointment. Someone should have come ahead of me to commandeer your back room."

The keeper swabbed out the inside of a stein, his hooded eyes raking Thorne with much less interest than his barmaids. "How do I know it's you they're here to meet with?"

Thorne tipped his head. "Do you know of many other silver-haired young men named Faer?"

Cistine hid a smile as the man's lip curled. He nodded to a dark doorway on their left, disguised behind leather cords. "Through there. Take the steps down. We'll keep your woman company in your absence."

"I choose my company for myself, thank you." Cistine snatched Thorne's arm and towed him toward the doorway this time.

"Feeling tense?" he teased while they elbowed through the crowd.

"I don't like taverns."

"I know." He was suddenly serious, hand hovering above the small of her back when they ducked through the tendrils. "I'd hate to think our allies know that as well, but we can't take any coincidence for granted."

A draft of cool air guided them down the short set of wooden steps and into a long corridor Cistine assumed ran beneath the street. She shivered at the notion of a dozen taverns stacked directly above their heads, her thoughts spiraling to caved-in roof beams and bloated corpses and the taste of death in a shattered home.

Thorne took her hand and slowed their progress. "Nothing is going to happen to us. As much as they're testing us, these are still our allies."

Cistine heaved in a slow, steadying breath—and laced her fingers with his. "I know. It's not them, it's this tunnel."

Thorne eyed the ridge of ghostlamps glowing above their heads. "If your luck is frail enough that this could all come crashing down on us, I might be better off going on alone."

She socked him in the ribs, pulling her blow at the last instant when she remembered his wound from the assassins. Smiling, they continued, passing through the tremulous light to the door at the hall's end. Thorne paused with his hand on it. "Remember what I told you about conduct."

Cistine smoothed her dress again. "Everything."

His smile glowed in the dimness, warming her from the inside out. "Hold your head high, Cistine. You are a born leader. Now show them what Talheimic royalty is made of."

He opened the door.

CHAPTER FORTY-THREE

THE MEETING PLACE was warm in most regards, high-walled, framed with candle niches and hearths. A long table dominated the center, surrounded in high-backed seats occupied by no less than eighteen men.

Yager and Traisende, gathered but not speaking to one another.

The Chancellors were easy to pick out from among the Tribunes—an older, pale man and a younger, dark one, dignified by their postures and frowning faces and their seats at one end of the table. The Tribunes around them varied in age and build and color, yet their eyes all had the same piercing intellect—like Thorne's, but colder. Cistine masked a shiver as Thorne shut the door.

Every head swiveled. It was difficult not to wilt under those stares, to remind herself she was a *princess*, by no means their inferior.

Cistine raised her chin and gripped her wrist in her other hand at the small of her back, meeting each pair of eyes steadily—imitating Ariadne's cool, unrevealing stare while the two Courts measured the man and woman who'd called them here.

Finally, the older Chancellor said, "You're late, Thorne."

He inclined his head. "Forgive me, Chancellor Bravis. It's difficult to move swiftly through city streets when the Court in session is hunting your head."

"Yes, your ongoing feud with your father." Bravis had a pensive, bearded face full of crags that vanished into his thick umber mustache. "And who is your lovely consort?"

When Thorne tensed, Cistine replied, "I'm as much the reason you're here as he is."

"Truly."

"You've been Sillakove's allies these ten years," Thorne interjected. "Given us aid, helped us evade my father's watch. You would never have risked this journey if you weren't curious what's changed. Will you hear us now?"

Bravis glanced across the table at a dark-skinned Chancellor who watched the proceedings in silence. They conferred with no more than a glance; then Bravis sighed. "Sit."

They took the chairs at the table's opposite end, Cistine's belly fizzing with anxious energy. Thorne gestured to the Chancellors in turn.

"Chancellor Bravis, head of Traisende Court. Chancellor Maltadova of Yager."

"We know your name, Thorne," Bravis said. "But your companion…"

"My name is Cistine," she supplied. "*Princess* Cistine Novacek of Talheim."

Maltadova's heavy brow lowered further. His men gazed at Cistine with ravenous intensity, and if she hadn't been clutching every inch of her composure, furiously aware of how her hands and feet were placed, how straight her spine was, she would've squirmed.

As it was, she still shifted slightly. So did Thorne, brushing arms in their close-fitting seats.

"Talheim," Bravis mused. "Your father and his people were told never to return after the truce went into effect."

"I'm aware. And Talheim honors its promises, so you understand I wouldn't be here if it wasn't under dire circumstances."

"Talheim's circumstances, dire or not, are no concern of the Northern Kingdom's."

"They're of concern to Kanslar," Thorne said. "Especially when the most prominent daughter of Talheim is risking her life and reputation to help unseat my father."

Maltadova sat back slowly in his chair. Bravis frowned. "Are you really?"

Cistine bobbed her head. "Chancellor Salvotor is a threat to us all. Thorne has informed me of his intentions with the other Courts and how he's managed to infiltrate them. I doubt his hunger for conquest will be sated once he has absolute power in Valgard." She considered a moment before adding, "I admire the strength of your Courts...particularly you yourselves, Chancellors. To have not only resisted his advances, but to have been clever enough to root out his spies thus far is a testament to your cunning."

Bravis smiled coolly, but Maltadova's eyes narrowed in suspicion of empty flattery. He remained silent when Bravis said, "Salvotor is neither as astute nor as circumspect as he thinks himself. It's been simple so far to smell his spies and traitors among Traisende's courtlings."

"But he'll never stop searching for ways to outwit you," Thorne said. "He covets your Courts desperately."

"Why?" Maltadova spoke for the first time, his voice unnervingly sharp.

Though her hands shook so badly she had to press them to her thighs, Cistine forced herself to hold his gaze. "He wants to unite you all under a single name, then march against Talheim to find the Key."

Bravis smoothed a hand over his mouth. Maltadova's eyes darkened. "The Key to the Doors is only a myth."

"It's real," Thorne said. "Confirmed by the *visnprests* who were present at its forging. My father knows this—and he knows Talheim safeguards it. So does Bravis."

Maltadova's eyes snapped to the other Chancellor, who shrugged. "It was before you took the Judgement Seat."

"Salvotor is advancing," Cistine said. "And if he manages to capture me as ransom and unite the Courts, he'll force all of you to war against *my* kingdom with my imprisonment as leverage against my father."

Maltadova shook his head. "I fought in the last war. That is not a fight we will win."

"Not without great loss of life, anyway," Bravis said. "And my life, I'm rather fond of. All right, Thorne. What is it you need?"

"We all know I can't make public accusation against my father," Thorne said. "But you can. If you challenge his right to sit in the Judgement Seat, it may be the first step toward diverting conflict."

"And what are we to challenge him on?" Bravis asked. "His dealings so far have been clandestine, and none of his spies have agreed to testify before they've come up mysteriously dead. He's a madman, but undoubtedly a clever one."

Cistine brushed her thumb over her healed knuckles. "What about the things he's done to his body? The reinforcements in his skin?"

Bravis stiffened. "I beg your pardon?"

Thorne rapidly explained the armored state of his father's flesh, setting off a storm of tense murmurs among the Tribunes and Chancellors alike.

"Of all the arrogant, dangerous..." Maltadova struck the arm of his chair. "We knew he'd done something to his face, but *this*...how is this possible?"

"Experiment after experiment. You know my father is fond of those."

Bravis slouched, resting his elbow on the chair and draping his long fingers against his mouth. "I can see what he's thinking. Make himself invulnerable, then take control of *our* Courts by force."

"And control the augments," Cistine added. "That's what this is about. Finding the Key and opening the Doors to obtain absolute power over all augmentation."

"I can't fault him for that. Any one of us would do the same if we found that Key." Cistine leaned forward to argue, pulse thudding in her wrists, and Thorne brushed his fingers down her arm—an unspoken warning to hold her composure. "But the Courts, that he thinks he can take us by *force*..."

Maltadova scowled. "Sheer arrogance. It cannot be tolerated."

"Then stand against him," Thorne urged. "Make a public case to strip his title. Without the influence he holds at the head of Kanslar, his dreams of conquest die."

"With or without his title, Salvotor is still a threat," Bravis warned. "If he took word of his disbarment as a call to arms, with those reinforcements under his skin…"

Thorne's face was firm, his tone unyielding. "Leave him to me."

The fire guttered, painting the walls with long fingers of dancing light.

"And what does Talheim offer in this affair?" Maltadova asked.

"First, and perhaps most important to all of you," Cistine said, "we won't hold Valgard responsible for Salvotor's attempt to use me as ransom against my kingdom."

Bravis froze. Thorne reclined slightly in his seat.

"In addition, I'm prepared to overlook any notions of Valgard uniting its Courts and going to war against Talheim for the Key," Cistine added. "We'll call it unfounded hearsay."

"Our Courts have not even spoken of this matter," Maltadova warned.

"Yours haven't," Thorne said, "but the ones my father has sway in, you can trust *they* have."

"So, given all that…" Cistine spread her hands on the table. "I'm prepared to offer an alliance. Not just a tenuous truce, but a real treaty between the Northern and Middle Kingdoms that will reverse Salvotor's plans for war. I'll help you remove him from power, and in exchange Kanslar Court has already agreed to stand behind Talheim against King Jad and the Southern Kingdom of Mahasar."

Bravis scoffed. "Promising the power of your old Court to another kingdom while you're still in exile? I see arrogance is hereditary, Thorne."

"I'm not being arrogant," Thorne retorted. "You know the High Tribune's title is still mine, no matter how badly my father hoped to bury that inconvenience. It's why you've put support behind me in the wilds."

"Then we remove Salvotor," Maltadova murmured, "and you return to your place."

"Where I remove my father's infestation from the other Courts and return power to its rightful hands," Thorne nodded. "And then offer Talheim my full support as Chancellor."

Stomach fluttering with delight, Cistine smiled at Thorne. He didn't return her glance, but his jaw ticked, fighting a smirk as Bravis and

Maltadova exchanged a heavy glance.

"You all know how and why the Courts were created," Thorne said— and he went on, Cistine thought, for her benefit rather than theirs, "when the last of the Elder Kings turned tyrant, the territories each selected a tribe to infiltrate Stornhaz, to bring the King to his knees."

"Yes, and the five tribes who survived became the five Courts, and their leaders became Chancellors." Bravis rolled his hand. "Your point?"

"Consider that: the tyrant King. The Courts defying him."

The room hushed for a moment.

"That's what Salvotor will do," Cistine said. "He's making himself King. When will your tribes rise up and defy him?"

No one at the table had an answer, each man prompting the others to respond through nervous glares.

It was Thorne who broke the awkward silence. "The tribunals were created to give a voice to the people if the Chancellors ever became too much like kings ruling with iron fists. My position exists to prevent my father from becoming too powerful. But a man can't destroy a king, or a Chancellor who *thinks* himself one, alone. I need your support. *We* need your aid."

Cistine's heart bloomed with pride; that was the concise, powerful statement of a leader regardless of exile; of a man with success resting just at the tips of his fingers.

And then Bravis said, "No."

Cistine's hope and eagerness guttered into shadow.

"No," Thorne echoed, his tone just as flat.

"Attacking Salvotor and trying to unseat him would be as dangerous as open war with Talheim. We risk exposing some sort of weakness in the courtroom and showing him we've helped you all these years. I know what your father did to you was gruesome, Thorne, and the future you're fighting for is better than his plans. But I can't make a public show of my feelings on the matter."

"I know you've already risked much, offering supplies and weapons to us," Thorne said carefully, "but that isn't enough if we want to end this conflict while we're all still alive to enjoy the peace that follows."

"If our aid isn't enough, then maybe you don't deserve even that."

"Bravis," Thorne insisted, "he has to be stopped."

"You mean you need him turned out to the cold, outside the protection of his Court."

"If that's what it takes."

The Chancellor shook his head and pushed back his seat. When he stood, so did his Tribunes. "I'm sorry. Sorry we *all* wasted our time coming here. You have nothing to offer us as a weapon against Salvotor, just like you haven't these last ten years. Talheim's offer of friendship isn't enough to stake my Court or my reputation against. But I won't unmask your whereabouts to your father, either. Consider *that* my mercy."

Maltadova rose as well. With a sinking heart, Cistine watched the two Courts file out; as quickly as they'd begun, the negotiations were over.

"What did we do?" she moaned. "Where did we go wrong?"

"Nowhere." Thorne's voice was as emotionless as his face. "They know the risk if they reveal their alliance with Sillakove. Bravis is thinking of his own Court, as he should."

"How can you be so calm about this? We needed someone who could get close to Salvotor—why aren't you furious with them?"

"Because," Thorne stood and offered his hand to her, "it's not over."

Too furious to be mystified, she stalked ahead of him all the way through the back avenues of Veran to the inn. Her brief hope for more allies, not only against Salvotor, but against Jad, slowly burned away.

She was still fuming when they reached the door to their room, where the entire cabal greeted them—though Maleck and Ariadne should have been guarding the streets outside.

The first indication something was wrong.

"We have company." Quill announced. "Half of them arrived after you two left, and the others just showed."

Cistine peered past him, her stomach dropping; for there, framing the parlor like it was theirs to command...

The envoy of Yager Court.

CHAPTER
FORTY-FOUR

Tʜᴇʀᴇ ᴡᴇʀᴇ ᴊᴜsᴛ as many women as men in the room, but the Yager courtlings outnumbered the cabal two against one. They were already weighing those odds: Maleck and Ariadne with their hands hovering at their backs, Quill with his fingers grooming the daggers on his hips, Tatiana unbuttoning the flagon case at her side, Julian drawing his sword.

With one word from Thorne or Maltadova, the parlor would explode into combat.

Cistine tightened her fists and sized up their opponents: all of them brown-skinned and long-limbed, every frame cut with solid muscle. If it came to a fight, regardless if Yager's courtlings held a flagon, it would be bloody. Most likely, people would die.

Then Thorne sauntered to the table, plopped down in one of the chairs, and flipped his heels up on its edge. "Still putting on airs, I see."

To Cistine's shock, it was a woman—Maltadova's age at least, dark braids trimmed in silver—who spoke: "You played your part well at the negotiation. I commend you for that."

Thorne's eyes were ice and shadow. "I swore an oath, didn't I? I'll keep your Court's secret always."

"And so you have. That is why we are here tonight."

"Thorne." Quill's voice remained cool, his gaze flicking across the men.

"What's going on here?"

"You're facing the true Yager Court tonight, *allet*."

And as the men inclined their heads and bowed backward, the women stepping forward to surround the table, Cistine finally understood; not only what Thorne meant, but his warning back in Hellidom that Yager would both test her and welcome her more than any other Court.

Test her, because she was a princess.

Welcome her because, like them, she was a woman in power.

Tatiana's jaw sprang open. "*How?*"

Their leader smiled a lioness' grin, sharp and confident. "We select for our *valenar* those with the keenest minds from all the schools of Stornhaz. They memorize the words spoken in meetings like the one your High Tribune hosted tonight, and they report to us."

"To the true Tribunes," Maleck murmured. "Yager Court is overseen by women?"

"It has been for decades, if not centuries." Thorne held out a hand to the eldest woman. "You're addressing Chancelloress Adeima, who took power when her predecessor fell in the war against Talheim."

"How long have *you* known about this?" Ariadne's brittle tone strove to hide shock.

"Since I was a boy. Aden joined with the wrong woman and the truth came out in the pillows."

"As it often does," Adeima sighed. "High Tribune Thorne has kept the secret of Yager Court for most of his life...a secret which has allowed us to root out his gutless father's attempts to overthrow our Court."

"Salvotor impresses himself on the men," Tatiana grinned. "But they're not the ones he should watch out for."

"No. They are not." Adeima snapped her fingers, and three slender bodies brushed aside the curtains to the balcony and stepped into the parlor—archers in dark, close-fitting hoods and mouth coverings, with bows primed but arrows aimed at the floor.

A quiet snarl ripped from Quill's chest. He flung an arm in front of Tatiana as she tensed and settled back on her heels.

"Peace," Adeima said to them. "We didn't come to threaten any of you, least of all your women. In fact, it's for a woman that we've come." Her eyes lit on Cistine, whose heart staggered in her chest. That stare was flint and spark and flame all at once, setting intrigue coursing through her.

The men drew out the chairs for the Tribunes, and as they all sat, the archers slung their bows over their shoulders and dragged down the cloths that masked their faces. Cistine clapped her hands over her mouth, and Julian swore.

"Liv?" Cistine said between her fingers. "Astrid? *Ingrid?*"

"Aren't you surprised?" Astrid laughed. "You must've thought we were such plain, silly courtlings back in Stornhaz."

A nervous laugh escaped Cistine. "Well, I didn't want to insult your intelligence. All those questions you asked me back then, about Thorne...you already knew him!"

"We didn't know precisely what he was doing," Liv admitted. "Communications had been scarce for months. But capturing women and holding them against their will just didn't seem like him. We had to know the truth to report back to our Chancelloress."

"*Thank you,*" Cistine said. "What you told me before I went into the courthouse saved my life."

"Yes, and we're all eternally grateful for *that*," Tatiana scowled. "But why are you here tonight?"

"I came to meet her for myself," Adeima said. "The woman my *valenar* claims is the Princess of Talheim."

Every shrewd eye from Yager Court fixed on Cistine, and heat flushed through her body again from scalp to soles. Maleck stepped up to one side of her, Quill to the other, hands still casually braced on their weapons. Ariadne and Julian flanked them. But Cistine knew what Adeima's piercing gaze searched for: a princess cowering behind the might of her friends, or a queen who'd faced Traisende and the consorts of Yager in the tavern today.

She rested a hand on Quill's elbow, brushed Maleck's arm, and stepped forward. "Then it's me you're looking for. Princess Cistine Novacek of Talheim."

"Princess," Adeima echoed quietly. "Sit."

Only one seat remained—between two Tribunes, across from Thorne and angled toward Adeima. Cistine gathered her wits along with her skirts and slowly approached the table; Maleck drew the chair for her and she sank down. When he squeezed her shoulder, she leaned into the touch.

The cabal arranged themselves against the walls, deceptively casual with their hands still near their weapons.

"Maltadova has already informed me of the negotiations in the tavern." Adeima took his hand, brushing her thumb over his knuckles. "Or should I say, the lack thereof."

"Though not for lack of trying." For the first time, there was an edge to Thorne's voice.

"Trying only matters in affairs of the heart and skipping rocks," one Tribune said.

"It wasn't as if we could force everyone's hand," Cistine said. "Not unless we wanted to behave like Salvotor."

Quiet fell.

"The meeting in the tavern was never meant to be the end of it," Adeima said. "Our men would not decide our steps for us, which meant the conference would not decide the course of this alliance either way. Thorne was testing us."

The High Tribune smiled. "A bit."

"Then where does that leave things?" Cistine demanded. "Will you help us stop Salvotor's cruelty?"

"And what, precisely, has he done?" another Tribune asked.

Another test, to learn how informed she was—whether the Princess of Talheim was a figurehead only, a tool used by Thorne to gain the women's trust while he secretly shielded her from conflict.

Cistine stepped up to the challenge. "He's left the Blaykrone territory defenseless." One woman flinched, pain lashing through her amber eyes. "We've already rescued one village from dire straits, but there will be more. When winter comes, when food is scarce and entire cities are buried in avalanches and carts are stranded on the roads, Blaykrone will suffer the worst of it."

The woman who'd flinched gripped her throat now, a small whimper sliding from her mouth. Adeima cut her a quieting glance. "And the purpose of this?"

"Me," Thorne said. "That I surrender to him, and my rebellion dies with me."

"Because you love Blaykrone. How did he learn of that, I wonder?"

"It doesn't matter how Salvotor found out," Cistine said. "If he's capable of finding out secrets like Thorne's, he could easily learn yours. Will you help us unseat him before that happens?"

"I want to help you, but trapping Salvotor is no simple matter," Adeima warned. "A feud between father and son isn't something we can convict a Chancellor on."

Tatiana scoffed. "He whipped Thorne raw more than once. Convict him on *that*."

Thorne grimaced. "Tati."

Sympathy carved the lines around Adeima's mouth. "Abhorrent as that is, it's still not enough to carry the weight of conviction in a trial."

"What about buying weapons out of season?" Cistine asked. "Would that capture a few ears in the courthouse?"

Adeima's eyes narrowed. "Now, that would be interesting."

"He's done it. And not just any weapons," Thorne said. "A man named Devitrius has been amassing *Svarkyst* steel for my father out of season. We intercepted a shipment he bought during Chancellor Benedikt's time."

"Clear proof that Kanslar has infected Skyygan Court," Maleck added.

Adeima swore under her breath. "*Svarkyst*. And who does he intend to use it on? His bothersome son?"

"Not with as many shipments as we've intercepted," Ariadne said. "He likely has enough steel to equip an army."

Maltadova scowled. "An arsenal of that sort can only have one purpose."

"The conquering king wants to bring *us* to heel," Adeima mused icily. "With weapons to cut through the armor of anyone who resists him."

Cistine laced her fingers tighter. "This isn't just Thorne's problem.

Even if Salvotor has what he wants from us, he'll continue to take from Valgard, from *you*. There's no end to this as long as he holds a place of power in the Northern Kingdom."

"The *Svarkyst* steel has certainly seen no hands in Stornhaz but his," Adeima said. "It's the first I'm hearing of it. But to stand in Court, there must be proof. A testimony. Something in writing, perhaps. A witness."

Thorne looked up at Ariadne. "We should be able to find someone in the Black Coast mines who would name Devitrius so Yager can draw the connection between him and my father's personal retinue."

Cistine watched the anxious faces around the table—Yager's Tribunes, wary to confront a Chancellor who'd already sunk his fingers into the other Courts, who could easily bribe a tribunal with threats and offerings.

They would need more than evidence. It would have to be personal.

"I hope that this would all be enough for Yager to prove it has honor," she remarked.

"You think this a matter of honor?" Adeima asked.

"I do. Where was Traisende's sense of honor when Bravis chose his own Court's future over all Valgard? The Courts first came to power because they saw injustice being done at the hand of a king, and they wanted to find the balance. No...they *were* the balance."

Julian cleared his throat, but Cistine didn't heed that subtle warning. Passion lifted her voice as she leaned forward, gripping the table's edge.

"I *know* you've seen that injustice. You can't even show this kingdom the strength of your brilliant women in positions of power because you would be ridiculed and mocked, if not attacked and cast out. That's why you allied yourselves with Sillakove, isn't it? You shared Thorne's dream of a better Valgard, and that dream has been dying for ten years while Salvotor drags this kingdom down the road to Nimmus. And who's tried to stop him?"

Half the table jolted when she slammed her palm on its surface.

"*Fight*," she snarled. "Fight back! In the courtrooms, in the streets, in *any* way you can. Stand with us...not in the shadows, but in the light. Prove why Valgard *should* have a Court governed by women, because you were the first to stand by what you knew was right, even when the risk was too great to fathom."

She met Thorne's eyes across the table, anchored to the pride glittering in his gaze.

"Help us save both our kingdoms," she said, "and I promise you, Talheim will never forget this."

Silence embraced the room. The Tribunes looked at their *valenar*, and the cabal glanced at one another. Cistine wanted to wipe the sweat from her neck, but she dared not move—especially when Adeima's eyes pinned her flush to the seatback.

"Here is the bargain I will make with Sillakove," she said at last. "Bring me a witness and destroy those mines when you do it. Make certain there is no hope of Salvotor gleaning a single blade more that can harm my Hunters."

"If you want the mines destroyed, you'll have to provide the augments to do it," Thorne countered. "My cabal has already sacrificed enough resources fighting a battle alone against Salvotor that is Valgard's to wage."

Adeima pressed her lips together. "We will leave enough flagons to destroy the tunnels. If you manage to do this, I'll see to it that the Courts move to disbar Salvotor and Devitrius at once."

"And if the others won't stand with us?"

"You mean Bravis? Leave him to me. All he needs is a bit of a nudge to do what's right for Valgard."

"And for Talheim?" Cistine interjected.

This time, the Chancelloress fixed her with a truly penetrating stare, sharper even than Queen Solene's gaze whenever she caught Cistine sneaking away from archery practice. Those eyes blazed with an internal, nurtured fire—and Cistine *craved* it. She yearned to make others feel the way the Chancelloress left her now: acutely conscious of her place, her status, and unable to deny that she was in the presence of a leader.

She schooled her features to match Adeima's—that same calm, unaffected heat, the same tilt to her eyes.

The two women measured one another in silence. Then Adeima said,

"Not for Thorne or his Court, but because of you, Princess Cistine...because of the love you hold for your people. If this comes to pass, Yager will stand with *you* against King Jad."

Cistine glanced at Julian, her heart soaring with pride, with glee—and found him slouching stone-faced against the wall, staring at the floor.

Some of her elation fizzled as Thorne sat forward, sliding his boots from the table. "Whether you do this for our sake or not, Sillakove thanks you. *I* thank you, Chancelloress. Where do you want the witness delivered?"

"That will be forthcoming. Send your raven when you arrive safely wherever it is you hide away. I'll return him with instructions."

Thorne inclined his head. "You're as wise as you are powerful."

"So Maltadova tells me." Adeima rose and gestured to her women. "Say your farewells."

Before Cistine could stand, Liv, Ingrid, and Astrid enveloped her in an embrace that smelled of cloves and wood polish.

"It's wonderful to see you safe," Astrid said. "We couldn't be sure if the fire in the teahouse was enough of a distraction to help you escape."

"Not all of us did," Cistine admitted. "Ashe was captured."

Liv frowned, pulling back. "Your guard?"

"We believe her to be a prisoner of Salvotor," Maleck said. "We've yet to search Detlyse Halet."

Adeima studied Maleck's face with the same wariness most people did. "I can inquire of the Lightless Pit on your behalf. Women do not leave other women in Salvotor's clutches."

Relief shredded the shadows in Maleck's gaze, and his hand clasped Cistine's shoulder almost tight enough to hurt. "You have our thanks."

Adeima dipped her head in farewell and glided to the door. The Tribunes and their lovers fell into step with her, pausing when she did, just short of the hall. "Thorne, you may want to harvest some *Svarkyst* steel for yourself. If your father is reinforcing his flesh with armaments as you told Maltadova and Bravis, then before long, the only way to stop him may be with that indelible steel."

Then she was gone, taking her Court with her. The door shut at their heels, its creaky hinges cackling at the stunned cabal.

"Did that truly just happen?" Maleck muttered.

Cistine rose, framing her hot cheeks in both hands. "Unless I'm dreaming."

"Well, if you are, could you dream away the kink in my back?" Quill stretched and swung his arms loose. "That Chancelloress was right, Thorne. There may only be one way to end this."

"We'll discuss that later," Thorne said. "For now, we piece together a strategy. I hadn't intended to sack the Black Coasts. Not yet, anyway."

The blades on Ariadne's belt shifted with her feet. "All the same arguments stand. There are Blaykrone workers there, and innocents from Veran."

Thorne's eyes darkened. "I know. But many more people will die if my father has his way. From Blaykrone especially, as we've already seen."

While he and Ariadne debated the logistics, Julian slipped up behind Cistine, startling her from her reverie of reliving the meeting over and over in her mind. "You must be ready to sleep after all that."

"Not really." Her bones still vibrated with the rush of adrenaline. "Why did you look so furious before?"

Julian wrapped his arm around her waist. "That was an awful lot of friendship you promised them for not being Queen yet. They might take advantage of that, especially if they're hunting for the Key."

"And King Jad might take advantage of our weaknesses in the meantime, making the Key a moot point. I would rather treat with Adeima than face someone as mad as King Jad without her."

The storm in Julian's eyes did not abate. "Your father might not approve."

"Papa isn't here. *I* am negotiating for Talheim's future."

Julian shook his head. "You'll have to learn to communicate these decisions with me *before* you make them, once I'm King."

Quill clapped his hands, startling the retort straight from Cistine's mouth. "Well! That was pleasant. I could use a drink."

"You're all free to go," Thorne said, releasing Maleck and Ariadne from their watch duty. "Tatiana, *behave*. I'll join you soon, there's something I need to look into first."

Quill cuffed his shoulder. "Just don't have all the fun without us."

"You know he's incapable of having any fun without us at all," Maleck replied.

"You, of all people, hardly know the meaning of that word," Thorne shot back. "Save a drink for me."

The mischievous smile Quill and Maleck swapped made Cistine fear for the sanctity of that drink. Grinning, she started forward, but Julian gently pulled her back. "I think we'll stay in tonight. You all go and have your fun."

She swiveled to stare at him. His smirk sent a shiver down her spine—not a pleasant one—as the cabal looked around at one another and shrugged.

"Your loss." Quill whistled Faer in from the balcony and led the cabal out, already bantering as if the tense meeting had never happened. As if another battle wasn't mushrooming on the horizon like a late-summer storm. Only Ariadne looked back, gaze lingering long on Cistine.

The moment the door closed, she whirled to face Julian. "You have to *stop* speaking for me!"

He blinked, hurt breaking in his eyes. "I just thought you might want a moment alone together. It's been nice to have that lately."

Cistine struggled not to seethe at him. "Julian. I *do* want to spend time with you. But I've never gotten to drink with the entire cabal! I am perfectly capable of deciding *for myself* whether I want to be here or there."

Julian frowned. "You don't drink."

"I just went chest-to-chest with a Chancelloress." An aftershock of disbelief rocked through her when she spoke the words. "I faced a secret ruler of Valgard, I made myself heard, and I helped us seize a chance for the cabal *and* for Talheim. Maybe it's not a bad time to have a mead or two."

Julian folded his arms, scowling. "You have no idea how uncomfortable it makes me, the things you choose to do with your time lately. The way you spoke to those women...gods, Cistine. Not just the alliance you offered, but the *way* you did it. You didn't sound like yourself."

She rubbed her temples, a dull ache mounting behind her eyes. "*Yes,* I did. You may not like this part of me, but it *is me*. And if we're going to be married, you have to accept that. Otherwise you'll make us both miserable."

His eyes narrowed. "So your unhappiness is all my fault now?"

"I did *not* say that!"

Julian flicked a hand, turning away from her. "You know what, Princess? Do whatever you like. I'll just be here, like I always am, waiting for you to put the pieces together."

Angry heat budded in the corners of Cistine's eyes. She thumbed it away and quietly cursed. "We can't keep doing this."

"Doing what?" Julian flung himself in her abandoned chair, his back to her.

"Arguing this way! Then you insult me and we make amends without ever really addressing the issue. I don't want another apology when I come back, Julian. I want things to *change*."

"You want me to accept that my princess drinks and fights now? That she doesn't pick up books and hasn't *wanted* to in weeks?" Julian retorted. "Forgive me if that *change* takes time getting used to. I didn't realize I was marrying a lush."

Cistine stalked forward a step. "*Julian.*"

"Just leave. Go do whatever you want."

She halted, weight balanced forward, hands in fists. Unlike Quill, unlike *Thorne*, she couldn't wrestle the tension from Julian. He would never deign to release his anger that way. He would sit here in solitude and simmer, and she could choose to stay until his temper cooled.

She wondered what it said about her—about *them*—that instead she hurried out and slammed the door behind her.

The inn's spacious front porch was not deserted when she stepped onto it, still reeling with anger: Ariadne leaned against the railing, straightening as Cistine emerged. "That was quick. But not as quick as I expected."

Cistine rubbed her face with both hands. "I need a drink."

Ariadne slid an arm around her shoulders and pulled her close. "Don't we all, *Logandir*?"

CHAPTER FORTY-FIVE

CISTINE AND ARIADNE met the rest of the cabal in a tavern dripping with iron chandeliers, its street-facing windows welcoming in the cool breeze. Barmaids rotated to and from a counter bisecting the open floor, the rowdy echoes of card and dice games floating from the second-level balconies.

Ariadne steered Cistine to the counter with a friendly, protective arm around her shoulders. The others were already halfway through their first round of drinks—Cistine hoped Tatiana's was only water—and Quill was in the midst of telling a joke that had her in side-splitting laughter when Cistine wedged herself between him and Maleck. Breaking off midword, Quill slapped her on the back. "Ha! So, you *did* come. Pay up, *Storfir.*"

"Mal, you bet against me?" Cistine pouted.

Maleck flicked a mynt down the counter into Quill's open palm. "I bet on the likelihood that Julian's arguments would be...persuasive."

Cistine's ears grew hot. "There was no persuading happening."

"Good," Ariadne said crisply, and picked up her own glass of water. "Let's drink."

For a while, that was all they did, the cabal making their way through a third round before Cistine finished her first. When she called for her second, Tatiana said, "Make it two."

"Tati," Quill warned. "Don't."

"I can handle *one* drink, Featherbrain," she snapped.

Quill's face shuttered with annoyance. Maleck and Ariadne looked away.

"I could make my night's wage on your cut of the counter alone!" The barmaid plunked down steins for Cistine and Tatiana, then slid an unsolicited round toward Quill.

He grinned at her, his eyes sparkling with mischief and mead. "I'm more interested in what happens *after* you receive your wage."

The woman cocked a smile his way. "Stay long enough, *jekk*, and you just might learn."

Ariadne rolled her eyes. "Here we go again."

"What did she call him?" Cistine asked after the woman sashayed away.

"Handsome," Maleck said into his stein. "Roughly speaking."

Quill swept his hair back from his brow and shot an arrogant glance at Tatiana, who was too preoccupied with her tankard to notice.

They shared one another's company until that barmaid's shift ended and she brought the fifth round with the laces of her corseted top undone to the third bracket and her hair loose around her shoulders. Once she planted herself in Quill's lap, Maleck drifted off to occupy himself at a card table; Ariadne broke up two brawls in as many minutes and prowled the room eyeing for more; and Cistine sat on her own at the counter, sweating at the flirtation between Quill and the barmaid whose name had yet to come up in conversation.

No one else seemed to notice when Tatiana put away her fourth stein of mead with no signs of slowing.

Quill looped an arm around the barmaid's waist and propped his chin on her shoulder. "You know, as a well-traveled man, I can say with good authority you may be the loveliest woman in Valgard." He glanced at Tatiana from the corners of his eyes, but she only snorted when the barmaid giggled.

That charmer's mask slipped. Quill gripped the woman's waist and lifted her off him. "Excuse me." He retreated hastily to the door, and the barmaid, laughing, finished his stein.

Tatiana turned on the stool to face her. "He has rotting warts."

The woman's eyes widened. "I beg your pardon?"

"He's hoping to get you too drunk to notice. Get out while he's gone."

The barmaid's rosy-cheeked grin paled into shock. "Oh. Oh, *stars*. Thank you for saying something."

"My pleasure."

"That was a lie," Cistine chided while the barmaid hurried around the counter and vanished through the tavern's back entrance.

"How would you know?" Tatiana slid from her stool and relocated herself next to a band of sailors from Veran's quay. In seconds, she'd struck up a playful rapport with the tallest and burliest of them.

Cistine sat sipping her mead in solitude until Quill returned and scanned the bar, eyes wide. "Where did our friend go?"

"She had a...prior engagement."

Quill didn't answer; his eyes had found Tatiana flirting with the sailor, and when she swung her leg over the man's lap, Quill picked up his stein, finished the dregs in one draw, and excused himself again.

Cistine looked between his retreating back and Tatiana's blank mask under the provocative tilt of her lips, and tossed her hands. "*I give up!*"

"At long last, she concedes," Thorne's joking voice startled her as he slid onto the stool next to hers. "To be fair, that was a good run. I stopped trying to understand them years ago."

"What are they *doing* to each other?"

"You'll have to ask them, if you're feeling bold. I always wondered the same thing—what in the stars would keep someone from reaching out to the one person they wanted most in the world?"

"You see it, too?"

His smile was warm like ghostlight. "Every day."

Cistine slid the rest of her mead to him, and he accepted with a grateful toast. "Where were you?"

"Making certain Bravis didn't double-cross us. His concession came too quickly for my liking. Either he's struggling under the pressure from my father, or he's already caved."

"Which do you suppose we're dealing with?"

"The former, thankfully, which buys us some time. If we pull off this siege on the Black Coasts, it may be enough of a crutch to keep Traisende standing against Salvotor's advances."

"But Ariadne mentioned that all the same concerns exist as before. Which means the prospectors, the miners..."

"All in danger," Thorne agreed quietly. "You once said you wanted me to tell you what a siege on the Black Coasts would be like if it ever came to that. Do you still want to know?"

Perhaps it was the mead that gave her the courage to say she did, despite the hammering in her chest.

Thorne rubbed the side of his neck. "We'll do everything we can to chase the workers from the mines. But when we collapse the tunnels to prevent them from reaching the ore, there's no question people will die."

"Good people, or bad?"

"Neither. Just simple men trying to make a wage. Even the Vassora."

Cistine rested her face in her hands. "This is awful."

"It is. I despise that it's come to this, but Adeima is right to want the mines collapsed. These people are outfitting Kanslar, and every Court influenced by them, for conquest."

"But they don't know that! They're fulfilling shipments so they can feed their families."

"I know. Which is why I have a very specific request to make of you." Thorne swiveled his stool to face her. "I swore I would never lie to you again, Cistine. We're going to face a battle inside those mines—and, yes, we will face casualties."

Cistine swirled her smallest finger through a blot of condensation on the counter, painting loops to match the snarl of emotion in her belly. "Thank you for being honest with me."

"Of course. Now I need *you* to be honest."

The somberness of his tone had her tucking her hand, and her betrothal ring, under the counter's edge. "Yes?"

"I need to know where you want to be during the siege. If you even want to be part of it. With a bow in your hand, you'd be useful in the tunnels picking off the Vassora and anyone else who attacks us."

Cistine's guts writhed at the thought of shooting men who were there to defend themselves and their livelihood. "Thorne, I can't. I don't think I'm ready to kill that way. To go into battle. I'm sorry."

"Don't apologize." Though soft, his tone held fierce. "*Never* apologize for your compassion. If I'd had a choice, no one in Sillakove would've ever had to kill. We didn't get to choose after what my father did to us, but *you* still can, and I will fight to my own death to ensure no one ever makes it for you."

Cistine laid both hands under the counter this time. "What else can I do to help?"

"I could send you in ahead of us. If you posed as a miner, you could spread a rumor for the workers to evacuate. Normally, I would send Maleck to do this days in advance, but any hint of our intentions ahead of time and the Vassora will be prepared for us. I'd rather not risk Yager's flagons in a battle of that size."

"Would it really save lives, or do you just want me to feel useful?"

His mouth quirked. "Sometimes I forget that in Talheim, peace gives you the luxury of stroking someone's pride. Yes, it will save them. Not all of them, but each life is important."

Cistine breathed deeply through a spurt of nervous energy. "Then I'll do it."

"Thank you." His smile in full force now, Thorne finished off Cistine's mead. His eyes traced the tavern—tallying the number and location of his cabal—and he shot to his feet when he spotted Tatiana swiping another tankard from the sailors. "Nimmus' teeth. After I told her..."

Cistine snagged his elbow. "Let me. I don't think it's a lecture she needs tonight. It's someone to talk to, and it should be me."

Thorne gazed down at the hand looped through the bend of his arm, the ring that glinted on her finger. "At your command, Queen Cistine."

The words sent a flutter of raw nerves through her, but Thorne's smirk took the edge from them before he pushed through the crowd to find the others.

Cistine's eyes tracked back to Tatiana. She'd given up on the sailor and taken his stein off to drink alone again, gazing absently across the tavern. Cistine's heart ached at that flat stare, those vacant features that once brimmed with so much humor and passion.

She had to do *something*.

Hailing the barmaid for a third stein, she slid down the counter and plopped into the stool next to Tatiana. "I'm going to sit here."

"Obviously." Tatiana didn't spare a look up from her own drink.

Cistine nodded across the tavern. "Why did you do that to Quill?"

"You mean with the barmaid?"

"Well, and the sailor."

Tatiana scowled. "Don't you dare hold *me* in contempt. Quill's done the same to me more times than I can count. Tonight, he started it. With *her*. Fair's fair."

"I don't hold either of you in contempt. I just don't understand why you do that to each other, when you're clearly—"

In love.

She couldn't bring herself to say what she'd seen when Tatiana was shot with a poisoned arrow and Quill came running to find her, terrified and thirsting for blood; what she'd known ever since that day above the falls, when the mention of Tatiana chased out the specters of Quill's suffering. What had only been confirmed when Tatiana incited his wrath in Starhollow to draw him from his own misery at Pippet's fury and tried to take his place going into that broken house in Geitlan—to protect him, just as he'd protected her tonight from the Yager archers.

Tatiana scoffed, licking droplets of mead from her fingertips. "We do it because it's all we can do. It's what we've always done."

"Always," Cistine echoed—a question that wasn't a question.

The warrior raked her with a ruminative stare, a small, empty smile gracing her lips. "Maybe it's just the mead, but you look exceptionally lovely tonight. So I'll indulge you." She spun the stein between her palms, staring into its sloshing depths. "I met Quill when I was a little girl. His father was a Tribune and his mother...I don't remember what she did, but she was too busy for him, so they usually left him at another Tribune's house, with Thorne, whenever his cousin watched him."

"Aden?"

"Got it in one." Tatiana toasted and drew from the stein. "My mother and Aden's worked in the same house of healing. One day she just decided that if Aden was already chasing two rowdy boys, he might as well chase me, too. It was always the four of us after that, all the way until Thorne, Quill, and I went to school together. Salvotor shoved Thorne into the hardest classes to move him quickly through the ranks, so then it was Quill and me against the world. Before I knew it, we were spending every waking moment together. For *years*."

"And then Salvotor took him?"

Tatiana nodded slowly. "It was the first time I realized Quill wasn't...invincible. You watch someone pull through the worst card matches, the hardest tavern brawls, and you start to think nothing can touch them. But when he dragged himself out of Detlyse Halet...I thought that was the worst I'd ever see him. And then he brought his sister to Hellidom, this little infant, both of them soaked in blood." Glazed with memory, her eyes branded the far wall. "I will never forget that day."

"I understand that, and how it changed things. But I still don't know why you push him away, if it's meant to be you two against everything."

"Because that's what I do, in case they haven't told you. I keep people at arm's length."

"Why? Because even a tinker's daughter can't fix *everything*?"

Tatiana rooted her in place with a cold look. "Who told you that?"

"Maybe it's what I see with my own eyes! We were friends before I went to Stornhaz, I don't care what you say to me, and ever since I came back you've been treating me like you couldn't care less if I live or die. But I think you *do* care, Tatiana Dawnstar."

"Not so loud, *stars*!" Tatiana grabbed her by the back of her neck and towed her down between the stools, breath hot and putrid with mead. "Let me make this clear: I *don't* care. I *do not care* what happens to you."

"Why not?"

"Because I *can't!*" Tatiana snarled. "I can't keep loving things that break! Why do you think I did what I did to Quill tonight? I can't stand seeing him with his hands on some other girl, but I can't let myself get close enough to *be* that girl. Do you understand that? If I keep losing these things, watching this cabal suffer, it is going to tear me apart!"

She released Cistine and sat back, wiping her mouth on her arm.

"Self-preservation," she murmured. "It's how I survive."

Cistine's throat clenched at Tatiana's sunken face. "No. That's how you die so slowly you don't even realize it's happening."

Tatiana snorted. "You only say that because you've never been hurt the way I have."

Cistine steadied the anger in her voice before she replied, "Ashe."

Tatiana froze with the tankard halfway to her chapped lips.

"Don't you think I wish I didn't have to hurt like this?" she added, tears bubbling up her throat. "Like I've lost a piece of myself every day she's gone? You aren't the only one who's ever felt pain, Tatiana! But we don't heal it by separating ourselves from everyone we love."

"Don't tell me it wouldn't be easier if you didn't miss her."

"Life isn't about doing what's easy, it's about doing what's right. And I know, as much as I'm hurting, it wouldn't be *right* to treat the cabal like dirt just to make myself hurt less. If I learned tomorrow that Ashe was dead, I would be glad for every day I spent with her. I wouldn't live in regret for the rest of my life. Can you say the same?"

Tatiana set the stein tiredly aside. "What do you want from me, Cistine?"

She snatched Tatiana's hands and squeezed them. "I want *all* of you, Tati. Your hurt, your temper, your smiles and wisdom. I want to talk about our problems while we root through your closet. I want to read books of Valgardan lore and drink tea and discuss politics and augmentation together. I want..." she choked on an unexpected sob. Tatiana stared at their joined hands, tears plopping from her own cheeks. "I want my friend back. The first person who taught me to love Valgard and didn't make me feel like I was failure for what I didn't know. Who saw *me*."

Tatiana lifted her head, weeping silently and steadily. Cistine freed one hand and brushed those tears away.

"I want you to teach me how to fix things, how to fix *us*," she added. "Because I'd rather die tomorrow knowing we're friends than go home to Talheim thinking you hate me."

"I don't know how," Tatiana rasped. "How to love things I know are going to break. That are *already* broken."

"Yes, you do know. It's why you can't let Quill go. This is what you *do*, Tati, it's who you are. You fix things. It's time for you to fix your own heart. Let me help you."

Tatiana's lips quivered, and she shuddered violently from head to foot. Then she vomited straight into Cistine's lap.

It was a slow task hauling Tatiana back to the inn. Three times, they paused while she emptied her stomach into the gutter and Cistine held her waist and twisted her hair from the nape of her neck; by the time they reached the private parlor, Cistine sweated and panted as well, Tatiana gasping with laughter at her own uncoordinated disgrace. They tumbled into the room to find it quiet; no one else had returned yet, and Julian was asleep, much to Cistine's relief.

She deposited Tatiana onto her bed and snatched the empty fruit bowl for her to vomit into one last time. Purge complete, she worked on removing her friend's armor.

"This is humiliating," Tatiana laughed. "Look at me...a cabal warrior. I can't even undress myself."

"Don't be modest. You've wanted this to happen since we first met."

"Well, you're just so deliciously adorable." Tatiana draped an arm across her eyes.

A bolt of clarity struck Cistine at those light, empty words: Tatiana's flirtation was another layer of hurt, an imitation of intimacy feigning the closeness she craved. Because when they had been *truly* close, bonded deeper than just Thorne's training regimen forcing them together, the flirting stopped and honest conversation took its place. She prayed they would find their way back to that again.

She helped Tatiana crawl under the covers, retrieved a cup of water, and sat next to her while she buried her face in the pillow. "When you wake up tomorrow, Tati, please don't ignore me. *Please.* Let's talk, let's go and shop...anything. It's time to mend this."

Tatiana moaned into the fabric. "I may not be much for talking tomorrow. Or shopping. Or being a person."

Cistine held her breath.

"But, maybe the day after," Tatiana relented. "When I'm not as sick."

Cistine kissed the top of her head. "About Quill," she said against her hair, "you shouldn't lie to him about how you feel. Or to yourself. It's not fair to either of you."

"You're one to talk," Tatiana mumbled.

Cistine blinked, fisting her hand sharply—the one that wore the ring. "I don't know what you mean."

Tatiana sputtered with unsteady puffs of laughter. "Don't think I haven't noticed the way you look at him."

"At Quill?"

"No, you liar." Tatiana rolled over. "At Thorne."

Then she was snoring.

CHAPTER FORTY-SIX

A SHE HARDLY SLEPT the night before the chariot race, between practicing with Aftan in the evening and running with Aden after dark. The arena already rattled overhead when she belted on her armor after a quick scrub bath, echoing a storm of gossip about the newest sponsored fighter appearing in today's race. Up in the stands, the people wanted to know who the sponsor was; in the catacombs, the other fighters speculated which fortunate soul had snatched a sponsorship.

Through the bathing-area gate, a guard shouted at her to move quicker. Muttering under her breath, Ashe grabbed her racing turban and stepped through the gate to find Nimea waiting for her as well.

"Come to wish me luck?" Ashe jibed as the guards led them up the corridor.

Nimea snorted. "It isn't luck you need out there, it's a stars-damned miracle. The last so-called race winner died an hour after the end, trampled by his own horses."

Ashe managed not to wince only because Sander had already warned her of the brutality awaiting today. "I'm sure I'll be fine." She bundled her hair up into the turban. "Where are the others?"

"They claim not to care if you live or die."

"A sense of comradery worth dying for."

"The last time we invested our hearts in anyone outside ourselves, it brought us to this place. They can't afford to care."

Ashe scoffed, but said nothing. She knew what that was like—she shouldn't care about anyone in the Blood Hive, either.

And yet...

When they neared the staging room, Nimea slowed. "They're letting some of us watch...as if that's supposed to encourage us to find sponsors."

Ashe paced backward away from her, hooking the turban's mouthguard into place. "Why wouldn't you? Doesn't this look so exciting?"

Nimea rolled her eyes. "Don't let them kill you."

"Not if I can help it!"

But once she was locked alone in the staging room, the guards vanishing into the arena above, Ashe's nerves jangled again. She danced one foot on the stone floor as she sat, clasped her hands, and bowed her head in prayer—but no words came. The True God seemed so far away. *Everything* was far away except the pounding of her heart and the body-shaking roar of the arena.

Footsteps approached from the catacombs, and Ashe was almost relieved not to be alone with her thoughts. She lifted her head and lounged on the wooden seat, feigning carelessness as a pack of fighters entered through the gate, unaccompanied by guards.

The other sponsored racers.

Six men, built similar to Andras, clearly better fed and cared for than the other fighters; Ashe had never seen any of them in a match. They moved together like a pack of wolves, forming a semi-circle before the bench.

A twinge of warning strummed Ashe's guts. She sat taller, spread her arms on the seatback to make herself seem broader, and slowly tilted her head. "So! Who's prepared to race?" None of them spoke. "Well, that's unfortunate, because I certainly am."

The man directly before her bent at the waist to peer into her eyes at level. "Who is your sponsor?"

Ashe arched a brow. "You tell me yours and I'll tell you mine."

His eyes slid swiftly to one side—toward Ashe's *injured* side, where the lips of skin had closed into a scar over the arrow wound.

When Ashe lunged to her feet, the man caught her throat and slammed her against the wall, driving the strength from her body. "Your sponsor. Who is it?"

He loosened his hold just enough for Ashe to draw breath to speak; she pulled up her knee and drove it into his sternum instead. When his hand sprang from her throat, she dropped and feinted to one side, trying to get clear of their bodies, but the pack closed her in against the wall.

The Traisende-sponsored fighter responsible for that arrow wound in Ashe's side crowded closest, the stink of his body corrupting her breathing space as he flattened her to the wall. "One more sponsored charioteer is one too many."

At first, Ashe didn't realize she'd been stabbed.

But she felt—*heard*—the knife twist against her leather armor and knew that wasn't right. Steel shouldn't penetrate a leather vest. It should've stopped the blade.

God almighty, it was *inside* her, digging among her intestines, gutting her like a *fish*.

A furious roar quaked the room, setting the fighters backward on their heels, and for an instant Ashe thought it was her own scream of shock, of *rage* that they'd used this dirty, underhanded coward's tactic, trying to remove her from the race before it began. But it was not her voice, because that caught in her throat with a glottal hiccup when the black knife whipped out, blood pouring from her armor.

That snarl of world-ending fury...

That was Aden.

He smashed into the fighter who'd stabbed her, driving him into the wall and hurtling the blade from his hand. The others scattered wide as the Lord of the Hive bloodied the man's face in two swift strokes, plucked up the weapon, and stepped over Ashe.

When had her knees hit the ground? Why couldn't she stop the bleeding?

"You are dead men," Aden growled. "All of you have just taken your last breaths, and that will catch up to you with more agony than you can possibly fathom."

A horn blasted in the arena, signaling the race to begin. Aden threw the keys to one of the fighters, ordered him to unlock the gate and then toss the ring back. The keys skidded in front of Ashe's face, her cheek somehow resting on the stone floor now.

"Get out," Aden spat. "And pray to the gods for the mercy that you die under the chariot wheels today. If you return to this Hive in one piece, you will not stay that way for long."

The men shuffled out, and Aden's face swam into vision. "Ashe. Can you hear me?"

Dully, she could—him, and the crowd, screaming with joy as the charioteers mounted up.

"I have to get out there." Ashe dug her limbs into the floor and forced herself, swaying, up onto her knees. "Sander's horses...the race..."

"You're done. You aren't racing."

"I have a contract!"

"Ashe!" Aden grabbed her face with one hand, steadying her wobbly head. "I can see your insides. *You are not going out there.*"

Her breath stopped. She didn't look down, didn't want to see—he was lying, she wasn't even in that much pain, no worse than the shrapnel in her leg on the Vingete Vey.

"Then they win," Ashe gasped. "If I stay down here..."

"You aren't staying, either."

Aden wrapped his arm around her back and swooped her up. With the change in height as she left the ground, a black tide covered Ashe's face, soaked her eyes and nostrils, and poured down her throat.

Darkness. Warmth. An herbal smell, rough hands, bright eyes—

Clarity roared back like a thundering avalanche, burying her in agony as candles flared to life around her. She lay on Aden's bed with him crouched above her, unlacing and yanking open her vest, then rolling up her shirt. Something dark red and globulus heaved through her skin.

"Keep your eyes on me, Ashe. Do *not* look, do not close them." Easier ordered than obeyed, but Ashe couldn't find her voice to tell him that. "This is a *Svarkyst* wound."

His weight vanished. Ashe struggled to sit up, retching as blood flooded her side, her guts flirting with the edges of that hole, wanting to escape...

"*What is going on here?*"

Ashe collapsed with a groan. She didn't need to see Sander to recognize his voice clashing with Aden's, a flurry of words passing in and out of thought, out of reason. She hadn't realized how much she missed lying on something softer than stone, softer than sand. This bed devoured her whole.

A firm blow against her cheek lifted her from the mattress.

"Don't fall asleep," Aden warned. "You know better."

Sander knelt on one side of her, Aden on the other, and his hand slid under her head. He sat her up against his shoulder.

"Do it," he said to Sander.

The scowling Tribune yanked on a pair of thick, armored gloves and unclasped something from his belt, rolling it between his palms.

A glass vial. A gods-forsaken *flagon*.

"No!" Ashe thrashed to escape the heinous power that should not have been—and screamed so loud her throat tore as a new pain, deeper, visceral, ripped through her body.

"Do it!" Aden shouted again, hand covering Ashe's brow.

The vial of augmented energy cracked against her wound.

Fire flooded her body—then ice, then lightning. Ashe screamed again, sobbing at the pain that hurled itself against her ribs, climbed them to her throat, her shoulders, into her head. Aden wrapped his arms tightly around her, stopping her from fighting loose and running from them, straight into the arms of the Undertaker—allowing the augment to begin healing what was broken inside her.

Unconsciousness so dark and deep, like a well to the center of the kingdoms...Ashe had only known it once before: after she fought an augur boy alone during the war.

She couldn't call his face to memory. He'd cornered her while she took watch alone, his gangly shadow of a body the speartip of the patrol sent to assassinate Prince Cyril and King Ivan. In just a few blows, he'd disarmed her and knocked her bloody into the snow.

The only thing Ashe could recall before she passed out was how she'd screamed into his face that she was not afraid of him. That stroke of bravery had sent him running into the trees.

She'd woken hours later back in the camp, Prince Cyril sitting by her side. He'd told her how they ran off the rest of the patrol because her fight with the boy alerted them to the coming danger. She'd been asleep for many hours after; she hadn't even stirred when they patched her wounds. All she knew of the time between were dreams of snow and shadow and blood, and that augur boy's dead, wide eyes with light trickling back into them.

And now she knew nothing but shadows and screams and anger, waking in the bed's gentle embrace with a pillow under her head and blankets enveloping her body.

This was not death. This was Aden's room.

Slowly, she rolled onto her back, body throbbing from the inside like she'd been set on fire, and towed up the hem of her shirt. Her fingers explored the skin above her hip, probing the rigid scar rising from the flesh. It felt weeks old, or months. Certainly not hours.

She was healed. Because of an *augment.*

Swallowing a curse, she peered around the dim room; the candles banked, and no one had bothered to relight them. From the far side of the room's broad center column—

Voices. Familiar.

"I knew because Aftan led the chariot from the arena." Sander's light accent, bitter with rage and affected with alcohol. "Given what's transpiring in the Hive these days, it wouldn't take a brilliant man to deduce something happened to her."

"Clearly not." The sarcasm in Aden's voice was going to get them in trouble. "I'm glad you came when you did. Without that augment…"

Neither of them spoke, and Ashe's insides twisted with nausea; she'd never thought she would owe her *life* to an augment.

"How much do you know about what's happening in the Hive?" Aden's question drew Ashe from her spinning thoughts.

"I think we both know who shot you now. And *I* know that the rations are being poisoned."

Aden's silence was like a death knell. Ashe waited for the storm to break in its wake.

"That's why she's been sharing her meals with me." The softness of his tone, where she had expected roaring rage, surprised her. "She knew."

"I told her. Before you ask, no, there's nothing I can do to stop it. It's Tyve poison, slow-working, so I have no proof of its presence until the fighters begin to die off. And by then…"

"It will already be too late."

Liquid splashed into a cup. Ashe knew it wasn't water.

"As if we didn't have enough to contend with down here," Aden growled, "now we're a part of this power struggle between you Tribunes."

"Don't sound so condescending. Your own cousin is High Tribune of our Court."

"Which is the very reason I can safely condescend to you. I know Thorne wouldn't play with lives this way."

"Maybe not. But I don't have the luxury of being Thorne."

Ashe tried not to scoff. Clearly, Aden didn't know his cousin as well as he claimed if he thought Thorne wouldn't use others for his own ends the same as every other Tribune.

A chair scraped, and Sander said, "I should go. Word will be getting around by now that I'm her sponsor, with the way neither of us appeared at the race. Best to stomp these fires before they burn out of control."

"And as of this moment, we're bitter enemies again," Aden said with a touch of the sardonic.

"Before we are, let me impart a bit of advice: damn your pride, keep eating the meals with her, Aden. That woman is trying to save your life—

Nimmus only knows why. Don't take that for granted."

A beat of quiet, and Aden snorted. "Someone's made you soft."

"I'm sure you have your suspicions as to who."

"Stars, don't I. Now get out."

Sander must've obeyed, because Aden moved to Ashe's side of the room, peeling open drawers and shutting them again. His armor rattled into place, and she rolled over to face him. "What are you doing?"

"I'm going to have a word with the men who did this to you."

"Aden, don't. Noaam will never forgive you."

"It's not his forgiveness I'm in this place to beg for. Stay here as long as you need to recover."

Aden strapped on his leather vest and strode out of the gate.

CHAPTER FORTY-SEVEN

A WHIRLWIND OF planning followed the cabal's meeting with Yager, the first day full of so much map-reading Cistine and Ariadne both battled headaches by the end of it. The second day, Cistine woke to Tatiana standing over her bed.

"Battle armor," she said in greeting. "Let's go."

They shopped on the border of the Aliment and Steel Houses for hours, searching occasionally for armor and talking without end. Though the conversation stumbled at the beginning, with the rising sun and the addition of hot tea came new honesty from Tatiana.

"When did you start feeling like you had to run instead of fighting things that scared you?" Cistine asked while they browsed racks at a small armor shop.

"Curious as always, aren't you?" Tatiana's retort lacked any true heat. After a moment, she sighed. "I don't know. My whole life, maybe. Take things with my father for example. He's a brilliant man, and I think he knows it, but his naivety thwarts him. He invents all these things...weapons, household items, even augwains...augment-powered metal carriages that used to ferry people over those high bridges in Stornhaz."

Her fingers stilled on the rack, eyes shrouding with anger. Cistine chose not to say anything.

"Anyway," Tatiana went on, "Papa invents these things, and then investors come slobbering at his door. He's always too quick to enter into business with them...no contract, nothing signed. And they steal his inventions over and over again."

"That's awful!" Cistine exclaimed so loudly a patron shushed her.

"It is," Tatiana said. "Watching that happen ever since I was small, I suppose I came honestly by the feeling like everything we have is just made to be taken away from us. And what happened to the cabal only proved it." She stepped away from the rack, shaking her head. "But the other thing about my father is how he's determined to focus on the good rather than the bad, even when he can't rise above his station. He's always so sure his next invention will be the one that makes him famous."

She turned to Cistine, lips tipped in a funny, small smile.

"You remind me of him that way," she said. "And maybe I could do with a bit of seeing the good myself."

"Well, it sounds like you have an excellent teacher in your father."

"Not just him. Don't pretend to be modest."

Cistine stuck out her tongue and perched her hands on her hips, surveying the disappointing racks all around them. "I know why we haven't found anything suitable yet. I should commission my armor from Tariq."

Tatiana tossed up her hands in mock-surprise. "Well, no *wonder*! I suppose you'll just have to live in that training armor until we go back."

"I suppose I will." Cistine motioned her from the shop. "Since *someone* vomited all over my only dress."

Tatiana groaned as they stepped into the bright sunlight. "I have a drinking problem."

"I've noticed. And about that..."

"I already told Quill yesterday, I'm done," Tatiana interrupted. "Too much at stake, and if Thorne knew about the other night..."

Cistine didn't bother to tell her that he knew—or that she'd convinced him to give Tatiana another chance even while she nursed a headache and chewed on ginger root the day before. "If you do it again, someone will have to tell him. He has his reasons for wanting you sober."

"I know, I know. And like I said, I'm *done*. No more flasks, no more taverns. I'll tell them to close my tab for good back in Hellidom. And if things do get out of hand, Quill has my permission to intervene however he thinks best." Her jaw worked, chewing over her next words before she spoke them. "I'm lucky I still have him."

"Well," Cistine said, "you have me, too."

Tatiana squeezed her arm. "Much as that terrifies me when I know you'll go running off into danger again...it's good. I missed you. A bit."

They were both smiling again when they returned to the inn, slowing to greet Julian at the parlor door. He offered a nod to Tatiana and a hand to Cistine. "Talk with me?"

Reluctantly, she took his hand and walked with him past the table where the rest of the cabal was gathered around the coastal maps again, and down the steps to the seating area.

Julian pulled her onto a couch and wrapped his arm around her shoulders. "I'm sorry about the other night. I was just rattled. Seeing you that way with the Chancelloress...that was new."

"It's new to both of us," Cistine said. "But you have to embrace it."

"I know." He grazed his thumb over her ring. "I overheard Thorne talking to the others today. You're going into the mines ahead of us?"

Cistine's stomach turned somersaults at the notion, but she refused to show her nerves. "It was my choice. Don't hold this against the cabal."

"I know, I won't. But I still think it's a choice you shouldn't have to make. I just keep reminding myself how much better things are going to be when we go back to Talheim. Especially once everything is officiated between us."

Cistine's heart drummed, an oddly unpleasant sensation. "Oh?"

"I'm going to ask your father to teach me everything about how to be King. And you...you can do *whatever* you want. No more sneaking into tunnels, no more having to train, no burden of rulership. I'll do everything I can to relieve you of that pressure, so you can go back to living the life *you* want. The one all this responsibility is draining from you."

Cistine's cheeks chilled as the blood drew from her face.

He wanted to remove the burden. To take it from her. The power. The responsibility. Her crown.

For a brief glimpse, she saw the life Julian intended for them: him with the heavy circlet on his brow, her curled up in chaise by the bedroom window, reading endless stacks of books and drinking tea. The same future she'd dreamed of for most of her adolescence; the one she'd felt her parents were robbing her of with every formal ceremony and event they forced her to attend.

And yet...

That crown. That power, to stand in the presence of Chancellors, to bargain with High Tribunes, to protect her kingdom with word and deed. That was as much a part of her as her love for books and dresses.

And Julian wanted to take that away. He wanted her to sit aside, a beautiful ornament, sleek and pampered and doted on. To waste the muscle she'd grown with Quill; to forsake the discipline she'd learned from Ariadne; to lay slack the knowledge Maleck and Tatiana had imparted; to give up the leader's bond she'd forged with Thorne.

The future he was striving toward could only come to pass if he wrestled Cistine's crown from her hands. And a few months ago, she might've given it away to him without a fight. But now... "What if I don't want that future?"

Julian's brow creased. "Then why did you agree to marry me?"

Cistine didn't know if it was the gods' humor, the simple course of life, or her own disgusting luck that the cabal stopped talking just then. That they all heard his question.

Dead quiet penetrated the room like a blade. Slowly, Tatiana and Quill revolved in their seats to face Cistine and Julian.

"I'm sorry," Tatiana said. "I must've misheard you."

"Did you say *marry*?" Quill demanded. "As in, the Talheimic equivalent of *valenar*?"

Julian grinned. "Didn't Cistine tell all of you?" He held up their entwined hands. "She agreed to be my wife."

Cistine squirmed as the cabal all exchanged long, stunned glances, silently asking one another the same question she'd asked herself countless times during the past week.

Why *hadn't* she told them?

Maleck was the first to speak, with a small, refrained smile. "Congratulations on your happiness."

"Yes, we're leaping for joy...right along with you," Tatiana said slowly. Ariadne fixed Cistine with an inscrutable look, brows faintly narrowed.

Quill's gaze was trained on her as well. "I assume we're invited to the wedding?"

"We'll see how the details come together," Julian hedged.

Thorne stood, and at the scrape of his chair, the room fell silent again. Cistine's cheeks heated until they pulsed, and she could barely meet his eyes.

"All the gods' best to both of you," Thorne said. Then he excused himself and went out onto the balcony, passing Julian and Cistine without a sideways glance.

Julian didn't seem to notice the tension in his absence, or else he didn't care. While the cabal bombarded him with questions about wedding rituals in Talheim, she slid her hand free. When he didn't claim hold of her again, she stood, mumbled an excuse, and escaped onto the balcony as well.

She was glad for the distant burst of the Agerios on the rocky shore, the churns and shouts of Veran below, and the privacy afforded by the gauzy lavender drapes when she leaned against the railing beside the brooding High Tribune. "I'm sorry. Julian shouldn't have barged into it like that."

"It's none of my concern," Thorne said.

"It is if it resurrects the pain of the woman you broke with."

He swiveled sharply, locking her with that branding stare. "You think this has anything to do with me? Or how I feel?"

"Doesn't it? You told me once you were going to forge the *valenar* bond, and it ended in disaster. I can understand how a betrothal would bring that loss back, even if you don't have a practice like it in this kingdom."

Thorne stared at her for a long moment, his gaze inscrutable. Then he nodded toward the archways. "Tatiana is most likely dreaming about this wedding, however it's done. You should be with her for that."

Cistine's chest tightened. "Of course, because *that's* how I want to spend the rest of my time here. Planning the details of a wedding, when I should be looking for the Key, or a way to overthrow your father, or helping Maleck find Ashe."

"And if we had all those things tomorrow, what then?"

"What do you want me to say, Thorne?" she snapped. "I suppose I would! I'd plan a wedding to someone who wants me to be complacent and quiet for the rest of my life...someone I care about, but I know he sees me a certain way, sees my *future* for me, and...Thorne, *what?*"

His stern brow relaxed. "You didn't come here to console me. You want me to talk you out of this."

Cistine folded her arms to hide the gooseflesh racing across them. "I'm wearing his ring, aren't I?"

"I think we've all worn ceremonial attire before."

Huffing, she looked away...but that forced her gaze to snag on the ring, a symbol of beauty and devotion that suddenly weighed her finger like an iron chain. "I'm fond of Julian. I've always been."

Thorne nodded to her hand. "Then why are you shaking?"

Tucking it out of sight, she scowled at him. "I despise how well you notice everything about everyone."

"Not everyone. Just you."

She faced him, propping her elbow on the railing. "And what do you notice tonight?"

He mirrored her posture down to the tip of his head. "What I've always seen: a princess willing to sacrifice her desires for the good of her people. A woman prepared to forfeit what she wants for what she *believes* her kingdom needs."

"We both know the feeling of that, I think."

"True. I suspect we do."

Cistine rubbed her knuckles on the iron, her burst of frustration fading into the sounds of the sea. "What do you think of this? Really?"

He was quiet, and she held her breath, uncertain what she wanted him to say. Of what he *would* say, or why—after their wrestling match in

Starhollow. After he'd kissed her brow on the walk from Geitlan. After she'd screamed his name and run to him—heedless of death bearing down on them both—when the assassins attacked.

"If you're happy, then I'm happy, Cistine," Thorne said at last, so softly his voice was one with the distant waves and the night wind. As if these things were pulling him away from her. "Are you happy with this betrothal?"

Cistine glanced into the parlor, where the cabal—even Julian—ate and drank together, their laughter floating between the drapes.

She did not reply.

CHAPTER
FORTY-EIGHT

NEARLY DYING TOOK a toll on the body. For a full day, Ashe did nothing but sleep; when she woke at long last, the candles had clotted into low pools, more a legend of light than the truth of it. The sound of heavy belts and pieces of armor hitting the floor roused her; then the mattress depressed, and she sank with it, tumbling down into slumber again.

She woke on the bed's edge to the candles relit, looking down at Aden where he slept on the floor.

Her brain as dusty as one of the old books Cistine loved, Ashe studied the Hive Lord, looking for wounds and finding only bruises and blood-frosted knuckles. Whatever fight he'd started on her behalf, he'd clearly walked away the victor.

He'd been gone for a day, gone to battle for her. That was three Valgardans who'd been ready to fight on her behalf when they all should've been at one another's throats.

It was unfair. None of it made sense. Maleck ought to despise her for the part she'd played in the war. Thorne's cousin should be as vicious as Thorne himself. Sander should've let her die before he wasted one of his precious augments on her.

Yet here they were.

Ashe draped her arm over the bedside, and with her thumb, flaked away the damning evidence of Aden's judgement against the other sponsored fighters from his hands—as if that would spare him the lash that was coming.

Though he stirred at her touch, he didn't open his eyes; a mark of his exhaustion. And then Ashe, too, was asleep again.

She woke the third and final time to the scrape of angry voices.

"I have furious sponsors clamoring at my doors," Noaam seethed from around the stone wall, barely beneath a shout. "We have an understanding with these people, Aden!"

"I thought so, too," Aden replied, level and calm as if his outburst in the staging room had never happened. "But they broke the truce first. Their fighters stabbed Ashe. They nearly killed her."

A beat. "Let me in to see her."

"I don't think so." Aden's voice conveyed his posture perfectly: body cocked in a casual slope, shoulder pressed to the doorway, arms folded, barring Noaam's way to her. No trace of weariness or exhaustion left in him. "She's resting, which is what she needs after this ordeal. We'll keep this between us, Noaam."

"You've humiliated me again with what you did to those fighters. You know what that means."

Aden sighed. "Let's get this over with, then."

Their footsteps retreated before Ashe managed to throw off the blanket and crawl to the foot of the bed. She staggered up, dashed out into the corridor, and looked both ways, but Aden and Noaam were already gone.

No chance to plead for mercy. No chance to tell Noaam he was punishing the wrong fighter.

Ashe cursed aloud and rubbed her face with both hands. Maybe if she could find Sander, have him tell his part of what happened, Noaam would reduce the sentence.

She'd barely set foot from the corridor when a hand curved over her shoulder, wrenching her back. Exhausted though she still was, Ashe already had her fists up and flying before she finished a full pirouette. Her knuckles bit into Nimea's cheek, knocking her head sideways, and the other woman doubled back with a shout. Ashe barely pulled back from the second punch in time. "Don't sneak up on me like that!"

"And don't *you* give me orders!" Nimea's eyes sizzled with rage. "I've been looking for you! Where have you been?"

"Recovering." Ashe let her arms drop. "I never made it to the race. You were right, it's dangerous for sponsored fighters."

"Maybe so," Nimea said. "But it's more dangerous for the rest of us."

For the first time, Ashe doubted that. "What do you want, Nimea?"

"There's a rumor spreading that you're sponsored by Sander. Of Kanslar."

So much for putting out the fires. "Is that troublesome for you?"

"I don't understand why you accepted his offer. Sander was always friendly toward Thorne."

Ashe frowned. She hadn't suspected *friendship* between them when Sander said he planned to use her to reach Thorne. But she hadn't really pushed the subject, and right now she didn't care to obsess over Sander's motives; she didn't want to indulge Nimea's suspicions either. Because with a *Svarkyst* wound pulling the life from her, Sander had saved her; and Aden, whose cousin she was helping the Tumult hunt. And Nimea had been nowhere to be found.

"Look at it this way," Ashe said. "Now if you ever need someone to spy on a different Kanslar Tribune, you have me."

She shoved Nimea aside and went to find a guard who could fetch her to Sander.

"I'm afraid there's nothing I can do. My hands are tied." The Tribune's tone was light, unaffected as he leaned against the gate above the staging room—the farthest the guards would let him come. "Aden is Noaam's to punish as he sees fit. And he's riled him up quite a bit this time."

Perched on the steps, Ashe braced her head back on the iron bars and grimaced. "He deserves to be knocked on his ass for plenty of things, but not for this."

Sander's gaze raked over her, bright with curiosity. "Don't tell me you're growing fond of him."

Ashe rolled her eyes. "Where I come from, we try to repay a life for a life." Just like Aden had done during her match with Kalman. Were they really so different, her and this Valgardan Hive Lord?

"Unfortunately for your sensibilities, there's no place for sentiment like that in Siralek." Sander folded his arms and rested his back to the gate, squinting up at the cloudless blue sky. "Aden will just have to endure."

Mirroring his posture, Ashe flopped against the iron, glaring into the room where she'd nearly met her death. "That wasn't the stance either of you took when I was bleeding out on that bed." Saying the words—reliving that blurry cacophony of time—did not help her feel as bold as she'd hoped.

"I'm afraid you're much more valuable to me than the Lord of the Hive."

"Fortunate for me."

"Doubly fortunate, because I'm going to offer you a piece of advice." The pitch of Sander's voice changed, so even without looking Ashe knew he'd swiveled his head toward her. "The way you shouted for *Maleck* at your first match. The way you ran to Aden during his. And what you're doing here today—"

"I know, I know. Weakness."

"On the contrary," Sander said. "Hold tight to that. It takes a warrior of true mettle to remain themselves in this place. What Aden did to those fighters...despite what you may believe, that was not Hive justice. That was *his* measure of right and wrong. And sooner or later, you'll be challenged to weigh out yours." He shrugged up from the gate, his voice floating back on the dry air. "Just remember what was given for you when the time comes, hm?"

He left her alone with that troubling missive, her gaze fixed on the place where she'd nearly died.

CHAPTER
FORTY-NINE

THE BLACK COASTS were like nowhere Cistine had ever seen before, a maze of sheer-sided basalt columns and stark ridges gleaming damp under the midday sun. Sweating in her plain, heavy shirt and dark pants, she trailed the cabal through soaring shadows and jagged pockets of light within a half-mile of the mine shaft's entrance, where they halted in a shelter of stones for their final preparations.

Tatiana circled Cistine, tugging at the angles of her cobbled-together miner's attire. The bulky clothes hid her curves and made her look—as Julian had sulked that morning—like an average-height boy. "She's fit."

"Remember," Maleck said, "spread the word like a fire, not like a secret. There's no need to tell every man you come across. Trust them to warn their friends."

"Find a bucket of ore first thing and carry it with you," Quill added. "That way you'll blend in."

"You have exactly two hours before the Vassoran watch changes," Ariadne reminded her. "That's when we strike."

"Save as many as you can," Thorne said. "But when you see the shift change, get out."

Julian scowled at them and brushed forward to take her chin. "Just be careful. Watch out for yourself."

His fleeting kiss made Cistine acutely conscious of the ring she had left behind at the inn—and the strange sensation when she'd taken it off and left it on her bedside table.

She couldn't afford to think about that now. She smiled when Julian stepped back, and touched Nail's hilt on her belt. "I'll see all of you soon."

"One last thing." Thorne offered a handful of basalt dust. When Cistine nodded, he smoothed it gently onto her cheeks, across her brow, and down the bridge of her nose.

"Well?" Cistine said. "Do I look like a miner now?"

"I still see a queen."

Pulse thundering, she squared her shoulders and picked her way down the shore's gravelly lip toward the distant mouth of the shaft.

The mines were far more intimidating than the brutal heights and perilous plunges outside. Cistine's hands trembled the moment she entered the dimness, cut only by ghostlamps strung on cords along the shaft walls, though no one gave her a second glance. She wedged her feet into the heavy boots provided on shelves, then followed a train of workers into the cliffs.

It was everything she'd envisioned, a dark artery of pocked stone reinforced by angular wooden beams opening after a span into a cavern of ledges and columns, heights and depths she couldn't see the end of. The miners broke away toward smooth paths with wheelbarrows propped beside them and stations full of picks and chisels—and, to Cistine's relief, small wooden buckets for toting ore. She snatched up the nearest one and ambled to a stone spire; no sooner had she halted beside it than a miner began to load the bucket full of ore.

"Are you from Blaykrone?" Cistine asked.

"Yes," the man grunted. "Less talk, more work."

The barrel dipped with the next load of ore, and her arms with it, but she forced her voice through gritted teeth. "You and your friends need to leave. *Now.*"

The man chuffed with humorless laughter, pressing the chisel tip to a particularly stubborn clump of ore. "Not if my family wants to eat."

"If you want to live to see them again, you'll go."

He hesitated, his gaze tracking to the knife at her hip.

"Something is coming," Cistine whispered. "These mines will be a bloodbath in a matter of hours. If you value any lives here, especially your own, you'll escape as quickly and quietly as possible."

"And why should I believe you?"

Cistine offered a silent prayer to the gods. "Because I bring this message from High Tribune Thorne."

This man of Blaykrone stared at her, eyes wide and jaw slack, familiarity and belief bright in his gaze. "What does the High Tribune want with these mines?"

"To stop them from being used to enslave Valgard."

Ruddy face paling sharply, he took the basket of ore from her arms and pressed his hammer and chisel into her hands. "You must take your message to the other shafts. Leave the rest of this cavern to me."

Tools in hand, Cistine slithered through the small, hollow tunnels from chamber to chamber, hunting for men from Blaykrone in every cave and passing the message quietly to them. Some scoffed and waved her off, and she didn't waste time arguing with them. But the ones who listened helped her; room after room, they spread the word to their companions. And with everyone who agreed to pass those whispers along, who told her where to go and how many caverns there were, Cistine's fear slaked a bit more and her determination swelled.

It was hopeless to think she could reach them all in less than a full hour—half the time in, and half to return—but she was still shocked at how quickly the minutes evaporated when she heard the familiar brush of wings on the stale air. Faer soared down the long loop of tunnels, alighting on her shoulder with a triumphant croak, and Cistine slammed to a halt.

Quill's signal. She had less than an hour to return to the surface.

But there was just one more mining hollow to conquer, full of men who had no idea what was coming. Maybe they wouldn't believe her...but maybe they would.

She could almost hear Julian hissing in her ear, warning her to get out before battle broke inside the Black Coasts; before everything the cabal had feared, all their reasons not to sack these tunnels in the first place, came to fruition.

Before Cistine was buried alive. *Again.*

Faer dug his talons into her shoulder, almost a warning, like the last whisper of reason passing from her mind.

"Go back if you want," she said. "It's just one more cavern."

When she broke into a run down the shaft, Faer tightened his grip and swayed with her movements.

Cistine burst into the last cavern without preamble and shouted, "All of you, get out!"

The men looked up sharply, one or two exchanging confused glances, and no one so much as stepped toward her.

"This mine is going to collapse!" Cistine cried. "No one is safe. Get out by order of the Vassora!"

To her breathless relief, they laid down their tools and jogged toward her. Catching her breath in great gulps of victory, she led them like a queen's army up the shaft toward safety.

There were far less workers left behind than she'd anticipated; it seemed most had believed the words of their friends if not from her. Tears of joy pricked her eyes at every empty room they passed and every one where the remaining men saw their companions trailing her, took notice, and fell into step. She'd never been so glad to walk into danger, had never considered any risk as worthwhile as this one.

Faer's grip tightened suddenly. He bleated a warning call.

The Vassora were distinctive with dark armor and darker blades where they separated from the shadows between mining hollows and fanned into the corridor ahead of Cistine and the miners. For a terrified heartbeat, she could only think of Ashe facing men just like these above the sewers, as fearless and sharp as a sword herself.

But Cistine was no sword. And she had no sword.

"So," a guard growled. "You're the one who's been spreading lies of a mine collapse to all the men."

The miners began to murmur. Cistine swallowed, but it didn't clear the dryness of her throat.

The guard jerked his head. "Seize the woman."

Cistine whistled, and Faer lifted from her shoulder. She hurled herself forward as he speared toward the guards, and when one drew his sword and raised it to cut the raven from the air, Cistine crashed into him. They toppled to the floor, and she managed one good hit to his crooked nose before iron fingers banded her biceps and wrists, snatching her arms behind her back. Two men hauled her to her feet, writhing and flailing; Faer was already gone.

"Back to your stations!" The guard thundered as he staggered to his feet. The miners' whispers turned to grudging complaints, and Cistine's heart plummeted.

"No...please, *please* listen to me—you have to get out!" she shouted. "You're all in danger!"

The guard backhanded her, and blood flooded Cistine's tongue. Through watering eyes, she watched the miners slump back to their cavern...back to their labor.

Back to their tomb.

The guards dragged her up the corridor where Faer had vanished, into the next nearest cave, and smashed her up against a pillar. While she struggled to catch her breath, bobbing above the riptide of pain coasting through her back, they drew her arms behind the pillar and bound them.

Quill's voice whispered in her memory, rousing through the pain, and Cistine flexed her wrists when the men tied the bonds.

The leader of this Vassoran band circled around in front of her, his bearded features full of fury. "What's this rumor of attack? Who's coming to these mines?"

"No one," Cistine panted. "I just...wanted the day off from working."

"I find that difficult to believe, seeing as we have no women working in these mines at present." He stripped the shawl from her hair, yanking out several threads with it. "Who are you, and why are you sending the workers away?"

Cistine spat out the blood pumping from her split lip. Though her knees quivered and her bowels trembled, she would not betray the trust the cabal and Yager Court had placed in her. If it was a princess who had won those things, then a princess she would be, like her mother who'd made madmen of her captors in Mahasar's capital so long ago. "Maybe I intended to destroy the mines. Maybe I didn't. How will you ever know?"

"I think you would prefer to tell us outright. Other methods can be...messier. And prolonged."

Bile scalded her throat. Her knees buckled at the notion of *torture*.

"I came to destroy the mines because I *know* what you're doing. *Who* you're sending these weapons to, and why." The words emerged bolder than she'd expected. "But Chancellor Salvotor will never make this kingdom his own, no matter how many *Svarkyst* weapons he has in his arsenal, no matter how many Courts he infiltrates. Valgard's beating heart belongs to its people, and those people will find a way to fight back. Because others fight *for* them."

The amused lift of their brows and the narrow slant of their eyes told her she should never have spoken.

"So, that's what this is." From the pouch at his waist, the lead guard drew a glass vial of rippling purple essence. "I have the perfect send-off for you...something to repay the blood you and your cabal shed from our brothers and sisters in the Izten Torkat."

Cistine dipped against the restraints, the rope slackening when her knees finally gave out. Every warning Thorne, Ashe, and Maleck had given of what augments would do to someone unarmored, someone like *her*, screamed through her all at once.

Why had she chosen sentiment over wisdom? Why had she told Tatiana she would wait for Tariq to tailor her armor?

"Don't," she whimpered, "gods, no, *please*..."

"Killing the messenger sends the most powerful message of all."

The guard hurled the flagon.

With one last powerful flex, Cistine slid her hands from the loose bonds and dropped to the side as the glass broke—and lightning discharged.

Icy-hot light pierced through the cavern, and with a crack of resonate thunder, stone slabs broke from the roof. But Cistine didn't feel that, didn't even feel the heat, or her hair standing on end, or her body burning.

She felt the same sensation as when Thorne used light to blind the assassins; the power went into her, *through* her—hugged her bones, filled her veins, seared her eyes, her blood, her very heart. If she screamed, it had no voice. If she wept, there were no tears. The lightning burned off everything but her very core, and Cistine flamed like a dying star, pulsing hot and fading, pulsing and fading, and then...

Nothing.

The augment spent itself. It winked away.

And she was still *here*.

The guard stared at her smoking clothes, her disheveled hair, in horror and revulsion and shock. "What in the *stars*—?"

The cavern floor rocked—a distant explosion. Another flagon unleashed.

Gathering her frayed wits, Cistine pulled out Nail and flung herself at the guard, clubbing him over the head with all her might. Without looking back to see if the others pursued, she ran toward escape, trailing vapors of smoke from her shoulders.

God's mercy was the only explanation she allowed herself to consider as she charged through the corridors, screaming herself hoarse at anyone who hadn't been scared out by the crack of lightning and the boom of thunder when the Vassora unleashed an augment against her.

And she'd *survived* it.

She stumbled and fell to her knees in the second cavern from the mouth of the mines where shadows slithered among the pockets of light, people shouting everywhere, yelling at *her*. When a hand grabbed her elbow and towed her upright, she lashed out wildly with Nail. They'd bound her like an animal, tied her and tried to execute her as a warning to the cabal, and she would *be* an animal, she would bite and claw her way free—

"Cistine!" Ariadne caught her wrist. "You're going to put someone's eye out if you keep flailing like that!"

Her sharp voice cleared Cistine's vision enough to see they were all here, flagons and weapons in hand, grim-faced and bloodied already.

"What in the stars happened to your clothes?" Ariadne demanded.

Hysterical laughter burst from Cistine's lips. "The Vassora caught me."

Her eyes narrowed to ruthless slits, grip tightening around Cistine's wrist, then springing away. Julian darted forward, pulled Nail from her grip and jerked her into his arms; but Cistine's eyes were on Thorne, and his were on her.

The panic, the *pain* in his face, when he took in her singed clothes and damaged mouth...

"Get to the surface." His voice was rough but the command gentle, sparing her from seeing what he would do to the men who'd subdued her.

Cistine squirmed free of Julian, took Nail back from him, and darted past the cabal. When Faer descended on her shoulder, she almost wept; the comfort of his weight, and knowing he'd signaled her friends to arrive before they were meant to, for her sake, was too much to bear.

She stumbled from the mines, fell to her knees on the shore, and vomited into a tide pool. Her hands, bracing her weight as she retched and waited for another surge of bile, swam into focus, scuffed with basalt and dust, and still steaming from how close the augment had come.

No. Not just close. That power *had* struck her, the evidence clear now in the daylight. She was missing an entire sleeve of her shirt, the fabric ripped down one side, her pant leg mere tatters held together by strong threads and the boot *melted* around her foot.

And yet she was alive. Somehow, the skin beneath was unmarked, the only pain in her damaged mouth.

Cistine rolled onto her haunches and tried to yank off the boot, this horrific evidence of something she would never be able to explain, to herself, to the cabal, to *Julian*. Faer glided onto the round stones beside her, skipping and croaking as Cistine wielded Nail madly, slashing the boot apart, prying the strips away from her foot and spreading her toes through the threadbare stocking.

"What was that?" she sobbed. "Faer, what just happened to me?"

The raven nipped her fingers until Cistine stroked him, still staring at her foot. She'd never heard of anyone surviving a killing augment without armor; Maleck had said it would end her life in seconds, and her clothing certainly hadn't endured it.

So why was *she* unscathed?

A current of power ripped through the Black Coasts, quaking into Cistine's bones. Sense jolted back into her: she was too close, too exposed. If the Vassora survived the cabal's fury for what they'd done to her, she would have to fight again. And right now, she couldn't.

Her whistle was shaky, but Faer flapped up to perch on her shoulder again while she jogged down the coast, her exposed foot tearing open on the rocks. She laughed with raw disbelief that lightning harvested from the wells of the gods themselves had left her feet unscathed, but simple rocks could shred them.

When she slowed and sent Faer up the cliff face to keep watch, some of her trembling finally eased. She paced away the rest of it in a tight, repetitive loop among the columns, desperate to be done with it all—these mines where Devitrius had done his secret dealings, the hole into the Black Coasts, and the things she had seen there today. Things she couldn't explain.

A half hour dragged by, and apart from tremors that rocked the stone and black sand on occasion, nothing moved. Even Faer was uncommonly still, invisible among the dark rocks above.

Come.

Cistine sat up from her resting place with her back to the cliffside, head turning irresistibly back toward the mines.

Come and see.

Why did that call have a twin voice to the augment's power when it struck her, singing the same irresistible song?

She slowly pushed herself to her feet and limped back toward the mine shaft, following the whisper that grew stronger with every step she took down the crescent shore.

Come. Come. Come and see.

Cistine's belly dropped when the mines came into view; she slowed and finally stopped. And she waited.

A violent quake ripped through the shore, hard and near enough almost to put her down on her knees. She staggered half a dozen unsteady steps toward the mine shaft, then halted, arms banded around her middle, counting minutes by the beats of her heart.

But the cabal didn't emerge.

"No," Cistine breathed. "No, no..." Her gaze blurred, her mind conjuring up the horrific, life-ending possibilities—finding Tatiana with limbs severed, Maleck's chest crushed, Ariadne's wise eyes forever closed, Quill's white hair turned bloody, Julian's head severed, Thorne...

Thorne.

He was there, leaning wearily on the cave's mouth, the sunlight pouring across his augment-shocked hair. One side of his face was masked with blood and his precious dragon-scale armor was torn, hanging from the side of his body. His waist clattered with weapons crammed into his belt and jabbing his sides.

But he was here. Which meant the cabal must be close behind.

Groaning, Thorne unbuckled his belt, let it fall to the stones, and looked up at her with exhaustion graying the bright blue of his eyes.

And for the first time in her life, Cistine understood what all the books meant, all the things she'd ever read about captivating sunsets and starshowers and the glory of a sunrise, and how it could take someone's breath away, an anchor and freedom all at once; how seeing the beauty of life at the right time could change everything. All the poems and prose she'd giggled about with her handmaids at thirteen, fourteen, fifteen years old...they all made sense to her right then.

And when she reached Thorne, when she wrapped her arms around him, buried her face in his chest and felt the quick, steady thud of his heart—when she knew he was alive, that they'd both survived, yet again, the impossible—she started to sob.

A low growl of concern shook Thorne's ribs, and his arms circled her in return, shielding and supporting and comforting all at once. "Are those tears for me?"

Cistine trembled at the brush of his fingers through her hair. "When the tunnels collapsed, I thought you were..."

If she said it, if she heard the words aloud, she would lose whatever strength kept her on her feet; so she set the notion free, leaving it unspoken.

"So did I," Thorne said. "When Faer returned alone."

Cistine pressed her hands flat against his back, against the dips of his scars, the places where his dreams were whipped from him. He shuddered at her touch, held unnaturally still for one breath, then arched his spine gently into her hands and curved his body over hers. Daring himself to submit to her fingertips against those markings; letting her touch those vulnerable places unearthed by the battle in the cavern.

"How many?" Cistine croaked. "How many miners died?"

"Don't ask me that," Thorne said. "Two hundred and sixteen. That was how many we counted escaping the shaft. That was how many you *saved*."

Cistine's knees quaked. She'd done that—sent over two hundred people from harm's way, and nearly lost her own life doing it.

She'd never felt more like royalty than she did in that moment.

She had never felt more like a queen.

Rocks rattled. Steps shuffled on stone, and Julian's voice reached them, haggard and smoke-choked: "Princess?"

And Cistine finally realized what she was doing.

She had run to Thorne before she even looked for Julian. She was leaning into his embrace, and his hand was stroking her hair, and she didn't *want* to pull away. Some part of her, driven mad by the day's calamity, wanted to press a kiss against Thorne's bare shoulder before she drew back. Before she *forced* herself to let go of him, so he would release her.

She went to Julian, and he wrapped his arms around her instead, kissed her temple and settled his chin on her head as if nothing was wrong.

One by one, the cabal streamed from the mines. Their armor smelled of char, of the augments that had collapsed the tunnels; all of them, even Julian, carried their body's weight in *Svarkyst* steel. The last that would ever be mined here, at least in this century, without their machines to boor deep holes through the devastated shafts.

"The witness?" Cistine asked.

"The foreman escaped with the others. When we cornered him, he agreed to meet us at the inn," Ariadne said. "Thankfully, he remembers Thorne."

Thorne, who would not look at Cistine as he picked up his belt and slung it over his shoulder, whose heat still stamped Cistine's body, whose calm, soothing voice echoed in her ears.

And standing there on the brink of all the chaos they'd caused, of a task done well and one of Salvotor's footholds broken forever, Cistine knew Tatiana was right about her. She was a liar, deceiving them all, but mostly herself.

And she knew what she had to do.

CHAPTER
FIFTY

YOU WANT ME to testify against Devitrius—and *Chancellor Salvotor.*" The foreman's question clanged as hollowly as a spoon dropped on the table; the silence thickened after it, and Cistine looked around at her friends. They were all still dressed in their armor, though Thorne had donned one of his dark shirts. Cistine held a chilled water pack to her bruised mouth; Maleck and Tatiana numbed sprained limbs and stitched wounds as well. And Quill, both eyes blackened, his heels flung up on the table and his arm around Tatiana's seatback, cleared his throat and looked at Thorne, who sat back with folded arms.

"As foreman, the orders for weapons all passed through your hands," he said. "Devitrius is a member of my father's personal retinue, but he's been posing as a weapons broker for Chancellor Benedikt of Skyygan Court."

"Buying *your* steel out of season," Ariadne added coolly, "and passing it to Kanslar, who shouldn't be able to initiate weapons deals until their constellation rises."

The foreman—Józef, Cistine reminded herself tiredly, a man with a name and a family—passed a hand through his salted dark hair. "We did make several sales with Devitrius. But I swear to you, we had no idea he was a member of Kanslar."

"Few people do," Thorne said. "My father prefers it that way so he can make bargains like these."

"If I agree to testify to this in the Courts, what then?"

"We pass you along to Yager Court," Tatiana said. "They've agreed to bring the case to trial if we produce a witness with proof Devitrius made the trade out of season."

"I have proof," Józef said. "Hand-written contracts at my home."

"And *we* can prove Devitrius is your father's man," Maleck said to Thorne. "We've intercepted enough correspondences between them to make a sound connection before a tribunal."

"Finally, some use for all those letters other than making us lose sleep at night." Quill cracked his knuckles gleefully.

"I'll escort you personally to your home," Thorne said to Józef. "We'll retrieve the documents and bring you somewhere safe to await Yager's word."

"You might as well bring everything you can carry," Tatiana suggested. "It's possible Salvotor has other agents brokering weapons deals out of season, maybe even in Tyve. Let's see what we can root out."

Thorne's mouth curved in a tired smile. "It's good to have you back."

Her bright eyes flicked to Cistine. "It's good to be back."

When Józef and Thorne slipped from the room, Maleck's eyes fluttered shut. He slouched away from the table and collapsed in his alcove. Tatiana quickly followed suit, and Julian disappeared to the balcony, as quiet he'd been ever since the mines.

Cistine had a good guess as to why.

"You look ill." Ariadne leaned forward, frowning. "What's the matter?"

"Nothing," Cistine sighed.

Quill slid a cinnamon stick between his lips. "When has that ever been true? You can tell us."

She stared at the knots in the tabletop and slowly peeled the pack from her jaw. "Do you think Julian and I are right for each other?"

She didn't have to lift her gaze to know Quill and Ariadne were looking at one another, or to sense how heavily they weighed the question.

"Do I believe you could survive a joining without murdering one another?" Ariadne said. "Yes, I do, which is more than can be said for many Valgardans."

"But could you be *happy* with him?" Quill snorted. "Not in this life or the next."

Defensiveness rose in Cistine, but she forced herself not to argue; instead she rode that crashing surf until it slammed into her heart, leaving her exhausted again. "Because he undermines me."

"Because you're going to exhaust yourself if you spend your entire life fighting to prove every choice to the one person who should support you most," Ariadne said. "You're better off celibate than that."

Quill nodded. "Too much effort."

"Shouldn't love be worth that effort?" Cistine argued weakly.

"If this is the battle you're having," Ariadne gestured between Cistine and the balcony drapes, "then it's not really love. Infatuation, perhaps. Idealism at best. But not love."

And that was the heartbreaking truth she'd wrestled with ever since Julian asked her what they were doing if not putting one another first. Because putting him first had become such a chore, a distraction from everything else she had to do. Loving him and being the person Talheim needed her to be were not the same; they never had been.

Her fascination with Julian had always been a welcome pastime when her destiny as Talheim's sole heir seemed so overwhelming, but now she was stable in her position, and if not entirely prepared, then at least secure in what her future would bring. Meanwhile their courtship had devolved into a constant struggle to balance head and heart, authority and intimacy. And she was so gods-forsaken weary of fighting him, trying to patch holes in a ship they kept ripping apart with their arguments.

She stood, limbs and heart heavy. "Thank you for being honest with me."

"Is that all?" Quill's eyes gleamed, and Ariadne folded her hands on the table's edge. "Or did you want to talk about what happened with the Vassora today?"

Cistine swallowed. "What's there to discuss? They bound me and attacked me, and I—"

Escaped. Survived the impossible.

"We saw the state of your clothes," Ariadne murmured. "If they tried to—"

"They just wanted to scare the truth from me," Cistine assured her. "That was all."

And maybe it wasn't a lie. Maybe the lightning *had* missed her, and her clothing had been ruined by just a taste of its heat from afar. All the more reason to have her armor tailored as quickly as possible, if even a nearby brush of augmented lightning could do that to her clothes.

"You're sure?" Genuine concern replaced the cocky offhandedness of Quill's tone.

"Absolutely." Cistine's cluttered mind was already moving away from this conversation, out toward the balcony, into that star-studded night.

Before she followed it, she stopped at her sleeping alcove.

She'd never seen Julian look so lonely. He leaned against the railing, collar undone, sleeves pushed to his elbows and forearms braced on the iron bar, legs crossed at the ankle and one boot toe balanced behind the heel. Even in leisure, his posture carried a kiss of his Warden's training, a man of the sword and of service to Talheim.

The son of Rion and Eboni Bartos, the chosen heir of Practica, the son planned for times of war. Talheim's intended King.

Cistine's chest ached at the sight of him, and she almost went back inside, almost gave herself cause to doubt.

But it was not fair to him, to the man who'd left flowers on the kitchen table, brought her orange-blossom tea, searched for knowledge of the Key at her request, and always made time for her. Who'd defended her in battle and safety...who'd proposed marriage to comfort her. He always thought he had her interests at heart. And now, even if it pained her, she would consider his.

She leaned against the railing beside him, and they gazed toward the Black Coasts.

"Interesting day," Julian remarked.

Cistine let out a long breath. "It was."

"How's your jaw?"

"Sore. No worse than after a good match with Quill."

"Right." Julian's voice was soft. "Sometimes I forget you take blows regularly now."

There was room there for an argument, but Cistine let it go. And in the absence of conflict, there seemed to be little to say.

Julian leaned back, curling his hands on the railing. "There's more than two hundred miners drinking in this city right now wondering what they're going to do with themselves tomorrow. I'm thinking I'd like to join them."

Cistine took a deep breath. "Before you go..."

"Not going to stop me, Princess?" It was a stab at humor, but neither of them laughed.

Cistine turned to him and opened her palm, the rose stone glowing brilliantly between their bodies. "I came to give this back to you."

"I thought you might." There was no frustration or shock in Julian's voice. Only quiet, resigned sadness.

"You...you did?"

He nodded. "Ever since you went into that meeting with the other Courts, ever since we met with the Chancelloress, I knew it was only a matter of time. You said things, did things there that I didn't realize you were capable of as a woman. But, as a queen..."

"That was who I had to be." Even as the words left her lips, Cistine knew as long as they were betrothed or courting, it would always be this: his opinions, and her defending herself from them.

"I know it was. And the princess I couldn't stop thinking about in Practica, the one I tried to forget with all the tavern girls and stable hands in town—she was brilliant, and beautiful, and kind and generous. She was strong in her own way," Julian said. "But she was always a princess, you know?"

He took the ring from her, weighing it in his hand.

"You're becoming a queen, Cistine," he said. "A strong one. And as a Warden, I'll serve that queen until the day I die. But I don't think I can marry her.”

She should've felt sorrow at those words, but there was only relief. After everything that had happened, everything soured between them, they'd finally found something they still agreed on.

“The proposal was supposed to set things right. Put them back how they were at the beginning, with the girl who turned to me for everything. For advice. For protection.” His eyes were starlit fathoms as they turned from the ring to her. “But you're not that person anymore, because you don't want to be. And a ring isn't going to turn back time, it isn't going to change that. It will just chain us to each other, force us to try to save something we both know has been dead for a while now. And I don't want to spend the rest of our lives fighting. I'd rather serve as your Warden than argue as your husband.”

He was letting go. He wasn't going to fight for her. And for that reason above all else, Cistine knew she'd made the right choice.

“I'm sorry we couldn't be right for each other, Julian,” she said—and meant it. “Maybe in another time, another place...”

“Maybe,” Julian said. “If we didn't need different things.”

She understood that, too; Julian was a warrior who needed someone to protect. And there was someone out there, a girl like she had once been, who wanted nothing but books and tea and quiet things, and would keep wanting those things for the rest of her life.

Cistine hoped Julian would find that girl, and love her deeply, and defend her, and that she would cherish him in all the ways he deserved. Because somewhere, there was someone Julian could be with, and they would both have what they wanted. And be happy.

Cistine hoped there was someone like that for her, too.

But the moment was wrong to tell him all the joy she wished him, and the ache too fresh to be soothed by notions of the future. So she curled Julian's fingers over the ring and squeezed his hand. “In that place...that lifetime...I'll always find you.”

He kissed her bare knuckles one last time. “In that place, or any other, I'll be at your side.”

∾

The night brought tears Cistine hid in her pillow as memories of every touch, every moonlit patrol, every whisper of the future she and Julian ever shared crashed through her. She questioned her choice a dozen times, touched her thumb to the empty base of her marriage finger, and cried some more.

And then finally, with tears spent, she slumbered and did not dream—not even of him.

Morning brought light, and color, and resignation.

Morning brought screaming.

"What in the *stars* happened to you two?"

Quill's roar yanked Cistine out of bed, disheveled, dry-mouthed, and swollen-faced, not knowing where she was or why she was there until she heard Józef's frantic voice: "We were returning from my house when they attacked!"

Cistine stumbled out into the parlor to find everyone except Julian gathered at the table. Thorne was slumped in a chair, gripping the armrest while Maleck stripped off his tattered shirtsleeve and exposed the torrent of blood pumping from a wound across his biceps.

Cistine covered her mouth with both hands.

"Who attacked you?" Quill turned his hair across his head, eyes sparking.

"Who do you think?" Thorne growled.

The assassins.

"Where are they now?" Tatiana demanded.

"Two are floating out with the tide," Thorne groaned. "As for the third..."

A hopeless glance between them, and Cistine's stomach plunged. There was every chance the assassin was lurking nearby, waiting to follow them from the inn and finish what he'd begun with Thorne's arm.

"They're almost as good at tracking as Aden," Ariadne muttered.

"That being the case, we're not going back to Starhollow," Quill said.

"Should we even go back to Hellidom?" Cistine demanded.

Thorne pinched the bridge of his nose, grimacing as Maleck rinsed and dabbed his arm with a cloth. "We can pose as travelers stopping on our way from Unsverd to Lataus. We won't go home until we're certain no one is following us."

Józef cradled his face in his hands. "I'm not certain I can do this."

"You have to." Pain harshened Thorne's voice. "If Salvotor overtakes all five Courts, he can do away with assassinations *and* the rule of law. He can kill whomever he wants."

"But this has gone too far for *us* to ignore," Tatiana snapped. "The forest was one thing...one incident. But this? They won't stop, Thorne."

"I know." His eyes rolled shut, a groan escaping his gritted teeth when Maleck rinsed his arm again. "While we wait for Yager, we hunt them."

"We'll have to leave soon," Ariadne said.

Thorne gestured to his arm. "As soon as this is bandaged."

"It's going to be a long, hard ride to Hellidom," Maleck warned.

"I can endure it. Just make the bandage *tight*."

The parlor doors eased open, and Julian slipped inside; judging by the light shuffle of his feet, he hadn't expected anyone else to be awake. He froze just over the threshold with his weight braced on the door, bloodshot gaze and clipped movements betraying his inebriation. "What happened?"

"Assassins," Quill said curtly.

Julian blinked. "*Here?*"

"In the streets." Quill whistled, and Faer flapped up from one of the couches, settling on his arm. "We're leaving as soon as Mal puts Thorne back together."

Julian's gaze jumped to Cistine, and her stomach clenched. On a different day, she would've gone to the comfort of his arms. But now... "You need to sober up. We have a long journey ahead of us."

Though his gaze lit with a flash of belligerence that would've come out in harsh words from her suitor's mouth, her Warden and subject only said, "Yes, Princess."

Tatiana passed Cistine on the way to her alcove and squeezed her hand, and she was glad beyond words for that simple touch. She couldn't wait to be back in Hellidom, sleeping in her own bed, training on the rock top, gardening, and plotting Salvotor's downfall and the aid to be sent to Talheim. She couldn't wait to hug Baba Kallah and sink into the smell of cherries and sugar from her clothes.

She couldn't wait to go home.

While the cabal broke apart to collect their belongings, Cistine went to the table and offered her hand to Thorne. Pale but steady, he accepted it, and she hauled him to his feet.

"Is Julian all right?" he asked.

Cistine watched him weave tipsily toward his sleeping alcove, her cheeks heating. "He will be. I returned the ring last night."

Thorne was quiet for a moment. "I'm sorry."

Cistine glanced around at him. His face was cool stone—unreadable. But if she had to guess... "No, you aren't."

His eyes flicked to the side, then locked onto hers. "For the pain you're both going to feel, yes, I am. But otherwise..."

He did not finish that thought.

CHAPTER
FIFTY-ONE

A SHE SAW NOTHING of Aden after her recovery. It was Sander, not him, who chose her next fight—a simple show against a man purchased from a Valgardan slave-market, to prove to the crowd that Ashe was not in any way hampered by the attempt on her life. She won the fight almost too easily, given she'd been bleeding to death a week before; a sour part of her wished the augment hadn't healed her so well, so she wouldn't be reminded with every effortless swing of her blade that she owed her life to the very power her people had stolen from the Northern Kingdom.

A single shadow lurked in the staging room at her return, and Ashe's stomach knotted at the thought it might be Aden who'd come to wait for her; but to her disappointment, Nimea stepped from the darkness when the gate clattered shut, murder flashing in her eyes.

Ashe sighed. "What now?"

She grabbed Ashe's elbow and hauled her away from the arena, through a series of side corridors she'd never visited before. They walked for many minutes before Rez's quick, unsteady breaths fractured the stale silence; then Andras, huffing like a bull in the dark. And though she could neither hear nor see him, she suspected Tobor was nearby.

Nimea released her at last. "We just received word—Kalman and one of the other fighters are dead, yet again. And Thorne is still alive."

"Why does this keep happening?" Rez hissed. "We send out our fighters wherever *Ashe* dispatches them..."

"And they die," Nimea finished.

Ashe cursed through gritted teeth. She didn't have to see Nimea's face to know the woman was regarding her in a different way than usual—a far more dangerous one. "It isn't my fault your fighters are no match for the cabal."

Nimea's fingers fastened in Ashe's collar, forcing her against the wall. With a slash of rage, Ashe felt herself being smothered once again by that fighter in the staging room. "Enough, Ashe. We have to end this before anyone else dies."

"I'm trying!" Ashe snapped. "Once they leave this place, it's no more in my hands than any of yours whether they live or die!"

"Perhaps," Tobor interceded softly, "what we need is not a battlefield, but a small intrusion. It won't be as satisfying, but it will end things."

Slowly, Nimea's grip loosened. "Are you volunteering the talents you learned from Tyve?"

Fabric rustled—the sound of a shrug. "If you send me somewhere Thorne's guard will let down, I can end this in one stroke."

Ashe felt their focus pressing on her from every side, a choking wave of ruthless intent. Her place among them was tenuous now, fractured by two failures, by dead friends and paths to nowhere. They knew *she* knew what to do next. But to give it....to put so many in danger— "I need your vow on whatever honor you have left that *no one but Thorne* is harmed."

"And the cabal," Rez said.

A flicker of Maleck's face lit through Ashe's mind like ghostlight in the dark; this time, rather than retreating from the memory, she leaned into it. "No. If I give you the information about Thorne, it's for him only. Do I have your word?"

Andras breathed a shaky curse. Nimea's fingers twitched on Ashe's collar as she deliberated. Ashe held her breath.

"Only Thorne," Tobor said. "I give you my word. The others are piecemeal. Worthless once he's dead."

Ashe breathed out in slow increments. It was a risk, a terrible one, trusting a Valgardan's word; but if she didn't give them something, they'd stop trusting her. They might even leave her in this corridor to die. She had already tasted what this Hive was capable of, and she didn't want another knife to the ribs.

The sooner she stopped this charade and pointed them straight to Thorne, the sooner this would be over for all of them.

"Hellidom," she said. "They make their home in Hellidom."

CHAPTER
FIFTY-TWO

ASHE DID NOT sleep well that night or the following one; it was almost a relief to be woken from her restless slumber in the middle of the night with summons from Sander, delivered by a blank-faced guard.

It was unusual for him to send for her on such short notice. Stranger still that the guards did not lead Ashe to the houses, but deep into the booth-market of Siralek where the nomads traded for items or sold their wares from three-sided stalls and open tables despite the ungodly hour.

Ashe welcomed the distraction, the time away from the Tumult's piercing stares...and away from the concern for the people of Hellidom that had wormed its way into her chest over the past two days. She brushed the thought off as they slowed beside a booth full of blown-glass sculptures. A man lingered close by, his hands folded in the small of his back. A flash of brown skin at his wrists and shoulders, and Ashe knew.

"If it's a shopping companion you want, I could recommend someone much better than me," she said. "I'm not always in the mood."

"Nor am I," Sander replied. "But when one has twenty-seven women to impress, one must always be on the hunt for trinkets." He signaled the booth's steward for five blown-glass roses, each a different color.

"Then I hope you didn't invite me along for advice on what to buy them, either. Otherwise they may all end up with ornamental daggers."

"What makes you think they wouldn't appreciate that?"

Ashe arched a brow at the gaudy gifts wrapped by the boothkeeper. "I think I have an idea what kind of woman attracts your interest, Tribune."

"Oh, do you now?" With the satchel of glass tucked tenderly under his arm, Sander tilted his head. "Walk with me."

The guards melted into the crowd so perfectly, Ashe almost felt alone with Sander, and she was surprised the notion didn't bother her. She owed him the scar over her hip, after all. She owed a Valgardan her life.

"I'm sorry about the chariot race," she said. "My guard slipped. It won't happen again."

Sander waved a hand bedecked in rings. "I'm afraid the race is the least of our worries now. All of you may be dead by month's end anyway."

Ashe's mouth went dry. "*What?*"

Sander beckoned her into a cloth-draped refreshments tent, the smell of cardamom and hot honey greeting them just over the threshold. He wound his way through the thin crowd of patrons toward an empty lump of cushions in one corner, and Ashe followed him, her head spinning too much even to protest when he ordered food and drink for them.

"What did you mean we may all be dead soon?" she demanded when they were settled.

Sander carefully set his glass trinkets aside. "Noaam held a council with all the known sponsors this morning. Apparently, he's grown rather uncomfortable with this power struggle, and he's aware by now that sponsorships have given the other Courts something of a boot in Siralek's door. So now he's arranged a very particular fight meant for nothing but pure, unadulterated slaughter. Siralek hasn't held a melee like this since the war with Talheim, when overcrowding became such an issue."

The boothkeeper returned with drinks, and Ashe took her mug—some hot milk concoction with notes of cinnamon, nutmeg, and honey—and sipped it carefully while she watched Sander's face. He'd ordered the same drink, but didn't touch his.

"What a melee involves," he went on, "is a group of fighters placed through a pattern of obstacles. First they face a gauntlet of trials...pikes, flames, and the like. Those who manage to survive fight one another. And those who survive the man-to-man combat are torn to pieces by the arena beasts."

The hot drink scalded Ashe's throat and soured in her belly. Slowly, she set the cup between their cushions. "So it's a sieving process."

Sander nodded grimly. "There are no survivors in a melee, though they draw the greatest attention of all matches. Men will travel from as far south even as Blaykrone and Lataus to witness one. The sheer killing show, the *amount* of bloodshed, it's...quite a remarkable sight." But even he, under his naturally-tan skin, had gone pale.

"And the sponsored fighters are the elect this time," Ashe murmured. "All of us."

"Everyone Aden didn't kill after the mess they made of you."

"How many *did* he kill?" Ashe had found no one yet to ask.

The Tribune sighed. "Three of the six who cornered you. The rest are in considerably less profitable fighting positions than before the race, but Noaam want them for the melee as well."

"He'll lose an awful lot of sport in the long run."

"Yes, well, I'm afraid this may be all my doing," Sander admitted. "It was a tenuous position Noaam was in before us, tenuous but true. It wasn't until he realized the *Kanslar* Tribune over Nordbran managed to sponsor *you* that he saw the beginning of the end."

Ashe's breaths quickened. "This is about me?"

"It's about all of us, and how Noaam feels threatened by us...and he should. He perceives the best way to maintain his family's chokehold over Siralek is to demonstrate that we, his fellow Tribunes and the other sponsors, are not outside his grasp. And he is not above sacrificing his *own* sponsored fighters to lessen our influence here." He blew on his drink and sipped it, watching Ashe over the rim. "In short, Noaam took my sponsorship of you as a declaration of war. And he intends to strike surely and swiftly enough that it will be quite some time before any of us can recover. Before there will be anyone alive worth sponsoring again."

Ashe sat back hard on the cushion. "I appreciate the warning, though

I'm not sure how anyone prepares for something like this."

"You pray you've done enough good, somewhere, to see Cenowyn rather than Nimmus when you open your eyes in the beyond."

Ashe stared numbly into her drink when the boothkeeper returned with some kind of hot dough balls slathered in molasses and sugar. Sander picked at them, but Ashe couldn't remember what it felt like to have an appetite.

"For whatever it's worth," Sander added, "having watched your fight against the Viperwolves and the way you dashed to Aden's aid, if anyone in this stars-damned place stands a chance of seeing Cenowyn, it's you."

There was no comfort in his words. He didn't know what she'd done with the Tumult, the hate and vengeance in her heart that suddenly mattered so much less, knowing her days were numbered.

It wasn't Cenowyn she wanted to see, it was Cistine. If only to tell her goodbye.

It seemed she would not be given the chance.

Betrayal still numbed Ashe's burning nerves when she wove her way toward Aden's chamber near dawn. Sander had purchased lamb skewers with tomatoes and garlic cloves for their breakfast, but she was still full with the hot churn of rage and fear.

Siralek had turned on its own fighters, the best it had, and offered them up as a sacrifice to the gods. All her carefully-laid plans were unravelling, and she couldn't see a way past it yet. If she survived the gauntlet, the other fighters would be waiting. And if she killed every last one of them, she would still have to find a way to best a flock of beasts. And if she somehow accomplished *that* miracle, it was likely a Tribune would put an arrow through her heart. Maybe Sander would do it himself to spare her any further agony.

Three paths to freedom, and yet they'd all gone nowhere.

"Off with your sponsor again?"

Ashe halted at the echo of Nimea's voice from behind her and turned to face the scowling fighter. "Keep your voice down."

Leaning against the arched stone wall, Nimea watched her with feral intent. "Or perhaps you were visiting with your Hive Lord savior. I hear Noaam released him today. Pity our reprieve's over."

There was too much scorn in those few breaths for her to remark on, so Ashe settled on the one that infuriated her rather than the one that sent relief kicking her ribs. "*Savior?*"

"I heard in the staging room before my fight with Tobor today what he did to those sponsored fighters who gutted you. They found the last pieces of them this morning."

Ashe fought back a grim smile. "It was well-deserved." And it was less fighters they'd have to face in the melee.

All at once, she didn't feel like smiling anymore.

Nimea's brows slid up. "You must be so grateful to him, swooping in to avenge you."

Ashe folded her arms. "What's that supposed to mean?"

Lips twitching, Nimea shook her head. "Nothing. Difficult as you may find this to believe, I actually came to thank you for your help—for giving us Geitlan and Veran and Hellidom. I know it hasn't been easy been for you, enduring my suspicious friends, but there's no doubt in their minds anymore that you're one of us." She shrugged away from the wall and clapped Ashe on the shoulder. "Tobor is out there, on his way to Thorne. This will all be over soon. Once that *bandayo* falls, we'll be free to tear down everyone who's ever wounded us...beginning with Salvotor."

She retreated down the hall, and in her absence Ashe dragged both hands down her face, cursing under her breath. Now of all times was not when she needed Nimea's support and gratitude; not with the melee closing in, and not when strange prickles of unease still rode the current of her pulse whenever she thought of Hellidom.

Nimea was right about one thing, at least...it *would* all be over soon for Ashe. One way or another.

Heaving a sigh, she dropped her hands—and froze.

Aden bent around the corner of the corridor mouth, silent and unshakeable as a death sentence. His eyes bored into her, promising Nimmus, promised every sort of pain she'd ever known, and then some.

Because he'd heard everything.

And now that she'd given them Thorne's home at last, now that she'd given the Tumult the truth they craved, Ashe had no doubt Nimea precisely planned it that way.

CHAPTER FIFTY-THREE

NEITHER OF THEM spoke on the torturous walk back to Aden's chamber. Ashe wanted to ask him if he was all right, if he had been recovering or still suffering for the past week, but it didn't matter. Maybe he'd been healed by his patroness—at a price. Maybe he'd been looking for Ashe to confide in today, someone who knew his secret and didn't hold it above his head.

It didn't matter. Because when he slammed the gate shut behind them, there was no warmth in the gesture, nothing but rage in his eyes as he leaned against the iron bars.

"What have you done."

No inflection. Not really a question—or, if it was, not one he wanted the answer to.

Ashe folded her arms and took a deep breath to quiet the black abyss of panic slowly yawning in her chest. "What did you hear?"

"All of it."

Teeth gritted, Ashe waited for him to realize what he already knew.

"All those times you said you gained nothing from Nimea about what she and her comrades were planning. That wasn't true."

Ashe shut her eyes. "No."

"How much do you really know?"

"Enough that it doesn't matter anymore."

"Tell me everything," Aden growled. "Everything you should've told me weeks ago."

Ashe hesitated—but what did it matter? He couldn't stop any of it. From here in Siralek, he could not keep Thorne alive. "They want to kill Thorne. Devitrius is supplying them with weapons once they leave Siralek."

Aden rubbed a hand through his hair. "They'll never reach him through blind attacks. They must've learned that by now." He stilled, eyes widening. "But if they kill the others, if they incite his anger by way of his loyalties..."

Ashe folded her arms and set her jaw against the same guilt that spiked in her chest every time she thought of Maleck these days. "What's done is done."

Aden's eyes narrowed, reading something in her tone that the words themselves did not convey. "What did you give them?"

"Hellidom," she said, and Aden blanched, lifting forward from the gate. "I told them they could reach Thorne in Hellidom."

She had never felt anything like this silence before, dark and malignant and steaming with fury. Her heart slammed into her ribs; if Aden hadn't been blocking the gate, she might've fled.

"Why?" Aden said. "*Why?*"

"Because I'm not here to spy for you!" Ashe burst out. "I'm a Warden of the King's Cadre, trained by Rion Bartos himself. And I'm protecting my princess!"

"By betraying *Thorne?*"

"He betrayed her first! This is retribution. The first rule Rion ever taught me: you only defeat an enemy when you're ready to match him blow for blow!"

"Who is this Rion and why should either of us give a *damn* what he says?"

"He's my commander, the closest thing to a true father I've ever known," Ashe spat. "He trained me. Everything I am as a Warden, everything that enabled me to survive this pit, I owe to *him.*"

"And here I was under the impression you survived by your *own* merit." Aden raked his hands down his face. "Stars damn it all, I never should have entrusted this to you. Talheimics are *incapable* of letting go of a grudge."

"You're blaming Talheim for this?" Ashe barked. "I would never have accepted this mission if you'd been honest with me from the beginning about who Nimea really is!"

"A part of Thorne's hidden Court? Is that what she told you?"

"Yes! And when he and his precious cabal fled Stornhaz, he betrayed the rest of them to Salvotor—to this place! He's the reason they're here!"

"Thorne did not betray them. He would've died before he gave Salvotor their names."

"Don't lie for him. Why else would any of them be here if not because Thorne betrayed them like he betrayed Cistine?"

"He didn't!" Aden roared. "*I did!*"

The candles guttered between the skulls.

Ashe stared at him, coldness biting into her cheeks and neck as the blood fled from her face. "You—*what?*"

"Salvotor knew Thorne was keeping something from him. He knew I was part of it, like I was part of all Thorne's affairs. So he baited me...tricked me. He told me my *father* was still alive." For the first time Ashe had ever heard, Aden's voice cracked. "My father, the man I aspired to be—the man whose memory still keeps me from becoming a Blood Hive beast like the rest of them. Everything good left in me, *I* owe to *him*. And when Salvotor offered me his whereabouts in exchange for names..."

He broke off, and broke his stare, gazing at the dead candles on the walls.

"It was a lie, but I believed it," he snarled at last. "I told him about the support Thorne had begun to rally. A Court within Salvotor's Court, of which we were all part. I gave Salvotor everything, every name, for that one hopeless chance...and it was all a ruse. He was not even *alive*. Thorne was whipped, Baba Kallah's leg broken, Ariadne was violated and nailed to a door, Quill imprisoned in Detlyse Halet and Maleck carted off to stars-know-where...for nothing. Because of *me*."

Ashe took several steps back from him. "*You* betrayed them?"

"I was desperate to save my father...desperate enough to believe Salvotor's false evidence." Aden shook his head, shook the memories away. "But even when we fled, even when it was *hopeless*, Thorne wanted to go back for them. Bleeding, his back broken open, he still wanted to free Nimea and the others."

"And you let them go on believing *he* was their enemy, when it was *you?*"

"I've tried to convince them of his innocence. They've never listened—I didn't know their hatred ran *this* deep after a decade," Aden rasped. "I came here years ago to keep watch over them, to try and free them, because Thorne told me it was the only way I could prove my remorse for what I'd done. I didn't know Devitrius had given them a means to reach him...or that *you* provided them the places, the names, the *weapons* against him! Your loyalty was meant to be to me, to finding and preventing this...not ensuring his death!"

"Don't lay the blame on my shoulders! You started this when you told them I'd been with Thorne—you did this yourself!"

Aden's eyes widened. "What in Nimmus are you talking about? I never mentioned your involvement with Thorne!"

Ashe's mind scrabbled through that conversation with Nimea in the dining hall the first night she met the Tumult. "No, you did. You *had* to. Nimea only let me into their ranks because of that."

Aden's gaze fell suddenly blank. And Ashe knew.

Devitrius.

He'd spread that rumor. Stirred up Nimea's interest in Ashe and pushed them toward one another with his wicked tongue, beginning that first night when he brought Ashe to Siralek just for this.

Because Salvotor had known she wouldn't betray the cabal outright, wouldn't lead him to them after he wounded Cistine so terribly—even worse than Thorne. So he'd sent Ashe to the one place and the only people whose hatred of Thorne matched hers, whose vengeance would feed her fire until it burned away her control. Her common sense. Just like he'd used the thought of Aden's father to burn away *his*.

They were no different at all, Ashe and the Hive Lord. She'd fallen for precisely the same ruse.

Shame whipped through her, so hot and quick it slung words from her lips: "None of this would've happened if you hadn't betrayed your friends! You're a liar, a coward, Aden...and you deserve to be in this place. You sent these people here to die!"

"You think I'm unaware? I'm here to pay the price for what I brought on them! This is not about saving me, it's about protecting Thorne."

"Well, now we both have his blood on our hands," Ashe said. "You kept the truth from me, and I sent assassins after an innocent man!"

Innocent.

She hadn't thought of Thorne that way, not once, after what he did to Cistine. But now her mind betrayed her just as wickedly as Aden had, recalling like a taunt how Thorne had gone into the jaws of battle to find Cistine, just like he'd run to her in the Izten Torkat when they fell over that edge together. He'd put his body between her and danger, even a threat of his own making; as guilty as he was of deceiving Cistine, he'd also come to save her.

And if Aden was telling the truth, that was what Thorne did: he broke things, and then he made them right if he could. Like he'd tried to come back for Nimea and the others, even though that hadn't been his fault.

No. It had been the fault of the man before her, the one she'd worked with, dined with, and fought alongside. The one she'd spared, the one whose release she'd pleaded from Sander. The one she'd worried over constantly for the past week.

And he'd kept all this from her.

Ashe couldn't look at him. There was nothing to say that would even graze the first edge of the hurt beating in her body or the guilt that trapped her in a fist.

Thorne would die because of them—the destructive force that was Ashe and Aden.

Blinded by shame and shock, she stormed toward the gate, shoving

Aden aside. "You did this. You. Not me."

"We're both to blame," Aden said. "Both guilty. If Thorne dies, then we killed him. Because I trusted you."

"No," Ashe spat. "Because you *lied* to me. And to Nimea."

She left his chamber. And this time, it was she who slammed the gate.

CHAPTER
FIFTY-FOUR

THE WARMTH OF the sunlight fanning across Cistine's shoulders clashed with the cold wind slipping under her collar, leaving no doubt that autumn was marching down from the north. She sat back on her heels, wicking off the bit of sweat gathered at her temples and surveying her handiwork—fruits plucked for canning, vegetables harvested for a spate of recipes Baba Kallah had written out. It would be a busy few days, but she welcomed the distraction. Now that they'd returned to the Den, Hellidom mercifully confirmed empty of enemies, things were beginning to feel normal again. Soon enough, Yager would send for Józef so the trial against Chancellor Salvotor could be underway.

Heart pounding at the thought, Cistine stacked her baskets and wove toward the Den, letting the water wheels' familiar creak soothe her frayed nerves. She had too much on her mind lately—training, cooking, cleaning, the assassins, Blaykrone's troubles, and Józef, Ashe, *Julian*…

She shook the thought of him and his distance and silence from her mind when she toed the Den's door shut behind her. A whisper moved on the wind of its closing.

Come and see.

She'd been fighting that familiar call since the moment they stepped foot back in the Den and greeted Baba Kallah. She didn't like to imagine it was stronger than when they left for Geitlan...so loud she could almost believe it was not only in her heart, but in her mind as well.

She reached the kitchen with her load of baskets so high she couldn't see around it, and she only knew she wasn't alone when a deep laugh sounded just ahead of her. The top two baskets vanished, and Thorne peered at her over them. "Hungry?"

She kicked his shin. "You know the answer to *that*."

At the table, Ariadne snorted quietly, glancing up from the map she and Thorne were assessing, demarcated with lines and pins—places where the assassins had attacked and possible points of origin.

"Anything?" Cistine asked carefully as she and Thorne lined the baskets on the counter.

"Nothing definitive, I'm afraid," Ariadne said. "The points of attack suggest a hideaway somewhere in the Vaszaj Range, and yet..." her eyes flicked to Thorne. So did Cistine's.

He sighed. "Their attire suggests they hailed from a warmer climate. Kroaken or Nordbran."

Cistine frowned. "So we have no idea of where to find them or how to confront them?"

Thorne chuckled, mussing her hair. "Easy, *Logandir*."

"We'll find them," Ariadne said. "But not before Maleck finds you."

An aberrant breath brushed the back of her neck, and Cistine whirled, smashing her fist into Maleck's chest. He didn't even flinch at the blow. "Don't do that!" she yelped—then froze.

He was holding a stack of letters between two fingers. One was addressed to her.

"Yager?" Cistine breathed.

Maleck flicked the letters apart—one to the table, one into Cistine's hands—and propped his hand on the cabinet above her head while she tore open the heavy envelope. Thorne folded his arms and reclined against the counter, watching her read Liv's tidy scrawl aloud.

"Dearest *Yani*...Yager sends its regards. I hope the weather is favorable where you are. It's cold as death here in Stornhaz already, but in the east, it's far warmer." Cistine swallowed, pulse racing again. "Astrid and Ingrid just returned from their mission. They noticed some Kanslar activity near Keltei Temple, but as for Detlyse Halet..."

Her throat closed and her fingertips grew numb. She lowered her arm, and Thorne caught the letter by the corner, freeing it from her grasp to finish reading: "There is no trace of your friend in the Lightless Pit."

Maleck's hand slid from the cabinet, his arm draping over Cistine's shoulders and drawing her against his side as the kitchen blurred before her eyes.

Ever since Jovadalsa, she'd hoped so desperately that as terrible as Detlyse Halet might be, it would hold the answer; that they were merely being kept from Ashe by time and circumstances, not that she was still absolutely missing. They were just as far from reaching her now as they had been when they fled from Stornhaz.

"Training," Maleck murmured against Cistine's ear.

She let him turn her toward the doorway, realizing only when he did that Thorne had taken her hand. When she looked back, meeting his troubled gaze, she could hardly believe it was pain he felt for her. But there it was, shining in his eyes.

He gave her fingers a quick squeeze, and let go. With a fleeting smile, Cistine hurried after Maleck—fighting with all her might not to look inside Ashe's empty room.

"What do we do now?" Cistine panted over the echo of beating steel.

Maleck didn't answer right away, walking her through a series of slow strokes with the knives they held—Nail in her hand, Remany in his. They never moved through these drills faster than a crawl, just as when he'd had her testing the weight and balance of knives in the weapon room. And yet his measured approach allowed her to become aware of muscle memory, her arms learning where to bring the blade to block, her eyes already quicker to find places she could pass his guard—which she did now, sliding Nail gently into the hinge of his elbow.

Maleck stepped back. "Now we turn our eyes elsewhere. I had a thought last night...the desert prison, Siralek. Though it would be unusual for Salvotor to send a Talheimic prisoner there, where she could rally her strength, it has merit."

"Rally her strength?"

Maleck held her gaze, turning the knife over in his fingers. "In Siralek, prisoners are pitted against one another in matches to the death."

Cistine winced and raised her weapon. They moved through the drill again—faster this time, with her on the offensive. "I imagine it would be well-guarded, then. Difficult to look into."

"Naturally. But I may have some connections that would prove useful, as I did in Jovadalsa."

Cistine faltered at the thought of what another encounter like that mean for Maleck. And for Ashe, if she truly was in such a prison.

"Cistine!" Maleck snapped, and she barely swung Nail in time to block as he switched from defense to attack. "*Concentrate.*"

She pushed thoughts of a fighting prison from her mind and plowed forward, forcing him to back away. They swayed across the rock top, repeating the same pattern of thrust, block, parry, over and over. It was slowly beginning to feel like habit, to feel natural down to her bones.

Then, abruptly, Maleck said, "Sheath."

Confused, Cistine nevertheless obeyed, sliding Nail into its scabbard on her hip. "Why are we stopping now?"

Fingers clamped down on her ribs from either side, tickling her so hard she shrieked like a bird and spun around, half-laughing, half-swearing, aiming a blow at Quill's side. He casually stepped from reach, Faer sulking on his shoulder—exhausted and cranky from his flight to Starhollow and back again.

"Just what do you think you're doing here?" Cistine demanded in mock-outrage. "You had your way with me this morning!"

Quill's brows jumped, and Cistine flushed, but to her relief he simply thumbed his nose and gestured into Hellidom. "Time to meet Tatiana and choose your battle armor. Remember?"

She hadn't—the letter about Ashe had scattered her thoughts like seeds on the wind—but now excitement and relief warmed her core. Facing augmented enemies would make sense if she had armor to protect her. She could finally put the incident from the Black Coasts out of her mind.

"You're both coming," she decided. Ignoring Maleck's quiet litany of excuses and Quill's groan of protest, she grabbed their arms and dragged them down from the rock top with her.

CHAPTER FIFTY-FIVE

THEY SPENT MOST of that evening in Tariq's shop, where Tatiana had already been browsing an hour before their arrival. Six new outfits hung from the crook of her arm when they found her.

"Not a word," she warned at Cistine's grin. "This isn't about me. This is about *you*."

Cistine didn't mind that in the least, even when they all fell to arguing about which reinforcements were best—steel silk, serpent scales, or animal hide. She browsed the racks of armor in their varying color and design, plated with protective casts that would conduct certain augments better and protect against the elements in unique ways, but there was one set she returned to again and again.

"Red adder scales," Tatiana explained when she found Cistine standing before the rack, arms akimbo, staring at the armor. "A little less flashy than I thought you'd like."

"Those scales are the real thing, by the way," Quill drawled. "Adders are heavy, and so's that armor. But for good reason...it's so tough, most blades can't get through it."

"Even *Svarkyst* steel would have difficulty at the first stroke." Maleck agreed. "It's the less-expensive cousin to dragon's hide."

Cistine ran her fingers over the slippery-smooth armor, her stomach clenching. It wasn't until she touched those dark, shimmery layers that she understood why it appealed to her; its lay resembled a King's Cadre uniform. "This is what I need my armor made of."

They left the shop not quite gloomy, but silent, the three warriors clearly in tune with Cistine's melancholy. She clutched the receipt with Tariq's written vow to have it finished as soon as his other commissions were cleared, and tried not to feel Ashe's spirit haunting her steps. As if this new armor might be the only way she would ever feel her Warden with her again.

"I need a drink," Quill announced suddenly. "Who's with me?"

Tatiana swung her bags over her shoulder. "Early bed for me. I have guard duty with Józef first thing tomorrow."

"Pity you, Saddlebags! He's insufferable when he's bored, and he's already torn through almost every book in the Den."

"At least he enjoys Baba Kallah's company," Cistine offered.

"That woman has the patience of a god. Well, enjoy your restful night without us, Tati."

"Oh, I *will*." She winked at Cistine and sashayed away.

They arrived in Hellidom's only tavern to find it bustling with the day's hunters and workers, making a challenge of finding a table. When they sat, Cistine had to tuck her bag between her knees to avoid blocking anyone else's seats. Before the first round of mead arrived, Quill reached into the pocket of his open vest and slid a square of paper to her. "Faer brought this. I think Pip forgives us for leaving."

Cistine unfolded the paper and burst into laughter. Crude though the sketch was, there was no mistaking the entire cabal—Quill with his mismatched plumage, Thorne's head snow-white, Maleck with a faintly-penciled scar over his right eye and flowers braided into his hair. Pippet had taken the most care detailing Tatiana's golden dress and dark locks, Ariadne's swords, and Cistine with a white gown and a crown of stars on her brow, standing next to Pippet herself—also crowned. Two princesses, holding hands.

Cistine slid the picture to Maleck. "It feels good to be forgiven."

A smile tipped his lips. "Yes, it does."

"Cassaida and Helga both send their love, too." Quill hung one arm over the back of his chair. "Geitlan's people should be able to last the winter in Starhollow. We'll rehome them in the spring."

Cistine took her mead from the barmaid with a quiet *thank you* and waited for her to depart again before she replied, "Hopefully by then, the danger to Blaykrone will have passed."

Quill's eyes darkened. "It had better. Magnus and his archers are working themselves to the bone, and it's barely enough. There's still no aid but ours being sent to Blaykrone. Flooding below the Izten Torkat, wildfires near the Unsverd border, and bandit raids—real ones—on the Vingete Vey. Apparently, the Vassora withdrew from the road to *reinforce* Stornhaz."

Maleck's eyes slid up to his friend. "Salvotor."

"Naturally."

Cistine grimaced. "Adeima *has* to write to us soon. Blaykrone can't take much more of this, and the archers can't be everywhere at once."

"Well, we could help too, if Thorne divided us," Quill said.

It was an argument they'd had often and heatedly on the journey home from Veran. Quill and Thorne had nearly come to blows over it, and they already knew which side of the line Cistine came down on.

"*No*," she said, which was the same thing Thorne had told them. "The attacks on Blaykrone may be Salvotor's way of drawing us out into the open so those assassins can finish the job. This cabal has to stay together for now, or we'll be slaughtered."

"Agreed," Maleck said.

Quill polished off his mead in a few swift pulls, then picked up Maleck's to refill as well. "Right. But other people are being slaughtered in the meantime."

Cistine rested her chin on her hands, her gaze trailing listlessly around the tavern while Quill went to the counter. He was right—and eventually Thorne wouldn't be able to endure the injustices in Blaykrone, even for the safety of his warriors. He would go himself, if he wouldn't send anyone else, and try to put out fires, dam floods, and stop criminals with his bare hands.

She cast up a silent prayer that Yager would write to them before they reached that point.

But that prayer burned up, turned to dust, and floated away from her thoughts when her eyes fixed on the table beside the counter, where a circle of men gambled and laughed together.

"Drink up, *Storfir!*" Quill banged the steins down, slid one to Maleck, and flopped back into his seat. "What did I miss?"

"Cistine?" Maleck said.

She couldn't draw a full breath, couldn't tear her gaze away from those gamblers and the barmaids who attended them.

Or from Julian.

There he was, playing cards, laughing and drinking like these were old friends he'd gambled with often, though she'd never seen him so comfortable among Valgardans. There was a woman perched on his knee, and he ran his fingers absently through her hair.

The mead climbed Cistine's throat, burning and sour, and her eyes heated. She was dimly aware of Maleck and Quill swiveling to follow her gaze—and growing very, very still when they saw what she did.

Quill's fingers slowly tightened around his stein. "I'm going to kill him."

"Would you like us to remove him from the tavern?" Maleck offered, and Cistine knew at one word from her, he'd be across the room and yanking Julian from his chair. He'd find a decent excuse to put him out in the cold, even if it gave the people more reason to fear Maleck himself.

Cistine sucked in a harsh breath as Julian absently laid out a card, then kissed the barmaid's shoulder, just like he'd done so many times to her. The foolish, selfish memories dug into her mind, setting her heart wailing when Julian won that round, pulled the woman around by her waist, and kissed her full on the mouth.

Cistine couldn't believe the pained sound that escaped her throat at the memory of how that kiss felt when it was hers alone to cherish.

"Cistine," Quill said—then shoved back his chair. "Nimmus' teeth, I'm not going to sit here for this."

"Quill, no." She grabbed his arm. "I'm the one who did this. I gave him back the ring. I can't fault him for moving on."

"In your presence," Maleck growled. "With no respect for your heart."

"He doesn't know I'm here."

Quill slowly sank back down and picked up his stein again. "He never deserved you, anyway."

Cistine tried to drink her mead and focus on the conversation when Maleck and Quill turned it to talk of Hellidom and Starhollow and how Helga had mentioned some chest pains while she worked and needing more help from Geitlan's people than expected. But her eyes skimmed back to Julian, so relaxed and happy—as if he'd already forgotten her. Even though he'd been so withdrawn on the journey home from Veran, here he was, in the taverns like he had been before their courtship, six steins deep with his chin hanging over the barmaid's shoulder.

Cistine scraped her chair back. "I'm going home."

Quill and Maleck rose at once. "So are we," Quill said.

"No. Stay and drink, you earned it after all that shopping. I'll be all right."

She was at the threshold when she thought she heard Julian say her name; but she ignored him, escaping into the street, and the moment her feet touched the road the tears started. She wept all the way back to the Den in fury and grief: grieved for the happiness that was gone. And angry that she couldn't seem to let go of the person she'd *chosen* to give away.

Her face blotchy and hot, eyes itching, she slammed the Den's front door shut and made straight for her room. Her only hope was to sleep and wake with her composure intact again; but all notions of a swift escape were dashed when she arrived in the kitchen to find Baba Kallah standing at the stove where a kettle boiled. Józef occupied the table, flipping through yet another book.

"Tea is nearly ready, *Yani*." Baba Kallah's tone brooked no protest.

Cistine stopped trying to sidle toward her room and slumped into a chair instead. "Tea would be lovely, thank you."

Baba Kallah retrieved three cups and filled them with steaming apple tea, placed one before Józef and another before Cistine, then lowered herself into the seat beside her. "These come fresh from Hellidom's newest merch. A desert spice blend with valerian. He claims it's soothing to the weary mind and brings good sleep."

"Do I seem weary?" Cistine couldn't dredge up enough humor to make the joke convincing.

Baba Kallah frowned. "Just as weary as Thorne. You know, this tea was meant as a gift for him...a welcome tribute to the man who safeguards Hellidom." She nudged Cistine's arm and winked. "But I don't think he would mind us drinking it, do you?"

Cistine smiled weakly and shook her head.

"Well, I intend to make good use of it." Józef helped himself to the tea in a long, deep gulp, then hacked at the heat, banging the cup down and fanning his mouth.

"Men," Baba Kallah laughed, turning to Cistine again. "It's nice to have you all to myself for a moment. Thorne's told me about what you did in the Black Coasts."

An arc of unease twisted down Cistine's back. "I hope he didn't tell you *everything*. I was a mess at the end."

"We're all a mess. But you transformed that mess into something beautiful."

"It's true." Józef wheezed, sweating and red-faced from the hot tea. "You...greatly impressed the miners, risking your life for theirs. It's no wonder they call you *Logandir*."

Cistine stared into her mug, the spicy, herbaceous aroma curling through her nostrils. Her skin tingled with the memory of her confrontation with the Vassora—the lightning sizzling near her body. "I'm just glad to save lives...to be useful."

"You have always been useful." Baba Kallah drank deeply, then brushed her knuckles along the arch of Cistine's cheek. "Why do you cry?"

The floodgates unleashed, and she told Baba Kallah—and, to her mortification, Józef—how she'd parted ways with Julian in Veran, and what she saw in the tavern. The front door clattered open and shut somewhere during the story, and Julian's familiar footfalls stumbled into his room. She dropped her voice and struggled to go on, and still Baba Kallah listened, her forehead faintly pinched, drinking her tea while Cistine's grew cold, and her tears cooled with it.

Finally, she was calm again.

"I'm sorry." She wiped her face on her sleeve. "I'm just starting to realize that the choices in a queen's hands are fathoms different from a princess's. It's not about parcels and parties anymore, I'm making decisions that will impact my kingdom, my future, and my people's lives."

"Yes," Baba Kallah said. "And it is a heavy burden. But you've made the right choice, for Talheim and for yourself."

"I didn't think making the right choice would hurt so badly...that letting go of Julian could hurt as much as all our fights."

"Choices like these are never easy," Baba Kallah said. "But it's better to have a little pain now in the parting than a lifetime of it in your marriage. Just look at my *valenar* and me."

Józef groaned suddenly and slumped against the table, falling deeply asleep in the middle of their conversation.

Baba Kallah chuckled, picking up her mug again. "Some men can't hold their tea."

She stopped.

Her hand rattled—and the cup crashed from her grasp, shattering on the table, as Baba Kallah toppled from her chair and collapsed on the floor.

CHAPTER FIFTY-SIX

SCREAMING, CISTINE LUNGED to her feet, hurling aside the chair. "*Thorne!*" She dropped to her knees, feeling for Baba Kallah's breath. "*THORNE!*"

Baba Kallah breathed, but shallowly. A faint freckling of foam hung about her lips. Cistine scooped an arm under her bent shoulders, sitting her up and shaking her. "Baba...Baba Kallah!"

Footsteps thundered down the stairs, every one thudding in Cistine's chest. The door in the hallway slammed open, and Thorne appeared, hair ruffled, dark shirt and pants wrinkled as if he'd slept in them, and Cistine sobbed his name.

Hurling chairs aside, he dropped down beside them and cradled his grandmother's face in his hands. "Baba Kallah?" To Cistine's relief, the old woman's eyelids flickered at her beloved grandson's touch. "What happened?" Thorne's eyes leaped to Cistine's face. "Cistine!"

"I don't know! We were drinking tea, she just collapsed..."

Thorne bellowed toward the opposite doorway, and before she could comprehend what he'd said, Maleck and Ariadne bolted into the room. Behind them, rumpled and wild-eyed, Julian appeared—a commander's son used to rising at the sound of revelry, skidding to a halt at the sight that greeted him. "Oh, gods, what *happened?*"

Thorne pointed to Józef. "Check him!"

Ariadne darted to the table, pressed her fingers to the man's neck, and cursed. "He's gone, Thorne."

Cistine gaped at her. Their witness—the man who could validate the contracts with Devitrius, all the knowledge about Salvotor's movements along the Black Coasts and the deals with the *Svarkyst* shipments—gone. Just like that.

Maleck picked up Józef's cup, sniffed its contents, then dropped it with a low curse. "Poison."

Cistine wove on her knees. The tea...

"Did you drink it?" Thorne's fingers tangled in the back of her hair, dragging her head around toward him. "Cistine! *Did you drink it?*"

"No, not a drop!"

"Do you know where it came from?"

"It was a gift." She squeezed Baba Kallah's shoulders. "A tribute from a new merch..."

A gift of poisoned tea. For *Thorne.*

The assassins.

She met his wide eyes, the realization searing the air between them.

He kissed Cistine's brow swiftly and scooped Baba Kallah up in his arms. "The merch who gave it to her—*find him.*"

Ariadne vanished, Julian on her heels, as Thorne carried his grandmother down the hall. Maleck offered a hand to Cistine, and they chased after him through the foyer, past door after door on the right-side corridor. Quill and Tatiana jutted their heads out when Cistine and Maleck ran past.

"What's going on?" Tatiana yawned.

"Baba Kallah's just been poisoned," Cistine choked.

They were at her back before she'd taken another step, rushing after Thorne and Maleck into Baba Kallah's sparse, simple room, where Thorne had laid her already against the pillows of the canopied bed. He sat her up, as Cistine had, so she could breathe. Maleck hurried to examine her, and Cistine slipped to Thorne's side. He stood back from the bed, still close enough to touch his grandmother—first her head, then her shoulder. Then his hand hunted for hers and squeezed. She returned the gesture, but so weakly...

Cistine started to pray.

Maleck swiveled toward Thorne, and in that grim, uncompromising stare, Cistine saw again the man she'd met on the Vingete Vey: a tender spirit faced with battle, retreating behind locks and barriers to escape his pain.

Thorne's hand tightened around his grandmother's. "No."

"I've never seen poison of this kind before. The smell is like *zivmeglas*, but the effects..." Maleck shook his head and touched Baba Kallah's arm. "It's slowing the flow of blood through her body like ice."

Cistine's mind raced. "What about using a blood thinner?"

"We have none here. And even if we did, thinners take hours to go into effect."

"Then why are you still sitting there?" Thorne's voice was blade-sharp. "Go and find some!"

"Thorne. She doesn't have time."

Behind Maleck, Tatiana let out a strangled half-sob smothered by her hand. Quill wrapped both arms around her shoulders from behind and kissed her temple, his eyes trained on the bed as if he feared he'd blink, and Baba Kallah would be gone.

"Józef drank more tea than she did." Maleck smoothed the hair from Baba Kallah's brow. "I suspect that's why he went first. But even so...minutes, Thorne. At best."

Dry sobs ripped from Cistine's throat. "What about a healing augment?"

"The ones we have will mend broken flesh, but they can do nothing for poisons. We brought none of those with us from Stornhaz."

Thorne's chest rattled in low, agonized gasps, as if *he* had been poisoned, as if *his* blood was firming up in his veins. Maleck rose from the bedside and Thorne took his place, tucking the hair behind his grandmother's ear. He searched her face with scavenging eyes, looking for hope somewhere in those pained folds. "Baba."

Her eyelids lifted slowly, and she raised her free hand and crooked a finger. "Cistine. Come here."

She tasted tears again as she sat on the bed's opposite side, her back against Thorne's, and took Baba Kallah's other hand. Her mind rebelled against the path her heart was already taking—the slow, dark slide toward accepting the horror before her. What she felt in that hand, so cool where it gripped hers.

"You do not stay here." Baba Kallah's gaze staggered between them. "You do not mourn forever. You go, and you fight, and then you have peace." She lifted their hands and brought them together, clasped between her own.

Cistine's heart stumbled, her eyes meeting Thorne's over their joined hands inside the cradle of Baba Kallah's final embrace.

"You have peace *together*." She kissed their entwined hands. "*Stornjor*, you...you are a better man than your father ever was. And you, Cistine. A queen...so long before your time."

Cistine pressed her lips together and shook her head.

"*Yani*." Baba Kallah freed their hands and touched Cistine's face. "When your day comes...I will be there. I will always be."

Thorne braced his hands on either side of his grandmother, leaning his brow to hers. "Baba. *Don't* leave me." It began as a command, but it ended a plea; a child begging his first and greatest love not to go.

"Never." But Baba Kallah sank more heavily against the pillows.

Thorne got to his feet and dragged his hands down his face, then back through his hair. Watching him step away from the bed, from the pain, Cistine almost didn't feel the faint tug on her hand. She almost turned too late to catch Baba Kallah's stare.

When the old woman motioned to her, Cistine leaned low enough to feel those trembling, cold breaths against her ear.

"*Sillakove*." The Old Valgardan word danced with power and enchantment on Baba Kallah's tongue. "Thorne is...our Star..."

The wind left her on a soft sigh, and she went limp against the pillow.

Tatiana sobbed, Quill cursed, and Maleck took two steps back and sank to his knees beside them, casting an arm around Quill's back. Thorne left the room without a word to anyone. In the hall, something cracked—wood. Bone. Then all was silent.

Cistine leaned her head against Baba Kallah's breast, and for many minutes she tried not to feel anything—the grief, or the guilt, or the devastating relief that she hadn't touched *her* tea, that she wouldn't be the next to die with Thorne's hand around hers. With the smell of orange and cinnamon wrapped around her, she searched for dark, void peace.

You have peace together.

"Thorne." Cistine sat up and turned to the cabal, still crashed on the floor, still holding onto one another.

"Go." Maleck nodded to the doorway. "He needs you."

Dazed, she followed not a call, not a sound, but her heart's own sense of where Thorne would go.

She found him outside the Den, past the garden, on the river's stone bank where he'd fallen to his knees. He stared at the crashing rapids, his back heaving and collapsing with surges of uncontrollable grief and rage Cistine couldn't truly fathom. Her own grandmother had died when she was young, so long ago she was little more than an absentminded fragment from a story, a woman of powdered sugar and book dust who'd come and gone with Cistine's early years. But Baba Kallah had been Thorne's longest and most powerful pillar.

The tears came again, silent, breathless sobs when she touched his back and sank down beside him. He didn't face her. He stared down at his hands, open on his bent knees—hands that had clung to his grandmother to no avail. Then he spoke the words Cistine already knew: "It was meant for me."

Silence, for a long moment.

"It *should* have been me."

"Thorne, no! *No.*" She slid her fingertips up the curve of his back. "Baba Kallah would've chosen this if she knew. Her life for yours, always. She loved you."

"I know. But without her..." he slowly drew his legs from under his body so he sat on his haunches, sprawled, his arms linked around his knees, head sagging. "Without her, I can't..."

Cistine slid her arm around his shoulders. "Let me help you. Don't shut me out of your grief, Thorne."

He was still, head bowed, only the wind shifting his hair.

Then he leaned into her, leaned his whole weight against her side and rested his head on her collar, his tears seeping into her training armor. With her free hand, she clutched his face to her chest and stroked his hair from his brow.

All around them, the night deepened, clouds smothering the stars.

Cistine woke on her bed with no memory of falling asleep.

It took a moment for everything to crash over her—the sensation of Baba Kallah's fingers around hers and the old woman's last breath still tickling her cheek. She whimpered with grief, pulling the blanket snug against her chin, and a hand squeezed her shoulder. Thorne was sitting on the bed behind her, his knee pressing her back. She wondered if she should say anything, ask if he needed to talk, or cry, or hit something.

A throat cleared from the doorway, and she kept her eyes shut as Thorne's legs unfolded and his weight slid from the bed. "Report."

"We have him." There was no triumph in Maleck's voice, no satisfaction...no emotion at all. "Julian and Ariadne found him trying to escape Hellidom on horseback."

"Give me his name."

"It's Tobor."

A breath of shock Cistine didn't fully understand. "*Tobor?*"

"I could hardly believe it myself. He's changed, but it's him."

The silence was perilous—the quiet of a man standing on a cliff, deciding if the leap was worthwhile, the risk of perishing for the chance at success.

Then Thorne said, "Break him."

CHAPTER FIFTY-SEVEN

I T TOOK A full day to prepare the pyre for Baba Kallah's body, the world a blur of endless, pounding grief where Cistine saw nothing of Quill and Maleck. Wherever they had taken the false merch named Tobor, it was far from sight, beyond earshot, and she was glad; in the warm embrace of the unusually-silent Den, she gave herself permission to weep while she kneaded bread dough, to sob into her hand when she made tea for herself and Tatiana, who sat blank-faced at the table and watched her work.

"I don't know how you can stand this," Tatiana whispered. "How you can think this is better than feeling *nothing*."

But she didn't go hunting for a flask. She came to the stove and wrapped her arms around Cistine instead, and they cried together for the love they'd lost.

That evening, with the pyre prepared on the Nior's banks, they sent Baba Kallah to rest in a brilliant dance of scarlet-gold flames. Cistine stood with Tatiana, gripping her hand, and Julian on her other side, fists folded in the small of his back, head bowed, hair hanging into his grief-stricken eyes. Across the pyre, Ariadne looked on with hands on her belted weapons, fighting tears. And Thorne, beside her...his expression made Cistine's stomach churn. All that rage, all that grief from the night before was gone. Dark circles coiled around his dead, dim eyes, the iciness no longer sparkling in their depths.

When the pyre was consumed and the ash had blown away toward the overcast sky, the people of Hellidom trickled away. Few spoke to the cabal; Cistine doubted they knew what to say. Even she was lost for words when she and Thorne walked side by side behind the others back to the Den.

When they entered the kitchen, drawn there by an unspoken accord, they found Quill sitting at the table, gnawing on a cinnamon stick while he fed breadcrumbs to Faer, and Maleck, slicing Cistine's loaf of cinnamon-orange bread. For once, the smell didn't entice her, but Thorne's stomach audibly growled.

Quill swung his boots off the table and stood, clapping Thorne in an embrace and murmuring something in his ear. Thorne dipped his head as he pulled out his usual chair at the table, and his eyes dragged almost unwillingly to the empty seat Baba Kallah always occupied at his right hand.

Cistine looked to her own chair between Ashe's empty setting and Julian's seat. He wouldn't look at her, scraping his thumbnail fastidiously on the tabletop. So she sat beside Thorne instead.

To her relief, he didn't order her from his grandmother's chair. In fact, he didn't stop looking at the seat even after she sank down into it. He startled slightly when Maleck placed a full plate of bread before him. "You need to eat, *allet*."

After a long moment, Thorne started to trim the crust.

"Quill," Tatiana said hoarsely. "What's the word?"

Face grim, he sent Faer up to perch on his shoulder. "It's not good. Tobor has connections now. He's not that awkward Tyve-loving herbalist we knew from Stornhaz."

"How far does this spread?" Ariadne asked.

"High and far." Maleck took his seat across from her. "These assassins have all come from the same source, with the same purpose. They've been tasked with killing Thorne or killing us to drive him from hiding."

"My father did this," Thorne said.

"Through Devitrius. And through Nimea. She leads the assassins from inside Siralek."

Thorne slammed his hand down on the table so swiftly Julian looked up and locked eyes with Cistine. Her stomach crumpled. That was twice in as many days she'd heard of that place. And if there was any possibility Maleck was right about where Salvotor might've sent Ashe...

A stroke of uneasy thought brushed her mind. She thrust it away.

"Nimea didn't know about Hellidom," Tatiana said. "How did she find us? Who could've told her?"

Thorne and Maleck stared at one another down the table, both deathly quiet, something terrible in that knowing stare.

"Thorne." Ariadne's voice trembled slightly. "No."

"Aden's been there for five years." The words wrenched from Thorne, each one hanging heavy with pain. "Trying to find a way to free the rest of Sillakove."

Quill grimaced. "You don't think he—?"

"Whatever else he did, Aden would never have given up Hellidom. Not unless she tortured it from him on his last breath."

Ruthless, damning silence crashed down over the table.

Quill slammed back in his chair. Tatiana shook her head. "No. No, *don't* say that."

"It's the only way she could've learned." There was no inflection in Thorne's voice. "No one else outside this cabal who knew we were here."

Maleck drummed his fingers on the table, gaze fierce, mouth taut. "Nimea must be stopped. It will be dangerous, but not impossible to reach her within the Blood Hive. I'll deal with this."

Cistine wondered if the rest of the cabal saw that hint of a plan starting to form in his face—or the way he met her eyes down the table and nodded faintly.

Julian reclined in his seat, folding his arms. "About Yager. When do we tell them Józef is dead?"

Quill turned his filthy hair over his skull. "As soon as we do, it's all over. Maybe we ought to find them and tell them in person. As least then we can negotiate face-to-face."

"Negotiate for what?" Thorne said. "We have nothing to implicate my father. Nimea did him a favor without meaning to: her assassin destroyed two of the most valuable people in Valgard. Almost three. It's over."

"Thorne," Cistine murmured, "don't give up."

He swung a sharp stare onto her, and she held beneath it. She knew he was furious, but not with her.

After a moment, he slumped again in his seat. "I ignored the assassins until it was too late. My father played Devitrius, played Nimea and used Aden...and now us. He finished what he started with Baba Kallah's leg, and I don't..." he fell quiet and dragged a hand down his face. "I can't *afford* to underestimate his position. He's beaten us. He beat us years ago."

Thorne left the table, the distraught cabal looking around at one another. Cistine had never heard him sound so hopeless...and judging by their faces, neither had they.

Baba Kallah's death and this notion of Aden dead as well had fractured something deep in his spirit, leaving him caught like an animal in a trap, bleeding out. As if it would be some mercy if the hunter came along and put a spear through his liver—and finished the job.

It was almost of their own accord that Cistine's feet carried her to Maleck's room half an hour after the cabal broke apart. In that short time, he was nearly packed; when Cistine knocked and he hailed her into the room, she found him folding the last of his provisions on top of his satchel.

Her empty stomach twisted, and she sank down on the edge of the bed. "How will you travel?"

"By barge and horseback." His reply was prompt; he'd thought this through, likely since the moment the notion occurred to him that Ashe might be in Siralek. "It should take little less than a fortnight. I'll surveil the arena, learn of its inhabitants and their whereabouts, and then..."

Silence. Given the grimness simmering between him and Quill, and what they'd managed to glean from Tobor, this reckoning would be brutal.

Cistine picked at a loose thread on the bedspread. "I wish you weren't going." She hated how her voice cracked, how weak it sounded; but with the taint of pyre smoke still clogging her throat, her eyes itching with unshed tears, she had no pretenses left.

Maleck belted the satchel shut and rested his forearms on it, peering at her. "The cause is good. For Aden, whatever's become of him, even if just to send him off on a pyre...and for Ashe, if she's there."

Cistine shivered. If her Warden *was* in Siralek, what state would Maleck find her in? Would she be just another tragedy waiting to befall them?

Had *she* been the one tortured to betray the cabal's sanctuary?

When she said nothing, Maleck rounded the bed and settled himself beside her. "What is it, *Logandir*?"

"I don't know." Cistine rubbed the vicious chill from her arms. "I just feel like something awful is going to happen...something worse than what already has. Did you see Thorne's face when he left the table? And the whole cabal, the state everyone is in..."

"I see them more clearly than they believe," Maleck said. "And I see you. I see how they need *your* strength. This dark path Thorne treads, I know he does not walk it alone as long as you're here. And that gives more hope for us all than you will ever know."

Heat crept up Cistine's neck. "I can't replace his grandmother."

"True, you're too young for that." Maleck rose again, offering his hand. "But you cannot be matched or measured in the good you bring. *That* is why I can go, even knowing Thorne suffers. Because there will be no lack in my absence with you to help carry the burden."

A film of tears blotted Cistine's sight as she took his hand and rose. "There *will* be a lack. I'll miss you, Mal."

"And I you, Cistine." He pressed a kiss to her head, fleeting and full of warmth; then he was gone, in the rustle of his lifted pack, his shadow-light steps carrying him off toward Siralek...and whatever grimness waited there.

CHAPTER
FIFTY-EIGHT

Two weeks passed, hot and fast as a desert storm. Word slowly trickled through the catacomb walls of what was to come; then the arguments began, and the daily stabbings as sponsored fighters tried pick one another off.

In between long, solitary training sessions, Ashe watched her back constantly—not just for them, but for Nimea and Aden, neither of whom approached her after that disastrous day in the halls. She forced herself into fitful slumbers, always with a rock clenched in her fist, braced to rise and defend herself. But word of Aden's assault on the last fighters to corner her spread as well, and for a fortnight, no one dared attack.

One more thing she owed him. One more thing that left her in greater disbelief and despair the closer the melee came.

There were twenty-seven sponsored fighters crowded in the staging room the morning of the match, ripening the air with the tang of fear. For once, they had no weapons as they waited; and with her back and shoulders to a corner where no one could creep up on her, Ashe measured her opponents.

Most of the men were larger than her. There were only two other women: Briet and Dilja, who she'd fought alongside against the Viperwolves, and neither of them would look at her. Ashe refused to look at Aden either, across the breadth of the room, though she could feel his gaze on her when a guard at last descended the exterior steps and fitted a key into the gate.

"The moment you set foot in that arena, don't stop moving," the man ordered. "If you hesitate to consider the course, you have ten seconds, and then you're shot. When you pass through the gauntlet, take up your weapons and fight."

He opened the door, and the fighters at the forefront surged through to the crowd's booming cheers.

Ashe held back. Those fighters would have a better choice of weapons, but she would see how they crossed the course—and that was more valuable now. Dilja, Briet, and a handful of others lingered with her, but Aden was not one of them.

Within thirty seconds, the death screams started.

Ashe cast up a prayer, and across the stream of bodies, caught Briet's gaze. Then they both turned into the tide and let it sweep them up the steps under the darkest, foulest stormy sky Ashe had ever seen, and into the gauntlet.

Hastily-constructed wooden platforms like gallows hung over gaping, pike-infested maws. Beyond them, great vats of burning-hot coals belched shimmery heat into the air; Ashe could smell the steam, different from the arid scorch of the desert wind, when she hit the netting around the platforms and started to climb.

Behind her, Briet screamed. With one hand woven into the net, Ashe twisted back.

Dilja had stopped running. Arms spread, a faint smile on her face, she looked up toward the Tribune's box.

An arrow slammed into her heart, and she toppled, dead of her own choosing.

Briet screamed again, and Ashe shouted, "Briet, here! *Move!*"

The girl darted across the sand, swung up into the netting, and scrambled beside Ashe onto the wooden platform. It swayed under the weight and thrust of so many bodies taking flight into the gauntlet itself, a forest of unsteady wooden posts and awnings over the perilous drop to a sharp or simmering death. Ropes hung from the posts, and many fighters were already swinging across on them. Some, with shaking arms and unsteady hands, fell. Pikes punched through their bodies with sickening splatters.

Ashe and Briet racked between their fellow fighters and leaped at the ropes. Ashe's palms chafed when she caught the braided twine, but then it was smooth going. She'd trained on ropes courses with the Wardens countless times, preparing to climb and vault Astoria's rooftops in pursuit of criminals. This, she could easily manage.

If only she'd been alone.

Another fighter lunged from his rope to hers, sending them barreling forward in a heart-stopping swing. Grabbing the twine high above Ashe's hands, he kicked her wildly, trying to send her plummeting to her death.

But this was not where Ashe would die.

When the fighter's foot cracked her ribs this time, she released the rope with one hand, snared his ankle, and jerked him down. She let herself slide as well, using her weight to drag him, ripping his hands free and letting him fall among the pikes.

To Ashe's left, Briet shrieked in terror; the man who'd taken her rope stomped her fingers loose and dropped her into the pit. Without pausing to think, Ashe kicked off a pike's tip and swung forward, snagging Briet by the wrist and banding her to her own rope. It wasn't how the melee was meant to be done, but Ashe no longer cared; she wouldn't let another Valgardan fall to their death like Noaam wanted her to. Today was all about defying, even to her last breath.

She led Briet in a series of quick, hard leaps from rope to rope, to the second platform where they could take their footing for ten seconds and look ahead. The vats simmered before them, some with charred bodies roasting inside, their vicious stench bringing Ashe's arm to her face. She could barely see through the mirage of steam toward the distant platform teeming with swordplay. She wondered if Aden was among those fighters, or if his body burned below.

"Ashe," Briet hissed, jostling her arm. The other fighters were almost across the pit, a murderous slant to their eyes as they closed in.

"We need to move." Ashe shoved Briet's shoulder and they lunged out onto the second set of ropes, skimming from one to the next so quickly Ashe's palms bled. These were the first of many wounds she was bound to incur, and they were nothing. They *had* to be nothing.

Alighting on the next set of platforms, she steadied Briet beside her and examined the obstacle ahead—a long, narrow beam between stakes driven into the hard sand a fatal distance below.

Ashe led the way out onto the beam. Two steps. Then five.

A slice of metal, a whistling rope, and from her left a battle axe fell, attached to the twine's flailing, frayed end, screaming toward her face. She dropped, swinging under the beam and back up to the far side to avoid the axe's biting edge. But now weapons dropped from posts on both sides of the beam, cleaving the air with their wicked, notched metal, and Ashe could only run with all her might, ducking, wobbling, trying to avoid row after row of flying, lethal steel.

Her feet hit the opposite platform, and she whirled back to meet Briet. Somehow, with acrobatic grace, the other fighter had managed to stay close on her heels. She sweated and panted, but her eyes flashed with new vigor as if, for the first time, she thought she might survive until the melee's end.

They fled across the third platform and took a running leap to the fourth and final stage where other fighters had already taken up the choicest weapons and gone to battle. Ashe hit the platform, tucked, and rolled toward the nearest weapon: a rusted sword, its edge bitten by countless stronger steels. Briet hefted a polearm, their eyes met.

Someone would kill her today. Someone would likely kill Ashe. But they would not end one another.

Sharp, keening pain broke through the back of Ashe's arm, and blood slapped the wooden boards as she stumbled against the railing, bounded back up at once, and whirled to face her attacker—one of the men who'd cornered her in the staging room the day of the race, though he'd had *two* eyes back then.

Ashe grinned, letting herself enjoy this confrontation, because it was *deserved*. And when they clashed blades, metal shrieking under the cacophony of the wounded and dying, Ashe was pure Warden once more.

Once she'd begun dueling, it was impossible to stop. She threshed her way into the fight, plucking off any warriors who were distracted in other circles, and the cluster started to dwindle. Gaps bloomed between the twists of armored arms and legs, and when the tally of the dead outnumbered the living, Ashe knew the crowd would grow bored. Soon, they would want to see bodies mercilessly torn to pieces.

She kicked her opponent off the platform, whirling away before she heard the crunch of his bones on the sand below—and she came torso-to-tip with a sword that aimed at her back. It hadn't met its mark because the wielder was already dead.

Because *Aden* had decapitated him.

He was stained with blood, his muscles contoured in sweat and shadows from the overcast day...a true lord of sand and carnage, his chest heaving as he braced his steel double-handed. It dripped blood from many dead, the freshest from the man who'd meant to run Ashe through.

They stared at one another, no humanity in Aden's eyes, only raw, killing force. Only the need to have her death for himself after what she'd done.

She raised her sword—

A low groan throbbed through the arena. A winch creaked, and those distant gates where the Viperwolves had emerged during the women's match slowly lifted. A hoarse, animal bellow shuddered through the air, and a pocked mountain of knobby hide thundered into the arena, gobbling the sand as swiftly as a horse's stride, though Ashe didn't know how. It was almost as tall at the platforms.

"Dahadts," Aden swore. "Get down! Get off the platform!"

Ashe ran, grabbing Briet as she bolted past her and sliding down the steps with her hands on the wooden railings. She hit the arena, scrambling away from the five berserk animals who slammed into the wooden posts like storm-force winds. The platforms buckled under the surge of massive tusks, bone-hard bodies, and thousands of pounds of muscle and hide; the vats overturned, the coals rolled and struck wood, and suddenly the arena was burning. The creatures charged straight through the flames and into the pikes, bowling some over, others piercing their flesh.

Ashe counted only ten, including herself and Briet, clawing away from the destroyed gauntlet, and she'd never heard a crowd so wild with excitement. Their voices cracked with ecstasy as the Dahadts circled and charged again—this time toward a lonely figure stepping forward to face them.

Ashe wanted to scream at Aden to get out of their path, but her voice refused to leave her throat. Perhaps this was his choice, like Dilja, to lay down his life before they could take it from him.

The Dahadts were ten meters away. Five.

Aden whirled into the space between one creature and the next, sword chopping neatly across their brows, and they plowed face-first into the sand. His blows had sliced in with no resistance at all. A weak point.

"You saw him!" Ashe bellowed. "Strike their foreheads!"

All the fighters bounded from cover at the walls, but before they'd even reached the three surviving Dahadts, a warbling cry slowed their feet. Ashe turned back to the gate, Briet beside her, with the bleak realization that this was not even the start of what the arena would hurl at them.

A multifaceted ribbon of creatures streamed from the gates. Wildcats with sleek gold and strawberry pelts; Viperwolves, screaming that hair-raising cry; man-sized serpents and scorpions, beasts of pelt and fang Talheim had no equivalent to.

Ashe slowed her breathing, gathering her wits and courage—knowing any of these animals might be the one that tore out her throat or poisoned her, that sent her to her knees for the last time. But she was not afraid. Her spine felt banded in steel, her limbs as steady as iron rods.

"Don't let your weapon stop," she whispered to Briet, just as Lord Rion had once whispered to her. "It doesn't stop until they're all dead, or you are." She glanced at the girl. "Are you ready?"

"I am." Though her words shook, her stance was strong.

"I am." Aden's voice was quiet as death's arrival on Ashe's other side, stepping forward to face the charging hoard beside them.

Ashe brought her weapon up before her, and with a scream in defiance of this place and the people who'd sanctioned them all for this death, she leaped into battle once again.

There was nothing graceful in this combat; it was pure, bloody slaughter, Ashe taking as much as she gave. Brutal claws raked her breast, tore into her back, scoured her face and thighs like a lash as she drove into the animals. Fangs punctured her armor, barely breaking the skin before she tore free and kept swinging at anything colorful, anything that coiled and sprang toward her, toward Briet, toward Aden. She hacked through body after body, severing muscle and bone until her arms shook with exertion. Every few minutes, they dodged another Dahadt, but some animals weren't quick enough to get out of the way. Nor were the fighters.

Cheers surged and ebbed as Ashe plunged her blade behind the shoulder of yet another wildcat, tossing its body aside. She stumbled clear of the fight, blood soaking her brow and sliding into her eyes, and looked wildly around the mosaic of dead bodies glowing on the dull sand like colors ripped from the loveliest painting in the Northern Kingdom. So much death, and somehow it still wasn't over.

"Ashe!" Briet sobbed.

Heart climbing her throat, she whirled toward the skeleton of burning platforms. A serpent twice her height had the girl cornered between flagrant beams, its head weaving forward, preparing to strike.

Ashe flung herself at the creature, wrapped an arm around its sleek, scaled body, and clambered up its neck. Gripping with her knees, she docked off its head in two deft strokes. A fountain of blood spewed skyward, setting the crowd into a frenzy as the glistening body coiled up in a heap.

Briet bent forward, gripping her knees and rocking her head up to smile at Ashe. "Thank—"

A Dahadt crashed over her, snapping her body beneath its shield-sized feet like a straw doll. Briet's head jounced on her broken neck, and then she disappeared under a cloud of dust as the beast moved on.

Ashe was frozen, stunned, for one moment too long.

A Viperwolf crashed into her, talons raking her side and teeth plunging into her shoulder. She screamed in fury and pain, hammering her blade toward the beast's head; it released her shoulder, caught the weapon in its teeth and wrenched it from her grasp. Ashe barreled her weight against it, tossing it onto its back, and staggered away from it. Bloodloss twisted her instincts into cobwebs, pain crashing again and again into her head.

Her knees hit the sand. The Viperwolf got to its hooked feet, shook off the stun of its fall, and bolted toward her again, and with a bellow Ashe hurled herself toward her fallen sword, rolled over, and swung at the Viperwolf's vulnerable neck. It collapsed, dead on the sand beside her, but she felt dead, too, her insides rearranged by the nauseating sight of Briet trampled, by the pain and hot venom and blood pulsing from her shoulder.

The arena beasts prowled closer, enticed by the hot metal scent of her wounds, and near the gauntlet's fuming wreckage Aden cut down the last fighter and turned to find the carnivores had given up pursing him for weaker prey.

The tip of his sword fell to graze the sand.

Of course he would not help her. Not after everything she had done to the people he cared for most.

Gasping for breath, Ashe struggled to put her feet beneath her, but her limbs trembled and her eyes stung and *gods*, she just wanted to be done with this place, with everyone and everything in it. But she didn't want to die.

A wildcat coiled, rocked its weight, and sprang—straight into the tip of Aden's polearm as he vaulted into the circle of predators and plunged his weapon through the feline's chest. With a powerful heave, he slung its body to the ground, ripped the blade out, and ran it through the belly, staking it to the sand as a warning.

The other beasts recoiled.

"Get up," Aden growled at Ashe.

"Why?"

"Because I said so."

That familiar, stubborn answer. Slowly, Ashe stumbled to her feet, and Aden put his shoulders to her, completely exposing himself. It would be so easy to draw her sword across his neck...to give him a quick death and then let herself be torn apart.

But she couldn't; because there was no reason for him to be here, to surrender his back to her while he stared these animals down, one savage creature to all the others. No reason at all when she'd already put a knife in him, into his beloved cousin through him.

But he'd come back for her. Like Thorne had gone back to Stornhaz and pulled Cistine from the Chancellor's hands. Like Maleck had called her name from that sewer. The same way Aden had put himself here to begin with, even under his patroness, for the sake of the Tumult who despised him.

A pit opened up in Ashe's stomach. These Valgardans—these impossible people—

She'd been so gods-damned blind. About them. About *herself.*

She put her back against Aden's and faced the creatures, and the pace of their circling slowed. In quiet concern, they regarded the unified force before them.

With a war cry like nothing Ashe had ever heard before, Aden tore into the creatures on one side, blades whistling and riving and plunging, and she followed his lead. The crowd's feet and fists pounded, a death drum resonating in Ashe's chest as she brought down the creatures, tossing some into the burning gauntlet, meeting others blade-for-fang and dancing around their defenses until she found their vulnerabilities. And as bright desert lightning cracked across the sky—as the pregnant clouds started to drip a gentle cadence of rain, cooling Ashe's hot skin—the animal ranks dropped.

Twenty. Eighteen. Twelve. Four.

She decapitated another Viperwolf, put her blade through an adder's eye, and heard someone's startled scream in the stands. She spun on heel with the last burst of her energy, bringing her blade to rest on the hinge of Aden's shoulder just as his settled against her throat.

They froze. In a massacre of dead animals and people, with the fire blazing beside them and the rain increasing in tempo, puffing small clots from the sand...they stopped.

Ashe's chest heaved so hard she thought her heart might fail. Aden breathed just as quickly, his bare torso jerking with every exhalation. Ashe didn't know when he'd lost his armor, or why. She just knew how easily she could kill him.

And even with her blade against his neck, she couldn't do it.

She should have hated him. Hated every Valgardan. But they were not all like their feckless Chancellors, just as she was not as clever as her Commander, as her King. None of this was as simply cut as she tried to believe when Devitrius dragged her to this place. Some blinded fighters for cheating and gave up their own bodies to save others. Some sacrificed augments to protect the lives in their charge.

Some came back when they didn't have to.

She could do just one last noble thing: if she was going to die anyway, she wouldn't go with the blood of a man who'd saved her life seeping through her hands.

Aden's eyes, still locked onto her, softened suddenly.

"I'm sorry," Ashe said. For the arrows that would strike them. For the lies. For Thorne, for all it mattered after what she'd done.

"I know."

Aden let his sword fall into the sand. Ashe followed suit. The dull thud of her weapon leaving her fingers peeled away her strength, and her legs buckled, but she refused to fall to her knees again. She would die on her feet, facing him. Just like that first day.

She waited for the archers in the stands to draw their arrows as ten seconds came to an end.

"*Mercy!*"

A thin cry from somewhere in the crowd. Something jerked in Ashe's chest, deep and fierce. Her pulse stumbled, not from dread, but—

"Mercy!" The cry came again, strident, cleaving the rain, and Ashe wondered if she was hallucinating from bloodloss, exhaustion, and adrenaline. Until she saw the disbelief in Aden's eyes.

He whipped toward the stands, toward that voice, as the call spread—

taken up on every side by these sated, stunned people, who'd witnessed a fight today beyond what they expected. This was not truly mercy from them; they wanted to see these two warriors brutalize themselves and their opponents, over and over, until they killed whatever kernel of goodness had made them drop their blades.

But then a new voice joined the call. Not pleading...*commanding*. "*Mercy!*"

She turned to face the Tribune's box, where Sander had risen, one sandal perched on the wood. And in his eyes, Ashe saw something new: a vow in that smile, a wild joy, as if they stood on the precipice of something beyond reckoning.

And then again, from the arena wall above their heads. "*Mercy.*"

Ashe looked up.

Hazel eyes scorched her, rooted her to the sand. She could not have fallen to her knees now if she wanted to, couldn't have spoken his name if she tried.

So Aden said it for them both. "*Maleck?*"

The heartbreak, the agony in his voice, the *wonder*—

And then there was a shout, louder than the chants for mercy, and Noaam surged to his feet. "Stars damn this! This is not a pretty race in the City of a Thousand Stars, this is a *melee*! I am the ruler of this Hive, and you will do as you were told! Archers, ready your bows!"

Maleck gestured with a deft cut of his hand, and Aden snapped backward, shoving Ashe toward the catacomb gates.

Fire exploded in the stands. Ashe did not see where it came from, as Aden dragged her away from the arena. Up above, Maleck charged toward the Tribunes' box, Starfall and Stormfury unleashed from his back. By the time she revived from her shock enough to struggle, to follow an urge beyond reason to scale that wall and cover Maleck's flanks, it was too late. Aden thrust her into the staging room and snarled, "*Stay right here.*"

He slammed the gate, trapping her inside.

Ashe hurled her palms against the iron so hard it flaked rust, and roared in fury that after everything, he'd leave her here, locked up like an animal while the arena burst into flames and the spectators broke away in screaming knots; while Maleck and Sander started something horrific in the stands.

Was he leaving her to die while he made his escape? Or had he locked her inside to protect her from Noaam's archers?

No one, not even Lord Rion when she was twelve, had ever pushed her out of harm's way. Had ever taken a fight from her—*twice*.

Ashe backed away and coiled up, ready to fling herself at the hinges, at any weak spot no other fighter had yet found. Instead she stepped into the cold kiss of a blade at her throat.

The fog of rage spiraled away like a dust funnel, leaving Ashe sharply aware of the sweat puddling in the dip of her throat, the knife that nested just above the hinge of her shoulder—and the hand on her arm yanking her around, slamming her back against one of the support pillars.

Nimea loomed before her, hair framing sunken cheeks and desperate eyes. Her cardigan hung from sculpted bones, the knobs of her shoulders protruding against her pale skin as if she'd given up eating days ago. Ashe's arm twitched up—a Warden's instinct surging to defend itself—but when the flick of Nimea's wrist sent the blade's edge burrowing deeper against her flesh, she went still.

The Tumult leader twisted her free hand in Ashe's collar and jerked her up from the wall. "*Walk*."

She marched Ashe away from the chaos above, through the long, dark halls, past countless flocks of hustling fighters. By the time they reached a deserted corridor Nimea deemed suitable for this exchange, Ashe's back and underarms were soaked with nervous sweat and her mind had conjured a dozen methods to disarm and escape from Nimea—all silenced when the butt of the knife slammed her skull, sending her to her knees. Her teeth rattled, numbness claiming her limbs for a moment; when the feeling returned to them, Nimea had her on her back, the knife against her throat again.

"What did you do?" she hissed.

"I don't know," Ashe slurred. Confusion bubbled in her head, hot and putrid like swamp gas.

Nimea gripped her throat in one hand and shifted the knife up to brace against Ashe's jawline. "Don't lie to me again."

She gasped in enough air to wheeze, "I don't *know* what this is about!"

"Tobor!" Nimea roared. "Tobor is dead!"

The shock that deadened Ashe's limbs this time had nothing to do with a physical blow. She slumped, staring at Nimea wide-eyed.

"Someone brought Tobor's head in a sack to Noaam," Nimea hissed. "Now that *bandayo* knows what we were doing, sneaking out of his Hive, and he's scenting for blood on the wind. They're coming for the Tumult."

Maleck. Maleck had brought that head to the Tribune. That's why he was here.

"Did you hear me?" Nimea tightened the knife, drawing a small stroke of blood from Ashe's throat. "*Noaam knows.* His retribution will be the end of us! This is all your doing! You sent *my people* into the jaws of Nimmus! You plotted this somehow with Aden!" The knife pressed tighter. "Stars, I *knew* it! After he avenged you, after you gave him the shield in that fight. He was supposed to kill you, but I saw you two up there just now...him, just as ruthless as he's always been, and you, the beast-slayer and rain-dancer at his side. Why did he spare you after you gave us *everything?*"

"Does it matter?" Ashe rasped, and Nimea flinched in shock. "We were wrong about Thorne. He isn't the person either of us thought he was."

"I know him!" Nimea tightened the knife against Ashe's jaw. "He betrayed us to *rot* in this festering Nimmus!"

"I'm sorry," Ashe said—and some part of her meant it. "I'm sorry about your friends. I did want to help you, I wanted Thorne dead."

Nimea bent, straddling her, knees digging Ashe's hips. "And now?"

Now...

"*Nimea!*"

She whipped back on her haunches, still pinning Ashe with the knife pressed to her larynx. Ashe craned her head against the floor, escaping that brutal edge, looking toward the corridor mouth—toward Aden, his body bent forward into the shadows as if at any moment, he would spring. His eyes were fixed on them, full of unnamable emotion. Ashe couldn't believe it was desperation, not for her sake.

"Nimea," he repeated much more softly, "put down the knife."

"Do you really think I'm that much of a *fool*?"

"I've never considered you a fool. You've been my cleverest opponent these last months...even more cunning than I believed, to have poached Ashe from my trust to yours."

"What did you want with her?" Nimea demanded. "Was she your spy? *Was she, Aden?*"

"Yes. I've been watching your movements for some time."

The knife tightened again, and Ashe swallowed.

"Why?" Nimea growled. "This obsession...our little dance. What has it meant to *you*, Hive Lord?"

"Everything. You and the Tumult have meant everything to me, because I put you here, and I thought I could find a way to get you out."

Nimea's knife slackened. "What?"

"Your imprisonment was my fault," Aden said. "And after half a decade, I couldn't live with the guilt. I came here, I surrendered myself to Salvotor of my own choice to make penance. To do what I could to defend all of you, or at least make certain you didn't die alone."

"Defend us? If you're the one who put us here, then you *destroyed* us!"

"No. I didn't save you. And I understand now that I couldn't. I came far too late for that...years too late."

Nimea's wet, harsh chuckle coincided with the mortal press of the knife, drawing speckles of Ashe's blood. "You don't know what it means yet to feel the sting of being *too late*. But you're about to."

"Nimea!" Aden barked, and by some feral Hive instinct, she froze again. "Don't do that. Put your blade into me. Not her."

Nimea's eyes were fixed on Ashe, madness bubbling in her gaze—the look of a woman whose plans had all shattered under her feet, who was crashing into a chasm with no end in sight.

Ashe understood that feeling perfectly.

"You have no heart, Aden," Nimea said. "What does it matter if I kill your spy?"

Aden swallowed audibly. "She isn't my spy. She was my friend. And I will *never* leave a friend to die in this place."

Ashe's head snapped back against the tunnel floor, straining to look at him again.

My friend. Was that what she'd begun to feel toward him, too—the man who saved her life, stole her fight, dined and trained with her? Had another Valgardan slipped past her guards while she looked the other way?

Aden's gaze held hers, full of intent.

"Friend." Nimea licked her parched lips. "Well. Now you can suffer what I suffered when you sent *my* friends to die."

The knife cleaved down—straight into Ashe's hand as she thrust it between them, against the serrated blade just above the crossguard. She screamed as the ruthless steel sliced deep into her palm, but when she bucked her hips and twisted, Nimea lost her seat. Ashe hurled her against the wall, and as they grappled for the knife, a shadow broke into the tunnel behind Aden, slamming him to the ground.

Andras. Nimea's lookout, her last and strongest friend, caught Aden in a chokehold; and when his appearance distracted Ashe, Nimea's fist connected with her face, opening the fountain of her nose.

Then they were fighting for their lives against what remained of the Tumult.

The sulfuric burn of battle coursed through Ashe's body for the second time that day, picking up speed as she and Nimea aimed blows at one another's soft parts, trading the knife hand to hand, slashes ripping open their arms and legs, their breasts and sides.

Desperation bubbled almost into panic in Ashe's chest. She'd survived the melee—she couldn't become a victim buried in these tunnels. Not at Nimea's hands.

That battle-hardiness and rage rose and rose, cresting when Ashe rammed Nimea into the wall, disarmed her again, and kicked the knife up into her own hand.

She plunged the weapon into Nimea's middle.

The Tumult leader hiccupped with shock and agony. Her fingers encircled Ashe's wrists, tightening beyond believable strength. Andras cried out and Aden howled with pain. Eyes fixed on Nimea, Andras pinned him to the floor, held his head in both hands, and gave a deft twist.

CRUNCH.

Ashe choked, but didn't speak. Staggered, but didn't run to him.

With a last smile, Nimea folded down at Ashe's feet. Aden slumped. Andras let go of his head—and toppled forward, dead with a beautiful, jewel-crusted dagger plunged into the back of his neck, drawn from an equally dazzling sheath still clutched in Sander's fingers.

"What an unpleasant individual," he choked. "I've never smelled such a stench in all my life."

"*Aden*," Ashe hissed, darting over Andras and taking a knee beside the Hive Lord. She gripped his shoulder and shook him, and though his body wobbled, his head started to lift. That horrific sound hadn't been his spine, his *neck*; it had been his attacker's as the knife pierced bone.

A concussion rocked the Hive, and Aden groaned, pushing himself up to glare at Sander. "Where's Maleck?"

"Holding the line." Sander beckoned to them both. "On your feet. We must leave—*now*. The Vassora have just stormed the catacombs."

CHAPTER FIFTY-NINE

"WHAT IS THIS?" Aden growled as Ashe dragged him to his feet.

"I believe it's a rescue," Sander said. "And it's the only way we all get what we want. The Vassora have been dispatched to deal with the Tumult, who they believe are responsible for the madness in the stands just now. Let's not wait around for Noaam to realize your friend Maleck was involved, hm?"

The floor pitched and swayed under her feet, and Ashe steadied herself with one hand against the wall, ripping the jeweled dagger from Andras's neck with the other and passing it to Aden. Together, the three of them dashed from the corridor, leaving Nimea and Andras to be buried under stone dust shaken down from the roof.

They ran through the smoke-strangled corridors where arena-trained criminals launched themselves against the Vassoran ranks like weapons themselves. The dead were everywhere, an echo of the melee, and Ashe couldn't leap over all of them; some she trampled as they bolted toward the staging room. Most of the bodies were blackened and shriveled by augmented fire, but a few she recognized—Hadessa, her body still smoking faintly; several of the guards who escorted Ashe to and from her meetings with Sander; fighters who earned the right, again and again, to live one more day in this dark place where the eyes of the gods never looked.

Now it was their tomb.

Sander yelped suddenly, doubling back and slamming into Ashe as a Vassoran guard skidded into their path. The man's eyes fell on the Tribune and rounded with recognition; Aden hurled the dagger into his throat, silencing his shout. Then he took the lead, carving down any resistance that came in their way.

The walls around them lapped with unnatural flame. The corridors rocked under spires of stone that jabbed the floor and roof into pieces. Even lightning, bottled in these tight passages of rock and sand, raised Ashe's hair from every stroke in the distant rooms.

This was the war, the tundra and the fields of southern Valgard all over again. Ashe tasted the tang of battle on her tongue, blood and adrenaline and bile, and almost gagged. The walls rippled with shadows, turning from dark stone to white ice and blood and dead eyes blinking from a young, ashen face looking back at her—

She didn't realize she'd halted until Aden twisted in front of her, his hands on her shoulders, one still holding that blood-soaked, jewel-studded knife. "We can't stop!"

We have to keep going. That was what Prince Cyril had told her in their ramshackle camp after she woke from her confrontation with that augur boy. *That's all we can do until it's over.*

"The tunnel is collapsing!" Sander cried.

Aden swore, wrapped an arm around Ashe, and bundled her through the staging room, up the steps, and into the arena. Once her feet hit the scorched sand, the damp, fresh air striking her face, sense returned. She shrugged off Aden's grip and led the charge to the outer gates and the figure waiting beyond, robed in shadows, swords dripping blood from the harness on his back.

Ashe slowed. Nearly stopped. Breathed his name.

Then the gate swung open and she hurtled through, Sander behind her, Aden after him, and Maleck slammed the bars shut and threw a wedge of metal into the gap, barring the way back into the arena where more fighters poured out to battle the Vassora in the open.

Sander led them between the nomad tents where people pointed at the flagrant arena and cried out in shock, or gathered their belongings and fled. Few noticed the four bodies racing down the dusty streets toward sanctuary.

The world sharpened into focus when they were safe inside Sander's dwelling. He exchanged rapid words with his pale-haired, stern-eyed steward while Ashe took stock of their surroundings: strangely bare this time, the cushions all heaped up in a corner and the walls divested of spoils.

Sander cuffed Aden on the shoulder and led him up the steps two at a time to the airy room above. Maleck did not follow them; neither did Ashe. Panting, they stared at one another.

His face was smoke-scorched, the ends of his long braids singed, a cut marring his cheekbone. But his hazel eyes were sharp, and they held her in place, sagging against the door. She'd thought she'd forfeited him by now, finally severed that bond after what she'd done. But here he was, staring at her, his hands hanging open at his sides, eyes taking stock of her wounds and her mere presence, looking at her like this was all a gift. And in that moment, Ashe felt *everything*.

"My limp's completely healed," she croaked. "In case you hadn't noticed."

The next instant, she was engulfed in the smell of clean water and charcoal and cedar, and Maleck's augment-scarred arms were around her, pressing her to his chest. And while Ashe had never been keen on physical affection...gods, he smelled so *good*, like forested places and fresh air and *freedom*. Tears pricked her eyes as she rested a hand on the small of his back.

"I searched for you." His voice was harsh. "Every day that I could. And all this time, you've been here. Forgive me, Ashe."

Forgive him? Ashe sputtered with sharp laughter and withdrew. "There's nothing to forgive. You're *here*."

Maleck set her back at arm's length, hands hovering at her shoulders. "You were...magnificent. In that melee."

Ashe coughed out a harsh laugh. "I was exactly what this place tried to make me."

"Yet you spared Aden."

"Would you have forgiven me if I hadn't?"

Maleck's gaze held hers for a long, uneasy moment. "I did not come here to judge what you've done, Asheila."

The sound of her full name, spoken so softly—it was dangerous. Dangerous what being so relieved in his presence was doing to her.

Ashe withdrew from him and jerked her head. "Let's go, before Aden and Sander kill one another."

But they didn't seem close to doing it. They stood in oddly-companionable silence at the window in the room above, watching the Blood Hive burn. Knees weak at the latest of all these strange sights, Ashe dropped onto the nearest couch; Aden turned to meet her gaze, and after a long moment, came to sink down beside her.

"Nimea cornered you in the staging room," he said, as certainly as if he'd seen it happen.

Ashe eyed him sidelong. "Where were *you*?"

"Trying to help Maleck."

"I could've helped, too."

"I knew Noaam would aim his arrows for you to break me. I wouldn't leave you to suffer for this feud between us."

She snorted quietly. "He must've been preoccupied these last few weeks if he really thought it still mattered."

"He saw us in that arena as clearly as they all did."

Ashe gripped her knees, bending forward. "Why did you save my life?"

"Letting you die would have been easier," Aden admitted. "And maybe I considered it. But I've had a fortnight to think on what you said...my place in what happened with Nimea. And I don't want to be the coward anymore." He mirrored her posture, inclining, head bowed and gaze fixed on the floor. "You had every right to believe what Nimea told you, and every reason to despise Thorne because of it. She was honest to her truth, even though she was misguided. I wasn't misguided, yet I was dishonest. What was done to Thorne by this Tumult...that was my doing. You lashed out as an extension of me. I couldn't let you die for my mistakes."

"I'm as much to blame as you are," Ashe muttered. "I let someone else's rage feed my own, even though I knew I was putting innocent people in danger. I can't blame you for what I've become in this place…I did what I did because I *wanted* to. I hated Valgard and all its people."

"All of us?" Aden gave a chin nod toward Maleck, posted beside Sander now at the window.

Ashe grimaced. "Enough of you to make me care less what happened to the ones I didn't."

"And now?"

Once again, that question left her speechless.

"Just…thank you," she muttered at last. "For not taking the kill when you could have. And for coming after me when you realized what happened."

"And you. For not putting your blade in my back."

Perhaps that was all they would ever manage. Perhaps that was the fullest extent of what it was to befriend a Valgardan. But at least she was alive for it.

Sander cleared his throat. "Join us, will you?"

Across the breadth of Siralek, the arena was awash in splashes of scarlet and peach, billowing with black smoke as thick as a dust storm. More and more nomads collapsed their tents and fled. Camels lowed and horses whinnied with fright as their masters dragged them away.

"This is going to go beautifully," Sander murmured after a long moment.

Ashe blinked at him. "You've lost your mind."

"Oh, not in the least." He turned a violent grin on her. "What I've done thanks to the gruesome gift of an escaped fighter's head is pushed Noaam to the uttermost, and now he's shown his penchant for violence—and his unwieldy hand over the arena. A melee was a risk he willingly took, but this? Riots and catacomb stormings and insurrection below his very feet? I'm about to have everything I wanted."

"Is this your way of saying our contract is over?"

Sander's eyes narrowed slightly. "Not over. Complete. I'm leaving tomorrow at dawn, as soon as the Vassora have the riots under control. I've been summoned, I have no choice…some large assembly near Jovadalsa, all the Kanslar Tribunes demanded there. And I'm sending *you* home. As far as anyone will know, the Hive Lord and Siralek's latest novelty were killed in the riots tonight."

Ashe glowered at him. "Why are you doing this?"

"Because I agreed to it," Maleck said. "When Sander confirmed you were both here, and alive, I vowed that if he retrieved you from the catacombs he would have an audience with Thorne."

"You're endangering Thorne for *me*?"

"For both of you." Maleck looked at Aden. "It's time for you to come home, *allet*."

Aden's back shuddered in a long breath. "You don't know how long I've waited to hear that."

They embraced, and Ashe was left facing Sander with his infuriating smirk and too-smug posture. "What is so gods-forsaken important that you're risking everything to reach Thorne? What does he know that you want so badly?"

"It's not what he knows, it's what *I* know. After a decade, I've finally found something that can topple Salvotor from the Judgement Seat."

Ashe's heart lit like a stroke of lightning. Aden withdrew from Maleck and turned a cool glare on the Tribune. "What is it?"

"Something I'll only discuss with Thorne himself. Tell me where to find him, and I'll be there just as soon as my business in Jovadalsa is complete."

Maleck blinked owlishly. "In Jovadalsa, then."

Sander's lips quirked. "Still not going to reveal where he's been all this time?"

"Never."

"I'll just have to settle, I suppose. I'll have horses brought to the door for you. Best you escape while there's still chaos. We'll meet in Jovadalsa in, shall we say, three weeks?"

"Best make it a month," Maleck said. "We won't be able to travel swiftly in the more populated areas."

"But of course. How foolish of me," Sander chuckled. "You're used to living the life of a wanted man."

He vanished down the steps, and Maleck's gaze raked over Ashe again, settling longest on her hand. "May I see?"

She offered her wounded palm. Sweat had run into the cracks, but she didn't feel it, nor the hurts from the melee. Shock numbed everything, even when Maleck retrieved Sander's pitcher from the table and rinsed the wound with the same gentleness he once tended her injured leg...a kindness Ashe didn't deserve.

"So. You delivered a severed head to Noaam?" Aden said blandly, leaning against the wall. "That's the flare of dramatic I would expect from Quill or Tatiana."

"The head was for Sander. I thought it might be enough to capture his attention. Giving it to Noaam was *his* thinking." A flicker of humor crossed Maleck's features when his eyes jumped to Aden. "I remembered that he once admired Thorne, and I took a risk that perhaps he still did...and that he'd leap at the opportunity to show Noaam a poor caretaker of the Blood Hive."

"You risked even more than Noaam with this insane gesture. Why show your face at all, Maleck? Unless something drastic has changed in the last five years, you're still one of the most wanted men in Valgard."

His countenance darkened, rage and grief colliding in his eyes. "It was retribution. Nimea's people nearly killed Thorne twice. And the third time..." he swallowed. "The third, they came *far* too close."

Ashe's stomach cringed. "What did they do?"

Maleck shut his eyes as if to shut out the pain. "Baba Kallah was killed."

Ashe jerked from his grasp and covered her mouth, bile surging up her throat. Aden slumped back against the wall with his hands wrapped around the sides of his neck, horror glossing his eyes. "*Kallah?*"

"Tyve poison, delivered by Tobor himself. Thorne believes you dead, Aden...that they broke you to find us. But I would not accept that unless I saw your corpse with my own eyes. And here you are."

Here he was. Alive. But Kallah...

Aden grimaced at Ashe. Maleck followed his gaze.

Her nape prickled, a lie branding her lips. But this was Maleck—the only other friend she had in Valgard, the one she'd entrusted Echelon to. The one she had brought with her into this dark place, who she'd had to fight not to be afraid for when she sent the Tumult after Thorne. Now the consequence of Ashe's vengeance was stamped into his devastated face, the grief for Baba Kallah turning his eyes to unfathomable waters. And even to save her own dignity, she could not be the cause for more untruth and suffering.

She'd done enough.

"It was my fault," she said, and Maleck's eyes widened. "I gave information I shouldn't have given to a woman named Nimea, and she—"

Maleck raised a hand. His face had gone white. "Why?"

Just one word—but the *ache* in it.

Ashe's eyes grew hot. "Because I was desperate. I hated Thorne for what he did to Cistine...I never meant for Kallah to be caught in the middle of this."

Maleck's eyes flickered. "Cistine nearly died along with her. She had the same poisoned tea in her hand."

Ashe stared at him. And stared.

The words didn't want to make sense.

"Cistine," she rasped, "Cistine and Julian stayed with you? With *Thorne?*"

"Every danger he's faced, she's been at this side."

Ashe broke down with a moan, clutching the wall for support. "No. *No*, she was furious with him, she was supposed to go *home...*"

She had sent assassins after the cabal. After Thorne. After Maleck. And after *Cistine*, who'd found a way to do what Ashe never could; to forgive the High Tribune, to make amends with him over his mistakes. She had been putting her princess and Julian in danger all this time, and she hadn't given the possibility a fleeting thought in the depths of her rage.

"I didn't know," she said. "Maleck, I'm *sorry.*"

Maleck shook his head and stepped away from her. "As am I. I thought you'd grown to trust us."

To trust me.

The words hung unspoken. His pain-stricken eyes flicked to Aden, then back to Ashe. Then he turned away from them, descending down the stairs, and something more than freedom tugged Ashe on his heels. Something stronger than compulsion or shame or escape set her feet to the steps after him.

Something she didn't dare dwell on. Because with the agony and betrayal in his eyes, she knew that fragile, unbelievable thing was already broken.

CHAPTER SIXTY

WITH THE PASSING weeks, the shroud of dark grief slid from Cistine's shoulders. Her mind was no longer content to languish in memories of Baba Kallah's ever-dimmer touch, or her eyes to seek the windows and door day after day in hopes for Maleck—and Ashe—to appear. The ache of productivity possessed her instead, and she buried her rage toward Devitrius, Salvotor, and the faceless Nimea in cleaning, gardening, and dragging Quill to the rock top.

It was during one of those sessions that she learned who Nimea was— a dancer who dreamed of a better Valgard, who'd been captured and thrown into the Blood Hive of Nordbran, now twisted to do the will of the very man who put her there.

Cistine raged in silence and solitude the day after Quill told her that story, her stiff fingers scraping dust and grime from the bedchamber corridor until her nails bled and her cheeks flamed with anger. And still she couldn't scrape away the years, undo the cruelty of time—erase what Salvotor did to Nimea, and what Nimea's people had now done.

That was where the call finally found her again, down on her knees waxing the floorboards, its soft fingers stroking her mind from a furious reverie.

Come, it whispered.

Cistine ignored it. No aberrant beckoning would change what had happened to Nimea, to Aden, to Baba Kallah. Nothing would numb this grief, and nothing took the edge off but *movement*. So she couldn't stop, would *not* stop—

COME!

She sat back on her heels, chilled as if the wind lashing the roof had suddenly found its way inside. Her heart thudded as she slowly looked over her shoulder. Somehow, that call seemed to echo from the dark door at the end of the hall, one through which she'd never gone, and never thought twice about what lay behind it.

Come and see.

She set the polishing rag aside, got to her feet, and with a quick glance to ensure no one stirred in the rooms around her, she slipped through door. The stairs beyond were cool and dark, and in the silence the tug on her mind sharpened, a plea and a command braiding together every step up the long, steep flight into another lightless corner of the attic. She spread her arms and inched forward, trailing her fingertips through the blackness until she encountered the solid, curved edge of a wooden shelf—then a glass jar.

Then another. And another.

Cistine selected one from the very top and backed away until the light from the hall brushed her back and sides, striping the bottle's face.

An augment flagon.

Gods above, it was beautiful, opalescent and thick, dark as the night and shimmering like bottled starlight. The harnessed power gifted from the gods themselves danced like music inside glass crafted specifically to contain it—a fatal power that could only be harnessed by the things the gods had created first, before man, before the world was truly the world...dragons and spiders and desert adders with glittering black scales like Cadre armor.

Creatures made of something other.

Mesmerized, Cistine watched the nacreous liquid swirl, and wondered which augment this was. Lightning, fire, water...something to rattle the bones of nature, something that harnessed the winds, something to break the stars.

Come.

Why did it seem as if the flagon itself sang to her?

Come closer...

Her ragged breathing and that call were the only sounds in the gloom.

Come and see.

"Nimmus' teeth! *Cistine?*" Quill's holler from the base of the steps startled her so badly she jerked, and the flagon fell from her fingers.

And smashed against the floor.

Darkness roared through the room, a blinding, wind-whipping gale, booms and banners of shadow enclosing her in a thunderous fist. She screamed, but the darkness took it, took everything, her breath, her voice, the very air from her lungs.

But she wasn't dead yet. The blackness wrapped around her, screamed back at her to open herself and embrace it and hold on, to cleave to it as it cleaved to her, burrowing into flesh, into bone...

A voice knifed the darkness, and the shadows coalesced, peeling off the walls, the shelves, away from Cistine's skin. She twisted toward the smallest pocket of light, gasping with relief, and found Quill and Tatiana standing there, fully armored. The darkness boiled around them, affixed to their reinforced threads; natural gloom returned, barely broken by the light from the hall.

Cistine's knees struck the floor.

Tatiana reached her first, following the sound of her descent, shedding her jacket and throwing it around Cistine's shoulders. Quill was on her other side in an instant, his hand on her head. "What are you doing in here? This is our flagon store—it's all we have!"

"Quill." Tatiana interrupted, shallow and shaky. "Look at her. She's not wearing armor."

Quill's breath snagged audibly in the dark. "What."

No inflection. Hardly a question. The beginning of a thought that met a brutal end, cut down by the metal edge of shock in his voice.

"It's nothing," Cistine panted. "I'm sure it's happened before, to someone in Valgard, maybe during the war, or...after..."

Quill and Tatiana were too silent.

Her heart imploded, a dying star glinting out of existence. "Hasn't it happened before?"

"Not to my knowledge," Tatiana said. "And you know how I love Valgardan history."

"That augment," Quill said just as quietly, "should've ripped the skin from your bones. It's called ravaging darkness. We use it to confuse enemies, but it also fights against them. Without armor, you...you should be *dead*, Stranger."

Just as she should've been dead on the Black Coasts. Not only from the lightning itself, but because it was *augmented* lightning, and she was just herself, without anything more than bare skin and bones to offer. An ordinary princess of Talheim.

"What does this mean?" Cistine asked.

Tatiana's hand tightened once more. "We don't know. Maybe someone like Maleck..."

"Please, don't! Don't tell Maleck, he can't go down that road again. Don't tell anyone. They have enough to think about with...with Baba Kallah, and Aden, and I just...they have *enough*."

"How do you expect us to keep this from them?" Quill demanded. "You just survived the ravaging darkness in a *dress*, Cistine. A stars-damned dress!"

"Maybe I owe that to both of you! You got here so quickly, and you took the darkness—"

Tatiana pressed a finger to Cistine's lips. "It just doesn't work like that."

She clenched her fists on her knees and shrugged off Tatiana's hand. "Listen to me, both of you. This doesn't worry me. *I am not worried.* I'll decide when to tell the others, because it's *my* life and *my* problem. Do you understand that?"

"I don't like this," Quill warned. "You don't play loosely with augments, Cistine. Nothing good will come from it."

"It's going to cost you," Tatiana agreed. "Keeping secrets like this."

She swallowed a sharp bite of fear. "And that's my price to pay when the time comes. For now, don't breathe a word of this to the others. It's my story to tell, when I choose to tell it."

Quill's breath rushed out in a quiet curse. "Fine, Stranger."

"But don't think we won't be reading up on this," Tatiana warned.

"As long as you keep it to yourself." Cistine struggled to her feet, still woozy, heart pounding. Quill hopped up and steadied her with a hand to her elbow, and Tatiana wrapped an arm around her waist.

"I'll take her from here, Featherbrain," she said.

Only then did Cistine realize why Tatiana had given her the jacket the moment she came upstairs; the darkness had indeed shredded the dress from her body.

Cistine did not leave Tatiana's room until her hands stopped shaking from the second anomaly with the augments. They drank tea, and Tatiana loaned her a pair of soft silk pajamas and read with her by the fire. Every so often, the sparks of a thought trailed up her spine, then winked out; she tried not to wonder why she had sensed the flagons themselves beckoning to her.

It was too much all at once; she had to turn her focus elsewhere.

She slipped out well after dark, leaving Tatiana sunk into books and maps, and felt her friend's gaze trailing after her until she shut the door. Despite the peace of the night and the lack of conversation about her brush with death, she was grateful to escape the bedroom corridor for the silent foyer—where she nearly collided with Julian.

Judging by the glaze in his eyes, he was already soused in mead—and dressed for a night out of the Den. He'd spent less and less time here since Baba Kallah's death. No more researching the Key, no more flower bouquets or meals together. She would have to put him to task again soon, for Talheim's sake. For her own sanity and his. But tonight, she was too tired for yet another argument.

He watched her with bloodshot eyes. "Hello, Princess."

"Julian."

He towed a hand back through his dark hair. "Are you...did you need something?"

Her voice lodged against the back of her tongue. She needed peace. Stability. She needed him to start researching the Key again. She needed him back as her friend, the one with whom she'd begun to share an easygoing rapport between the fluster of their new romance and the strain of contention at the end.

But with his drinking, his gambling...he was facing specters of his own.

"Not really," she said. "Are you all right?"

He shrugged. "Not really. But I will be."

They looked away from one another, and it occurred to Cistine that this was the first time they'd been alone since Veran.

"Listen," he said after a moment. "About what you saw, the night Kallah—"

"It doesn't matter," she interrupted, then gentled her voice at his wince, "it really doesn't. Nothing else does now that she's gone."

"I know. I can't stop thinking about her, either," he muttered. "I keep finding myself sitting at the table, waiting for her to walk into the kitchen. When you were caught up in training all the time after Stornhaz, did you know she ate lunch with me every day?"

A pang of gratitude and grief clenched her heart. "She did?"

He smiled forlornly back down the hall. "I think she knew how lonely things were. She made this place...warm."

And now it wasn't. Despite her best efforts, Cistine's attempts to polish and brighten up the Den made it no less frigid, because the cold didn't come from the onset of winter; it came from the absence of the brightest light within these walls.

"I miss her," Cistine whispered.

"So do I."

They looked past each other's shoulders again, and Cistine didn't know what to say, or how to say anything even if the right thought did occur to her. So much had changed in such a short time.

"I'm...I'm really glad you're all right," Julian murmured. "I know I shouldn't have run out with Ariadne to catch the merch, after...I should have stayed and made sure you were safe, but I just..."

"You did exactly what a Warden should. You helped catch Tobor. And I was where I needed to be, too."

"Right." Though she hadn't mentioned comforting Thorne that night, or Baba Kallah's last words to them, something in the morose tilt of Julian's eyes made her think he knew far more than what she admitted...perhaps he always had. "Well, I'm going out. Take care of yourself, Princess."

And then he left her in the hallway, feeling lonelier than she ever had.

CHAPTER
SIXTY-ONE

CISTINE TRIED TO return to training the next day, but she and Quill moved sluggishly through their paces, giving up before sunhigh—leaving her day full of nothing but heaviness again. When she sat on her bed that night with Tatiana, thumbing blankly through books, the words all blurred before her weary eyes.

"This is ridiculous." Tatiana slammed a dusty cover shut, startling Cistine from a blank stare at her own book. "Neither of us is really reading."

Cistine sighed. "We could try to ply Thorne with food again."

"Speaking of ridiculous causes."

"Have you seen him?"

"Not really. You?"

Cistine shook her head. "I just can't help thinking there must be *some* way to reach him, but he won't talk to me about Baba Kallah. He needs something to jolt him awake."

"Maybe we should tell him about your little accident in the attic, then."

Cistine glared at her. "I was thinking something more personal. Like his Name?"

Expression drawn, Tatiana gathered the books of Valgardan lore. "He's never told any of us what it is. That Name was the reason for Baba Kallah's broken leg...the reason Salvotor hated her so much in the end. Thorne always felt it was best kept a secret between them."

"It was just a thought."

"Not a bad one. Names are powerful things. But that's exactly why he never trusted anyone with it except Baba Kallah." Tatiana settled the books against her hip. "If it's any consolation, as much as all this hurts, I'm glad you dragged me back into it. So I can be here for Thorne and the others. And for you."

Hot tears washed across Cistine's vision. "Really?"

Tatiana nodded. "So, if *you* need to discuss anything...anything at all. Baba Kallah, Julian, or Thorne, even, I'm here."

"Thank you, Tati."

She smiled crookedly and left the room. Alone again in the thick silence, Cistine stretched out on the bed with her arms curled under her chin, eyes drifting shut—

Movement.

There was someone on the balcony outside her room.

She bolted upright, hand flying to Nail under her pillow, and a scream was already on her lips before she recognized that head of silver hair.

For an instant, she hesitated; she still didn't know what to say to him. But there he was, standing in the same place where he and Baba Kallah had taught her so much about Valgardan law and conduct, about augments and energy and how to be queenly.

Gathering her courage, Cistine slipped out to join him.

Thorne sagged against the railing, his head on his folded arms, and he didn't look up when she settled against the railing beside him. She matched his posture and leaned her chin on her elbow, watching him.

After a moment, he inhaled a long, wet breath through his nostrils, hiding tears. "*Aden* is gone."

It wasn't what she expected him to say, but maybe it was easier for him to face his faraway cousin's fate than his grandmother's. Even so, he spoke the words with an agonized lilt, as if for the first time he truly faced the crushing implications of Tobor's confession and what Maleck had gone to avenge.

Cistine drew a tremulous breath of her own. "Do you want to tell me about him?"

"What is there to say? He was like a brother, he helped raise me...his home and Baba Kallah's arms were the only sanctuary I had from my father's cruelty and my mother's indifference." Dull laughter shook from him. "And now Salvotor's taken both from me."

Heart clenching tight like a fist, Cistine slid her hand toward his arm, but caught herself just short. "Thorne..."

"Did anyone ever tell you why he betrayed us?" he interrupted. Mutely, Cistine shook her head. "It was because of *his* father. Salvotor offered him a trade, our names for the lie that he was alive—and he took it. For ten years, I've thought Aden was a fool. I've asked myself, asked the *gods* why he couldn't perceive the lie. Why couldn't he accept his father had been dead for a decade? Why couldn't *Aden*, of all people, realize Salvotor was bluffing, and choose us over him?"

His chin scraped his elbow in a slow headshake.

"I understand it now," he murmured. "If my father came to me and told me Baba was alive, that I could see her again...I would break. I'd give him what he wanted. Aden wasn't a traitor, he was the truest of us all. And I sent him to his death for it."

He buried his face into his arms again, his next words raw, edged with tears.

"I lost them *both*."

Cistine's heart cracked in grief for this new blow dealt when he already buckled under so many; and for Aden, who would never hear for himself the understanding in his cousin's voice.

Finally, words came to her. "When I was a child, someone set fire inside the Citadel. One of my father's enemies...he's had a few since I was born. They set the blaze outside my bedroom window."

Thorne's shoulders tensed. Cistine wished she hadn't seen that; it made her wonder if she ought to keep speaking. But here, against the Nior's music and the crank of the water wheels, she had a point to make.

"No one was harmed," she went on, "but it destroyed the garden. I remember hating fire for months after that. I didn't like to sit by the hearth with my parents. I didn't even want a candle lit in my room. It drove Ashe completely mad."

She paused, mind wandering for an instant with melancholy conjecture—how things might've been different if Ashe were here for this, as she'd been there for the miscarriages and the death of Cistine's grandmother.

But there was no one else. Only Cistine and Thorne.

"Anyway," she murmured, "I remember going out to the garden the following spring and finding tiny blooms everywhere. Seeds that had survived the blaze, coming up through the ground. My mother told me that even though fire ravages, what survives it often grows stronger than what came before."

Thorne's shoulders lifted and sank.

"I don't think I'm going to survive this." His words were calm and factual, like they were discussing another strategy, another battlefield he'd assessed. "I don't see a way forward."

"You could start by coming to supper every day or so. Your cabal loves you, Thorne. They want to help you, I know they do. Everyone here has lost someone close to them, except Julian and I, really. Maybe *I* can't speak to your pain, but they can."

Thorne couched his chin in the crook of his arm, looking away from her, toward the river. "Being near you has been the most difficult thing since that night. That's why I've been avoiding your company. I'm a selfish, stars-damned *bandayo*. And do you know why?"

Cistine wanted to tell him he was none of those things, but she knew he needed to say his piece. "No, Thorne, I don't."

"Because I was relieved," he said. "In that kitchen, I saw her...she was dying before my eyes. The woman who raised me, who saved me from becoming Salvotor, just like Salvotor became his father. I saw you both on the floor, and when Maleck said it was poison...when I *knew* she'd drunk it, the first thought that crossed my mind was still whether *you* had."

Cistine's breath caught.

"I was *relieved*," he growled, "even though she was still dying. Relieved that you weren't about to collapse in my arms next. And I am *still* relieved, every moment I see you drawing breath…and that terrifies me."

There was nothing she could say—not to thank him for valuing her life enough to be relieved, or to assure him it was all right to be conflicted in these ways, with this death. She didn't know what it was to mourn, especially a loss so sudden and violent. She had nothing but her heart, which ached for him, and her arms, which she slid gently around his back. She pressed her cheek against his shoulder, and his hand slid up slowly to clutch her fingers against his sleeve while sobs took his body in quiet waves; and she did not let go when he sank to his knees, gripping the railing post above his head, his face buried in his forearms.

She didn't know how long they sat that way before the balcony door whispered open. Footsteps crossed the wood, and a heavy weight struck the railing to their right. Cistine peeked open an eye and saw Quill sitting there, head tilted back, scowling up at the stars.

It wasn't long before the others followed: Ariadne leaning against the Den with her arms folded and head bent in silent prayer, Tatiana sinking down with her back against Cistine's, pressing her between her own slender body and Thorne's bulk.

None of them spoke; they simply sat with their High Tribune and watched the stars, their sorrow knitting them together—an intimate soulbond beyond any word or comprehension, because they had all loved Baba Kallah, and they all mourned her death. But their pain was their shield, and they raised it high, sheltering Thorne in their midst. If they couldn't speak to his pain, they would at least guard him while he struggled through it, back to clarity…whenever that would be.

Cistine laid her head on his back and shut her eyes.

Minutes passed. Perhaps even an hour.

It was Thorne who finally spoke. "This has to stop. This was a warning…the assassins were simply another way to reach me."

"How do you suggest we edit it?" Tatiana's voice rumbled against Cistine's spine with their backs pressed together. "We still can't reach him."

"True," Ariadne said. "But Thorne is right, this was all leading toward one end. I met with a group of merches who arrived from Jovadalsa tonight...they saw something out there."

Thorne slowly turned away from Cistine's arms and rested his back against the railing, staring wearily up at his strategist. "Tell me."

"Salvotor has assembled with the Kanslar Tribunes at Jovadalsa to assess the crime there...or so he says."

Quill cursed. Tatiana and Cistine both looked at Thorne, who'd gone pale as death, shoulders tumbling backward in shock. His head struck the railing. "He's tempting me out."

"He knows the assassins are finished," Ariadne agreed. "He knows about Geitlan and Veran...and now he may know what Tobor's done."

Cistine's heart thundered with dread.

"He's giving me the opportunity," Thorne said. "To surrender now, before anyone else is harmed."

"*No!*" At the power in that single word, emerging from Cistine like a punch, the entire cabal flinched. "Thorne, you *cannot let him win!* Baba Kallah would've hit you with her cane if she heard you talking that way. You have to stand for yourself...for *us!* Push back. This cabal needs you."

"I know that." An edge crept into his voice. "I know."

Cistine drew in deep breaths, slow and steady, sipping oxygen like mead and feeling it burn down her throat. "I'm relieved," she said, and this time he looked her deftly in the eyes. "I'm *relieved* I survived, because I know my fight is not over. And neither is yours." She rested her hand over Thorne's where it shook slightly on his knee, quivering with the tension of knowing his father was so close—and so untouchable. "Promise me, Thorne. Promise you'll let him strut around Jovadalsa and go back to Stornhaz empty-handed. He is *not* worth dying for."

Thorne held her gaze, icy eyes spearing her straight to the core. "Nothing in this kingdom is worth dying for, except all of you. I would never let anything happen to any one of you."

Relieved, Cistine smiled. And though Thorne didn't return it, she knew they'd made yet another accord.

CHAPTER SIXTY-TWO

THE NIGHT HAD deepened to core darkness and bruised shadows when the cabal retreated indoors again. Quill and Tatiana departed together, her hand linked in his towing him out toward the kitchen; Thorne lingered in Cistine's room a moment, looking dully down at her when she collapsed on the edge of her bed. But there was only warmth when he rested a hand on her shoulder.

"Thank you," he said. "For this night, and every one before it."

While she struggled to make sense of what he meant, he kissed the crown of her head, then led Ariadne up the steps to his loft.

Try as she might, Cistine couldn't sleep. She sat awake, knees gathered to her chest, watching moonlight trace the walls while thoughts of Salvotor's feckless maneuvers stoked the angry fires in her stomach.

When a throat cleared in the hall, she nearly leaped from the bed; her furious thoughts and racing heart quieted when she spotted Ariadne propped against the doorway. Exhaustion painted her features, turning her eyes to dark, unhappy pools.

"Thorne is asleep," she said. "I've left some herbs with him."

Cistine nodded, hugging her knees tighter, wishing she could tuck all her worries so small and hide them inside her.

Ariadne slumped her temple against the doorpost, guiding her knuckles against its grain. "You have been more a pillar for this cabal than you realize. And I thank you for it."

Cistine snorted. "I've hardly done anything." *Except shatter flagons and keep secrets.*

Ariadne shook her head. "This cabal...does not handle loss well. I won't say *I* handled it well. You saw how I reacted when Tatiana came home with an arrow in her shoulder. But this Den...it's strange. Being here these last weeks has offered some comfort, and we owe that in part to you. No one else is training, no one wants to clean and scrub or tend the garden. No one has enough appetite to make meals, but you do it all. And we...*I* am grateful for that."

Cistine's mouth wobbled into a smile. "Well, I'm glad to help however I can. I've never really lost anyone I was particularly close to."

Ariadne lowered herself onto the bed beside her. "Yes, you have. You've lost Ashe."

"But she isn't dead."

"I hope not. Even so...you know I have a sister who is also gone, but not dead. And these past months, I've felt like I lost Tatiana. I know that grief, and this pain for Baba Kallah, and I know the heart doesn't feel them any differently when the blows come."

Cistine nodded slowly. "It's never been a choice, though. I *have* to go on. This cabal needs me. Thorne needs me."

"And you endure these things like a warrior does. As a princess should, knowing there's no time to be broken with kingdoms to save. I want you to know I admire that, Cistine. Very much."

Cistine flushed with disbelief that *Ariadne*, of all people, would admire *her* strength—Ariadne, whose dreams had been shattered, who'd been ravaged by a man who was meant to safeguard her Order and instead impaled her to a door. "Maybe I'm following a good example."

Ariadne smiled, gentle and genuine. "I haven't been fair to you ever since you came to us. I didn't have any fondness for Talheim, and less for women I thought couldn't carry their weight. But you've reminded me of something I forgot after all these years."

"What's that?"

Ariadne leaned her weight back on her hands. "That once, I didn't know how to wield a blade, either. I preferred school and gardening to combat. I carried my weight in a different way, as you do. You may not be as battle-ready as us, but you're an anchor. A backbone. And that's something that outside of Baba Kallah, we've lacked for a very long time."

They were both silent, watching shadows sneak across the walls.

"Thorne is anxious," Ariadne finally said, shifting the subject to waters somehow both clearer and more difficult. "Obsessed with his father's movements. And the Chancellor is patient. Under the guise of stomping out crime in Jovadalsa, he could wait for Thorne until the end of his cycle. Beyond it, even. If not for our sake, then for Thorne's, we'll have to leave Hellidom."

Cistine gnawed the inside of her cheek. "Starhollow?"

"Maybe. Tatiana and I will review maps in the morning. For now, what we all need is sleep and prayer." Ariadne stood and squeezed Cistine's shoulder. "Remember, *Logandir*: royalty rises to the occasion. And for all of us, you have continued to rise."

She left Cistine sitting cross-legged, watching the darkness gather against the sweating palms of her hands. Then, eyes stinging, she laid down on her side.

Though sleep finally claimed her there, it was not restful. Always on the verge of dreaming, she saw Baba Kallah dying again, felt the old woman's last whisper ghosting against her cheek, a dream so vivid it brought her back to groggy consciousness again and again.

Near dawn, she gave up and padded into the kitchen for a scone and a mug of tea. She slowed to a tiptoe when she found Julian passed out at the table, elbow crooked around a mead bottle, head buried on his other arm. She had no strength left to be annoyed with him; she tried not to look at him at all while she chose a scone, brewed the chamomile in silence, and retreated back to her room.

By moonlight fading toward dawn, she returned to reading.

It had been weeks since she touched the book of Old Valgardan stories, scripted in runes Thorne and Tatiana took great pains to teach her. The words trickled back to memory, bringing a strange peace like she'd stepped back into that time of long summer days and training sessions, when things had been so much simpler. When Ashe had still been free and Baba Kallah still alive to discuss these stories with.

The scone was gone and the tea cold when she peeled through the last story, finger listlessly guiding under the words, and finally encountered it.

Cistine froze, finger stilling below a rune that blazed off the page as if caught in dawn light, sizzling with clarity that made her heart race.

She knew that word.

Sillakove.

Her lips parted in shock.

That was the word Baba Kallah had whispered with her final breath, its meaning crashing back to memory: a riverside fire, and Thorne's eyes across it, flames and ice colliding in his gaze while he told her about a collection of truncated epics Baba Kallah read him as a child, where he found the name for his Court.

Thorne is Sillakove, Baba Kallah had breathed with her last. *He is our Star.*

Sillakove. *Starchaser.*

He is our Starchaser.

Cistine snapped up from the bed and ran to the loft stairs, leaping up them two at a time, her heart crashing against her ribs. This was Baba Kallah's last gift to them both...something that knit them together, the very thing Cistine had told Tatiana she desperately wished they had.

"Thorne!" Cistine crashed through his door...and froze.

His room was empty. The window hung open beside the chimney, letting in the autumn chill. His blades, his armor, all of it—gone.

Nausea socked her belly, worse than the first blow Quill had ever dealt her, sending her hanging from the doorframe. She sobbed his name against her hand; then she spun on heel and tore down the steps so quickly her feet skidded on the last, and she crashed to her knees in the hall. Bones aching, she yelled for Tatiana, for Quill and Ariadne, hobbling into the kitchen.

None of them came. *None of them.*

"*Quill!*" Cistine screamed again, catching herself against the table as pain flared through her shins and kneecaps.

Julian woke with a grunt, scraping his head up from the table. Hair plastered to his brow, eyes dim with half-drunken sleep, he blinked at her. "Princess?"

"Where are they, Julian? Where's the cabal?"

He squinted one eye shut. "Tavern. Patrol. Why? What...what's wrong?"

"Thorne is gone!" Cistine's chest banded tighter than a corset, choking the words. "He's gone to kill Salvotor. *Alone!*"

The words sobered Julian like a slap to the face. He shoved his chair back, lunging around the table to grip her forearms, turning her to face him. "Where?"

"Jovadalsa. It's less than a day's ride from here."

"How long has he been gone? Did he take anything—weapons, augments?"

"Weapons, yes! Augments, I don't know. I don't *know*..."

"What do you need me to do?" Julian demanded, and she could've thrown her arms around him if not for the urgency crashing in her chest.

"I'm going after him. I know his Name, I can stop him. Make him see sense before he kills himself."

Julian swung his sword belt from the back of his chair, keeping his other hand on her arm. "I'm going with you. Horseback, or on foot?"

His grim, cool efficiency—the focus of a Cadre Commander to his Queen—cleared the panicked fog in Cistine's mind. "Horses. We can steal them and pay the merches later."

"Good. Get your weapons and meet me outside."

She had no time to pry over swords in the loft, to go to Tariq and beg for her armor early, or to find the cabal. She simply grabbed Nail, banded its sheath around her hips, and dashed out to meet Julian. Together, they raced away into the gray dawn.

CHAPTER SIXTY-THREE

THOUGH CISTINE PRAYED with every galloping mile that speed and time would be their allies, it was too late; her hope turned to unspeakable despair when she and Julian reached Jovadalsa's damp outskirts to the sounds of battle floating on the air.

They tied their horses near the bridge over the Nior River to the south and made the remaining journey through the Eben wetlands on foot, creeping up on an encampment of tents through which the sound of steel-on-steel rang. Julian's lips cut back from his teeth in an uneasy grimace; the son of Rion Bartos knew the sounds of combat when he heard them.

Cistine clamped down on her panic. She would not believe they'd failed unless she saw Thorne's body; until then, she had to plan.

They had little cover here aside from a few trees and shrubs with their roots moored deeply in the wetlands. They would be seen coming to and from the encampment unless Salvotor and his people had a reason to look elsewhere. She glanced at Julian, he looked at her, and they said in harmony, "Diversion."

Julian nodded. "An entourage of this size must've ridden in on *something*. I'll find the paddocks...classic distraction."

"I'll catch Thorne's attention." Julian opened his mouth as if to protest, and Cistine talked over him, "And then we all run back to the bridge."

"Leave the horses and ride the current west," Julian said. "Otherwise we risk leading them to Hellidom."

Cistine glanced toward the tents. "Ariadne is already considering Starhollow. We can meet them there."

Julian dipped his head. "I'll see you at the river, Princess. Be *careful.*"

"You as well."

Julian slunk off to the encampment's edge, and Cistine bolted toward the tents. There were enough to house at least two dozen Vassora, sprinkled with several finer tents for finer people—one even draped in stunning amber-and-violet silks, as if this was mere pageantry and the occupant had come to see a parade, not a slaughter... *Thorne's* slaughter.

The succinct strike of blades grew shorter as the Wild Heart of Fire burned through their camp, coming to rest behind the corner of a tent at the far edge, where the Vassora gathered. Interspersed among them were men in clean shirts and trousers, polished boots, and fine robes—the Tribunes.

And there in their midst was Thorne. Mud-spattered, soaked as if he'd swum across the river rather than taking the bridge, his silver hair swirled against the column of his neck and his armor heaved as he struck blades with his father.

It was the first time Cistine had laid eyes on Salvotor since Stornhaz; at the mere sight of his thinly-mustached face, his square jaw so like Thorne's, and his hateful eyes that were nothing at all like his son's, Cistine's half-deafened left ear throbbed. Her skin rippled with gooseflesh when she saw the dance of that glistering black *Svarkyst* steel in Salvotor's hands, a weapon that could shred Thorne's armor and kill him in a heartbeat.

But Thorne fought without fear, a relentless storm of killing skill entombed in flesh. He was glorious and deadly, blooded with the strength that could bring Salvotor to his knees; and he fought with all his might, just like in the Izten Torkat against the Vassora, and when he came for her in Stornhaz, and against the assassins. He struck without mercy against the man who'd stolen so much from him, who'd tried to mold him into a hateful vessel to fill with his own dark designs.

Cistine's mouth fell open while she watched them battle, skidding and spinning through the mud, and she knew Thorne could've won—if not for his grief, which made him reckless; if not for his rage, which stole his focus like a traitor's knife in his back.

Their weapons locked and father and son came together, matched for height. Salvotor's lips moved, spitting indistinguishable words, and Thorne's fingers tightened brutally around his blade. He reared back slightly to heft and swing; Salvotor headbutted him with a face full of inlaid scales and conduit threads, and Thorne cried out, falling to his haunches. Blood branched down the bridge of his nose.

Cistine slammed a hand to her mouth, swallowing a whimper. *Julian, hurry!*

Salvotor knelt before Thorne, plucked the weapon from his dazed fingers and tossed it aside toward the tents…only a few meters from Cistine's hiding place. Chuckling, he plunged his own sword into its sheath. "What did you intend to do, boy? Do you *ever* plan, or do you follow whatever thought comes to you first, like your grandmother taught you?"

Thorne's head shot up—straight into Salvotor's fist, which crunched his jaw and laid him flat on his back.

"*Did you have a plan?*" A snarl rode the current beneath his words. "Did you tell your followers you would kill me and restore balance to Valgard's Courts? Did you *lie* to them about that, too?" He took his son's hair in one hand and wrenched his head up so their noses nearly brushed. Cistine's heart fractured at the soft, painful huff Thorne made. "You have always known this couldn't end in my death, no matter how badly I *made* you want it. You would never become Chancellor with your blade in my chest. You had no plan to remove me from power. Does your cabal know *that*?"

Blood freckled Thorne's gritted teeth. He offered no reply.

"You have nothing," Salvotor decided at last. "A fair reflection of what you *are*. A man of nothing, who must pay a man's share for his crimes."

He released Thorne, letting him drop back into the damp soil, and got to his feet. "Put him on his knees."

Cistine's heart launched into her throat as a pair of Vassora swooped forward, taking Thorne by the arms and bowing him on his knees before Salvotor—facing the whip he unhooked from the belt of a round-faced, smirking man at the circle's edge. In the intimate cruelty of the smile between them, Cistine knew precisely who he was.

Devitrius.

Salvotor turned back, slowly uncoiling the whip. Though Thorne was dazed, blood threading across his nose and streaming down his lips, he thrashed weakly. "No. No, *no!* Please, don't—*please!*"

Tears slid down Cistine's cheeks, ripped from her control by Thorne's wild panic at the sight of that whip licking the ground. His struggles were fruitless against the hands that yanked his arms out to the sides. A third guard took up his own *Svarkyst* knife, slitting open Thorne's armor from nape to waist and laying it across his broad, scar-freckled shoulders.

Salvotor halted behind him. "One lash for each year you've defied me. Beginning with your first, when you turned to my mother's arms for comfort rather than to *your* mother's and mine."

He cocked his arm—

Baba Kallah's voice sighed to Cistine on the wind.

You must find your courage, Yani. *You must tap the wells of power in your own spirit, and fight.*

Coiling up and bearing breath deep down into her lungs, Cistine hurtled from her hiding place, yanking up the sword and charging forward, bringing every eye among the Vassora to her.

A hand closed around her throat from behind, ripping her to a halt. Nutmeg and cardamom and some other sort of spice, arid, almost cloying, stuffed themselves into her lungs. An arm banded her waist, trapping her against a man's muscle-hewn chest, and she caught the flicker of brightly-patterned robes from the sleeve that girdled his wrist.

"Do not fight," he said, "do not struggle, do not speak. Perhaps I can get you both out of this alive."

Then he towed her forward to face Salvotor.

It was the smallest mercy that when he saw her, the Chancellor lowered his whipping arm. Delight glittered in his venomous gaze, and Cistine wanted to vanish, wished she'd never moved from her hiding place. More than anything, she wished Thorne wouldn't raise his head.

But he did. His eyes found her—and widened with horror.

"Princess Cistine Novacek of Talheim," Salvotor said, and the man in whose hold Cistine hung tightened his grip just slightly. "It seems the duty of saving one another runs both ways between you and my traitorous son."

"Don't," Cistine begged, even knowing it was futile. "Don't hurt him."

"There is only one way to train rebellious boys—something my father taught me, as his father taught him. And his before him."

Thorne's eyes locked with hers, anguished and bloodshot, offering a silent apology for coming here, for facing Salvotor despite the promise he made—for bringing her into his father's reach again.

Cistine's tears welled over. It was not about her. It was not about the lies, about the betrayal...it was about Thorne, and that he didn't deserve this no matter what oaths he broke.

At the sight of her tears, his spilled as well. He breathed her name.

The whip snapped, and Cistine wrenched in her captor's hold, screaming with Thorne as he arched, the barbs biting into his back and tearing away skin. She squeezed her eyes shut when gore spattered the ground; she couldn't bear to watch more divots join the ones he was so ashamed of, so afraid to show. The sacred spaces she'd touched in the Izten Torkat, on the Black Coasts, when she saw him emerge from the mines and right then, she *knew*...

Even when she stabbed her elbow into her captor's muscular abdomen, even when she kicked and writhed and struggled to break his hold every way Quill taught her, he held her fast through twenty-eight lashes, each one jerking a cry from Thorne and a fresh sob from Cistine until only a mantra of "*Stop, stop, stop,*" tumbled from her lips.

And then it was over.

A hush fell as the last lash peeled back. The men released Thorne, and he slumped to his hands and knees in the mire. Blood stroked his flanks, plopping from his ribs and falling to the ground. His arms trembled and gave way, and he collapsed face-first into the mud. He didn't rise.

"Get up," Cistine sobbed. "Get up, Thorne! Oh, gods, no, no, *no...*"

Salvotor circled his motionless son, coiling the whip lazily and passing it to Devitrius, who flecked the blood from its end with his fingertips before he belted it on again. "This is what awaits any man in this field today who turns his back on Kanslar Court." His eyes flicked straight to Cistine—or perhaps to the man holding her, whose chest no longer rose and fell against her back. "Tribune Sander. Bring me that girl, if you would."

Thorne's voice cracked out, a battered roar rising from a throat ripped with yelling: "*No!*"

Sander froze midstep. Cistine's breath caught.

Thorne planted his hands and sat up slowly on his knees again, arms quivering. Sweat and blood and saliva fell from his lips, but he faced his father's hooded gaze in defiance—what little he could muster. "Finish it and *let her go!*"

Salvotor glanced between them. "You would die the Second Death for this girl?"

"I would die a hundred deaths for her. A thousand before I let you touch her."

Cistine's captor breathed, "*Selvenar.*"

Cistine herself was not breathing at all.

"There's only one Death left for you, boy," Salvotor sneered. "You've accomplished your purpose with your example today. It's time I rooted out Kallah's weak seed." He drew his blade from its sheath again, a purr of metal on leather as the serrated edge sprang out like mountains crowned with old blood rather than snow.

The Tribunes were all silent, but the Vassora cheered when the Chancellor stepped before his son. Thorne raised his chin with his old composure—the first glimpse of it since Baba Kallah died. But when his eyes found Cistine, that strength guttered.

"Don't watch," he said. "Cistine, look away."

But she couldn't. She had looked away from the whipping because she couldn't bear to see his skin shredded, the mockery of that lash. But not from this; she would never let him believe he was alone.

When she held his gaze, the composure drained from Thorne's features. He lurched forward like he suffered the whip again, sinking his fingers into the mud. "Cistine, don't give him the satisfaction!"

Salvotor checked over his shoulder that she was indeed watching, and she ached to spit that she wasn't watching for him. She wasn't even here for him. It was all for his fearless, reckless, unbroken son.

Sander was right. Thorne *was* her blended heart, her *selvenar*. She'd known it ever since they wrestled on that ledge above Starhollow—had sensed it long before that, when they traveled the Izten Torkat together.

That was why she'd come for him. Why she always would.

"Cistine!" Thorne's voice cracked. "*Wildheart*! Close your eyes!"

Her focus snapped back to him.

For a moment, she was not herself anymore; she was Maleck in the sewer below Stornhaz, giving up the pursuit of Ashe for a single word. She was Tatiana, drawn back from the brink of self-destruction at the sound of a Name given by this Tribune—Names that forged them all as a Court of their own.

Thorne roared that name—*Wildheart*—with the same power that called his warriors back from the edge.

And as Salvotor, unheeding, brought his blade arcing down toward his son's neck, Talheim's princess exploded.

Sander's sword was in her hand before her spinning kick to his ankles had finished dropping him, before the crack of her knee into his chin had finished resounding on the thick air. He tumbled from the impact, and she vaulted over him, catching Salvotor's blade at the hilt with hers and thrusting him away from Thorne.

The Chancellor's blade shoved back immediately, but Cistine's arms did not quake. Her muscles firm, her shoulders rolling with the press of his might, she planted her feet and stood her ground before Thorne. When Salvotor adjusted his grip and bore his weight down, Cistine drove her foot into his stomach with all her strength and thrust him away from them.

Perhaps in shock, but more likely in ruthless delight, Salvotor didn't send the Vassora to subdue her when she stepped back to Thorne's side. His hand curled around her waist and he brought himself slowly up, leaning into the strength of her.

"You threw your son aside," Cistine seethed at the Chancellor. "You have no place and no power in his life anymore. But I do. I know his Name, and that makes him *mine*."

Salvotor's mouth leaped open—

Wood smashed. Mud and grass burst into the air as horses slammed into the tents, bringing them down in droves of wood and hide. Trampled under flying hooves, the pelts disappeared into the mire—along with the Vassora who failed to flee before their desperate, galloping mounts.

Julian.

Tribune Sander, bleeding where Cistine had clipped his chin, struggled up and lurched toward them, and she tensed to fight two opponents at once. But he hurled himself on top of Salvotor instead, knocking him to the ground, shielding him from the onslaught of horses. Thorne jerked Cistine back from the breaking herd, and her gaze locked on Sander, flattening Salvotor into the mud. His eyes were fixed on her and Thorne in turn.

Run! he mouthed, and then shouted, "Chancellor Salvotor, stay low! The Vassora are securing the horses!"

Cistine tugged Thorne off to the side, and he faltered with an anguished grunt, unwinding his arm from around her waist. "Go. I'll slow you down."

Cistine spun in his embrace, chest-to-chest with him, and grabbed the pain-locked muscles at the hinge of his neck. "Listen to me, Thorne Starchaser. *Not without you.*"

At her words—at the sound of his Name—his eyes sharpened. He wavered and dipped, then clasped her waist again. At his nod, they ran, the horses surging around them and the Vassora and Tribunes tearing relentlessly away, toward Jovadalsa or into the open wilds of Eben.

And then the wind came. Not a natural gale, but a howling, relentless storm, the searing might of an augment blowing everything from its path, blowing them down. Thorne swung Cistine in front of him and fell, shielding her with what little armor he retained, as he had in the Izten

Torkat.

She didn't know what would happen when Salvotor reached them through that gale of wind. She only knew the vicious power was abusing Thorne's already-ruined back, and that after only a minute, this augment would destroy him just like lightning or ravaging darkness, with his armor nearly gone. But she could pretend she knew what to do, just like he taught her—because the wind couldn't hurt her as badly as it was hurting him.

Cistine laid her hand on Thorne's cheek, and when she pushed just slightly, he slid from above her. Barely-conscious, he tumbled to his shoulder in the mud, and she rose to face Salvotor.

He was only a few yards away, nothing left between them. Even Sander was gone.

Cistine's legs unlocked, carrying her forward. Behind her, Thorne stirred. He groaned her name and tried to sit himself up.

"Cistine! Thorne!"

She flinched but didn't turn when she heard Julian fall to his knees beside Thorne. "Get him to safety." Though her belly fluttered, her voice did not shake. "Do *not* come back for me, Julian. Don't come back for anything. I'll catch up."

She walked toward Salvotor, one deliberate step after another, and with every one she felt the cabal walking beside her toward this man who'd broken their lives. Quill's brashness. Tatiana's endurance. Maleck's quiet strength. Ariadne's unbreaking spirit. Baba Kallah's tenacity. And Thorne's endless determination to always have a plan, or pretend until one came to mind.

She could hear him shouting her name through the wind that stormed from Salvotor's body and lashed against hers, breaking with every stride like water around a boulder. It was exhilarating; not only the sensation, but the sight of the Chancellor's eyes narrowing, his face pinching with doubt.

She should be dead three times over from augments that failed to destroy her body. Her will. Her spirit.

"Maybe Thorne can't kill you and still rule in your stead," Cistine growled. "But I'm the daughter of your enemy. So I *can*."

She drew Nail and rushed the Chancellor.

Salvotor unclipped another augment from his belt and crushed it in his fist. Lightning raced up his arm, crackled across his shoulders, and climbed his face, sizzling purple in his smoky eyes as Cistine's knife plunged toward his heart.

The augment smashed into her, and though it didn't kill her, it burned like being dipped in acid. She screamed as it blew her off her feet, driving her body into the soil until she struck the mess of hides and wooden stakes that had once been the encampment. Dazed, blood flowing from the back of her head, she couldn't rise. She couldn't feel Nail in her grip anymore. Her body smoked, her clothing in tatters.

Salvotor stared at her, and for once, in his round-eyed shock, he was the perfect reflection of his son. "*That* was how he did it. Prince Cyril...that clever *bandayo*."

In the distance, Thorne roared with rage and heartbreak, if he'd realized the same thing his father did, some secret Cistine had yet to grasp through her blood-muddled daze.

Salvotor unclipped the next augment and hurled it straight against Cistine.

Blazing, furious light slammed into her body, the sheer radiance knocking her flat against the ground. She cried out until her voice broke, until it crushed her lungs and she could no longer breathe. Endless torrents of power spilled through her blood and marrow, through her entire being, burning away all the pretenses of who and *what* she was.

When it flooded away, leaving her gasping, weak, and paralyzed, Salvotor crouched beside her and took her chin in his hand. "I see how you are. My father made me into a weapon, as well. To think I wanted to use you to find the Key, when all along, it *was* you. The ritual the *visnprests* performed...it was no object that forged the Key, but Cyril's own bloodline keyed to the lids."

He stroked Cistine's bloodstained hair from her brow.

"You *are* the Key to the Doors to the Gods."

The hearing went out from Cistine's ears, and she could only stare at his gloating, triumphant smile.

"Take your hands off her!"

Julian's voice cracked through four octaves, his steps pounding the damp soil as he charged Salvotor from behind, blade in hand, yelling her name.

For a moment, the damp plains melted away. Cistine was five years old, curled on the Citadel's training pitch, clutching a wrist sprained from misfiring her bow, her chest heaving with sobs as Julian dropped his training sword and sprinted toward her.

Hold on Cistine, I'm coming!

Salvotor broke his fourth flagon and lifted his hand. Lightning coalesced again, braided together between his fingers, but Julian didn't slow. His midnight eyes were fixed on her, the same wild gaze that had so often danced with laughter, with desire, with joy and affection—now there was only rage reflecting on his steel.

"Julian!" Cistine screamed. *"Get away!"*

"Not without you!" he roared as Salvotor half-swiveled toward him. "Get away from her, bastard!"

"Julian, *no!*" Thorne cried out—one last, hopeless warning.

Power erupted. The shout was still on Thorne's tongue when lightning slammed into Julian and cleaved through his body in one deft, life-ending stroke.

Cistine's scream had no words as it blended into his anguished cry. The lightning set his body ablaze, warped his muscles, and burst through him; he crumbled to the ground, contours smoking, unprotected from augmentation the way Cistine had been.

Because she was the Key. And he was not.

She crawled to Julian, grabbing his shoulder and neck, sobbing his name, but she already knew. There was no pulse, no breath. No life in this body that had been so precious to her.

Julian was dead.

Salvotor grabbed Cistine by the waist and towed her away from him, and though she kicked and thrashed and shrieked his name, fought to get back to him, the augments had left her too weak to break free.

Blood-soaked, mired in grime, Thorne crawled after them. His hand extended, a desperate grasp, and Cistine reached for him in turn even as the panicked tears turned her vision to a mirage. Turned him to a vision far beyond her touch.

The fifth and final augment snapped loose, a maelstrom of many winds ripping her out of Thorne's reach. The last thing she heard was the bellow of her Name—a promise. A vow.

Then the wind stole her breath, and her consciousness with it.

EPILOGUE

SWEAT BEADING ON her brow, Tatiana watched the cards fall on the table. One, two, three—hers, Quill's, hers. She counted them the way she'd learned as a card sharp in Stornhaz; nothing good had ever come of that talent, just as her Papa predicted, at least not in comely circles. But here, among cheats and killers...

She slapped her hand down on the pile of cards. "*Voitaja!*"

Quill hurled his suit on the table, cursing. "How do you always know what card I'm about to lay down?"

She flashed him an enigmatic smile. She would never tell him she could predict *most* cards he would play based solely on the tell of his knife-sharp smile, the angle of his brows, the way he held himself. Some secrets even Quill was better off not knowing.

"Luck of the draw, I suppose." She leaned back in her seat. "Do the dance, Featherbrain."

"I despise you," Quill grumbled, sliding his chair back.

"You don't," Ariadne said from Thorne's usual chair. "And I doubt you despise losing, or else you wouldn't play against her. You've *never* won. The only way to save face now would be to stop playing altogether."

"I'm going to win!" Quill flipped over the empty scone bowl and plopped it on his head. "Someday."

Tatiana grinned at him, gathering the deck. "Never."

"A man can hope." He started the loser's jig around the table, and Tatiana couldn't bite back a cackle. It felt healing in her throat, on her lips. She'd carried the weight of Baba Kallah's death so heavily it suffocated her; she hadn't eaten for days, hadn't felt moved to do anything at all until Quill suggested a few friendly games of *Voitaja*—just like old times.

Old times were the ones she pined for right now.

Ariadne sat forward suddenly, brow pinching as she brushed invisible crumbs off the table. "Still no word from Thorne. Or Cistine."

Tatiana snorted. "Do you really *want* any? It's Thorne. *And* Cistine. Both missing."

"We're probably better off not knowing." Quill returned the bowl to the table, ruffled his hair, and reclaimed his seat.

"And Julian?" Ariadne asked. "He's gone as well."

Quill shrugged. "I haven't checked the tavern."

"True. There was really nothing to keep him here besides Cistine, so it wouldn't surprise me if he found other accommodations in her absence."

Tatiana grimaced. She needed to have a word with Julian; as an inventor's daughter who enlisted herself in a school of bright minds and brilliant futures, she knew what it was to be an outcast with no place among her peers. And to seek solace from the loneliness in a bottle of mead.

If anyone was going to help him, she supposed it ought to be her.

"Either way, I'd say it's about time." Quill picked up the next hand Tatiana dealt. "For Thorne and Cistine, I mean."

Tatiana rolled her eyes. "Only ever since Stornhaz."

"No. Before that. Maleck and I saw it after the Izten Torkat."

"It's not our concern what business they have," Ariadne warned.

The crooked slash of Quill's smile made something hungry rise in Tatiana's belly. "I'm just saying it will do a lot to solve the tension around here. Besides, Baba Kallah saw it, too. You know she did."

A burst of affectionate laughter rose from Tatiana's chest. "Are you joking? She would've pushed them into the Izten Torkat herself if she had the chance."

For several seconds, they regarded their cards silently. Ariadne loosed a quiet, long sigh down the table.

"So, what would that mean for Valgard," Quill ventured, "if they did?"

Tatiana looked up swiftly at Ariadne. She'd never really considered the notion: Valgard and Talheim, with a *joining* between them—

Before anyone else could speak, a shout echoed from the Den's foyer; the same voice that had given Tatiana her Name, that never failed to wake her from whatever slumber her fears or grief or anger sent her to, cried out for their help.

She was the first out of the kitchen, the first to reach the foyer where Thorne's dark silhouette sagged from the doorpost, just like that night she found him after he and Baba Kallah were punished by Salvotor—broken and whipped.

"*Thorne?*" Quill bellowed, shoving past Tatiana where she froze in the hallway, rooted by memory. "What in Nimmus—?"

He lunged and caught Thorne when their High Tribune sagged forward; his hands touched Thorne's back to steady him, then sprang away, tacky with blood. Thorne cursed in pain.

"Lean on me, *allet.*" Quill half-dragged him to a sofa on the room's edge and helped him down onto his stomach. Thorne scooped the decorative cushion against his face and groaned into it when Quill stripped what was left of his armor.

Tatiana's heart dove into her knees. His back—his raw flesh—looked like skinned game.

Ariadne bolted toward the attic, and Tatiana curled an arm around her heaving stomach, pressing her other hand to her mouth. Thorne's whole body trembled with every breath; Quill stripped off his own shirt and threw it over his ravaged back, then stooped low on one knee, curling an arm around Thorne's shoulders. "Thorne. Where and how?"

"You know how."

Anger pulsed like poison through Tatiana's body. She gripped her scarred shoulder and backed away two steps, slamming into the wall. "Cistine chased you to Jovadalsa, didn't she? Where is she, Thorne?"

He shuddered, and right then, Tatiana knew.

"She and Julian both came after me," he said. "Julian was cut down in the skirmish. I tried to bring his body, but I couldn't…I wasn't strong enough to carry him. And Cistine…"

Like a child hearing the medicos tell her father his *valenar* was dead of lung-rot, Tatiana wanted to bury her head, to block out these sounds, these inevitabilities—Thorne's next words.

"Salvotor took her." And then, even more softly, "She's the Key."

Quill's arm dropped away from Thorne's back, eyes blank with horror.

Tatiana could have *strangled* that stars-forsaken princess for doing this. First begging her to crawl from the comfortable gray numbness that cocooned her for so many weeks after their brief return to Stornhaz, then dragging her out by the tips of her fingernails until she had no choice but to throw open the cobwebbed corners of her heart and test their friendship…to see what that clever little gossip could do.

And now she was in Salvotor's hands, the man who defiled women and nailed them to doors, who took everyone they loved, everything they had, and *broke* them. He would break it all until Cistine was scared to love, scared to feel, because feeling was more terrifying than death, than seclusion, more than anything.

Ariadne reappeared in the doorway, flagon in fist. Quill stepped back from the sofa and she crouched in his place, shattering the jar. Silver threads poured around her knuckles like moonlight on ruffled water, and she placed her hand on Thorne's back, knitting his wounds shut.

Quill backed up into the hallway beside Tatiana. "Nimmus. The stars-damned *Key.*"

Tatiana palmed beads of shocky sweat from her face, trembling…not at the notion that the Key was a person, but that that person was sweet, innocent, tea-drinking, book-loving Cistine.

Cistine, who shot flagon-heavy wagons, who'd endured going face-to-face against Salvotor before, who'd survived the ravaging darkness in just a tattered dress and still ordered them around.

She cursed, meeting Quill's eyes, and the rapport between them snapped taut like a rope. He understood, just as she did, that this was why that augment hadn't killed Cistine. With or without armor, the Key could not be destroyed by the power of the gods..

She was something more. Stronger in some ways than any of them, but also inexperienced with pain and torture.

And now she was Salvotor's prisoner.

"Enough." Thorne's rasp jolted their gazes away from each other. He'd brushed aside Ariadne's hand and sat himself up, though the whip marks weren't entirely gone.

"These will still scar, Thorne," Ariadne warned.

"Good. I want them to. I want to remember every bit of this from now until my dying day. Remember that *I* did this to her—and to Julian."

Nausea stirred in Tatiana's belly—pain for a dead friend and a captive one. Quill propped his hand against the wall, his arm curving behind her back, and hung his head. "I hope we prepared her for this. She'll have to endure Nimmus until we get to her."

"But we *will* reach her." Ariadne straightened, offered a hand to Thorne, and pulled him up. The second he was standing, he was their High Tribune again—the one they'd left Stornhaz with, the one they would follow to the Sable Gates and back. And as he stood before them, eyes tracking from face to face, Tatiana's despair ebbed away, straightening her shoulders and lifting her head as it left and bringing her hand down from over her mouth.

Thorne's eyes promised a reckoning and success—even if it came in a storm of blood and battle. And he sealed that unspoken vow with guttural words that turned Tatiana's body to a weapon, ready for the fight:

"This hunt is *mine*."

End

A GUIDE
TO OLD VALGARDAN

Words:

Allatok – Heathen

Bandayo – Bastard (roughly)

Tajall - Infant (roughly)

Storfir – Big One

Stornjor – Great Love

Izten Torkat– Throat of God

Muunvat – Spit

Yani – Sweet

Sillakove - Starchaser

Selvenar – Blended hearts

Valenar – Blended blood

Svakari – The Betrayers

Kiralnave – The Chancellor's Fist

Malataranda – Sister of my Spirit

Jekk - Handsome

Creatures:

Viperwolf (CANID)

Dahadt (BEHEMOTH)

Arkhomar (SCORPION)

ACKNOWLEDGEMENTS

I T TAKES SPECIAL work to bring a novel into the world. In my experience, it takes a different kind, no less special, to make a successful sequel.

First, to God: for the answered prayers, for the random inspiration bursts, for the energy beyond what I ever thought I'd find. You truly give exceedingly more abundantly than I could ever ask or dream.

To Danny: for never thinking I'm weird when I need you to practice hold breaks or weird positions for a fight. For helping me see that *I* am enough. I never want another adventure without you.

To my amazing critique partners, Miranda and Cassidy: for punching through this book in one week. For dropping everything to go celebrate DARKWIND and treating me like family every single day. I could write a novel just full of gratitude to you two for all the things you've done. I'm a better person, a better writer, a better friend because of the lessons you've taught me. Thanks for letting me sneak in on your special days to share my babies with the world. YOU ARE A GIFT. <3

To Katie, Meaghan, Lina and Jenny: for agreeing to the flash beta round and being last eyes on this book. You helped bring courage and confidence back to this journey; I am forever grateful for your sweet hearts and stunning support.

To my family: for sharing me with the computer every day, for making space and time for my talents even when it pulled me away from you. For staying up until six a.m. to finish reading this book and sacrificing lunch hours to review it. For always encouraging, always loving, always believing.

To my Discord writing group: For being first eyes and cheerleaders, for telling me what worked and what didn't, for helping me unravel the first plot holes with our magic Discord brainstorm chats. No matter where our roads go, I'll love you always.

To all my friends and followers on social media: For being in the conversation, for teaching me, for supporting me, for sharing your excitement and hopes and dreams. I am rooting for each and every one of you. Always.

To Mina: For the car rides and mall adventures and sharing your kitchen table at 4:30 a.m., where I wrote Chapters 55 & 56 by candlelight and cried. Thanks for always being a safe space—not just your home, but your heart. I LOVE YOU!

And to my readers: For making space on your shelves and in *your* hearts for the cabal. I continue to be in awe of love and receptivity among this community. Every note and every review reminds me why I do what I do.

THANK YOU for giving DAWNSTAR a home.

See you in the next one! <3

Read On For a Sneak Peek at

THE STARCHASER SAGA
BOOK III

CHAPTER ONE

Six NAMES HOVERED like a vapor in the darkness above Princess Cistine Novacek of Talheim, pushed from her mouth in whispers while she rose and fell in steady curls from the floor.

"Thorne. Ashe. Quill. Tatiana. Maleck. Ariadne."

Her stomach throbbed when she raised herself up with her core and touched her elbows to her bent knees for the thirtieth time. The thirty-fifth. The fortieth. She kept her gaze on the ceiling bathed in freckles of ghostlight, pale like forks of lightning, like—

Cistine slammed down on her back and squeezed her eyes shut, but not quickly enough to dispel the image of Julian Bartos racing toward her, sword upraised, before the augmented lightning pierced straight into his body, pocked and blistered his skin, and melted his midnight eyes from their sockets.

Muscles burning, pulse pounding in the base of her skull, Cistine slowly sat up and peered around the cold chamber's dark hollows, mineral-licked roof, locked door, and the lonely bed where she'd huddled for the first several days of her captivity, rocked with grief-stricken dreams of Julian and the cabal. Then she'd started to hear them, whispers of their presence reminding her what they would have done if *they* were captured.

Tatiana would recite names and places to keep her mind focused. Quill would hone his muscles, preparing for a fight. Maleck would internalize the quiet and make it an ally rather than an enemy. Ariadne and Ashe would map the room and choose where to make a stand. Julian would tell her not to let them make a fool of Talheim's sole heir; to do her crown and parents proud. And Thorne would hold his head high, like a Valgardan High Tribune should, and make his captors feel they were trapped with *him*.

These thoughts had finally goaded her into core-tightening exercises and push-ups, then to drawing maps of Valgard's eight territories—Spoek, Nordbran, Kroaken, Lataus, Unsverd, Blaykrone, Eben, and Erdotre—with water from the drinking cup waiting on the steps every morning when she woke. While she did these things, the same gnawing reminder always lingered.

She should not be able to do any of them. She should have died on Eben's plains when she confronted Chancellor Salvotor of Kanslar Court. But she'd survived the unsurvivable because she was the Key.

She shuddered and shut her eyes, hugging her sore middle. All the excuses she made when augments didn't destroy her before were worthless that day on the plains; somehow, when the Doors to the Gods were sealed shut at the end of the war between the Middle Kingdom and the North, her destiny was forged—a Key to the lids that sealed the wells of gods-given power. So Salvotor had captured her and locked her away in this small room for *weeks*, waiting to discover the mystery of her.

Iron clattered as the chain on the other side of her door loosened. Cistine scrambled onto the bed, fighting to slow her breathing as a burly man descended the short flight of steps into the room. He was old enough to be her father, and as well-groomed as a King's Cadre Warden, silver-fletched hair, beard, and mustache meticulously trimmed, warm brown skin freckled with old scars, and slate-gray eyes solemn in the rosy light of the crushed ghostplants in his lamp.

He'd been here when Cistine first woke in this place, leaving a pair of muslin pajamas on the bed and taking away her shredded nightgown. He hadn't spoken a single unkind word to her, but there was a shadow on his brow Cistine didn't recall seeing whenever he left food and water while she watched through her lashes, pretending to be asleep. This time, he carried only a simple wooden box.

Unease curled in her stomach. "You're...Kristoff, aren't you? The head of the Vassora here?"

His brow creased. "In practice, if not in title." His voice was slow, warm, and husky—things she wished she could trust. "You've been summoned for supper."

"I thought I wasn't allowed to leave this room."

"You have a...guest."

She folded her arms. "I'm not feeling well enough for supper tonight."

Kristoff sighed. "You aren't being given a choice. Neither of us are."

"Will you drag me out?"

"No, but I will absolutely throw you over my shoulder. If you behave like a child, that's how you'll be treated."

Cistine almost jutted her tongue at him, almost reminded him she was not a child, but a prisoner.

The thought made her grow still.

A princess imprisoned. Like her own mother, Solene, and Julian's mother Eboni, abducted by Jad of Mahasar to goad Prince Cyril into starting a war more than twenty years ago. The clever women had plunged Mahasar's capital into disarray with manipulative words and playacting, turning Prince Jad against his father.

That was the legacy she came from.

The memory lifted Cistine's head high and drew her shoulders back. "I suppose I can make time for a guest."

Kristoff's mouth twitched, then firmed again when he opened the box. The dress inside was artfully-tailored lace and silk, floor-length, with long, sheer sleeves. It was also pale purple—the color inside a stroke of lightning.

Her heart jumped into her throat, and she shook her head.

"I don't like this any more than you," Kristoff grunted. "But things will be far worse if you don't do as you're told."

Bristling with more than just indignation, Cistine snatched up the dress and stalked to the small relief alcove at the foot of the bed. She loathed the clash of pale lavender against skin that had begun to lose its sun-kissed tan, as if the hours spent training on the rock top in Hellidom and tending her garden behind the Den had never happened. "Where did this come from? Should I assume this place has shops?"

"That gown belonged to my sister."

Tears pricked Cistine's eyes at the terrible heaviness in Kristoff's voice. When Baba Kallah died, she struggled to fathom the cabal's grief; yet now that she'd lost her and Julian both, she not only fathomed this man's agony, she *felt* it like a blow to the ribs.

For the first time, it occurred to her that the Vassora who often thwarted the cabal's plans might have their own griefs to carry.

She stuffed her feet back into her dirty slippers and stepped out to find that even while she took pains to hide herself, Kristoff had also turned his back, giving her all the privacy he could.

Cistine's fury softened. He was obeying his orders; that was not something she could fault him for. After all, why would he defy his superiors for her? She was only a tool of his kingdom.

"Should I twirl?" she asked.

Kristoff faced her, a strange emotion guttering across his face. "Come. We're short of time."

They stepped out into an arched stone corridor, the ghostlamp in Kristoff's hand bringing the only light for many paces. Cistine tried to decipher anything about her prison from the dark, heavy rock, which opened into a larger chamber at the corridor's end, the walls hewn in articulate lines and inlaid statues. Kristoff led her down another hall to the right, shorter than the last one and lit with a string of smaller ghostlit bulbs paving the way into a broad stone dining hall. Her so-called guest sat at the table, and at the sight of his face Cistine's knees turned to water.

Chancellor Salvotor.

ABOUT THE AUTHOR

Renee Dugan is an Indiana-based author who grew up reading fantasy books, chasing stray cats, and writing stories full of dashing heroes and evil masterminds. Now with over a decade of professional editing, administrative work, and writing every spare second under her belt, she has authored *THE CHAOS CIRCUS*, a portal fantasy novel, and *THE STARCHASER SAGA*, an epic high fantasy series. Living with her husband, son, and not-so-stray cats in the magical Midwest, she continues to explore new worlds and spends her time in this one encouraging and helping other writers on their journey to fulfilling their dreams.

Find Renee Dugan online at:
Reneeduganwriting.com

And on social media: **@reneeduganwriting**